STARVING FOR SIN

CAMIE PARRISH

COPYRIGHT

DEDICATION

In honor of the morally gray men that make my thighs cry.
Fuck you, Sir.

AUTHOR NOTES

I want to thank all of my amazing readers, friends, and family for supporting me while I tell the story of Athena and Ezra. This story is close to my heart because it shows a side of myself that I only let my closest friends see. Childhood trauma, drug abuse, and domestic violence all have been present in my life in some way.

Please be aware of the triggers you might find in this standalone book. Below is a list of triggers that pop up throughout the book at some point, but I do want to address one thing this book does not have. While I may cover childhood trauma in some form graphic dictions of child abuse or harm are not portrayed. This is not a plot line I write so you can be sure that child abuse, etc. are not mentioned here.

There is a brief moment where Athena recalls some of her past that include physical abuse. Athena at the age of thirteen is slapped, grabbed, and shoved by Cindy, her mother, but there is no mention of harsher abuse than that.

Triggers include but are not limited to- drug abuse, drug overdose, death, childhood traumas, sexual acts,

Erotic asphyxiophilia (breath play), knife play, Kinks including light BDSM, there is ABSOLUTELY NO rape, non-con, anything like that. Athena always has control over her body, and everything is consensual between her and Ezra.

** Please note that there will be talk about type 1 diabetes. I have first-hand knowledge of this condition and all information is coming from my mother who has dealt with diabetes her entire life. Using this particular medical condition was not made lightly however I did feel it was the best direction to go in since I have a personal view of the struggles it can cause.

My goal is to handle it with care and respect while also showing that life can continue with proper treatment. I'd like to thank my mother, Stephanie, for supporting me and providing me with information and advice about Type 1. All medical instances are situational and based solely on my mother's history and or past with her own disease. This story does not depict everyone's response to this condition.

TRIGGER WARNINGS

Contents

Triggers include but are not limited to- drug abuse, drug overdose, death, childhood traumas, sexual acts, Erotic asphyxiophilia (breath play), knife play, Kinks including light BDSM, there is ABSOLUTELY NO rape or non-con in this book. Athena always has control over her body, and everything is consensual between her and Ezra.

PROLOGUE
ATHENA - THIRTEEN YEARS OLD

MY CHEEK STINGS, the blood rushing to the surface, most likely bright red already. Cindy stands over me, her eyes are a deep pit of darkness, hatred swirls in them creating a whirlpool of spite that knocks me off my feet. Bringing gentle fingers to the side of my face, tears threaten to fall, but I hold them back not willing to give her the satisfaction of finally breaking me.

"Give me the fucking money you little bitch!" She yells, spit flying from her mouth like a rabid dog.

Shaking my head, my feet shuffle back until I'm flush against a door, Oliver's bedroom door, refusing to let her any closer to him. My angel. The only human in the world I love.

"Oh, you'll give it to me you stupid fucking child or I'll take him away." Her words are venom spewed from a cold heart.

"No. No you can't!" My words are pinched with pain.

She reaches for me knowing I won't move for the risk of

her rushing into his room while my little angel sleeps. Her hold is bruising on my arms, tightening with each breath I take, until I cry out from the harsh burn of her skin on mine.

"Where did you put my money, Athena?" Pulling me off my feet she brings me nose to nose with her.

"I- I don't have it I swear!" My lips tremble with fear, but below that somewhere deep inside the shadowed soul I bury is rage, hate, and over all pure sorrow.

Love. That's all Oliver deserves yet she hides away under abuse and neglect, burrowing her way into his skin only to cut him deep. I won't allow it not when she's broken me so irrevocably beyond repair. There's no saving the tattered, shattered pieces of me, but Oliver still has a chance. I just have to protect him from the inky black chains she suffocates us with.

"You petulant little fucking waste of space give me my goddamn money!" Shaking me with each word my head slams back with each thrash.

Wetness now coats my cheeks, the tears flowing freely from the continuous throb, my body pulses in tandem with my heart reminding me I'm still alive for now. Trying to wiggle from her hold I mumble a few words causing her to drop me to the floor, my back hitting the rough wood at the corner of the hallway wall. A piercing scream leaves me but it's the excruciating numbness chilling my bones that has my wail turning hollow and haunted.

"Shut your mouth!" Cindy grits out, sending a swift kick to my hip.

Biting down on the inside of my cheek so hard the taste of blood floods my mouth. I roll onto my hands and knees slowly moving off the floor to stand slightly away from the monster in front of me. My eyes shut briefly with a heavy exhale giving myself a small moment to pull my remaining strength together.

Turning I walk away slowly, my muscles fighting me with each step, my bare feet make across the ragged shag carpet under me. I keep my eyes on the floor counting each stain like they're stars in the sky guiding me back to a safe place. A true north, but it only ever leads to more suffering. I think my north star is tainted. Ruined.

"Hurry up!"

Her words sound further away, with each step forward my mind is slowly locking her out, until I hear nothing but a low buzz. Licking my lips, I feel a small cut at the corner of my mouth not quite sure when that happened.

Opening my bedroom door revealing nothing more than a twin mattress laying on the floor near the window and a small plastic three drawer container with a few items of clothing. I bypass them to open a small box hidden in my closet.

Shoving the small wad of cash into her chest I bolt out the door running through the apartment until I reach Oliver's room. Slowly opening the door my chest heaving, I peak around the wood of the door to see him sleeping soundly in his crib. Making sure not to wake him, I shut the door, and quietly sit beside his bed sticking my hand through the bars to hold his.

"I promise to never let her break you. No matter how broken I am I promise to always love you. It's okay bubs, sissy is here to keep you safe."

Tears continue to roll down my face, my head leaning against the bed, my eyes slowly closing with exhaustion. I no longer care to hide her money so she can't buy drugs. No. I hope she dies holding the cash that could feed her kids.

It's in this exact moment that my heart beats only for Oliver, and I swear then that no matter what happens to me he would be okay. I would burn the world down to protect him.

CHAPTER ONE
ATHENA

Today was hell watching my brother cry himself to sleep, just like the previous night and the night before that one. It's been three months since she left us here in the dingy apartment, with no food and even less furniture. How a mother could be so cruel and careless is beyond me, but in reality, this is nothing new. I have been raising Ollie since he was a baby, as if he was my own. Some people aren't meant to be parents and Cindy is bottom of the barrel fucked up.

My twenty-third birthday is in a few weeks; Sable wants to celebrate by going out to the club she works at, but who is going to keep an eye on Ollie? Trepidation seeps into my bones knowing that even with the part-time job I have on the days I'm not doing online classes, it isn't going to pay my bills. I will still have to get a night job.

Sable said she could get me on with her working two nights a week and the weekend, but could I really stomach working at the nightclub? Could I do this for Ollie?

Sable has been here for me through thick and thin since we were in grade school. Life dealt us both shit hands. Her dad becoming a drunk after her mother's death and my mom having an affinity to white powder. We both have fucked up family stories that made us closer than ever knowing that we had to stick together to make it in the Bronx.

Sable is a year older than me and has been working at the club for a year now, so she moved in with us once my egg donor split to help me keep up with the bills. I'm concerned about my baby brother, his nightmares have become more frequent showing no sign of getting better. School and work keep me from spending much time with him and I know that hurts him because he begs me not to leave when it's time for my shift at the cafe.

God, how do I care for a child when I still feel like a broken little girl? Who do I look to when things get hard? Why was this burden placed on my shoulders? Please don't make me work at a strip club when I haven't even kissed a man before.

I had plans to make it out of this shithole. College was going to be my way out to something bigger and better. But now? My vision is filled with pain, tears, hurdles I can't cross, and a little boy who thinks I hung the stars. Am I destined to let him down? Everyone always says the lord has plans for each one of his children, but this feels like something deeper.

~

The anger in my heart scares me but with nowhere to place my hatred I look upward to shout into the night sky, screaming my frustration to the wind.

My hand begins to cramp. Water falls onto the page of my journal, smearing the last word written. Wiping my eyes, my lip's part on a sigh knowing that my tears are futile. Closing the blue book covered in a soft floral design, I place it back between my mattress and box spring. I roll onto my back, letting my eyes scan the ceiling.

Soft snores come from the wall behind my head where Oliver, my sweet Ollie, is sleeping on his futon while Sable is out working to ensure her half of the bills are paid. My left hand sweeps under my pillow where I stuffed the wad of cash into the pillowcase, feeling to make sure it's still secure in the spot I left it.

The amount is dwindling down, just another reminder of what's needed of me. It's that reminder that sends a shiver down my back, leaving goosebumps in its wake. Muffled whines sound against the wall, getting louder with each moment. Sitting up I toss my legs over the edge of the bed moving to open my door when the cries become louder.

"I can't take this shit anymore. How am I supposed to be a mom when I never had one myself?"

Bare feet slap against the hardwood floor until I reach the room that butts up against mine, throwing the door open to reveal my baby brother thrashing around, crying for our mom.

She doesn't deserve his cries. The love he still holds out for her breaks my heart. Knowing that she will do nothing but continue to let him down.

"Mom... Mom... Mom." His whimpers are groggy, still full of sleep.

Making my way to his bed I drop down next to him, hugging him to me, letting his tears soak my tank.

"It's okay, Ollie. It's me."

His cries progress into sobs, shoulders shaking with the force of his sorrow. With each breath out, his sob's turn into a soft snore until he is back into a restless sleep. Swiping the sweat from his face, taking in the light dusting of freckles that dot his skin, he seems so peaceful when I hold him. Oliver has a way of bringing out the best in everyone he meets. His kindness knows no bounds.

"Sleep, bubs, tomorrow is a new day." My whispered breath fans his strawberry-blonde hair across his forehead.

My angel snuggles closer into my arms, his head resting in the crook of my shoulder, warm air brushing down my neck with each exhale. Each night that this happens the wall around my heart becomes stronger, building the iron cage higher until it's impenetrable.

Resentment clouds my mind, hardening who I am until all I can see is the little boy in my arms. It's then that I vow no matter what happens it is me and him against the world.

If the whore dares to come back, she'll be met with a coldness even she wouldn't know what to do with it. She thinks she can just throw us away like trash, to never care for again. Fuck that and fuck her.

Sable said she can get me a job with her working part-time to help build a nest egg for us, to get out of this shit-hole. Looking down watching Ollie's eyelids flutter with the movement of his eyes behind his lids. I hope his dreams are filled with light and love.

What I must do next is all for him, for the life we should have had. Tomorrow, I'm taking Sable up on her offer even if my skin crawls at the thought.

Goal one: Stack up money to take care of Ollie and myself.

Goal two: Finish school and get us the hell out of this place.

It's then that I come to the conclusion that I will do anything, everything, to make that happen with or without my pride. And on the off chance she tries to come back, I'll be ready to fight her for him.

"Shh. I'm here, bubs."

Tomorrow, I become the first virgin stripper in New York City and the reason is lying next to me.

CHAPTER TWO
ATHENA

The smell of coffee washes over me while I stand staring at the cracks that spread through the countertops. It reminds me of the time Cindy tried to redo the counters with fake wrapping to cover up the fact that this place is so run-down. As if the holes in the wall, barred windows, and peeling paint didn't draw attention to it. The machine finally finishes in time for me to pour a black coffee for Sable and make a hot chocolate with marshmallows in a cup for me.

Her sweet tooth is just as bad as her caffeine addiction. The only thing we can agree on in the mornings is that coffee and hot chocolate are life.

She hates mornings while I love being up in time to watch the sun rise. Don't get me wrong, I love the nightlife just as much as any other young party-goer, however, watching the world wake up is pure bliss.

"Thanks," a raspy voice says from behind me.

"Shit!" I yell, jumping from the sudden appearance of my best friend.

She slides her cup under her nose to inhale the aroma of Folgers strong brew, letting out a sigh, she finally takes a sip. Hissing, she sets it down, keeping her hands wrapped around the cup for warmth.

"Why are we up so early this time?" she asks.

Her brown eyes assess me. The sleep not quite gone from her face and I realize she must have woken up to talk to me about something because she is up earlier than normal.

"Ollie wanted to go to the park today but that doesn't explain what you're doing up so early." My eyebrow lifts in question.

Looking down at her fingers, she fidgets a little before she huffs out a gust of air that blows her golden-brown hair into her face. Sable is beautiful in a rare-natural-beauty-type of way with her brown hair cut short around her shoulders, caramel brown eyes, and small freckles sprinkled across her face and nose. She stands just shy of five eleven with long lean legs built for dancing. She is a total knockout with a small waist and big ass to boot.

The only thing she complains about more than her bank account are her boobs because even with all that ass she's still only sporting a B cup. Waiting for her to finally look up from the dark liquid keeping her gaze cast down, I ask what I need to know.

"What's on your mind, Sabby?"

Soft eyes meet mine. The show of emotion has my back snapping straight with wariness. Sable is anything but soft and mushy. The words bitch and snappy best describe my sassy bestie.

"You know I love you and want to help you in any way I can, right?" she says with caution.

I don't speak, instead I wait for her to continue, keeping my eyes on her face because she can't hide anything from me.

Reaching a hand out, she squeezes my hand. "I'm going to be moving out in a few months. It's time for me to find my own place..." She stops when I pull my hand away, backing away from the counter.

"T, don't be like that. It's not for another few weeks. I just wanted you to know in advance so you can plan for another option or roommate." She stares at me, giving me time to respond but I don't. I can't.

"I'm going to pay up on my share of the bills before I go to give you time to figure things out and I promise to still help out with Ollie when you need me. Come hell or high water remember?"

Tears well in my eyes at those words knowing what they do to me. She steps around the counter to come wrap me up in one of her bear hugs. Breathing in her sweet vanilla scent I let out a chuckle that has her pulling back to get a look at my face. The sight she sees must be enough for her to know that I shouldn't be alone with my thoughts today because she quickly offers to go to the park with Ollie and me for the day even when I know she must work tonight.

"Why don't you stay here and get some rest, I know last night was a long one for you. Your door didn't close until well after four in the morning," I tell her, even when my mind screams for her to stay with me. My codependency on my best friend has really gotten out of hand.

Shaking her head, she turns to head back to her room. "Get dressed and then wake up bubs, I'm going to jump in the shower. We can stop for ice cream on the way back!" she shouts down the hallway, closing the bathroom door behind her.

Opening the fridge, I pull out everything I need to make omelets minus the cheese. My hatred for the orange culprit still growing strong, even now at twenty-two years old. Cooking has a way of calming the anxiety creeping up my neck, my skin turning red with nerves. How am I going to live in this place without Sabby? She has been my anchor, the one person that has never failed me or Oliver. She has never betrayed us. She has never left us, nor would she leave us for a man.

The aroma of cooked eggs fills up the small kitchen, drawing in a tired little boy with messy curls and sleep-filled eyes.

"Good morning, bubs, you hungry?"

Letting out a wide-mouthed yawn. "Mm-hmm," is all I get before he slumps in a stool at the counter, laying his head on the cool surface.

Turning back to the task at hand I flip the gooey egg substance until its folded perfectly together. Can you really call it an omelet if it only consists of eggs, seasoning, bacon, and diced fruit? Either way, no one who has had my famous sweet breakfast has complained thus far so I must be doing something right.

Opening the door to the fridge I grab my secret ingredient to add a little sweetness, hopefully helping bubs wake up.

"Here, you better eat up if you want to get to the park

soon," I say, trying to push the smile on my face wider for him.

Grabbing a fork, I set his plate down then move back to the stove to finish the other two before turning everything off. I place the dirty dishes in the sink to soak while we are gone.

I start eating my omelet right when the bathroom door opens. Steam billows out when Sable walks out the doorway in gray leggings and a white t-shirt with her running shoes on.

"Mmmhh," she groans, coming up to snag her plate from the countertop. "I love when you cook your signature breakfast."

The grumble from her stomach agrees with her statement.

"It's what I'm here for... to feed you two needy brats." Swatting at her ass and ruffling Ollie's hair I sit down next to him, digging into my food.

We sit in silence the only sound is the clinking from our forks against the small porcelain plates we found at a garage sale. They're not even from a matching set. Putting the last bite of greasy goodness in my mouth I get up, place my plate in the sink with the other dishes, and head to the bathroom for a lukewarm shower. In this ragtag shithole that's the best we get around here but at least we have running water, there was a time when that wasn't the case.

"Ollie, make sure you get dressed when you're done. We can leave after my shower. Sabby offered to treat you to ice cream later."

Winking at her over my shoulder I see her eyes roll before the door closes, blocking her from view.

Finishing my shower, I walk from the bathroom to my small, closet-sized room in the back of the apartment.

What started as a nice, light cream-colored carpet once upon a time has turned into a deep tan color that shows the age of this place I call home. The urge to run, escape, is so strong my hand grips the doorframe, nails chipping the already ruined paint.

I can't run. I can't think like that, not when we are so close to being out of here. Taking in a large gulp of air, tightening my towel, I rummage through the piles of clothes until something clean pops out at me.

Black is my usual choice of color so when I spot my Nirvana black and gray shirt with a small hole in the arm pit, I pull it on, braless. Who needs a bra when you're a part of the itty-bitty titty community?

Snickering at myself I shuffle through a few pairs of jeans until I land on ones that haven't been worn this week. Laundry time is limited when cash flow is down, washing clothes in the tub is a last resort, but it has been done before.

Squeezing my size fourteen ass into a pair of jeggings is a feat but we make it happen. Making sure to grab my small, black leather wallet and sliding it in my back pocket, I sit on my small twin bed and pull on shoes before I go out there to join my two hellions.

"You can do this. Just ask her for a job. Don't be a wuss." Giving myself a pep talk to get my mind in the right place to have Sabby ask her boss to hire me.

Springs press into my butt cheeks causing me to shift on the mattress. My gray comforter with the moon phases on it giving me comfort when the room I'm in takes my comfort away. My affinity for the moon, stars, and night sky is unmatched.

Knocking has my head snapping up. "You ready, sissy?" Oliver's voice asks from the other side of the door.

"Yep, kiddo, just putting on my shoes. Go brush your teeth while I finish up in here."

The groan he lets out is heard even through the door. Boys and hygiene don't go together at his age. Getting him to brush his teeth is the easy part, it's getting him to take a shower that makes it seem like I asked him to pluck his eyes out while standing on nails.

"Don't make me smell your breath!" I shout before the sink water turns on from the other side of the wall.

My door opens revealing a smirking Sable. "Okay, Mom," she declares.

Once we are all done, dressed, clean, and ready to go we meet at the front door to head out into the chilly New York air.

"Park and ice cream, that's all, kid," I say, shutting and locking the door behind us.

CHAPTER THREE
EZRA

*S*ir, *your meeting starts in thirty minutes.*

Bailey's voice comes from the speaker on my desk letting me know that my two o'clock will be here shortly. My head hits the back of my Herman leather office chair when the warm mouth around my cock slips deeper down my shaft.

"Fuck, keep going." The groan that rips out of me has my muscles tightening.

Her whimpers can be heard from under my desk allowing her throat to swallow around my dick, dragging her lips back up and then down again. My right hand reaches under to push her head down more, the wet sound of her gag has my balls pulling tight.

"That's it, doll, open up for me," I growl out through clenched teeth.

My hips thrust up helping her take all of me until she pulls back, using her tongue to swirl around the head. Knocking on the door has her pausing but I take both hands on each side of her face giving me the perfect position to fuck her face until the tingling in my balls has me shooting down her throat.

She goes down one full stroke before coming up, making sure to clean every drop off me. She pokes her head from under the desk with a sly smile. The knocking gets louder. Bailey letting me know that my clients have shown up.

I push away from the desk to let Selene crawl out. Her ass nice and round right in my line of sight has me lifting her at the waist to slam her down on my lap.

"Ready for more already, baby?" Her voice is silky smooth, always so needy for me.

"Don't tempt me, CeCe. You know work comes first."

Her pouty lips turn down in a frown to put on a show of her begging. She knows I fucking love when she begs for me, it's evident in the hardening happening under her. Grabbing her by the throat, I lean her back against me before I address the woman at the door.

"Cancel my meeting, Bailey," I yell towards the door, making sure she can hear me. My teeth nipping at Selene's neck.

"But, Sir, your clients are here now."

"Fuck," I groan, shifting her off my lap to stand. I adjust myself turning away to fix my pants.

"Let's go, CeCe. Time to head out. I'll call you soon."

"You always do." She winks as she heads to my side door but not before looking back over her shoulder with a hungry look.

They're always hungry, the women. It comes with the success and money. One thing I have learned being the CEO of Finlay Executives, one of the highest paid companies in New York. Women will do anything for a man in a powerful position.

Sighing, I open my office door, meeting Bailey head-on as her hand moves to knock on my now open door.

"Oh, hi, Mr. Finlay, your meeting is all set for you." Her eyes turn down looking at the floor, her back ramrod straight.

I'll never understand the mousey little thing in front of me. Even if she is one of the best assistants in the business, not to mention the only one who hasn't run out crying after the first week.

"Thank you."

Keeping things short, I walk into the conference room on the top floor of my office building sitting in the center of NYC. The sleek look gives a professional appeal while the tech provides safety. After all, that is one of the main focuses of my business. We provide Security, P.I work, lawyers, and even bail bonds. Walking into the conference room I spot my younger, well, only brother, Eros, sitting at the table with two petite women dressed in sleek winter clothing.

"Good afternoon, my name is Ezra Finlay. It appears you have met my partner, Eros. Thank you for meeting with Finlay and company today."

Shaking both of their hands, I take a seat at the head of the large rectangular table made of steel.

My brother eyes me a moment, most likely wondering

what made me keep a client waiting but then again, he isn't one to turn away a free blow job, even when work is calling. Us Finlay boys have learned to have our cake and eat it too now that we busted our asses to get where we are. Giving him a slight shake of my head along with a smile, I turn to look over at our guests.

"Mrs.?" I ask, waiting for them to introduce themselves.

"I'm Emily and this is my daughter, Kaya."

"Emily, my partner, Eros tells me you and your family are looking for security, is that correct?"

"Yes, Sir. It's... well, it's my husband. Soon to be ex-husband. I've tried restraining orders, hiding, moving states, filing for divorce, everything but nothing keeps him away. Kaya is old enough that he has started to try to go after her as well and I just can't..." Her voice breaks off, pausing to collect herself.

She closes her eyes briefly; Kaya reaches out to rub her mother's arm and that sends heat down my spine watching a teen comfort her mother. No child should have to witness what she has yet I get clients with children who need help with this sort of thing at least twice a week. Emily pulls the strength of a fighter out sitting up taller, wiping her eyes, and looks me dead in my eyes.

"I want security or I want him dead. Either way this has to end because we can't keep running across the country moving every time I get a whiff of him getting closer." Voice of steel with no hesitation she just blatantly asked us to protect her or kill him.

"We don't offer that service, ma'am. It is against the law, but what we can do is provide protection for you and your daughter. Did you fill out the form that my assistant emailed over to you?"

Eros slides over a manila file that glides across the table

landing right in front of me, and says, "This is everything we sent over, I looked it over myself, I even had Bailey put it into the system."

Eros has always had a soft spot for these situations, which could have something to do with our childhood and where we came from. It's the entire reason we started the company we have now. It's what drives us to be better, do better, provide better.

"Thank you."

Looking over the forms I take my time gathering the information needed while taking quick glances over the folder to watch my brother comfort Emily in a way he normally doesn't do.

"Eros, please see Emily and Kaya to the closing office to go over the contracted information. I'll take their forms to our office downstairs to file it with the attorney."

I stand up and shake Emily and Kaya's hands. "Thank you for coming today. We will see to it that you are well taken care of."

Saying my goodbyes, I exit the door.

Placing the file on Bailey's desk I keep walking until my feet carry me to the elevator. Wanting to get some air I head down to the main floor, these domestic violence cases always hit close to home no matter how hard I try to keep my own personal feelings out of the way.

I may be an asshole who likes to fuck whenever I please, letting women beg on their knees for me while getting off to the sight of a red handprint on their pale flesh, but that's as close to harming a woman I will ever get.

The doors open to the lobby, displaying a pristine state-of-the-art area for potential clients to look over our services while using tables, WIFI, and dining area to work from.

I have found that most people want to work, they just

don't have the resources to do so, leading Eros and me to create a place to give the public while also bringing in new clientele.

Stepping out into the crisp, winter day my lungs take in the fresh air and the sun shining down on the city. Using this time to take a short walk to Central Park, this has become part of the routine in my daily schedule. Although Bailey would rather I not wander into the city during work hours, but she doesn't voice those concerns often.

Passing the afternoon traffic of people making their way around the city I get looks from everyone who walks by.

Women stare and the men sneer, both knowing exactly who I am and what I do. Finlay Executive isn't the only way this city knows me, being on the cover of a magazine with the title Sexiest Single CEO does garner some attention. Selene may have been under my desk mouth on my cock, but she knows the deal.

No strings, no overnight play time, and no jealousy. She has only lasted this long because she follows those three rules. The moment she doesn't is when she loses her spot at the top of my contact list, which would fucking suck considering she gives head like a porn star.

I finally make it through the crowd into the park taking a seat at the bench that always seems empty on this side. The metal is cold even through my pants, but I sit anyway because the walk was over five blocks. Large trees block out the sun providing me shade as well as casting a shadow over my face to better to hide from anyone who might try to walk up asking about the business.

Laughter erupts from a little boy who looks to be around nine or ten, sporting red hair and a gap-toothed smile. The two women chasing him look to be having more fun than he is. The smiles they are wearing shows their happiness.

Watching the three of them run around the swing set for a few rounds my mind drifts to when I was younger chasing my little brother around thinking nothing in the world could touch us. Now, as an adult I know that the little boy in those memories was naive with no knowledge of how everything would change in the blink of an eye.

After thirty minutes of ignoring my cell, I finally pluck it out of my coat pocket only to see it's Miles calling me.

"Yeah, man, what's up?" I ask my long-time best friend.

"We have a problem, meet me at the club," he states abruptly.

Ending the call, I slip my phone back into my pocket, glancing up to find that the three have already left the park.

Standing from the bench, to find my way to Miles' club down on 5th Avenue. His bar doesn't open until later tonight so I'm stuck wondering what he has gotten himself into.

Miles has been with me and my brother since our days in junior high. We met after fighting over a girl named Kinsley and have been friends ever since.

It takes me half an hour to walk to the club. The door opens to shouting coming from behind the counter at the bar, where Miles is holding one of his barman against the wood countertop by the throat.

His temper has always kept him in trouble. It's part of the reason we aren't able to hire him at the company, because we run background checks on all our employees and being family doesn't save you from the rules.

"Miles. What the hell is all this?" I shout over the noise.

The room goes silent all but the sounds of a young

woman whimpering behind Miles and not in the way Selene was under my desk.

This girl looks absolutely terrified with wide eyes, tear-stained face, and red marks up and down her arms. I can almost see the bruising start to form around her upper arms and wrists.

"What the fuck is this?" I yell to no one particular.

"That's why I called. Finlay Execs are about to have a field day with this one." He makes a show to slam the guy down against the bar to prove who he is talking about. "Take him into my office. He doesn't leave until I say so," he instructs his bouncer, who just walked into this mess.

"It's okay, sweetie, no one here is going to hurt you," I say in a soft voice trying to keep her calm.

"Ez, you need to take her back to the office to get cleaned up. She might need medical care."

My eyes bulge at his meaning when I notice her clothes torn and tattered in places that send me into a rage. My muscles straining to keep me in place. If I go in there to beat the life out of that man, she won't go anywhere with me and right now she needs us all to be calm.

"My name is Ezra—"

"I know who you are," she blurts, her voice so low I can barely hear her.

"Why don't you come with me back to my office to get cleaned up. We can see about getting my doctor to do a personal visit so you can be comfortable." Offering her my hand, I wait to see if she takes it.

"What's your name?" I ask, when she shies away from me.

"Sadie"

"Well, Sadie, let's get you cleaned up and away from everyone's prying eyes. What do you say?"

Not speaking she nods her head, walking around the bar to meet me on the other side.

Keeping my hands at my side to make sure she doesn't get spooked, I have Miles call Eros to send a car to me.

"You take care of the girl; I'll handle the prick," Miles states before he walks into his office.

CHAPTER FOUR
ATHENA

S *ex With Me* by Tramp Stamps blasts through the speakers, my hips swaying as I dance through the apartment with the broom in hand. Sable and I have been cleaning since we got back from the park while Oliver passed out on the couch.

Sabby slides on her socks toward me snagging my hips to stop herself from falling, our heads fall back in laughter that is drowned out by the loud bass of the song playing.

Dropping the broom, we spin around hand in hand laughing until we feel sick from the motion. It's not until the song trails off that we realize Oliver has woken up and is standing in the kitchen doorway watching us with a curios gaze.

"What kind of song is that?" he asks, questioning our choice of music.

"It's our theme song, right, Sabby?" I laugh, shoving her with my hip, making her trip over her feet and slam into the counter.

We all burst out laughing, doubling over. Pressing my hand to my stomach, I don't notice at first, not until his legs start to sway.

"Ollie, are you okay?" Sabby says, her voice filled with concern.

Standing up straight my eyes latch onto his just now noticing his pale skin with a slight sheen of sweat covering his face. "Ollie?"

My words have his baby blue eyes connecting with mine, his tiny hands shaking with effort when he reaches out to me.

Taking a step forward just in time to catch him as he falls to the floor. His eyes cloud over right as he passes out.

"Sable!" I yell in a panic, not knowing what to do or how to help my little brother whose body weight is fully in my lap now.

"I'm calling 911."

Looking away from Oliver's face, my best friend comes into view looking just as worried as I am. The bone deep fear for the only blood family I have left overwhelming me.

My breathing picks up but I remind myself that I can't help him if I can't keep my anxiety under control. A panic attack right now would not do either of us any good, not when we have no idea what's going on.

"Here." Sable hands me a cool washcloth to place on his head.

I use it to swipe up the salty sweat that has begun to bead around his forehead, brows, and upper lip. The sight of his skin turning an ashen white has a gut-wrenching fear taking root deep within my stomach.

"Where are they?!" I scream, feeling desperate.

Continuing to press the wet cloth over his head and face is the only thing keeping me focused. The simple task taking up all the thoughts in my mind.

"What did I do?" I mumble more to myself than Sable.

"T, this isn't your fault, he could be sick. We don't know why he passed out. Kids get sick all the time. No need to panic until the paramedics get here and give us a reason to."

She comes to stand behind me, placing a reassuring hand on my shoulder with a small squeeze to remind me that no matter what we are never alone. It's never just the two of us, not anymore. Sable, my sister by choice is here for us.

A loud knock sounds at the front door signaling that the paramedics have arrived. Sable gets to the door quickly, letting in the paramedics, who push a gurney through our narrow doorway.

The metal railing scraps across the already peeling paint, but I can't bring myself to care about this shithole when my brother has yet to wake up.

"Miss, please, move aside so we can assess the boy and take his vitals," the older of the two says, his tone giving off an air of arrogance.

Only giving them enough room to shift him off me I wait for them to tell me everything is fine, and he would wake up soon, the same hyper little shit he has always been. Instead, they start spitting out medical jargon that goes over my head. After ten minutes of them talking to each other without addressing me my patience runs out. Not knowing what they're talking about and what all these numbers mean.

"Can someone tell me what is going on? What's wrong with my little brother?" I snap.

"Calm down, miss, your brother is stable for now. We are going to transport him to the hospital for a full work up. It appears that his blood sugar is low, and he has signs of dehydration," the younger one says, his tone and demeanor kinder than his partner.

"What do you mean dehydrated? He had breakfast, water, and ice cream today!" My voice rises an octave, the panic coming back full force. The last thing we need is CPS sticking their noses in my business trying to say I'm unfit to care for him.

"The numbers don't lie, miss. His blood sugars have dropped. Add that with his skin reacting to our test tells us that he is dehydrated. Is your brother on any medication? Is he diabetic?" old guy asks.

"I... I don't know. He has never been tested for something like that. He has always been healthy like a normal ten-year-old boy. Please, just help him. Do what you need." Tears roll down my face, my head falling into my hands while the medics load him onto the gurney.

"I'm riding with him." My head snaps up when they pull the gurney up into the appropriate height to roll out the door.

"Where is his mother or legal guardian?" younger guy asks.

"I am his legal guardian." Standing, I look him in the eyes daring him to challenge me on that fact, knowing how these things could go. This could turn from bad to worse quickly if they have even a small amount of asshole in them they could brush me off and call child protective services on us.

They look at each other for a moment likely having a silent conversation about what the right call would be, but my brother needs help and I make that known, loudly. Finally, we are on the move, deciding my guardianship is a problem for another time, we head down the stairs lining the side of the brick building we call home.

They load Oliver into the back of their rig hooking him up to what looks to be an IV with fluids to help hydrate him and motion for me to climb into the small seat to his right.

"I'll stay here and wait for you to update me. Here's your cell, I grabbed it and your purse. Call me as soon as you know something. I love you, T." Sable's eyes start to water before she suddenly turns around, sprinting up the stairs disappearing into the apartment.

Watching the door shut behind her snaps me back to the now. The sounds of the machines filling my head until white noise is all I hear. Vision blurring the adrenaline is wearing off. A panic attack is a few minutes away. My body sways toward the bed my brother is lying motionless on.

"Whoa, miss, are you okay?" a male voice says from the front seat.

"I've got you," a second voice says from somewhere close, warm hands grabbing my upper arms pulling me up straight to shine a small light in my eyes.

The white noise gets louder, my vision scattered with black spots, unable to focus on the man's face in front of me. Closing my eyes, I start to take deep breaths counting to three and releasing. This is what I've practiced to get through my attacks.

"She seems to be having a panic attack," the one

holding me says. His voice pulling my eyes open. He releases one of my arms to reach somewhere behind me bringing his hand back with a small bottle of water. "Here drink this and take deep breaths. Everything is going to be okay. The doctors are going to take good care of your brother."

His smooth baritone soothes me into a false sense of hope but if it washes away the numbing feeling of dread, I'll latch onto it with everything I have. "Thank you." Voice shaky, I take the bottle, twist the top and down half the bottle before closing it and setting it to the side.

"How is he doing?" I ask, breathing in deep counting to three and releasing. While I practice this the younger guy who I can now fully see is the one sitting in the back with me, looks over my brother for a moment before filling me in on his condition.

Oliver's fingers begin to twitch as the medic says, "He's stable right now. The fluids are doing their job. Once they run some tests to see why his blood sugar dropped so dramatically you will have more information on what's going on but for now, he is alive and safe."

"I think he's waking up," I blurt, moving forward to clasp his small hand between both of mine. "Ollie, can you hear me?" The hope in my voice is noticeable.

"He might be groggy from the crash so give him a little time before you rush to ask any questions that might confuse or scare him."

"Ollie, it's me sissy. Can you hear me?"

"Mmmmm," he groans. His eyes flutter open a moment before they close again.

Before I can start to freak out again the rig comes to a sharp stop in front of the emergency room. The driver gets out to round the back of the truck. The back doors swing open to show a small group of doctors waiting to unload Oliver.

A tall female doctor or nurse reaches out a hand to help me from the back, I can hear her trying to get information from me, but my eyes are trained on the group who are currently moving my baby brother from the back of the ambulance, wheeling him through the double doors leading to the hospital.

"Miss. Miss?" The woman's voice gets louder next to me.

"Yes?" I snap at her, looking away from Oliver to look into the eyes of the person distracting me from what's more important. "I need to follow my brother; you can collect your information later." With that I walk into the hospital not waiting for her to chase after me. The doors to the hospital close, shutting out her nagging voice leaving me with the smell of antiseptic in the air.

Dear lord, please keep my baby brother safe I can't lose him too. It's with that small prayer that I continue moving forward, chasing after the group slowly disappearing down the hall.

CHAPTER FIVE
ATHENA

Diabetes. Type One Diabetes, to be exact. I keep repeating those words in my head. The doctor came in over an hour ago to tell me the news while my brother lay in the bed eating Jell-O still hooked up to the IV.

From what I have looked up so far, I have learned that Type One can be passed down to you from someone in your family and usually shows itself early in life. Just one more shitty thing we got from our tainted bloodline.

"Sissy?" Ollie whispers, picking up on my emotions.

"Yeah, bubs?"

"Am I like really sick? Sick enough to say home from school tomorrow?" he asks.

A small laugh escapes. The question floods me with relief because he is acting just like the pain in the ass he always is. "The doctors are going to get you everything you need to make you feel better I promise, bud, but yes you can stay home tomorrow to rest."

"Yes!" he shouts.

"Whoa. What's with all the happy shouts?" His nurse walks in with a big white-toothed smile aimed at Oliver.

"He was just convincing me to let him stay home from school tomorrow. What do you think? Does he need a day of rest?"

"It won't hurt for him to say home." She sends a wink my way. Taking his vitals, she writes a few things on her clipboard, continuing to check over different machines.

"Ma'am?" I ask.

"You can call me Nurse Jessie," she says, turning back to her paper.

"Nurse Jessie, is there a class or booklet with information on his condition? I don't know much about it other than he has to watch his blood sugar and even that confuses me." My voice hitches on the last word. The overwhelming feeling of stress getting to me.

"How do I do this? Will he be on medication for the rest of his life?"

"Sweetie, take a breath. The doctor is going to go over everything for you before they send you home. Yes, he will need to be on insulin while also taking his blood sugar test which is a small finger prick to make sure everything stays right where it is."

"And this medicine, is it expensive?" My hand starts to shake at the thought of yet another bill.

How much can one person take on to their plate before everything they are holding up collapses on top of them. The tightrope I'm walking on is starting to sway.

"Don't worry about that. Right now, the main thing to focus is the fact that we know what's wrong." Her tone reassuring me just a touch.

Once she's done taking his vitals and writing her notes, I take a seat next to Oliver who has been playing on my cell. Reaching my palm out for him to drop it in my hand.

"I'm going to call Sabby to let her know you're wake. You can have it back once I'm done." Raising my eyebrow to challenge the pout on his face, his smile finally breaks through. Shaking my head, I call her to update her on Ollie.

Twenty minutes later and a promise to call her with any more news Sabby ends the call to get ready for her shift tonight. She called my boss at the cafe to let them know why I missed my shift this evening, which saved the only income I have coming in. Luckily my schoolwork is all online this semester, so I can work on my courses at home with Ollie tomorrow.

Turning to check on Ollie from my spot near the door I see that he has fallen back to sleep, seeing his peaceful face so relaxed has exhaustion pulling at my eyes. Making my way to the small green leather chair with minimal cushion I sit next to him, letting my head rest near his hand. Taking his hands in both of mine, our hands folding together on the scratchy white sheet on the bed, my eyes start to drift closed.

The sound of the metal door clicking closed has my head popping up to see the doctor coming into the room with several forms and packets in his hands. The doctor is a tall six foot two or more man with black hair and broad shoulders that look like they could lift a car off a baby.

"Hello, Athena, my name is Doctor Howard. Why don't we go over some paperwork so we can get you and your brother home to sleep in your own beds." He gives me a warm smile.

"Thank you, please tell me what I can do to make sure this doesn't happen again. Was it the ice cream?"

"First, your brother will be insulin-dependent. You will need to keep track of his blood sugar. At this age, the guardian will need to keep up with his testing but at some point, he will need to learn to do this on his own. There will be foods, drinks, and snacks that he needs to be limited to as well. Being a child, he won't like it, but his health is more important than cakes and cookies."

Dr. Howard goes over the list of dos and don'ts that we will have to follow the rest of his life, everything he can and can't have, the medicine he will need, and everything else that goes along with it. My mind races with doubts that I can handle this. It's not until I look over at my sleeping baby brother that I shove that thought out of my head.

"Where do I get all of this equipment, testing strips, needles, and insulin?" I ask, knowing that this stuff isn't cheap or free, with no insurance this is going to be hard to get, even with the part-time job I have now.

"Here is a small supply to get you started. Here is a prescription for his meds, and what you will need to purchase. We can provide you with a coupon to get his first months set free but after that you will need to go to your pharmacy to get these items priced at their rate."

"Thank you so much for everything. Could you show me how to use this?" I hold up his testing items.

"Yes, I can go over all of that right now, the nurse is getting your discharge papers together, and then you are free to take him home."

Dr. Howard goes over everything more than once, answers all my questions, making sure to settle any worries that arise during this process.

It takes roughly thirty minutes to do all of this, get Oliver dressed, collect all our papers and new medical products for us to head out of the hospital where Sabby's boyfriend, Mike, is waiting for us out front with a ride home.

Looking back at those double doors closing slowly behind me, the feeling of walking away from there with my brother on his feet next to me, holding my hand has pure contentment taking over me. Aside from the diagnosis, new bills, and obvious new medical discovery things are better than they were hours ago.

Tonight, I'm going to talk to Sabby about working at the club on nights she isn't going to be working so she can help watch Oliver. It's the only practical way to keep us on our feet with Sabby moving out and the cost of insulin.

"Let's head home, bubs," I say, opening the car door to let Ollie slide inside.

CHAPTER SIX
EZRA

"Get your feet off my coffee table," I shout over to Miles, who has his ass planted on my couch. My nice, dark gray leather couch that seems to have a permanent Miles shaped ass print embedded into the cushions.

"Bring me a beer when you come back this way," he says, slinging his feet off the ebony stone table.

At least he did what I asked even if it was followed up with a demand for alcohol. In my Penthouse no less. I thought moving to the upper side of NYC would give me a chance to break away from always being the one to house our-less-than-respectably-clean-guest. Miles has always been around; through everything Eros and I have been through so having him here with me has never been a problem except when I have to clean up his messes.

"Did you handle the girl from the bar?" he asks around the swig he takes from his bottle, a few drops of the liquid dribbling down his chin.

"Yeah, she's in a safe house right now getting the help she needs. Doesn't look like this is the first time she has had hand marks on her, but it was the first time Luke hit her. She said he has never been anything but nice to her except for that day." My voice drips with disgust, my anger brimming the edge of my control.

"Luke won't step foot in the bar again. That's if he can still walk." The malice in his tone doesn't escape my notice.

Miles has always been all in when it comes to his feelings. That's what keeps him in trouble with everyone but us. Through all the tough macho bullshit he eludes Miles Grayson is nothing if not loyal and kind.

When we were younger, I trusted only him to watch out for Eros while I handled business to get us out of the streets and into a warm place to sleep. We crawled out of the ditches with cuts that run deep but Miles? He has scars so deep no amount of time will heal.

"Where's Eros?" he asks, not taking his eyes off the TV screen.

Grabbing the remote to flip through the channels looking for a game to put on I take a seat on the edge of the couch with a glass of whiskey in hand. "He stayed at the office downtown to keep an eye on a new client and her daughter."

He gives me a questioning look. The same question no doubt rolling through his head that I had earlier today in the meeting: what interest does he have in this woman? Not voicing my thoughts on the issue, we watch a White Sox game with small talk.

It's nearing midnight when the elevator door dings open, Eros walking into the foyer, tossing his keys into the small gold tray at the entry table.

"Where the hell have you been?" I ask.

"It's been a long night, Ez, let it rest." His eyes are bloodshot with a glassy haze, letting me know he's going to crash soon.

Shaking my head, I turn back to the TV, shoving Miles's head off my shoulder waking him up in the process. Sighing, I decide it's time to get some sleep, letting the guys know as much, I walk down the hall to my room.

"Lock up my apartment, fuckers," I toss over my shoulder.

The sound of teasing and laughter fade the further I walk toward my room. My apartment has three bedrooms, but the master is up a small staircase that wraps around the far back wall.

The stained wood steps take me to the top level where my room and the master bathroom are. The two extra rooms are downstairs with one extra bathroom in the middle. The guys will sleep here on occasion, but Eros has his own house outside the city where he likes to do fuck-knows-what with his land.

Miles on the other hand bought the building his bar is in and turned the upper half into his own apartment. We all have our own space but sometimes the space is too much, so we have family dinners on Sunday and if someone happens to stay the night? Well, we know where family belongs.

Opening my bedroom door, I take in a much-needed deep breath, I'm tempted to call Selene to come relax my muscles, even when I know that's against the rules we have set. Giving her that one opening would change the way she sees our relationship or lack thereof. Toeing off my loafers near the door my socks come off next, tossing them into the basket near the bathroom door.

My room is what some might consider lavish with a California king bed, forest green sheets and black comforter, decorated with gold accents through the room.

Those same people would have their jaw on the ground if they saw the large, bear-claw tub in my bathroom that also has a his and hers closet.

Stripping the rest of my clothes off I dump them into the basket on my way in the bathroom, the cold tile floor sending a shiver up my spine. Needing to shower the day off I turn on the water to let it warm giving myself a moment to let my thoughts take over.

Work has taken its toll on me, even when we have good outcomes with our clients, the burden of those who hire us weigh me down. Checking to make sure the water is warm enough I walk into the stone shower with a bench to my left. Warm water slides down my back from the rainfall shower head above me. I take my time to wash away the sweat and loosen the knots in my neck from today.

Stepping out of the shower, I wrap a towel around my waist, walking over to the small bar in my room so I can pour another glass of whiskey before hanging the towel over the bathroom door and climbing into bed. The liquid goes down smoothly leaving a trail of heat down my throat warming my chest.

My eyes feels weighted, sleep slowly creeping up on me, I stop fighting the thoughts knocking around in my head to finally let myself fall into a deep restless sleep.

It's not the sun peeking behind the satin curtains that

wake me, no it's the smell of fried eggs and bacon that wafts through my door causing my stomach to growl out its demand for food. That can only mean one thing, the guys stayed here last night instead of going home, but why the fuck are they up this early?

Heading to the kitchen after grabbing some gym shorts to pull on I hear them arguing over who makes better breakfast. Before Eros sees me, Miles has already spotted me rounding the corner. His subtle wink doesn't go unnoticed.

"Your food has nothing on my bacon biscuits, and you know it!" Eros says, waving his arms around with the declaration.

"Ezra doesn't even eat this shit. He usually hides it so he can give it to me. I'm telling you, bro, your food is trash." Miles has a blank look on his face, not letting his poker face slip.

"Bull! I'm going to go wake his ass up right now and prove your skinny ass wrong," Eros says, his tone getting serious.

"Who knew food was such a sore subject for you, little brother? Sorry to bust your bubble but Miles makes a mean French toast." Keeping a straight face, I keep moving into the kitchen until I reach the counter.

Spinning in place, he faces me with a stricken look of pure horror before saying in a low voice, "Are you serious?"

It's then that me and Miles crack, our laughs booming out of us while a stunned Eros stands there with his mouth hanging open and his eyes wide. The look on his face is priceless.

"You really think this meathead has better skills in the kitchen?" If it wasn't for the slight smile, I might be worried that he was hurt by our jokes.

I roll my eyes. "Nah, Miles's food is garbage I'm just fucking with you. Now, not that I'm not happy to see your ugly mug but what made you stay here last night?"

They both make eye contact, exchanging a knowing look like they're up to something I'm not going to like. Looking like twins with a mirrored expression, they both meet my stare at the same time.

"We're going out tonight and you're coming with us," Eros says and Miles watches me. Watching and waiting for my argument.

Before I can shake my head Eros states, "We're going to this club called Deadly Sins to see some dancers and have a few drinks. You're coming, even if we have to drag your ass down there ourselves."

"That'd be a pretty heavy load though," Miles smarts off.

"A strip club?" My right eyebrow dips in question.

"They prefer the term dancer, dickhead." Eros snickers, smacking me in the shoulder.

"Fuck it, I'm in. But I want a dance from the best girl they have." It's been a while since I've let myself relax and enjoy the hard-earned money we made. What's the harm in having a little fun before I call up Selene to take care of my needs?

"Fuck yes!" They say at the same time, creeping me out even more with their twin-like bullshit.

CHAPTER SEVEN
ATHENA

Standing in the middle of the bright room watching the girl's line down the wall at small, mirrored stations to get all dolled up, taking in everyone in an assortment of different outfits getting ready to take the stage, my heart-rate picks up. Nerves bundle in the pit of my stomach. The lights on top of each station blinding me in all directions. Make-up dust clouds the room mixing with the strong stench of cigarette smoke and a hint of weed.

"Watch it," a leggy girl snaps, pushing by me knocking me off balance.

I spin in a circle unsure where to move to and not ready

to get closer to the ones cramming themselves into tight stockings near the back of the room. No one has looked up from what they're doing to speak to me, if Sable was here she would know what I needed to do, but she is watching Oliver for me.

The tall, lean woman sitting on a stool in front of me lacing up thigh-high heeled boots peeks over her shoulder side-eyeing me, not bothering to stop what she's doing.

"You need something, red?" Her voice has a rasp that most girls would kill for. The plump red on her lips shine as she speaks, entrancing me with the movement. "You must be a green one," she says.

"Green?" Trying not to look too out of place, I straighten my spine, staring her in the eye with a look I hope conveys strength not fear.

"Yeah, honey. Green, new, fresh, you know?" Putting her laced-up boot on the ground she stands up in front of me. Her eyes wander down then back up. Slowly assessing me, finding me lacking, I'm sure.

"Yeah... Yeah. This is my first night." I reach my hand out to shake hers.

"My name is Athena." Putting on a smile, hoping that I can find at least one friend here to keep me from falling flat on my face in embarrassment.

Swatting my hand away she twists me in a circle, getting a good look at my body, curves and all, while snickering at my outfit. Stopping me when my eyes face her again, she twirls my waist length hair shaking her head at the wavy mess.

"You won't be making shit in this. The guys at Deadly Sins want to see the goods and they are good, you just hide them well. Come on, we'll get you all set up for the night and if you make it through the first round, I'll take you

45

shopping at Adam and Eve for a few things to wear on stage."

She takes me to the far back wall where there is floor-to-ceiling lockers that each have a small lock on the front. Opening the door to display over a dozen hangers with an array of different G-string outfits, fishnet jumpers, and more bodysuits than I have ever seen. Palming through them until she stops on a royal blue full body fishnet suit with a black top and thong to go underneath it.

"This will make your fire red hair pop beautifully without throwing you to the wolves your first night on stage. You have an amazing body. Have you ever danced on stage before?" Handing the outfit to me, she then leads me to a small stall changing area with no door or curtain.

"I used to dance Ballet." Taking the items from her I quickly change into it not worried about the other girls. I am used to changing in front of women, so it doesn't faze me in the slightest.

Whistling, she flashes me a big chiclet-white smile that shines against her dark skin. She is absolutely stunning in her ruby red bralette and thong that has diamonds hanging from the nipple area.

"That explains the toned legs. These men are going to eat you alive in this outfit. It hugs your hips perfectly!"

I follow her back to her small station where she introduces me to a few girls, and I learn that her name is Staci, but she uses Sasha on stage. They all give me their stage name urging me to let them pick one for me to use as well. We settle on Red because that's what Sasha called me when she first saw me, and it matches my hair.

After we get dressed one of the girls lets me where a pair of sexy black flats that go well with the outfit but have no heel so I can maneuver around the pole and stage without effort.

"Are you leaving your hair down or pinning it up?" one girl asks me. I think she said her name was Raven, due to her raven black hair that is tied back in a long fishtail braid flowing down her back.

Shaking my head, I reply, "Umm. Leaving it down."

Before I know it, I'm sitting on a stool in front of the mirror while two girls including Raven are working on my hair while Sasha applies silver eyeshadow on my eyes to make my emerald-green eyes pop out against my fair skin.

Once they're done they each step away, allowing me to look at the woman staring back at me in the mirror. Her eyes shine bright, the rosy color of her cheeks making her pale skin look softer, the wild, red hair she normally has is pinned on top of her head in a beautiful silver clip. The only hair left hanging down frames her face on the side with slight curls.

The person looking back at me is stunning taking my breath away in the process. They fuss over me for the next hour until the door leading into the room slams against the wall, letting in Vic, the manager of the club.

"What the hell is going on in here? This isn't the sister club get your asses up and out on that stage. Sasha and new girl get your asses out there now!" Spit flies from his mouth making my lip curl.

Sasha rolls her eyes and saunters past him without a second look, but he doesn't notice because his beady little eyes are on me, watching me sway over to him.

The sweat that builds over his eyebrows slowly slide down the bridge of his nose that looks like it's been broken a time or two. The odor coming off him makes my lip curl in disgust. Trying to hide the way he creeps me out, I stop a few short feet away waiting for him to give me direction.

He moves closer until his breath fans over my skin, sending shivers down my arms. "Who knew you were hiding all those curves under your clothes. I might just have to get a dance from you, what do ya think?"

His smirk shows a few rotten teeth. His fat hand grips my upper arm, halting my attempt to move back. "What do you say you give me a little pre-dance show?"

"Back off, Vic. You know how Sinclair feels about you trying to blackmail the girls for private dances, you would hate for him to hear about it again, your nose just healed from the last time," Raven warns him, pulling my arm out of his meaty hands. "Leave the new girl alone and do us a favor, go jerk one out before you come back, sound good?"

The other girls all giggle, Raven looks over her shoulder at me waiting for me to follow her, taking me to the back-stage area where we can spot Sasha dancing on stage while men of all ages and some women throw money at her feet. Some even get close enough to stuff wads of cash in her G-string.

"Breathe. It's just like a dance party with people watching. I heard you were a dancer before, it's the same thing with less clothes. You are here for one reason and that's money so go out there and fucking be a boss bitch. Take their money while they take home blue balls." With a slap on the ass and a "Good luck," she sends me out on stage where all eyes turn to me.

Without thinking, my mind blocks out everyone in the crowd until all I see is the ballet stage I used to dance on for hours at a time. Using the pole to my right as I move my body in different moves, being aware that some of them are closer to ballet moves than that of a stripper, I don't let that stop me.

Gyrating my hips to the rhythm playing in the club the muscles I no longer use release like a cannon until I find myself climbing the slick pole with motions I didn't know I was capable of.

Blocking out the yips and cat calls of everyone, my body continues to do what it was built for. Dancing has always been my comfort from everything that has scarred me, so I use this time to escape into a world where my brother is healthy with a mother who loves us.

For a moment I lose track of time and space until the song slowly drifts into another melody, Sasha makes her way to me with wide eyes and smile even wider, ushering me off stage before I have time to grab the money that is scattered across the stage.

"Don't worry about the money, you'll get it later. We have a girl that cleans the stage after each performance. Holy shit! You didn't say you could dance like that. You had them eating out of your hands!" She bounces on her toes, both hands squeezing my forearms in the process.

My cheeks warm not wanting to make a big deal out of it because this is only a means to an end for me. "I just did what I knew how to do without thinking."

We make our way back into the room filled with the other girls, Sasha gushing over my dance, demanding that I give them lessons on how to use certain parts of their body.

After talking with everyone for a bit, my ass plants on the couch against the side wall painted a deep brown. My thighs screaming at me for a hot bath with salt water to soothe the pain. It's been a while since I danced like that, but it was cathartic to let my body take over.

The night dwindles down, leaving only a few girls in the

back room. Changing into another outfit, Raven comes over to me, nudging my leg to give her room to sit. We talk for a few minutes before a small mousy girl with ashy-brown hair slinks over to let me know it's time to get back out there for my last dance of the night. Sighing, I slip my shoes back on to head out for another dance.

Whistles, whoops, and hollers meet my ears from behind the curtain begging for another round, but my legs are jelly at this point. Shaking my head at the stagehand, letting her know I am done for the night, I walk to the back room. Getting changed back into my normal clothes, I head into the office where Vic keeps our cash.

Back in my street clothes he doesn't bat an eye at me like he did earlier, and fuck if I'm not thankful for that.

"I'm here to collect my earnings, Vic," I say.

Tossing a clear baggy filled with bills tied by an elastic he doesn't give me a second look before he tosses over his shoulder, "That's one night's earnings minus the club's cut. You could make a name for yourself here with those moves, think about that."

Without replying, I walk out the door. I stop at the bar for a small glass of Malibu rum and pineapple juice, my go-to drink.

Waiting on Taz, the bartender for the club, a chill crawls down my spine, making me aware that someone is watching me. Not moving but letting my eyes trail the club from where I am I don't see anyone that looks like they are watching me, but I can still feel the stare on my skin.

"Here ya go, Red," Taz says with a wink before he makes his way back to a hot blonde at the end of the bar.

Sipping on my drink gives me an excuse to turn and lean against the side of the bar allowing me to see the entire room without looking out of place. It's then that I see a group of men sitting in a high rollers VIP booth near the front of the stage blocked off by a red velvet rope.

Girls are lined up just waiting for the chance to get railed by one of these three men. I don't blame them either because damn they are all sexy as sin in their own way.

They look rugged and business all at the same time. Dressed to the nines in fancy shit while drinking, whiskey bottle right there at their table. Before I can continue to ogle them, my eyes catch the one sitting off to the side. His frame the largest of the three but not in an obvious way, more like he is the type to go to the gym all hours of the night while the other two look lean and fit in a fighter or runner type of way.

What catches my eye about him isn't the way his black Henley shirt clings to his broad chest... no, it's the way his eyes track my every move, right down to the way my glass presses against of my lips, letting the cool liquid flow down my throat. *Fuck, is it getting hotter?*

He continues to watch me as the heat crawling down my spine into my core becomes too much. Spinning away, I set the glass on the counter hard, and toss a few bills into the cup on the bar before walking away. Before I get to the door, I look over my shoulder once more, knowing that his eyes are still on me. I can feel them like a warm caress.

That's it, I need out of this bar before I do something stupid like go over there and ask him if he wants to buy me a drink. *Get your shit together, Athena, you have responsibilities. Ollie needs you.*

With that thought I walk out the doors into the chilly night air, hailing a cab home. Crawling into bed, after a hot shower, the stranger's eyes are the last thing I see before sleep claims me.

CHAPTER EIGHT

EZRA

Watching my dick slowly enter Selene from the back, her stomach planted across the cool surface of my desk, ass pressed against my thighs, I move into her slowly waiting for my dick to get harder, but nothing has been able to get me there without thoughts of the woman from the club flashing in my head.

Selene moans, giving away the fact that she's either faking or likes half-limp cock, unable to get into it I take my eyes off the hair that isn't red.

Closing my eyes to picture the fiery goddess from the strip club. All legs, curvy, and red hair taking the stage with pure fire leaving all the men begging for more, my dick stiffens, getting harder than it has the past two week giving me what I need to get off.

Both hands grip onto her hips slamming in and out until the sliding of my desk across the tile floor has me slowing but not enough to stop the build-up of pressure in my balls.

Lifting my hand to slap her ass making a loud smacking sound I rub the red spot in tandem with my thrusts. Behind my eyelids Red dances to my movements showcasing her perfect ass with those wide hips that draw me in, needing a taste of her slick skin that shines under the neon red lights.

"Fuck," I groan.

Leaning down, I grip her throat shoving her down harder on my cock until my cum is spurting into the condom, her pussy squeezing me dry with her release. The loud moan Selene lets out has my eyes jolting open to reveal the brown hair spread across my desk. Pulling out of her to discard the condom I motion for her to get cleaned up in my connected bathroom.

Fuck, I can't even get off without picturing the minx who has had my dick hard for her since I watched her the other night.

"That was so good, baby," Selene purrs, her hands rub across my shoulders, leaning up to kiss the corner of my mouth.

"I'll call you when I need my dick wet again." My voice is clipped, not worried if I hurt her feelings. She needs to remember our deal. This is strictly fucking, nothing more.

Turning away, she seems to pick up that I'm done with her for now, Selene walks to the door to let herself out. Sitting down at my desk after cleaning it and moving it back to its place I breathe a sigh of relief that she's gone.

Needing to get my mind off this obsession I have with a random woman I focus on work and my clients.

It's not until the sun starts to set behind the glass of my office that I realize nothing has been done today with the way my thoughts keep drifting back to her. Maybe I just need to go see her again to get her out of my system or I can fuck her out of my system.

Not one to have a problem getting a woman to bed, I make it my goal to fuck her once and be done so I can get back to getting shit done around here.

Calling up Eros to see if he's up for a night out this weekend I leave a voicemail when he doesn't pick up then I head to the gym to sweat out this pent-up frustration. She has my dick by the balls twisting them up until it's useless for anything but her.

That just won't fucking work for me, I'll fuck her until my dick hates her, lighting up her pale flesh with fresh marks, before I turn her loose. The picture of her ass painted red has my dick twitching in my pants, pressing against my zipper.

"Fuck, I need to dig my teeth into her," I utter.

The elevator dings, opening to reveal a tired Eros standing there with Miles at his side both looking like shit. Eros sports the same red-rimmed eyes as the other night while Miles just looks like he has been rammed through the ringer.

"I see you got my message."

Pouring them both a shot we all stand around the marble counter in silence, each taking turns tossing back the warm amber liquid.

"Deadly Sins again tonight, bro? You have a kink you feel the need to share?" Eros perks up after the last two shots does its job.

"I bet he has a thing for tying up strippers. He looks like the type of fucker to do some shit like that," Miles jokes.

If they only knew how fucking bad. I need to see my hands splayed across Red's throat with her head thrown back in pleasure. Shaking off the mental picture I smack the back of Eros's head not giving them a response.

"I need to blow off steam from this week but if ya'll want to go home to sit around instead of watching a stage full of women fuck a pole for money then be my guest."

I can tell my tone takes them by surprise and damn if it doesn't shock me too but my need to see her again is consuming me, driving me to the edge, pulling my skin tight until I can't breathe. She's like a curse, a sin, deadly as fuck.

"Hell, yeah, we're down. We were just messing with you because it's usually you that's a stick-in-the-mud. Glad to see you finally do something other than bury your cock in that money-hungry-bitch Selene," Eros says. Always the smart ass.

Miles nods his head, never one to give me shit for who I stick my dick in, that could be because he has the worst taste in women. Always settling for the ones who bleed you dry but that's not my problem anymore. You can only try to help someone out so many times.

Miles never learns from his mistakes. His mind makes him believe he isn't worth a damn no matter how hard Eros and I try to convince him otherwise, so he lets women drag him down by the throat until he's nothing more than a shell. True fucking mommy issues.

"Saturday night?"

We all agree to go out on Saturday. Everyone breaks away to do our own thing, mine being cooking because out of the three I'm the only one that knows how to do shit, while Miles heads to put on a game before Eros has time to get back from his shower to steal the TV for a quick game on the Xbox.

After a while the kitchen is filled with the smell of steak, potatoes, and sautéed green beans, drawing in the two from the other room. It may not be Sunday dinner, but we still pile around the living room to eat, none of us up for conversation tonight.

Eros has been distancing himself lately, spending more time at the safe houses than the office, knowing I need to dig into what's going on but now isn't the right time, while Miles has shit going down at his bar that he won't tell us about.

He thinks we can't see it or maybe he wants us to see it so he doesn't have to address it himself. Either way, I can see him struggling with something big. The fear I have for my brother, blood or not, has me making a mental note to keep an eye on things. We eat in comfortable silence before we turn in for the night.

They end up heading out before I make it up to my room for a shower to wash Selene off me. It's been two days since Selene was spread across my desk, she hasn't bothered to reach out, not that I give a fuck.

I made it past lunch without looking at the clock, now it's a little after five, my patience is spread thin needing to see her again. Needing to lay eyes on her. Almost wanting her to not be there tonight so I can let this all go but just the split-second thought has fury spiking under my skin.

Every cell in my body is consumed by thoughts of her

driving me mad, the need for her body to be under mine has me jumping to my feet heading out the door. I don't stop to speak to Bailey before heading down to the lobby and out the door. Dialing up Eros to have him ready to go.

"Meet me at the apartment." Ending the call with nothing more than those words, I head to the penthouse to get dressed before we head out for the night.

They both meet me at the elevator a couple hours later.

No longer willing to wait to see the temptress calling to me I throw all common sense out the window. My fixation is going to drag me to hell, my perfect brand of Sin bottled just for me, my Sinner.

Two hours later we walk into the club to the same booth as before, taking our seats before we order two bottles of Middleton Irish Whiskey, the same bartender from the other night sending a sexy raven-haired girl to our table.

Once she realizes my attention isn't on her she moves over to Miles, who has her damn near begging for a rough fuck right here in the middle of the club. My eyes scan the stage just in time to see Red slink from behind the curtain, my mouth watering at the sight in front of me. And damn if she isn't a sight to be seen.

"Fuck me," I grunt.

Sitting up straighter, watching her take the stage my gaze tracks her movements, taking in everything from her red high heels up her milky legs to the green fishnet body suit hugging every inch of her body, my eyes finally make their way to her face.

Those emerald green orbs pull me in, her red hair layered in waves around her face down to her waist not pinned to the top of her head like last time, she rolls her shoulders before she starts to dance.

Every man in this room only has eyes for her right now and that has my blood boiling under my skin. She is fucking mine.

She is like a deadly sin calling me to her, Lust in the purest form, Greedy for her, I can feel Wrath pulling me under the all-consuming need to have my dick buried deep in her dripping cunt is overwhelming. Adjusting my hard dick not caring who sees, my eyes don't leave her body.

And when she dances? Fuck me, my mouth waters watching the way she moves on stage. Without thinking, my feet carry me closer, blocking the view for several pissed off men, not that I give a shit, until I'm right in her line of sight watching the way her thighs grip the pole picturing my face between them.

Eating her like a starved man in a desert. *Fuck I need to get out of here.* Turning away, not before I drop a roll of hundreds on the stage, I find myself back at the booth with two curious pairs of eyes trained on me.

It took everything in me to walk away without snatching her ass off the stage and tossing her over my shoulder, so I keep my eyes on her, but my hands grip the leather booth holding me in place.

"Why don't you buy a lap dance, looks like you need to loosen up," Eros jokes.

Before Red leaves the stage she catches my eye. Stopping dead in her tracks, our eyes meet holding her there until the other dancer pulls her off stage. The last view I have is of her ass swaying to the beat only she can hear.

She's mine. Even if I can only have a bite.

CHAPTER NINE
ATHENA

Waking up to the sound of something scraping across the floor has me bolting out of bed. Rushing to the door, I swing it open to see Sable scooting boxes across the floor, her gray sweatpants rolled up to her calves.

"What the hell are you doing up this early?" I say behind a yawn.

She eyes me from over her shoulder while continuing to push the large boxes over to a corner in the living room. It's become more of a storage area over the last few weeks. Just another reminder that she is leaving soon. My heart squeezes at the reminder.

"Sorry, didn't mean to wake you. There's hot chocolate in the kitchen." Nodding her head toward the counter.

The smell of fresh coffee and my favorite hot chocolate doesn't distract me from the fact that in a few short days my best friend is going to move out leaving me to live alone for the first time in my life. I'm going to be alone with Oliver in this apartment and I'm not sure how I'm going to manage without her.

Clearing my throat trying to push the emotion out of my voice. "Need any help?" I ask around the lump in my throat.

Sable, being the best friend, hears the edge in my tone, turns around standing to come wrap her arms around me. The moment she hugs me in her warmth the tears start to flow, her own not far behind. Standing there in each other's embrace we give ourselves a minute to grieve the loss of comfort we have built behind these four walls.

"Okay, that's enough. Thanks for making me cry, you bitch," she says as she laughs, shoving me off her to go back to moving the boxes around the room.

Heading to the kitchen for a much-needed cup of hot chocolate, I start up the stove and oven for some biscuits and gravy, turning on some music as a pick me up. We haven't discussed what our plans are once she moves out or how she will continue to keep Ollie on nights that I work at the club but somehow I know she isn't going to let me down.

Spotting the mail on the counter I open the ones addressed to me with Oliver's name on it, ones from his hospital stay and other medical visits since then, and I regret it immediately.

Panic grips at my throat looking at the amount on the bottom of the page, knowing there is no way in hell I'll ever be able to pay off that amount no matter how many nights I work. My hands shake while I try to stir the gravy. I try to push those problems out of my head for right now, those are issues for another day for tomorrow's Athena to worry about.

This Athena is making breakfast for her two favorite people and I'm going to sway to the music, sing off key, and keep my head up. Because letting Sable see me break before she moves out isn't an option and giving up on Oliver sure as hell isn't one either. It's time to boss the hell up for them both no matter what life throws at me.

We work on separate tasks letting the music play to ease the hurt and tension in the air, both of us knowing things are going to change no matter how bad we want them to stay the same.

It's not until I'm pulling the biscuits out of the oven that Ollie wonders out of his room, bed head and all, to grace us with his presence. Making sure to watch what he eats and to keep an eye on his medicine he has started to feel better but sometimes I catch him trying to sneak snacks he can't have.

"Morning, bubs." I say, sliding a plate to him at the counter.

Grumbling is the most I get before he starts to stuff his face with food, smiling I turn back to the stove to clean everything up, placing mine and Sables plates on the counter I wave her over to eat.

After a few bites she brings up a subject I'd rather not talk about in front of Oliver but she's been hounding me about it relentlessly so I shouldn't be surprised she springs it on me while I'm trapped in the kitchen with them both.

"Soooo... were you ever going to tell me about Mr. CEO man that keeps showing up to see you?" She side eyes me.

"I had to hear it from Sasha and Raven, who didn't spare the details of how he only comes in to see you and if you're not working, he leaves." Shoveling a bite into her mouth, she waits for me to reply.

"It's nothing, I don't even know who he is. It's not like he talks to me or asked for a private dance or anything." I roll my eyes at her.

"T, the man comes to see you every fucking weekend. He either wants to fuck you or kill or hell both. We don't know his kink, but either way you have him hooked. What are you going to do about it? Or better yet what are you going to let him do about it?" She wiggles her eyebrows at me.

"Sabby!" I smack her, motioning to Oliver, knowing that he is too young for this conversation.

"Go play, kiddo. Me and big sister here need to talk." Tossing him her phone she sends him to his room to play.

Great, now I know she's not letting me out of this.

"Sabby don't start with me. You know I don't have space in my life for anything but Oliver and you. I'm already juggling two jobs and school now you're moving, I can't deal with a man right now."

"No. What you mean is you haven't had to think about having sex with anyone since you became a mother-figure to your little brother and now you don't know how to let loose and lose your virginity." Her words turn soft at the end, and I know that she means well.

Sighing, I look down at my hands. "I don't know how to be anything other than who I am right now. Besides, it's the only thing I have left that belongs to me, that no one can take control of or force me to give up for someone else."

"T, look at me." She waits for my eyes to meet hers. "You can't sit your life out just so you can raise a kid that isn't yours. I know you have responsibilities to Oliver, hell so do I, but that doesn't mean you don't get to live your life the way you want to." She reaches out to hold my hand. "Now, tell me about this secret sexy man that has the club all in a fit about it. Raven almost came in her pants when she had to serve him drinks a week ago." We both laugh loudly at that.

Walking around the counter I pull her hand until we both take a seat on the couch, cuddling up with one of my fuzzy blankets from my collection, I tell her all about him.

"The way his eyes track me when I'm on stage lights my skin on fire, Sabby, it's like he is peeling off my skin to see what's underneath and it lights me up, even when I zone everything out, I can still feel his stare on my skin. My eyes find his before my feet even hit the stage some nights. Watching each other while I dance, and when men get to close, I swear I can feel the anger rolling off him in waves. Am I crazy?"

My words spill out of me at the memory of how it feels when he's near me.

"Damn girl." She breathes out, fanning herself. "It sounds like he wants a taste of you. When do you go back in?"

"I'm supposed to work tonight but you have to work tonight so I might call in." Looking away, I start to wonder how things are going to work if I can't find a sitter.

"Look, I wanted to bring this up later but since we are both on the schedule for tonight, I might as well tell you now. I spoke with the girls, and we all agree to help you watch after Oliver while you work. Whoever is off for the night will come stay here with him until you or I get home. Raven is off tonight so she can cover for me, if you don't mind, I can call her now to check."

Pulling my hands into hers she smiles at me in the way she always does when she knows I'm overwhelmed.

"I don't know. He's my responsibility I don't want ya'll to miss out on doing things to help me. I can figure something out."

"Stop it, Athena Marie, you have a family here willing to help you, so get over it and let us do just that." With that being her final word, she gets back up to turn the music back on and gets started on packing more of her stuff.

Knowing that this means I'm working tonight I go spend the next several hours hanging out with Oliver before I have to head into the club. Nerves swim in my stomach at the reminder that mystery man might come in tonight to watch me dance and that thought has my smile widening.

The sun is starting to set in my bedroom while I get ready for work tonight, trying not to think about a certain person, when Sable walks in letting me know it's time to head out soon.

Stopping in Oliver's room to tell him goodnight, I give him a kiss on the check that he wipes off, laughing I greet Raven at the door with a hug thanking her for everything. She pushes us out so she can take up a spot on the couch with a book in hand, one that I have read before, Shadow Beast by Jaymin Eve.

"I can't wait to see this man candy you have tracking your every move. Hopefully he might have a brother or two." She winks.

"You do remember that you have a boyfriend, right? Or is that an on again off again thing right now? It's hard to keep up with you two."

Pushing me, making me to trip, we giggle as we walk toward the club that's not too far from where we live. It normally takes me a little over half an hour but we make good time and end up walking into the club thirty minutes earlier than normal.

"There's my girl!" Sasha says, hugging me before she moves to Sable.

"Damn, you replace me already?" Joking, Sable drags us both to the dressing room where we get changed into our outfits for the night.

"Guess who's out in his normal booth?" Sasha faux whispers in my ear, knowing Sable can hear her.

He's here already! I shrug my shoulder, acting nonchalant, as my heart pounds a little quicker.

"Holy shit, he's here this early?" Sable gushes. Rushing to the door, she opens it so quickly that it slams against the wall, instead of stopping to see if it caused damage, she sprints down the hall to look past the curtain where the VIP booth is for the high-roller clientele.

My head sticks out a little giving me just enough room to zone in on his usual table until I see him and this time he's alone, the men usually with him nowhere to be seen, his eyes on his glass of Whiskey.

"That's *him*?"

"Sable! Keep you damn voice down." I yank her back away from the stage.

"Oh, please, he can't hear me over the music blasting in this place. Loosen up, babe, or I'm sure he'd love to handle that for you. Either way, hot damn that man is sexy."

Her and Sasha spend time fawning over the mystery man that has been in the club every night since I first took the stage, watching, waiting for me to walk out on stage. At first, I wasn't sure he was there for me, but after the first few times, I realized that he leaves shortly after I leave the stage, never stopping to see anyone else and never getting a private dance.

"When do I go on?" I ask the stagehand, who is off to the side watching us act like idiots.

After getting our times worked out, we head back to the dressing room, both hounding me on what to wear. We finally finish up our looks with the final touches before Sasha and another girl must head out. Sitting on a stool at my own table now that I've been here longer than a few nights, I take survey of my outfit wondering if it's too much, or too little to be exact.

"You look hot," Sable says, standing behind me teasing my hair in its long fishtail braid that brushes the tip of my tailbone.

Looking back in the mirror I see a woman that's strong, fierce, brave, everything that I'm not once I leave the stage. The person that walks out there and the person that's at home with Oliver are not the same. Here, I become someone who fights for herself, stands tall, someone who sees beauty in the mirror. Where at home, I see an abandoned little girl begging for someone to stay, for anyone to see her for who she is and want to stay with her for her, despite her family drama.

"T, you deserve the world, let someone see that in you." She kisses my head before walking away.

Breathing deeply, I stand, fixing my outfit around my breasts. I bend to strap on my signature red high heels that I have taken to wearing, and I head to the stage to entrance a man who has gotten under my skin in a way no one else has with only a look.

CHAPTER TEN
EZRA

The music vibrates the table holding my glass, the ice clinking against the crystal, the amber liquid thumping with the bass. Picking it up to toss back the last of my drink, the lights change from neon green to a deep red to match the dancer about to get on. All beams flash to the stage announcing Red making her entrance with the song

Pillowtalk by Zayn playing in the background.

"Fuck me," I groan, adjusting my dick for the tenth time today when my eyes finally land on my temptress. My own personal devil here to torture me, dressed in a tight as sin leather top with matching thong and sexy, red heels. She looks like a fucking seductress here to ruin me.

Walking in slow, tempting steps she finally looks away from the crowd, her eyes locking with mine, the bright green popping against the deep red and her pale skin, but it's not her wide, fuck-me eyes that catch my attention, no it's her breathing that picks up when she sees me.

We hold eye contact, her chest rising quicker with each step she takes, until she finally reaches the pole in the middle of the stage, that's when she breaks her gaze from mine to begin dancing for the men yelling her name.

"Sir, would you like another drink?" my waitress asks, her small hand reaching for the glass I'm still holding.

Handing it over to her with a nod of my head I can't even make myself give a shit that I didn't give her a response. Not when Red has my full focus up on stage moving her body in a slow rolling wave against the metal pole her small hands wrap around. Not able to stop myself I picture her hands gripping my dick right before her pale pink lips glide down my cock using her tongue to make twirls around the head wetting me from tip to base.

Grunting, I make another shift to prevent my dick from having a permanent zipper print on it. I watch her every move, imagining each one being done just for me. Knowing I have no choice but to sink into her until I'm balls deep to feed this craving, I start to make my plan on how to get my hands on her, mar her skin with my mark, embed myself so deep I'll have no choice but to forget all about her after.

The song starts to fade to a new one, Red and the dancer walk off stage, but instead of heading to the back like most of the girls they head over to the bar, the bar that's less than ten feet away.

The tall, lean girl with brown hair chopped to her

shoulders lets her eyes flick over to my booth as they walk by me with a wide smile.

"That's him?" I hear her attempt to whisper.

Red nudges her with her shoulder, glancing back at me when her eyes connect with mine she jerks back forward coming to a stop at the bar. Taz, the bartender, walks over to greet them with drinks already made.

Maybe I'm a masochist or just fucked in the head but nothing could pull my attention away from the way her lips encase the tiny black straw, watching the way her mouth sucks on it to pull in a sip, her throat working with each swallow.

"Here you go, sir." The waitress from before sets my glass down before hurrying away to another booth.

Picking it up and tossing it back in one go I stand, needing to get the hell of out of here before I decide to toss her over my shoulder in front of everyone, not giving a fuck who sees because this woman has dug her way under my skin.

I stop at the other end of the bar to pay my tab and leave a tip for the waitress I'm pretty sure thinks I'm an asshole, not that I give a shit because I am, but I leave her something anyway.

"Are you fucking insane, T?" A whisper-yell catches my attention.

"Keep your damn voice down!" Red replies, her raspy voice has my balls tingling. Damn she's a siren.

Not wanting to alert them that I'm listening at the other end of the bar I order another drink, waiting to hear her speak again just to feed my craving for her.

"You want to what?"

Looking around before she continues, I keep my eyes on

my phone that I've pulled out of my pocket, she passes over me without pausing.

"Oliver's hospital bills came in today, you're moving out, and I can't do this on my own. You didn't see the amount. I have no choice; this is the quickest way to get the money I need." Her voice holds so much emotion.

Who the fuck is Oliver? What fucking idiot would have a woman like her working here and paying his bills? My blood boils seeing nothing but red, whether that's for the fact that my Sinner here has a man or that he would let her carry the burden of taking care of his ass I couldn't tell you. All I know is she's mine not his, from the moment she walked out on that stage and danced for me.

"You're talking about selling your virginity. It's insane!" her friend, Sabby, as Red called her, says, her eyes bulging against her small face.

"I wouldn't just sell it to some random guy! I could have a private auction." Red's cheeks get pink with her words.

Shoving away from the bar my glass spills, the ice smacking the hard surface gaining the attention of several people on the other side of me. Tossing a few bills on the counter I walk away to get fresh air. Virgin. She said sell her virginity at a fucking auction. Over. My. Dead. Fucking. Body. A virgin? That word rattles around in my head slamming into my brain the whole walk home. Untouched. How untouched? Has my little sinner ever been licked? Has a man's mouth ever had the chance to taste her? What about this Oliver?

Fucking hell. If I thought I was obsessed before, I was wrong. Skin untouched by anyone else? A perfect canvas to paint red in all the ways I envision and fuck me my mouth waters at the images flashing through my head.

Her long legs gripping my head as I eat, lapping at her

center. Her hands gripping the headboard as I plunge into her from behind. Her ass red with my handprint. Her raspy voice calling out my name as her orgasm hits harder each time she crests that hill.

Red, I'm coming for you. I pray that you're ready for what's to come. My greed for her has my pulse picking up speed with each step in the cold night.

Sin baby, if you think anyone but me is getting the pleasure of owning every inch of your body, you're fucking crazy.

CHAPTER ELEVEN
ATHENA

"Don't leave me alone." Shaky words slip from my mouth. Wetness gathers in splotches on Sable's shoulder, a sign that the tears are falling freely now.

She pulls me in tighter. "I'll always be here for you and Ollie. We will still see each other at work and outside of work, I need to do this. Please understand."

Pulling in a deep breath with one last squeeze I pull away, wiping my face with the neck of my t-shirt before she sees what a mess I am, not that she doesn't know, she's a mess too. This beautiful girl in front of me, who has been in my life for so long, who is so profound, brave, smart, funny, is going to change the world one day.

Her kindness and strength have already changed me. If it wasn't for her, I don't think we would have made it this far.

"Promise me this won't change who we are. Promise it will be just the two of us forever like always, Ride or Die come hell or high water." My hands grip her shoulders, our eyes shining in a blur of tears and red-cheeked smiles.

A honk outside startles us, making loud laughs burst out behind the tears. The moment of distraction is just enough to have us getting back to carrying out her remaining boxes to the U-Haul.

Oliver stands outside looking over the railing that leads downstairs to the truck, watching the woman who is just as much of a sister as I am, small streaks of wetness track down his small face.

Not wanting either of us to see him cry he keeps his eyes trained on the truck being loaded but Sable sees him, so she makes her way over to kneel to his level.

Wanting to give them a private moment knowing my brother needs this I head down with the last of the boxes. I hand the final brown box packed full of bathroom stuff over to the man Sable calls her boyfriend, but he still makes my skin crawl with his seedy eyes darting around waiting and watching for someone to jump out at him.

Sable swears he's a good guy, but I can see behind the lies and good looks, this guy is hitting the needle hard and hiding it good enough to trick a street-smart person like Sable. Is she blind or in denial?

Turning away from the loaded down truck, the one hauling off every trace of Sable from my apartment, my apartment not ours. Because it's mine now, my shoulders feel heavy with the weight of it all.

The hairs on the back of my neck stand with the feeling of someone's eyes on me. Subtly looking around without moving too quickly I see a small, black Audi parked in the rundown streets of the Bronx.

Windows covered in dark tint blocking my view of the driver doesn't stop the feeling of their eyes roaming over my body, causing goosebumps to break out down my arms.

Before my mind processes what it's doing my feet move toward the curb, getting closer to the car until Sable shouts my name pulling my attention back to her. It is long enough for the car to rev it's engine and zoom off down the street.

"Who the fuck was that?" she asks, coming to stand beside me.

"Your guess is as good as mine but with a car like that I'll bet it's no one good. You don't come around here for anything good driving something like that."

Grabbing Oliver's hand ignoring his complaints, tugging him behind me leading us back toward the apartment. Shaking off the feeling of those eyes lingering on my skin, my thoughts are pulled back to the present when the back of the U-Haul is slammed closed, signifying the end of everything that keeps me sane in this world.

The door closing on me brings the fear to the forefront of my mind and sobs threaten to break free during our goodbye.

"It's not far and we will still see each other almost every day. Keep your head up. You're a goddess, let her out. Take everything you want." Her words are a loving whisper against my ear. With one last hug she climbs into the cab of the truck, flipping us off as they pull away.

"What do you say we go grab some ice cream to cheer us up? We can give you your medicine before we go. How does that sound?"

"Yea!" His fist flies to the air, saluting the ice cream gods.

I laugh under my breath, opening the front door to a quiet apartment that's a little emptier than the day before. Heading into the kitchen to grab cold insulin from the drawer in the fridge. Oliver has been a champ through all the changes in his life that had to be put into motion for him to stay healthy but the one thing that's the hardest on us both is the shot he needs in his stomach.

It takes us ten minutes to get the needle in place. His screams breaking my heart each time he tries to pull away from me, but the truth is I would listen to the wails of pain a million times over than ever see my brother turn that ghostly shade of white ever again.

"Okay, bubs, it's over and done with. Let's get some ice cream to take with us to the park, Raven is going to come hang out with you tonight while I work. I'll get pizza tonight if you promise to do as she says, deal?"

"Deal!" His voice seems so careless and free in this moment the brightness shining at me reminds me why I do the things I do at night.

I push the thoughts of the deal I plan to make, the contract I plan to draft out of my head because now is not the time to process all the things I'm giving up, saving my brother from his illness.

No, I can't go there. Not when we are so close to being able to drop the crushing weight off us. My choices could break me down into nothing but Oliver, I'm dragging him out of this hell even if it kills everything I am. I'd take on the world for the freckle-faced rug rat holding my hand as we cross the street.

"What flavor do you want, Sissy? I want them all!"

Rolling my eyes with a smile planted on my face, we make another block further before I see it... the black Audi parked down the street at the cafe next to the ice cream shop.

Worry barrels down into my stomach before I shake it off, realizing that this doesn't mean anything other than whoever the driver is likes the food at the cafe, I work at part-time.

The door opens to Izzy's Ice Cream shop blowing my hair away from my face, bringing the fresh smell of waffle cones to me. We place our order with the person standing at the counter. Oliver walks around looking at all the different flavors while I pay when the door dings with the entrance of a new customer.

"Welcome to Izzy's, sir, how can I help you?"

I move away from the counter keeping Oliver in my sight, when a deep, gritty voice speaks to the cashier. Each word sending a zing down my spine.

"I'll have whatever she's having." His words sound so secretive with a hint of rasp.

Turning around, I come face-to-face with the guy from the club. My eyes widening before I control my reaction with a polite smile, my head tilts to him acknowledging him without being rude.

"Ollie, let's go." My words come out quiet and small, sweat beads across my forehead, feeling his harsh stare into the back of my head. It takes everything in me not to turn back around. The stark gray eyes I'd be met with keep my head trained on the exit.

"Miss," the feminine voice calls from behind the counter. "You forgot your change."

"Keep it," I toss over my shoulder, tugging a squirming Ollie beside me.

"Thank you!" she shouts, and it's then that I notice that I just tipped her fifty bucks that I didn't have to escape the man that causes my blood to boil and my panties to drip.

"What are you doing?!" Oliver shouts yanking his hand from mine.

We come to a stop at the small bench near the entrance of Central Park. Oliver takes a seat trying to clean up the mess I made when I pulled him out of the store.

Seeing just how covered he is while his tongue laps up the rest that was left in the cone makes me laugh so hard my ribs hurt.

Oliver joins in laughing, spitting droplets of rainbow liquid from the sides of his mouth covering his shirt in small splashes. Proof that we are both a mess, him covered in sticky sweets, and I am a mess covered in nerves dipped in needy want for a man that shows up wherever I am.

Shouldn't I be scared that this broad-shouldered man seems to be following me? Even with that logic swimming around in my head the thought of his mouth on me trailing down my neck to my collarbone has a thrill shooting through me.

"Stop it, Athena. Get your head out of your ass. You are about to auction yourself off to the highest bidder. Now is not the time to fantasize about a man whose name you don't know."

"All right, go play for a while before we have to head home to meet Raven," I tell Oliver.

Sitting down, I watch him play for thirty minutes or so

hoping he tires himself out before I leave him to go to work but my eyes also track each breath, each slow movement, anything that would let on another episode like the last one.

It's close to an hour later before the hair on the back of my neck tingle with the presence of mystery man himself crossing over from the far side of the park entrance.

"Son of a bitch," I mumble to myself.

Oliver is on the back end of the playground tossing a ball with a few other kids so he can't see me waving my hand in the air to let him know it's time to head back instead it serves as a distraction and before I know it, the tall, clean-cut man steps up beside me, his build claiming the remaining space surrounding me.

The air around me gets thick. My chest rises with it, making my cheeks flush red. His eyes glancing down lets me know he sees it too.

"Red." His voice rasp so low it causes chills to cascade across my flesh.

"Don't call me that," I grit out, harsher than I thought I could manage. My body betraying me by leaning closer to breathe in his scent. The smell of cool winter nights and expensive Armani mix together creating one hell of an alluring smell.

"What? Red?" He tilts his head, taking in each emotion across my face, reading me like his favorite book.

"That's not my name and keep it down before someone hears you." Not mentioning Oliver directly.

His large frame turns to face me, caging the back of my legs against the bench, leaving me standing in an awkward position trying to maintain eye contact with him. The light gray of his eyes is encased in a thick circling of dark blue like the sand capturing the sea holding it at bay. Pretending I don't notice his hands fist at his sides my eyes stay trained on his gaze, wetting my lips I watch his pupils dilate with the movement.

"What should I call you then? Hmm." His words are barely heard behind the grunt he lets out.

"I don't even know you," I retort.

"What do I call you? Red fits but since you nixed that name, what will it be?" he asks, his tone bartering no argument. Pure power leaks from his pores, he exudes dominate sex appeal.

"Athena! Athena! Guess what!" Oliver shouts, running over to show me what's made him so excited.

I bite my tongue because Oliver just gave him what he wanted without even knowing what's going on. *Ah, screw it.* Oliver shows me a ball that one of his new friends said he could have before he races back over to keep playing. The smile that's slowly spreading on my face is swiped off with one word.

"Athena." He plays with my name, making it sound like something far dirtier than it is.

"Yeah, Athena. And who are you exactly?" My words don't match my tone because even to me I sound breathless.

His smirk pulls on something deep in my gut, heat pooling low in my core. "Ezra Finlay." He sticks out his hand expecting me to take it like a good little girl. Ha!

"Yeah, nice to meet you but it's time for me to head out." Walking away before I do something stupid like climb him like a tree. I don't make it more than a few feet before his voice hits my ear, "I'll see you tonight."

Ugh. That threat just soaked my thong all the way through. The promise of what that means has excitement coursing through my veins.

Looking over my shoulder, spotting him watching me

walk away, I toss out, "If you're going to stalk me at least ask for a dance then I'd get paid for being watched." Before I realize what I said his eyes grow darker, the black of his pupils expanding, sending slight fear into my bones.

My head whips around, my feet carrying me over to Oliver as fast as I can without breaking out into a run.

Holy shit. What did I just say?

CHAPTER TWELVE
EZRA

Hot water beats down my back, soothing my racing pulse. The urge to hunt her down and drag her ass into my bed is so overwhelming, squeezing my eyes closed tighter the image of her pillowy lips moving with her smart-ass words has my cock hardening. Pissed off at the fact Selene can't take care of what Athena does to me. *Fuck. Her name tasted so good on my lips.* I grip myself in hard angry strokes taking all the pain with the pleasure.

Letting the picture of her fucking my face with those thick as fuck thighs wrapped around my head take over. I use those images to fuck my hand until I'm spilling all over shower floor. My eyes pop open to watch it wash away with the memory of her soft, raspy voice that makes my balls tighten even with them spent.

My phone buzzes against the gray granite counter. Stepping out of the shower wrapping a black towel around my waist, I answer my brother's call.

"Yeah?"

"Hey, man, me and Miles are headed over to grab you. Are you home?" Eros says.

"Just getting out of the shower, what's up?" I ask, knowing they are never up to anything good.

"Quit playing around with your dick and get dressed, we're going out for drinks and fun tonight."

A thrill runs through my veins picturing Athena on the stage. Her long legs enticing me to call her over for a dance. Her words from earlier repeat in my head, *if you're going to stalk me at least ask for a dance then I'd get paid for being watched,* and damn if that's not the very plan I have for her tonight. If I had it my way, she wouldn't dance in front of anyone but me ever again. The thought sobers me.

When in the hell have I ever thought past the first fuck? I need to get this girl in my bed and out of my head before I do something stupid.

"Bro, you there?" Eros says behind a laugh. Miles' laugh can be heard in the background. "I didn't think you were actually fucking with yourself, either way stop playing with your dick were coming up now."

The call ending has me walking into my large walk-in closet that has a big, wooden, waist-high dresser in the center. The surrounding walls lined with clothes, suits for court and meetings, hiking clothes, and casual. I go for something comfortable. Grabbing dark gray sweats to toss on with a black Henley shirt and black Nike shoes.

By the time I'm stepping out of my room the elevator downstairs dings with the arrival of Eros and Miles, both dressed in similar street clothing. Miles in ripped jeans and a black sleeveless shirt where Eros wears dark jeans and a polo shirt.

"Well, well, look who's done yanking it," Miles says with a wide smile on his face.

I ignore the jab, opening the fridge to get us all a beer before we head out. They continue to rib me. Sliding the beers across the kitchen counter to them, I pop the top on mine, pressing the bottle to my lips letting the cold liquid go down smoothly.

Miles takes a sip of his before he sets it down. "Has she filed any charges against Luke?" he asks.

"Who?" I question, my eyebrows raise in confusion.

"Sadie, the girl from the bar that you had to haul over to your office because Luke got handsy with her. Is she going to press charges or at least tell us what the hell all that was about?" The tone of his voice is telling. We all have an issue with domestic cases, but Miles has his own personal issues with it.

"Right now, we are just giving her a place to lay low and recover from the beating he gave her. She had several healed fractures and broken bones that weren't set, so no I'm not pressuring her on doing anything."

Not getting the answer he wants, the beer in front of him is tossed back until the bottle is empty. Pushing away from the counter he storms out of the kitchen throwing the glass bottle in the trash harder than needed.

"Miles—"

I put my hand up, stopping Eros from following him into the living room knowing that he might need a minute to blow off the building anger. If Miles hates anything more than a man who likes to hit on women, it's women who let it happen repeatedly. He knows deep down that it's not easy or simple to leave but watching your mom be a punching bag at such a young age, not being protected from the damages or the rough hands of his dad, that builds resentment that never goes away.

Not when closure is impossible and the one person you want to blame or kill, probably both, is in the ground from drinking himself to death. Not that anyone around here gives a shit about the dead-beat bastard with heavy hands.

"You know how he is when it comes to this shit. It's one of the reasons we know he couldn't handle working at the company, just leave it be," I say.

Eros looks over his shoulder one last time, worried for his best friend before he jumps into fucking with me about my little temptress. The craving to see her is overwhelming, sending my patience out the window. My eyes drift to my watch to check the time, knowing the club doesn't start their star girls until later, but I would sit there all night just to see her. She has become my weakness, the thought of corrupting her pure untouched skin, my perfect sin to commit. My Sinner.

My phone starts to go off, so I pull it out of my back pocket seeing Selene's name on the screen. Fuck, she's called three times today already. I think about ignoring it, but I know she won't go away easily. She's becoming too attached lately.

"Selene," I say, detached from the conversation already.

Eros eyes me from the other side of the room before I shake my head, motioning for him to go find Miles.

"Baby, come over." Her voice comes out milky sweet and the sound sours my stomach.

"That's not going to happen, and you know it. We don't

do sleepovers, Selene. That hasn't changed." I keep my voice low.

She's silent for a few seconds before her tone changes. "You don't want me anymore, baby? Is that it?" she whines.

"I'll call you when I'm ready to fuck that mouth of yours and you'll be waiting for me like a good girl when I do. Until then, don't call my phone again or I'll paint that pretty ass red, do you understand me?" I state.

Knowing she'll do as I say, I end the call before she speaks. I have no intention of calling her anytime soon.

"What the hell are you doing with her?" Miles says, walking back in the kitchen with Eros following closely behind him.

Walking over to the fridge for another beer my feet change direction, opting for something stronger. Grabbing three crystal glasses with one hand and the bottle of brandy in the other, we each end up with a glass half full of amber liquid.

"Selene knows where we stand, she just needed a reminder. We all know none of us are fit to settle down so don't even try to tell me you don't have a list of women you run through. The only difference between me and you is you like to wine and dine them along the way and I like to skip to the good part, dessert."

Eros laughs knowing I'm right but it's Miles face that has the laugh catching in my throat.

"What?" I snap.

"You cut them loose when they get attached. The only reason you keep her around is because she fucks you like a porn star, but that girl is looking for a meal ticket. We all know it. You just don't want to lose the only good fuck you have left that's down with the dark shit you do behind closed doors."

I raise my eyebrow in question.

"Don't play dumb, asshole. We hear all about the kinky shit you're into. By all means, bust a nut however you want but don't drag her crazy ass around knowing all she is to you is a sure lay," Miles says, tossing back that last of his drink before heading to the foyer.

"That's enough talk about Ezra's fetishes. It's time to have some fucking fun!" Eros shouts with a laugh, slapping me on the back on his way to the elevator.

"We going to Deadly Sins again tonight?" It's a question but the craving I have to see her makes it sound like a demand.

"Nah, man, we have bigger fish to fry. Tonight, we're doing a little recon on a project that landed in my lap, but don't worry it'll be fun." He winks at me.

My hands ball into fists keeping me from choking the smug bastard in front of me. Thank fuck he's my brother because I'm itching to knock his ass out.

"You have us working tonight?" I snap. The venom in my voice takes them both by surprise and it should, my temper is always in check.

Miles stops before his finger presses the button to call the elevator to the penthouse floor. "Trust me. You're going to like this. It's going to take down an entire fucking ring of dirt bags if we can get the intel we need."

Miles's involvement has me wondering what the hell we're about to walk into. Miles stays out of company business unless he is directly involved, like with the woman at the bar but this, him willingly going with us to do recon. It doesn't add up, but I trust them with my life, so I let it go.

"This better be fucking worth it." Not seeing Athena tonight sours my mood before I hit the ground floor of my building.

Whoever they have us watching better be someone big or they're both going to be eating out of feeding tubes when I get done with them.

Miles drives his Denali, giving me time to picture her on stage dragging every man in the club into her trance. My jaw clenches. The overwhelming need to sink my teeth into her soft flesh taking over.

The drive takes no more than thirty minutes, leading us to a small building lit up with neon lights sporting a flashing sign that reads, Moe's Bar, real fucking original. A bar? Why the hell are we meeting a client at a shitty run-down dive bar with shit beer and cold food?

"What the hell is this? Moe's?" I demand.

The twitch of Miles's hand on the wheel is a show to his restraint when it comes to my temper. They have both been on the other end of my blows when I finally snap, so he must sense the turmoil in me.

"Just chill the fuck out and get your grumpy ass out of the truck. We can't afford to miss our chance," Eros states, snapping into business-mode. The bullshitting attitude is left behind, replaced with someone who is just as cold and hard as I am.

We all step out of the SUV, at the same time all three doors slam in the cold night. The gravel of the parking lot crunching under our shoes. We walk into the neon light shining above the building. Drunken shouts and hollers are heard behind the thick wooden door leading into the dusty bar.

"Let's get this shit over with I have things to do," I blurt, pulling the door open letting the smell of beer, piss, and cigarettes fill the air.

CHAPTER THIRTEEN
ATHENA

Seedy eyes take me in from the front row of the stage. The seats are filled by greasy men who smell of whiskey and lies, the ones they tell their wives when they come here after a long day at work. These are the types of men you turn away from while walking down the street at night in the darkest corners of the road.

The hooting and hollering of the few who throw bills on the stage floor make my skin crawl. The money not enough to make me okay with the looks they shoot my way.

Dancing past an older man to the left of the stage I accidentally get too close to the edge providing the perfect reach for his large, calloused hand to grab my ankle. With one rough yank he sends me to the floor. Then the shouting begins.

My head makes contact with the stage so hard stars line my vision, black spots blocking the view of the madness. I can feel a rough hand dragging me off stage, his other hand reaching up to close around my wrist in a bruising hold. The yelling and fighting gets louder, Sable's voice heard over all others, her screams alerting the bouncers and bartenders.

The pungent smell of whiskey mixed with cigarette invades my space when his face comes into view. Releasing my ankle, both hands are now wrapped around my arms squeezing tighter, the shouts getting closer. Blinking my eyes, I finally clear my vision enough to see the dark eyes staring back at me.

"Stop." My voice is weak, my head pounding in my ears.

Pulling me into him his breath fans across my bottom lip, making my stomach roll. Struggling to keep my eyes open, I force my body to move backward away from the bastard who is moving closer with each breath.

"Such a sweet thing." His voice has fear crawling across my skin.

The thoughts hidden behind his eyes is a tell on what he would do if we were alone.

My eyelids get heavier, pretty sure I have a concussion from the impact. My legs shake from pure exhaustion of the day mixed with what's happening now. His hands get tighter for a moment before they are ripped away from me so harshly my body is thrown backwards into the edge of the stage, my back slamming into the thick wood railing.

"Fuck!" Sable's voice sounds closer.

Slinking to the floor, several feet move away from me,

the bouncers clearing the space. Sable's face comes into view, red with rage.

Shaky hand reaches back to touch the back of my, head my fingers coming back damp with red liquid.

"Holy shit, we need a medic!" Sable shouts.

"Mmmhh." My words come out as a groan.

The panic added with the pain my body is in has darkness closing around the edge of my vision until it's all I see, my head falling back against the club's stage. The last thing I hear is Sabby yelling for help.

"How the fuck did this happen?"

"Where the hell were you?"

"Stop yelling. You're going to wake her!"

"Shhhh."

All the voices swirl together adding to the puddle of noises in my head. Shifting to my side I can feel the leather under me, letting me know that I'm most likely in the back room with the girls but who's the male voice?

"Get out. She needs rest."

That's Sable.

"No. What she needs is to wake up so we can check over her."

Bouncer?

"That head wound needs stitches"

Taz isn't at the bar?

"Shhh. She's awake."

"Athena? Can you open your eyes for me?" That voice belongs to my grimy bastard of a boss. The kindness takes me by surprise.

"Sabby?"

Blinking open my eyes takes time. The brightness making the headache building intensifying. The room clears from cloudy to sharp clearness packed with all the girls, two bouncers, Taz, and Vic.

"T, you scared the hell out of me." Watery eyes assess me. Her cold hands take in the damage from the attack, before the tears start to turn into pure rage.

"I'm okay. Just a little sore. I just want to go home; can I go home?" My eyes move slowly over to Vic, the question more for him than Sable.

A swift shake of his head is all I get before he storms out. I guess me being alive is good enough for him. Before he slams the door, he yells at the girls who are due on stage to get out there. One of the bouncer's trail behind him to keep the fucking animals out there at bay.

Sitting on the side of the couch Taz motions for me to lean forward so he can look at my head, his fingers prod at the wound gently, coming back dry.

"It's not deep but it did bleed pretty fucking good. Head wounds always do but it doesn't need stitches. You will want to take an ice bath because you're going to be sore as shit tomorrow." His face shows no emotion, but his tone gives him away.

Releasing a deep breath to calm myself my body screams at me when I sit up against the plush back of the couch. Only giving myself a few minutes to process everything I finally speak to no one in particular.

"I just want to go home to get clean and go to bed."

Sable steps closer kneeling down in front of me. "I'll take you home so you're not walking, I called Raven to let her know what's going on. Ollie is in bed, and I think it's best he doesn't know anything about this so let's get you in bed."

"Will you stay for the night? I don't want to be alone." My voice wavers with the adrenaline wearing off.

Three hours later me and Sable are sitting on the couch huddled together watching TV on my shitty flatscreen with a purple spot in the top right corner from Oliver throwing a ball when he was five.

Needing help taking a shower hits my pride right where it hurts although it's not the first nor the last time Sable has seen me naked. That's the type of bond we have, come hell or high water, we stick together.

"It's okay to go to sleep. I'll stay here until the morning," she whispers to the side of my head resting on her shoulder.

"Promise?"

"Always"

With the promise of not being left alone, abandoned once again, I release my hold on consciousness allowing myself to drift into a sleep so deep not even the constant present feel of those calloused hands could haunt me.

Dawn peeks just over the horizon casting the perfect glow in the living room. Sable is fast asleep on the other end of the couch, soft snores escaping with each breath. The stillness through our small apartment settles something inside me, reminding me of a time so far gone... a time when peace was a part of my life.

With Oliver still in a deep sleep from his busy day yesterday this gives me a chance for some alone time. Diving into my favorite book series about high schoolers running the town with loyalty, where family runs deeper than blood, I immerse myself into the world of secrets and lies to cover the stiffness in my muscles.

I'm only ten chapters in thirty minutes later when a groggy bedhead little boy stumbles into the room asking for breakfast.

"What do you want this morning, bubs?" I ask, giving him a little control back over what he's allowed to eat. So much has already been taken away from him.

"Pancakes?" His eyes light up but the sly smile that slides on his face means he knows that this might not be an option.

"Ollie..." I warn, knowing that he needs to watch how much sugar he takes in.

Sighing, he gives me those big puppy dog eyes that yanks on something in my heart. "Sissy..."

If I don't turn away now, I'll cave. He knows it and so do I.

"Dammit," I whisper under my breath. Laughing, I peek back over my shoulder on the way to the kitchen. "One pancake and no syrup. You can have some eggs and one piece of bacon though."

When a grin so big all his teeth show appears on his freckled face, I know just how easy it is to manipulate me and damn did he just win this one. Shaking my head as we go into the kitchen, Oliver takes a seat at the counter messing with a few Legos that were left there from last night. I pull out everything I need to get started with breakfast.

The smell of bacon is strong enough to pull Sable out of her dead sleep because it's only been twenty minutes and she finds her way in here to grab a hot cup of coffee.

"What are you guys doing today?" she asks, her voice filled with sleep.

"I'm going to take a hot shower before me and Ollie spend the day cleaning and watching movies until I have to go to work. Isn't that right, dude?" My 'dude' comment makes him scrunch up his nose. "What? I'm too old to call you dude?" I laugh.

"We have to clean?" he whines.

I nod, turning my attention back to the food before it burns. "Yep. It's cleaning and chill day."

"Ugh."

That's the only response I get while he gets back to messing with his toys. Sable watches me intently.

She's waiting for me to bring it up. Watching for my freak out, but she won't get it from me. Not after everything I've seen and been through. Last night was nothing new. The only thing that spooked me more than me hitting my head was the fact that this happened at work with bouncers and other men around that are paid to protect us.

"T—"

Raising my hand, I cut her off. "Not now." Motioning toward tiny ears, she knows this isn't the time.

"We need to talk about it. Are you seriously going back tonight? At least take a day off to get your head together." Concern fills her tone.

Plating our food, Oliver digs in as soon as the food reaches him. I signal for Sable to bring hers with her to the living room. We both take a seat on each end of the couch. Turning inward to face each other, realizing that this conversation needs all of our attention. This isn't just about last night, no, I have more on my mind than that.

This is also about the auction that I have planned and put together for this weekend. Sunday to be exact. Raven had a hand in helping me, Sinner Sunday.

"Sinner Sunday," Is the only thing I say. Watching the confusion morph into shock almost has a giggle breaking free.

She chews down a bite before speaking, "You really think you can go through with this? After being attacked last night, you still want to set yourself up for something like this?"

"I'm drowning in bills. This could really set me and Ollie up for a month or two if I can get a high enough bid."

My fork clinks against the plate, my eyes drop down for a split second until I swallow down my nerves, my back straightens with steel reserve.

"Sunday. I'm doing it Sunday. Raven has already put out the information to the regulars that she works with, and we have Taz keeping an eye on everything to make sure nothing comes back to bite us in the ass."

"This is prostitution!" she yells.

We both look over where Oliver was sitting only to realize he has finished his food and is now back in his room. Needing to reign in this whole situation I break down the plan with her, hoping this will make her feel better about the whole thing.

"Look at your arms. Hell, look at your head. You were knocked out eight hours ago."

"I know you're worried but look at my eyes. The bags under them are drowning me. The bills are killing us. We need more, and this could give us breathing room. I just want to breathe." Wetness tracks down my cheeks until the sobs finally break free.

Breaking down after all that's happened is freeing in a way that's impossible to explain but at the same time, I feel so weak for crying when I need to be busting my ass to get us out of this mess.

"Shhh." Sable moves over to my end of the couch, her plate now on the floor. She moves mine aside as well to hug me. "If this is what you really want then I'm with you no matter what but if you think you're doing this without me being there then you really have lost your mind."

My cries turn into laughs. Both of us laughing so hard we cry more. The tears not happy nor sad, just the shock of where life has led us.

Two young women struggling to survive by any means.

Putting ourselves in danger to care for the ones we love, when all along we could have run away from the responsibilities of it all.

I could never do that to Ollie. The image of the first time I held him floats into my mind, I'm doing this for him, for us.

Come hell or high water, I'll be there till kingdom come.

CHAPTER FOURTEEN
ATHENA

"At least Vic isn't always such a pig, letting you take the floor instead of working the stage," Raven says, hip checking me on the way to the private rooms in the back.

She's right about one thing, Vic didn't have to let me stay on the floor serving verses being on stage. Ever since I started here, he has kept me on a short leash. *The big ballers love you. They want to see you move. Your dancing captivates them. I don't see why you're surprised that ass keeps them begging for more.* All the small comments flood back to me just thinking about the creep.

"Red, over here," Taz shouts over the loud music.

We are getting ready to open the doors for the night. Having the bar set up, chairs and tables cleaned, and everything stocked because tonight is going to be one of the busiest. Deadly Sins is hosting a special on private dances to pick up clientele, but I think Vic forgets how unsafe that could make the girls with the prices being lowered.

The cheaper the dances the more the men get handsy. That's why we love the high rollers that come in here, they pay high price and follow the rules. For the most part.

"What's up?" I step up to the bar when Taz slides a Malibu Rum my way.

"Here. Take the edge off. I can see you freaking out from across the bar."

Looking over the glass at Taz I appreciate the way his black shirt clings to his wide chest, the cuff of his watch drawing attention to his large hands the way his veins pop against the deep red neon lights surrounding the bar. Blinking back into focus, my eyes catch his taking their time to assess me as well, so when he finally sees me watching my grin spreads.

"Thanks, Taz, anything I can help with?" *Like licking the sweat off your neck...* I shake the thought out of my head not needing those problems right now.

He smirks like he knows where my head was, he nods his head over to the booths. "Can you clean those last three for me? I need to get the bar stocked before we open in fifteen."

Clearing my throat, I nod and walk quickly to the three tables left of the entrance door. The same tables where Ezra and his friends sit when they come in. A shiver of excitement shoots through me with the very thought that he might come here tonight to watch me or to take me up on my offer that my big mouth spit out the other day.

With my mind on the gray-eyed mysterious man who has a tendency to stalk people, I don't notice when the doors open letting the crowd in with it. When I hear the chatter of entering customers I head over to the bar to drop off the cleaning rag. Rushing back to the dressing room to get cleaned up and ready for the night my mind drifts back to him, the only one who has ever made heat pool in my core with chills of anticipation covering my body.

Half an hour later the black lace boy shorts I'm wearing start to ride up my ass with each step I take toward the bar to grab more beers for a group of what looks like freshly-graduated college kids. My hands barely close around the last bottle when a girl named Sage, with long blonde and blue hair, and whiskey-colored eyes steps up beside me.

"There's a sexy ass man in room three requesting you."

Her eyes dart from me to Taz, the slight pause making my eyebrow raise just enough to catch her attention. Her gaze snaps back to mine before I have the chance to say anything and then she's walking away.

"Wait!" I chase her not quite able to walk as fast in these damn heels.

She sighs before spinning on her heels, the bright green and red glow of the stage lights making her jawline appear sharper, more angled, her eyes hard.

My mouth opens with a smart-ass remark not knowing what I did to earn a spot on her shit list but not giving a crap either way, but before the words are out, she cuts me off.

"Listen, I don't care why everyone is obsessed with you or why you get more stage time than the rest of us just stay the hell out of my way."

"What does he want?" Skipping over her comment I ask

what I need to know most. Am I about to give my first lap dance in one of the private cubes?

Rolling her eyes, pupils dilated almost covering the brown. "He wants a milkshake. What the hell do you think he wants, *Red*," she blurts, my stage name a curse lashing out at me.

What drugs has her wound so tight? Not giving her a response, I turn on my heels making my way to the back of the club where the cubes are located. Taz spots the direction I'm headed, his eyebrow dipping with an unknown emotion but before my brain makes the connection our eye contact is broken by a man ordering a drink for him and a woman hanging off his arm.

Rolling my shoulders keeping my head high, it takes effort to ignore the catcalls with a few touches so quick it's more of a whisper of air.

The cubes are lined in the back of the club. The walls glass tinted so dark you can't see in giving a sense of privacy but the cameras on the inside ensuring the girls are always safe. Security watches the camera, the men getting a free show having their cake while eating it too.

Passing the first two, ignoring the groans coming from inside, my feet jolt to a stop outside the third where I'm supposed to be. Admitting that it takes longer for me to enter than it should is a hard pill to swallow even before being attacked last night I had done well with avoiding doing private dances. Giving myself a second to breathe, I use those few moments to look over myself noting that even with the girls help the bruising is still visible when you look hard enough.

Stop stalling, Athena. Swallowing down the last of my pride my hand closes over the cold metal of the handle pushing slightly causing the door to creek open. The lighting is sparse. The black light above my head casting a glow from above making it hard to make out the man sitting in middle of the room. His harsh stare burning my skin, sending a zap of electricity down my spine.

His presence consumes every atom surrounding me, setting my body on fire. His face is covered in shadows blocking his features but the way the hairs on the back of my neck stand on end alerts me to who's sitting before me.

"Ezra."

Heart rate speeding up with each inhale, taking all the oxygen from the room. One foot moves into the room when his tall frame leans back into the plush leather chair halting my forward movement. I give myself a mental shake before the tips of my finger nudge the door shut, the click of metal making me jolt.

"You said you'd dance for me. I'm here to collect on that promise." Dark promises drip from his voice.

CHAPTER FIFTEEN
EZRA

My gaze trails down her face to her heaving chest, the rise and fall holding my attention. The feel of her stare lights me on fire. The hunger I had to set eyes on her turns to a low simmer now that she's finally within reach and fuck if it doesn't feel like my skin is a live wire in her presence.

The black light above changes colors once again settling on a bright green banishing the shadows finally giving us both what we want, what I needed, a full view of each other.

When her smart mouth tempted me with a private dance, I was well aware that she was being nothing more than bratty, those pouty lips spewing sass. Little did my little Sinner know just how desperate I was to get my hands on her.

"Of course, sir."

She keeps her eyes trained on me never wavering in her smooth, precise steps. The red heels making her legs look longer than they are. Fuck me, now all I can do while I watch her walk to me is envision her legs wrapped around my head squeezing me while she fucks my face.

Clearing my throat to clear the image I lean back in the chair, spreading my legs wide letting my hands rest on my thighs.

"I assume you know the rules?" Silky words spill past from her luscious, pouty mouth.

"No touching," I reply. The rule tasting like acid on my tongue.

"Mhhmm," she hums, finally reaching me.

Pillowtalk by Zayn starts to play from the speakers around the room signaling her that our one song has started. The devil himself hand-picked her to drag me down to hell. Her body riding the waves of each note, matching the tempo each roll of her hip's spears heat down to my dick.

My hands fist around my thigh attempting to keep them off her because I'd be damned if anyone or anything keeps me from watching the way she sings this song with each sway of her hips.

I thought the devil sent her to me but now? No, I was wrong. She is the fucking devil. My own personal demon filled with all the Sin my mind has conjured up for my own torture.

"Don't."

She peeks at me over her shoulder, her ass so close to

my dick if it wasn't locked in my sweats, I'd have it in her tight little pussy. Grunting, I drop my hand back down, gritting my teeth to keep myself in check, that possibility laughable.

"Red." I practically growl when she presses her palms on my inner thighs, hovering her thick hips just above my cock that's aching to slam into her.

In one smooth motion she turns, hooking both legs around me and the chair. Her arms circling around the back of my head. She's so close now that our breaths mix. Between us, the steady roll of her body brings her core inches from rubbing across the tip of my dick. My little sinner knows exactly what she's doing. I bet she can feel my dick getting harder, even though she isn't touching me. I can't wait to wrap my fist around her hair while I fuck her pretty mouth.

"You're a naughty little thing, aren't ya, Sin," I whisper.

"Sin?" Her question comes out breathless but not from dancing.

She's leaned over me with her mouth lined up against my ear.

"Yeah, Sin. You make me want to show you just how sinful I can be. And your mouth is going to look like heaven wrapped around my dick."

Her eyes pop open. The black of her pupils blown wide, her breathing starts to turn ragged. My girl likes the sound of that. Before she gets too far in her head my mouth slams over her lips, teeth clashing together with the force.

Her body tenses for a few short seconds, preparing myself for her to pull away, but then she shocks the shit out of me by kissing me back.

Taking what she wants her legs start to shake from staying hovered over me, but the moment she loses herself in this kiss they give out landing her right on top of me. All of me.

My hand slides from her throat to right under her jaw, tipping enough to open her up for my tongue to sweep in her mouth. *Fuck.* The taste of hot chocolate and cinnamon explode on my tongue making my dick jump in response.

"Ohhh," she gasps out.

It's only a second later that she finally remembers where the hell she is, the song is coming to an end. Jerking back our eyes meet, her lips glistening under the light before it turns a bright blue, the whites of her eyes almost completely covered with her dilated pupils. Using her shock to take in as much as I can knowing any second, she'll run.

"Damn, damn, damn," her chants come out shaky.

I let out a low groan.

Her hands rest on my shoulders, using me to push her body up when I see it. The bruises lined down her arms scattered in some places. Her attempt to hide them almost worked until she started to sweat off whatever coverup she used.

"What the fuck is this?"

Flinching, she fully pulls away from me. The wall behind her eyes slamming back down so quickly it knocks me off balance. Hell no, if she thinks I'll back off after tasting her she's fucking insane. Athena is mine.

"Athena, what the hell are these from?" I demand.

Her feet carry her backward toward the door. Jumping up before she gets her hand around the handle, we match step for step. One forward one backward until her ass hits the glass wall behind her.

Rage takes over until red is all I see. My fist closing around her jaw, forcing her to look at me when she speaks the name of whoever did this.

"I won't ask again, Sin."

I loosen my hold on her making sure she can breathe. Moving into her space, my lips trail up her neck sliding across her milky skin.

"Tell me. Who the fuck touched what's mine?"

"I'm not—"

Squeezing a little tighter to cut off her words, my teeth nip at her throat,

"Yet. You're not yet, but once I have my dick buried deep in your tight little pussy making it drip with every touch, every lick, every fuck, you'll be mine. Mine." She whimpers when my knee slides between her legs. "I can feel the heat from your pussy through my pants."

"Ezra," she rasps.

"Tell me who it was, and I'll let you ride me until you're done. Don't tell me and I'll have you begging me to let you fuck my leg, understand?"

How far is too far? Knowing that line, and being unable to stop at that line when it comes to her is two different things. Athena has my dick leaking like a teen hiding in the bathroom with his father's Playboy. Applying a little pressure, her mewls makes me harder, the thin fabric of her boy shorts soaked all the way through.

"What will it be?"

Pushing my knee between her legs harder, grinding it against her clit she starts to sway so I let her lean back against the glass all the way,

"That's it, baby, use me to get yourself off. Grind that sweet pussy harder. Come for me."

Breathy moans mix in with the song playing in the room, the light switching to a dull red casting shadows on her face. Taking her mouth in a deep kiss our tongues battling for dominance I use the distraction to bring my other hand around to her ass lifting her off her feet.

The tilt of her hips provides the perfect position for her pussy to slide up my thigh, the hand gripping her ass moving her up and down my leg.

"Ezra," she moans, my dick throbbing from her needy voice calling my name.

"Good girl, Sin, ride it out."

My teeth threaten to crack under the pressure of holding myself back from slamming her down on my cock. Thrashing her head back into the wall I trace the column of her neck with my tongue, the sweet taste of her skin driving me fucking mad.

Her orgasm builds with the shake of her legs as she uses me to reach the edge, but she still needs something to send her over. Knowing just what my girl needs my hand closes over her throat once again applying just enough pressure to give the illusion of not being able to breathe. Timing it with the next grind of her pussy on my leg, she shatters, her legs giving out completely under the pressure of her orgasm.

"Fuckkkk," she groans.

"Who was it?" I ask, letting my grip loosen.

"Some random old bastard from the club. He pulled me off stage."

Her eyes are glassy with her release, I wait for moment before I set her back on her feet to adjust myself in my pants, my dick still painfully hard. Not sorry that I used her orgasm high to get information I kiss her one more time before I walk back over to the chair to grab my shit from the table.

When I turn around Athena's eyes are blazing, the red in her hair glowing against her pale skin in the low light that has now turned an ashen white shade.

"Who the fuck do you think you are?" Her voice rises over the speakers.

It's almost cute the way her gaze tracks my movements, her hand now on her hip. The fucking spanking I'd give her if we were somewhere else. Not hiding my smirk, walking back up to her until she's right back against the glass, head tipped back to look me in the face.

Leaning down to speak in her ear, "I'm the man who just made you cum without ever touching your sweet little cunt. Next time, you'll be coming down my throat coating it with the taste of you, while my fingers are sinking into your warm pussy."

Red spreads from her neck up to her cheeks, the pink a stark contrast to her bright eyes. Backing away, I give her space to process my words. All thoughts of her being a virgin vanished when her soft skin touched me but now that word slams into me. *Fuck.*

"Athena—"

No other words escape before her hand lashes out striking me across the face.

"Oh shit," she mumbles.

Growling under my breath the little sinner in front of me stands tall, watching and waiting. "Oh, Sin, you better run."

With those last words she snaps out of it swinging the door open, bolting out of the dim room without looking back.

I keep my eyes on her until she disappears behind the stage assuming she's going back to where the girls stay when they aren't on stage or on the floor.

I think I'll keep my little sinner. My dick jumps in response to that thought.

CHAPTER SIXTEEN
ATHENA

S yrup drips down my chin onto the table where Sable, Oliver, and I are seated. It's the morning after my run-in with Ezra. The tingling between my thighs a reminder. Thoughts of him and his rough hands on my throat a distraction. Another drip of syrup, this time my French toast plops back onto the plate falling off my fork, when Sable eyes me from across the booth.

"What are you daydreaming about?" Her eyebrow rises in question.

My eyes track Oliver, watching him take a bite of his eggs, making sure the small phone he has is enough distraction for us to talk.

Lowering my voice, I reply, "Ezra showed up last night. Asked for a private dance and then things... happened from there." Hesitating, I look down at my plate picking up the fallen piece of bread soaked in sugary goodness.

Feeling the heat of her stare on the top of my head she waits for me to glance back up before she speaks.

"And you're just now telling me, why? Did he say what he wanted?" Her voice squeals with excitement.

Sending a kick into her shin, she yanks her knee into the tabletop grunting with the impact.

"Keep your voice down!" I whisper-shout.

I take the opportunity to shovel more food in my mouth, not quite ready to tell her everything, not sure I should at all. My skin still burns with his touch. My body craving more pressure from his body, his crude mouth turns me on. Not knowing I would get off on being talked to like that. Yum. Now flashes of his mouth slamming onto mine are taunting me.

"T! Holy fuck, what did ya'll do? You can't even focus enough to tell me." Wide eyes study me, looking for something on my face.

When she finally finds what she's looking for her mouth pops open, no sound coming out.

"Close your mouth!"

"You had sex with him?! What about Sinful Sunday?"

Slashing my hand through the air, my eyes bounce around the cafe' hoping none of the older customers overheard Sable's loud ass. Not spotting anyone looking over here with disgust I turn back to her, gulping down my sweet tea, wetting my dry throat.

"He saw the bruises when I got closer to give him his lap dance, then he fucking lost it. He demanded names and called me his, there was a feral look in his eyes." My voice so low I wonder if she heard me.

"Holy shit."

Wetting my lips, I smile. "We... umm." I pause, not sure what to call it. Hey, Sable, I dry-humped this random guy who has stalker issues, I loved it and want to do it again.

Yeah, nope. Or how about, he choked me and called me his property like I'm a piece of meat and my pussy clenched with each suffocating moment. She'd kill him and then commit me to a looney bin.

"Athena, we tell each other everything. You know better than to think I would ever judge you; did you have sex with him?"

Sighing, I shake my head. "No. Of course not but I did have the best orgasm of my life, without his hands ever touching me. At least not where I needed them," I say, looking away. I can feel my cheeks getting pink.

"You mean the best orgasm you ever had that you didn't give yourself?" She snickers.

My eyes roll so hard I feel a headache building. That, or Sable's smartass remarks are finally eating away at my brain.

"So..." She rolls her hands in a 'continue your story' gesture.

"He held me against the glass by my throat while I rode his leg. What else do you want me to say?"

She chokes on her water spewing some on the table, grabbing Oliver's attention in the process, cutting off the rest of our conversation.

"This..." She stops to cough a few more times. "This talk isn't over. You owe me a movie night and story time bitch," she retorts lightheartedly.

After that, we go back to eating our breakfast, more like

brunch, and talking about small things like her new place. Her and Mike have been arguing about little stuff ever since she moved in, and I can tell it's taking its toll on her. Lately her eyes are surrounded by dark circles, she's washing her hair less, and the exhaustion pours out of her. She has never been like this even when working doubles at the club all weekend. I'm starting to worry about her.

After we finish eating I make sure to check Oliver's sugar levels. Sable watches as I give Oliver his insulin in his stomach trying to use a different spot. I know he's getting sore, but he knows how important it is to take care of himself. After he has his shot and a juice packed, we all head to the park. This becoming our routine, to let Oliver play a while.

New York's weather is usually consistent. Unfortunately, today doesn't fall in that category, with the wind whipping our hair around in the warm air giving an almost spring-like feel.

"Oh, shit," Sable squeaks, grabbing my arm to halt our movement.

Looking from her face, I track her line of sight, leading me directly to a set of cool gray eyes. Son of a bitch.

"Oliver!" My voice is harsh, but it does the trick and grabs his attention. I motion for him to come back to us. "It's too busy today, why don't we go home and play video games?"

"But my friends are here." Disappointment lines his features.

Oliver has so little chances to make actual friends but here at this park has been the one place he always has someone to play with. Am I really going to let this asshole take that from us? Rolling my shoulders, I meet Ezra's glare head on. Screw it.

"Ollie, you stay near Sabby okay. I have someone I need to go talk to."

Oliver takes off toward the swings before my words fall from my lips. Sable nudges me with her shoulder giving me her famous, *I'll kick his ass,* glare before she slowly follows Oliver.

It takes a full two minutes before my feet move from their place on the sidewalk, not giving a shit when people snicker at me standing in the way. I stroll over to him, hating the way his full attention has my body coming alive. Loving it too? I need to stay far away from the broody bastard.

"Ezra." I try to sound annoyed but fail.

"Sin." His deep rasp sends shivers down my spine, reminders of last night.

"Don't—"

He cuts me off. "Don't what? Call you sin or make you fuck my leg?" His smirk shows his beautiful white teeth but the way his eyes darken with the threat it looks more like a snarl.

"Stay the hell away from me and my family." I jab my finger into his chest.

He's unfazed by my outburst. "What's Sinful Sunday?" His teeth grind with each word.

My eyebrows hit my hairline, eyes widening. "How the hell do you know about that?"

Reaching in his pocket he pulls out a small red and black card. Handing it over to me, he waits for me to finish reading it.

Sinful Sunday Invitation
Admission $1,000 Time 10pm
Auction for the Holy Grail – Starting bid is $10,000

Cash ONLY!

"Dammit." This has Raven written all over it.

"Want to tell me what's being auctioned, Sin?" His tone and stance tell me he knows just what the hell's at stake here.

Looking to the left my gaze lands on a few kids playing, keeping my eyes on them, I state, "None of your damn business."

It takes two beats. Two beats of my heart before he's crowding my space, driving me backwards until my legs hit something hard. Glancing behind me, my knees are pressed against a picnic table. Ezra's hands shake by his sides.

"What's being auctioned, Sin?" he demands.

And damn if my panties don't get soaked by being bossed around by this man. My breathing picks up, so close to him that my breasts graze his shirt. The small contact making my legs tremble slightly.

Ezra's presence is so overwhelming to my senses every touch, smell, sound feels like it will make my pussy combust. One small fan of his breath and I'm done. Pushed over the edge right here in the middle of Central Park.

"Me," I squeak

My voice is so low I doubt he hears the words, but his eyes are so fixed on my lips that I know he read them when his pupils dilate so wide the color is consumed by darkness, his tongue tracing the outline of his mouth.

Warm hands slide around my neck pulling my front flush with his hard body his smell overriding my every thought. The warmth from his exhale causing me to break out in goosebumps. Leaning down, he lets his lips trail across my cheek until they meet my ear his words making my thighs clench.

"Over my dead body. If you step foot on that stage to sell your tight little cunt to anyone, your ass will be marked red for a week."

"And what if I don't care what you say?" The way my words spill out on a breathy exhale he knows just how much he's affecting me.

"Don't step foot on that stage, Sin. I'd hate to kill all those wealthy fuckers who bid on your tempting ass." Studying me. "I was right. You are my own personal brand of Sin." Almost speaking to himself.

"Screw you," I reply.

"Oh, you will, and you'll be a good girl for me too, won't you. So, fucking good."

One hand moves to my throat, lightly applying pressure, the other drifts down to the small of my back. "So needy. I bet you're drenched for me, isn't that right, Sin baby."

I groan. The need to touch him, his skin, his lips, it's almost cathartic.

One moment his teeth are nipping at my neck, his lips leaving a trail of fire, and the next he's standing up right watching me intently while I try to gain control over my body.

"Have a good day with your family." The abrupt way he kisses my head, turning away to continue down the street sends warning signs to my brain and my body. This man is dangerous. I need to stay the hell away from him.

Why does that thought burn more than his touch? My skin cools with the absence of his body heat crowding me in, a numb feeling taking hold of me.

Sable watches me the entire walk over to the swing set knowing she wants to bombard me with questions on what just happened. Who is this man and how does he command my being with so much power? I need to know more about my stalker.

~

"Holy shit," yells Sable.

Jumping out of my skin, I curse under my breath. This woman will be the death of me one day with her loud mouth. We are seated on the couch, noses buried in our phones doing as much research as we can on one Ezra Finlay, owner and CEO of Finlay and Co., a company that houses a plethora of different titles: lawyers, protection services, private investigators, and other departments as well.

"He's loaded. Not only that, but this man is on the cover of a magazine with a headline titled the Sexiest, single CEO!" She thrusts her phone in my face, almost smacking me in the nose.

Gray eyes shine back at me through the phone. A form-fitting Armani suit clings to his biceps, Ezra's perfect white teeth blinding women with his smile spread across his face. My heart stutters in my chest. The feeling foreign and unwelcome. His striking looks mixed with those filthy words are an intoxicating combination, making my mouth dry but another part of me oozing.

"I don't care about his money. He has a possessive issue with something that doesn't belong to him. Me. He has it in his head that I now belong to him, his own personal toy to play with when he pleases." My words are grumbled from my rising frustration.

"He has no idea who he's messing with. I'm not easy prey but if he wants to dance in the flames, I'll show him just how bright I can burn."

My words are steady even when I can feel my mind start to crave his domineering control. Awakening something deep inside that's clawing its way up to the surface. The part of me that my pride wants nothing to do with, the part that yearns to be controlled.

Begging for someone to show me how to submit to their power. Allowing me to fall over the edge knowing he could catch me, even if by my throat. I only ever fall into the depth of his immense possession and pleasure. *I'm so fucked and the feeling of being trapped by Ezra Finlay has my core dripping with want.*

CHAPTER SEVENTEEN
ATHENA

"She's baking"

"I see that."

"Does this mean sissy is sad?"

My back is turned to the two culprits who think they're being quiet. Flour coating my hands, the feeling so familiar it settles something inside me. My fingertips roll the flour into small balls. Closing my eyes for a moment to force the voices in the back of my mind back down into pandora's box, praying it stays shut longer this time.

You're worthless.

She left you not him.

He will never need you as much as he needs a real mother.

How could someone love a street rat like you.

Words spewed with hate run on a loop through my head until all I see is a small broken little girl begging her mother to stay, to love her, hoping she would hold her through the nightmares. Unknown to the girl how harsh the world could be. But in that moment, she learned the hard way not to trust anyone who hasn't earned it. I can feel the anxiety start to climb, trying to claw their way out taking over my movements.

"Athena," Sable whispers, standing just behind me. Her soft hand reaches around me to grab the cookie cutter from my hand, placing it on the counter. Pulling me until my clouded eyes meet hers.

"Hey, look at me, you're here with us. Me and Ollie. Breathe in your mouth and out your nose," she says gently, her face serious while standing in the middle of my storm.

"Sissy?" Oliver's voice cuts into the white noise drowning out the static.

Taking in a deep breath on the exhale I finally move back to what I was doing without acknowledging what just happened. There's a form of peace in letting family wash away your demons. I'm thankful to have such an amazing best friend and little brother. My life wouldn't be the same without them.

"Would you like a cookie, bubs?" My voice enthusiastic.

I can see the wheels turning in his head wondering about his medicine at the same time not wanting to turn down one of my infamous chocolate chip sugar cookies. Three pans. That's how many cookies I've baked since three this morning unable to sleep.

"I can have cookies now?" Oliver asks, bouncing on his feet, keeping his face neutral in case I change my mind.

"You can have some of these cookies." I wink at him.

My laugh breaks free when a look of confusion turns to disgust.

"Sugar free cookies? No!" Oliver declares loudly, making me and Sable double over in laughter.

It takes a few minutes to gain some sense of control over our outburst, so I decide to let him off the hook.

"They have sugar. It's a sugar called Stevia, which is still sugar and you have to watch how many you eat but you can still have sweet food in moderation. Just promise me you will always tell me when you start to feel sick even when you don't want to stop playing with your friends."

"I promise." Oliver runs over to give me a hug.

My heart pangs when I no longer have to bend down to hug him. He's getting so big yet she's missing everything; his milestones, his brilliant jokes, all the moments I cherish she just throws away.

If tonight goes as planned, I'll not only be able to pay off his medical bills and get us out of this apartment, but I could fully adopt him as mine. The risk is high on reporting this to the state but if I can prove I make enough it just might work.

"All right, shorty, time to get dressed." Handing him two cookies, I point him to his room. "Go ahead and pack an overnight bag, you get to have a sleepover with Sable and Mike."

Unease seeps in at the thought of him sleeping some-where else but I trust Sable with my life, extending that to Oliver. I know she would never do anything to harm him.

While Oliver is packing an overnight bag Sable and I go over his insulin, what he can and can't have, and what to do if he starts to feel sick.

Nerves build in the pit of my stomach but tonight has

been in the works for a week now. Add the fact that it's officially my birthday, I have to make this go off without any issues.

"So, all you want for your birthday is to be dicked down, eh?"

Sable has always been able to spot when I'm spiraling so the joke does as it was intended. Both of us in hysterics.

"Happy birthday to my vagina," I declare, knowing she hates the word.

"Ugh!" Shoving me, she walks by me to make her way over to the couch.

We both plop down beside each other, still laughing before she looks at me from the corner of her eye.

Clearing her throat, she sighs. "Are you sure you're ready for this? And I don't mean the auction. You know he's going to show up. What are you going to do if he's the one to buy your contract?"

We had a contract drawn up with the basics on it, half up front and the other half after the deed is done. All they get is sex, nothing more, and I'm only signing off on a one-time deal. After all they can only pop my cherry once. The small piece of paper feels heavy in my back pocket folded like a used napkin instead of a sex contract.

"It's just sex, even if he does buy me. But what's to say he wins the bid? Raven said she has at least twenty men who paid their admission already. Anyone could out-bid him tonight."

I'm hoping someone out-bids him, but logic rears its ugly head reminding me that this is Ezra Finlay, CEO billionaire, and stalker extraordinaire. Or am I confused, and I want him to win while logic is on my side? Damn.

"I want you to call me if anything goes down that's not

planned. Taz will be there to guard you making sure nothing happens. The other girls will be there as well." I can see anger taking over her face. "Maybe I can switch places with one of the girls to make sure someone has your back."

"I'll be fine. Raven will be there, she is my guard dog. Oliver adores you. I need you to do this for me. Let's make a deal."

"Let's hear it." Sable giggles.

"Neither of us let it get past one in the morning without checking in with each other. Deal?"

She nods emphatically. "Okay. Deal."

We shake on it laughing the whole time. It's not until Oliver comes rushing out of his room an hour later asking about dinner that the time flashes at me from the clock above the stove, eight o'clock. Two hours until...

"We should head out."

Sable packs up some leftover food to take with them for the night, Oliver grabs his bag filled with his medical kit and a vial of insulin before he gives me a tight hug. Being away for a whole night won't be easy on either of us.

"Make sure to put your kit in the fridge when you get to Sabby's." I remind him.

We all make our way to the front door of the apartment, the light from the hall shining in through the small window to the left side.

Sable yanks me to her, wrapping me up in one of her warm bear hugs,

"Be safe or I'll be really pissed. I love you, come hell or high water," she whispers.

"'Til Kingdom come," I whisper back. She squeezes even harder before her and Oliver head out to meet Mike in the parking lot.

Locking the door behind me I welcome the reprieve from all the chaos.

Let Sinful Sunday begin!

CHAPTER EIGHTEEN
ATHENA

"Stop it," Sage snaps, smacking my hand away from my hair.

"Okay, okay, that's enough," I sputter

It's the same cycle repeatedly, me tugging at the curled strands around my face and Sage popping me for it. Both of us sitting under the harsh bright white lights of the vanity. She and Raven have been fussing over me for over an hour attempting to get me ready for tonight's auction.

"Fine. It's done with now anyway." She rolls her eyes with a soft smile, no malice to be found in her tone. "Take a look and let me know what you think."

"She looks freaking hot, Say!" Raven says, walking around the chair I'm in, looking me over with approval.

They turn the chair to let me see my reflection but when my eyes connect with the woman in the mirror, I'm stunned silent. Where I have wild red hair, she has perfectly controlled ringlets, my pale creamy flesh is marred with warm-colored blush and foundation, but it's my eyes that have me taking in a deep breath.

The emerald green shines like the brightest crystal against the smokey eye make-up Sage put on me. The dark gray color making my hair and eyes the center of attention.

"Holy shit." My voice is breathy with adoration.

"Damn right, my bitch is smokin'!" Raven says, cackling when Sage throws a blush brush at her head.

I'm still turning left and right admiring her handy work when Sage walks over with what appears to be a red leather jacket and black lace bodysuit. The jacket is long enough to reach my thighs but it's the beautiful black and red heels with a big red bow on the back of the heel that has me drooling.

"Whoa."

Settling it down on the couch a few steps away, her hands reach out to pull me up. The look in her eyes is one a mother might give her daughter on the night of their prom, knowing what normal teens do on those evenings. The caution in her stance has me pausing.

"Are you sure you want to do this?" she asks, almost sheepishly.

"I have—" I start but she keeps speaking. Her words spilling out of her.

"I'm with you no matter what you choose but are you sure? Because this is something all girls wish they had the choice to give away, but some are so eager to grow up they throw it all away. You have the opportunity to pick, hand-fucking pick, the person you sleep with for the first time and you're selling it."

Taking in a large gulp of air she pushes through, "We have grown to love you in the short few weeks that you've worked with us, so we worry. Just make sure this is what you want."

When she's done her and Raven wrap me in a warm hug, both trying hard to avoid flattening my hair, then they toss the outfit at me to change.

Once everything is in its place, I add a beautiful set of dangling earrings that look way more real than they are.

It only takes a moment to add a deep burgundy lipstick to match the deep red of the jacket before we're walking toward the door.

Taz's voice booms from the announcement speaker on stage. The club closed for the auction. How everyone pulled this off I'm not sure.

Sage and Raven flank me on both sides, leading us to stand behind the curtain waiting for my que to enter. After a few shakes of my shoulders, the tremors subside leaving adrenaline in its wake.

"Tonight, Devilish Desires has a special treat for you. Tonight, we host Sinful Sunday. A closed auction for only our top VIP clients. You will see waitresses stationed around the room to cater to your every need. The bar is open for orders; however, specialty menus are provided in each private booth with new prices for the evening." Taz speaks clearly with no hesitation.

"Before we introduce the Holy Grail, let's go over a few of the rules, shall we? First and foremost, there will be absolutely no fighting. We have guards throughout the club watching. Second, no touching allowed. Third, raise your numbers if you want to bid, do not under any circumstances get out of hand. And lastly, all money is to be paid before you leave here tonight with your prize." As he finishes, I swear I hear a little disdain in his tone.

"Okay, Red, this is it. Are you ready for this?" Sage whispers.

"Stop it! You're going to bring the nerves back. I need to do this with a clear head and no fear." Hugging her one last time before I head out, I say, "Trust me, this is nothing I can't handle."

I hope like hell that's true! No turning back now, Athena, get your head in the game.

"Now, the main reason you wealthy bastards have joined us. Let's welcome to the stage... Red!" Shouts, cat calls, whistles, and more reverberate through my body. The noise strong enough to have me vibrating in my skin.

Squeezing the girls hands one last time my head rises high, not willing to show weakness.

Each click-clack of the heels hitting the hard stage echoes in my mind, all other sound fading into the darkness. I can feel his presence before I make it past the curtain, like a powerful current of electricity buzzing across my flesh, sparking fire down my spine.

"Shit, shit, shit." Is my mantra with each step.

The stagehand opens the curtain letting in the array of colors from the lights overhead, momentarily blinding me. Blinking, the spots in my vision fade away until all I see are rows and rows of booths lined with privacy tents around the top as if they were in a classroom taking their state test.

I can see each of their faces, their body language, the sneers, but more frightening than that is what I don't see. Or who I don't see.

My body is aware of him being in the room, but my gaze

has yet to spot him among the men in the room. The lights go down until only a small spotlight is lit across my face moving from head to toe showing off every inch of me for them to see.

"Why don't you give us a little spin, Red," Taz says, motioning for me to walk in a circle by twisting his finger around.

A familiar song, *Belong to you* by Sabrina Claudio, plays in the background, giving me a smooth beat to move to.

Biting down on my lip hard enough to spill blood, my eyelids flutter as my hips roll to the sensual song. Each word etching itself into my skin.

My arms slowly raise above my head twisting and swaying, causing the leather jacket to slide open, revealing my entire front, the scrap of lace barely covering me.

In a final effort to sell them, I use the sexiest strip move possible, letting the leather glide down my arms giving myself goosebumps with the chill of the cool material. With a soft plop, it lands on the stage behind me, giving each pair of eyes the perfect view of my ass with the thong of the bodysuit providing a clear shot.

"Okay, let's go ahead and start the bidding!" Taz says, seeming distracted by my dance as well.

Using this time for the men to do business, my eyes track each shadowed corner looking for my stalker. The feel of his presence too strong to deny seeking out. My stare locks with several men's as they raise their cards in determination to own me. Fear creeps in at the thought of one of them having their hands all over me. Their dick inside me. Shit!

Not seeing Ezra sends disappointment through me. Surprising myself at the reaction of not seeing him.

"Twenty thousand," Taz yells.

Holy shit. Over a dozen cards fly up, Taz spouts more numbers, each time fewer and fewer cards go up, until there are only two men bidding for the right to defile me. Taz is spewing numbers left and right when the hairs on the back of my neck stand on end, firing awareness through my being.

Ezra's close. Each inch closer lights me ablaze, not knowing where he is sends a thrill through me, my heart starts racing. He's playing a game and I'm the prize.

"Two hundred and fifty thousand dollars," a deep voice says lowly from the back of the room.

Groans and scoffs sound from around me. The men not happy with being out bid, especially with this being a silent auction.

"Excuse me?" Taz questions into the darkness.

My chest rises and falls with exhilaration knowing who is standing behind the shrouded space coated in the dark shadows, embracing the cover of blackness, waiting and watching the show.

My steps falter when Ezra steps from behind the obscured booth making his appearance known. He continues moving forward toward the stage, time slowing down to allowing me to observe him.

Ezra is dressed in black dress pants, a white button-up shirt that grips his biceps and torso showcasing his every muscle and sharp edge. My eyes catch on the sight of his forearms on display from his sleeves rolled up just below his elbow. Purr!

The veins roll with the pump of his fist. The tension rolling off him feeds my inner demon, the one he claims calls to him. The image of those forearms caging me against the wall, his desk, my kitchen counter all slam into me at once.

129

"I said two hundred and fifty thousand dollars cash," he repeats calmly.

Taz's eye dart to me, standing just ahead of me at a makeshift podium made just for tonight. I can see his unease from my peripheral, but I keep my attention trained on the man making his way to me.

When Ezra reaches me, his hands lash out so quickly my head snaps back with the force of him throwing me over his shoulder.

It's then that the entire room erupts in chaos. The bouncers charge the stage while Taz stands there stunned for a moment.

"Put her the fuck down!" They train their guns on him.

Damn. Shit. Fuck. This isn't about to go over well.

"Ezra get your hands off me!" My legs swing from side to side trying to connect with something, anything, to thwart his forward movement.

His rough palm whips out, making contact with my bare ass. The thong eaten by my ass cheeks, the loud smacking sound silencing the room.

What the hell. I'm the only female who can say they have their ass on display, thong disappeared by their fucking cheeks, a red mark, and a wet pussy. Who the hell am I?

"I told you the rules and you, my little sinner, thought you could break them while I sat back and watched? Just wait until I get you to the back room. You better have a God to pray to, because I can assure you, baby, I'm no saint," he growls out.

Tossing a few wads of cash toward the crew he ignores the guns pointed our way and keeps walking toward the room the girls use to get ready. Raven and Sage are watching with wide eyes, but with one shake of my head they stand down. I'll deal with this bastard on my own.

"Put me the hell down, you asshole!" I screech.

Chuckling, his movement jostles me, the sound traveling straight to my clit. His fingers cling to my inner thigh, pressing me into him while he walks the tips of his fingers so close to my center, that the heat pouring off him engulfs me.

"Keep rubbing those thighs together, Sin and I'll be tempted to put something between them," he grits out.

We finally make it to a room in the back of the club where a man dressed in an all-black suit is standing by the door guarding it, I assume.

"Mr. Finlay." He nods, not sparing me a passing glance.

He didn't seem the least bit worried that his grumpy-ass boss had a half-naked woman over his shoulder, with his fingers so close to my pussy he might as well take a dip inside. Who the hell is this man?

The click of the door closing behind us echoes in the dead silence. My heart hammering in my chest but it's the pure anticipation rolling off me that has me taken back. Somewhere deep under the fear and anger hides a part of me that loves the feel of this.

Ezra stops in the center of the room sliding me down his hard body, every hard part of him, until the heels of my shoes hit the ground.

"I'd be a good girl and watch that pretty mouth. My control is slipping, and I'd hate to fuck those pouty lips right here." His lips are near my ear, the warmth of his breath whisping across my heated skin.

My lips clamp shut to block out the needy moan trying to escape.

"Good girl, Sin," he utters.

His hands spear through my curled hair yanking me back, sending pain through my scalp. His lips slamming down on mine takes the sting away. His kiss is like being drowned, wanting air so bad, but unable to come up to let the oxygen into your lungs, the pull to go deeper all consuming.

Using his tongue to pry my lips apart he invades every inch of my mouth to steal all that I have to give with this kiss. I can feel his control slipping, his teeth clashing with mine, looking for something to sink into, his body vibrating with need.

Shoving away from him, my legs wobble from the force of his overwhelming presence.

"Athena..." His voice is gruff.

CHAPTER NINETEEN
EZRA

Wide eyes bore into mine, the rise and fall of her chest draws my stare to her perfect frame. The beaded jewels lining the curve of her cleavage stand out against her creamy skin. Taking my time admiring the lace outfit she picked for tonight I follow the material down until it reveals her milky thighs that clench with the heat of my attention.

"Patience, my little demon," I whisper, taking a step toward her.

It takes a huge fucking effort not to mark her pretty skin with my teeth. The force of my hand, the pressure of my palms closing over her throat. That perfect shade of pink covering her flawless skin calls to me like the devil calls to his demons. Fuck, she might just be the devil.

"You can't—" she starts but with one look from me her lips clamp shut.

"Good girl."

Her teeth bite down so hard her lip turns a bright red, so close to breaking the skin that my dick twitches leaking with the desperation to fuck her warm mouth. She's going to look so fucking good tied to my bed, blinded and bound at my mercy.

"I warned you, Sin. Now you belong to me. Mine to fuck, play with, and touch whenever I please." One more step.

Her eyes darken with the movement. "One night. That's what you paid for, no more no less," she states triumphantly.

I chuckle. The dark sound makes her jump. "Oh, you think I paid a quarter of a million dollars to pop that little cherry of yours?" I laugh.

"Oh no, Sin baby, I want you for a month. Thirty days or you get nothing."

Licking her lips, the bottom one sporting teeth marks that make jealousy buzz deep in my bones. The desire to replace her marks with mine unbearable. Athena takes a step toward me, surprising me by the shear bravery of getting closer to a ticking time bomb.

"Why would you want thirty days? What's in it for you? How would that work?" she demands, the words spilling out.

I can sense the anxiety flowing off her, but I don't back down not when she's so close, her body heat chills my skin. The visible swallow is telling me what my nearness does to her, so I make the last step forward slow and deliberate, using my finger to lift her chin bringing those bright green eyes to mine.

"I get you. That's what I get out of it. I get to have you all to myself to do as I please until you're begging me to stay," I reply. "We'll draft up a contract to make it official if that's what you want, but you are mine, Athena. Understood?" Her pupils dilate.

"Yes, sir." Her words are almost a moan.

Fuck me.

"Say it again," I growl out through gritted teeth.

"Yes, sir." Her voice is firmer this time.

Gripping her throat, it takes everything in me not to bend her over right here and fuck her tight pussy and make her scream loud enough for everyone to hear. Stopping myself before this goes too far too soon, I lead her out of the room taking her to put something on before we go out into the cold of New York.

"I'll be standing right here, Sin, don't tempt me to come after you again. I enjoy it far more than you know."

She doesn't speak, her cheeks turning pink as she rushes past me in those fuck-me heels to get her things and I assume talk to the girls. Leaning against the wall it takes a little under thirty minutes for my girl to return but this time she's in gray sweats and a white, long sleeve crop top.

Son of a bitch, she's even more delicious dressed like this, my dick twitching in agreement. We don't speak on the way out of the club. All eyes are on us, the bouncers glaring and the bartender watching with hate behind his eyes. I know that look.

Nodding my head at him I make sure he sees the darkness in my eyes when it comes to my little sinner.

The doors open, letting the biting wind in, the chill nips at my nose as my hand finds the small of Athena's back, feeling the goosebumps spreading across her bare skin. Why the hell doesn't she have a coat?

"You always go out without a jacket?" I ask.

She ignores me for a moment, right before I go to grab her, she finally responds.

"Do you always buy your women?" she lashes back at me.

I don't let her see the grin on my face but fuck me if my girl isn't a little spitfire giving as good as she gets.

Leading her to my 2024 Audi RS7, the black tinted windows glinting under the streetlight. I can't see her face from this angle, but her steps falter when she notices that it's not the same car from the other day.

Yes, baby, I have more than one to take you down in.

"Nice car," she says, the attitude in full force.

"Keep it up, Sin, and I'll fill that mouth with something bigger than your smartass attitude."

She tries to cover her chuckle under her breath, but I catch it and damn if it doesn't make me smile. This woman will be my own personal hell.

Opening the door for her, she slides down onto the cream leather seats, the sight of her finally in my possession settles the demon rattling against his cage. Closing the door, I press the lock button for good measure until I reach the driver's side. Getting in I can sense rather than see her rolling her eyes, the darkness covering her from head to toe.

The drive back to the penthouse is silent, giving her time to come to terms with tonight. I mentally prepare myself to have Athena in my home. This isn't something I do, bringing women back to my personal home is against the rules I have set, but with Athena, it doesn't suffocate me.

It takes twenty minutes to reach the parking garage

connected to my building, her attention directed out the window the whole time. We both step out of the car once it's parked.

"Follow me." My words are final.

Huffing, she does as she's told. The excitement I get from that is unmatched. I can hear her steps pounding behind me in anger.

Stopping at the elevator to pull out my access card, my other hand reaches for Athena's, sliding our fingers together until they are intertwined. Her skin is soft gliding against my rough hands.

Once the doors open, I pull her inside letting them shut behind us. The walls of the elevator not allowing her to hide from me.

Looking into the mirrored wall across from me, my stare connects with hers. Her eyes bright and pupils blown with want, the look she gives me a stark contrast to her words.

My hand moves from holding hers to sliding across her thighs. The rough material of her sweats are preventing me from feeling anything, but that doesn't stop her chest from rising faster.

Reaching further, my palm covers her center until I can feel her heat through her pants.

"Ezra," she says breathlessly.

She's defiant. Fighting the way her body calls to me.

"Don't fight it."

Inching higher my fingers slip into the waistband and when they skim across bare flesh I groan.

"Fuck, Sin, you're bare under here."

Turning, my other arm cages her in by her throat, bringing her eyes to mine.

137

"Keep those eyes on me," I order, pressing the button on the elevator to bring it to a stop.

"I want you to fuck my hand. Now. Here."

Her tongue peeks out wetting her lips. My eyes tracking each movement. Her breathing picks up speed.

Pushing my hand further into her pants they finally meet the silky lips I haven't seen yet but fuck me they are so wet. Sliding my fingers deeper they barely reach the entrance before she tightens her legs, making me pause.

"Easy," I whisper, leaning in to kiss her neck.

My lips trailing her neck nipping and sucking distract her enough to allow one finger to slowly slip inside.

"You're so wet, so silky. For me."

I slide my finger inside her, coating my finger with her wetness. I pull out to draw circles against her swollen little clit. She's practically panting. My dick is twitching, the urge to bury it inside her increasing in intensity. Using two fingers to rub her clit repeatedly until she's shaking.

I move down, pressing my fingers inside her as I whisper in her ear, "My dick is so hard for you, Sin. I am aching to be inside your sweet, tight pussy."

"Yes," she groans, her voice raspy. The sound has precome leaking out the tip of my dick.

"That's it baby, ride my hand."

After my third thrust she presses her hands on my shoulders, her hips thrusting forward bowing her back, riding my hand chasing the fire that's building.

I pull back to watch her, the way her eyelids flutter, the pink shade covering her chest and face, her mouth opening in a silent plea. It has my cock weeping with want.

"Yes, Sin. Your pussy is squeezing my fingers so tight. I can't wait until you're gripping my dick."

My other hand applies more pressure to her throat the

redness creeping up her neck fueling me on. My fingers twisting and turning inside her tight pussy.

"Oh god."

"I'm not God, Sin," I growl out.

"Good girl, fuck yourself with my fingers. Come on my hand," I order.

"Ezra!" She tries to yell but my hold on her doesn't let her do more than a whisper.

Her pussy clenches as she reaches her orgasm, my thumb presses down on her clit, rubbing roughly adding a touch of pain knowing just what she needs. My grip on her throat doesn't loosen with the wave of her release, causing her face to redden but she doesn't stop fucking my hand.

"Mmmmm..." she groans.

She rides out the aftershocks of her orgasm. Her pussy clenching my fingers so tight I nearly come in my pants. She's so slick right now I bet I could glide my dick right in. Her hips are still slowly rocking against my hand, her eyes squeezed closed.

"Eyes on me, Sin," I demand. The need to watch her come down from her high, strong.

"Holy shit."

I let her neck go but don't move back. The beast inside me can't move from her orbit right now. My handprint covers her neck. The demon thrashes with excitement at the sight of her freshly marred skin.

It only takes a second before she comes back down, looking around at her surroundings, noticing that we are still in the elevator in my building.

"You asshole!" she shouts, shoving me off her.

I let her go, moving back to stand next to her again, I turn my head to face her, waiting until those bright green eyes finally meet mine, I bring my two fingers to my lips and dip them into my mouth, letting the taste of her coat my tongue. She tastes like ambrosia and wicked intentions.

The look in her eyes could light a lesser man on fire. Good thing I'm bathed in the flames of hell.

My girl wants me, but she wants to play first. *Game on, Sin.*

CHAPTER TWENTY
ATHENA

The doors ding open, revealing a large foyer donned with sleek tile flooring. The open space opulent and spacious. What sounds like a TV comes from the room ahead, bouncing off the walls bringing with it male laughter. Swallowing down my anxiety, my feet carry me forward, following each step mimicking Ezra's.

The ache low in my body finally fading away into a bliss that coats my skin. Flutters in the pit of my stomach take flight, like butterflies slamming against my insides.

"Whoa," I mumble, entering the large living area.

The far wall facing the city lets in lights from the buildings surrounding us, the wall made entirely out of glass, the corners of the room housing plants hanging from small hooks in the ceiling.

My gaze darts around trying to take in everything until they land on two men sitting on the couch laughing at something on the TV, but when Ezra stops beside the black leather couch, they both look our way.

"I see you brought home a friend," one of the men says, his blue eyes tracing my body, but his stare doesn't set me on edge like the others do.

"Eros, Miles, head out," Ezra says, his voice and tone final.

The silent one with darker blonde hair the color of dish water looks at me with a blank stare not showing any sign of emotion, nods his head then stands, signaling the other to follow.

Mr. kind eyes gets off the couch, but instead of following the other, he comes up to me with a bright wide smile on his face setting me at ease. I like this one.

"I'm Eros, this broody bastard's brother." Sticking his hand out, he waits to see what I'll do.

I can feel him, Ezra, stepping to my back pressing his front into me, watching with rapt attention. My hand slowly reaches out to grasp Eros's hand shaking it.

"Hi, I'm Athena, nice to meet you," I say.

"This asshole over here is Miles. Don't mind his manners, he's the quiet one." He looks over my shoulder. "You finally bring a woman home just to kick us out? Where's the fun in that?" He laughs.

Ezra stiffens behind me, so I give Eros an out.

"I need a shower." My words a declaration.

And it's true, after the grimy shit I did tonight add that with the wetness between my legs I could use a hot shower.

It's also the only way to get away from Ezra long enough to think of a plan, a way out of here, or a way to get what I want without losing too much. He wants to keep me, and I can't let that happen. Not when Oliver is my main concern.

"Not—" he begins but I quickly cut him off.

Whipping around, my finger jabs into his chest. "Ezra Finlay don't start with me. I need a hot shower to wash this fucking day off me. Where is your bathroom?" For good measure I stomp my foot.

Eros bursts out laughing, his blue eyes shining with mirth at the thought of someone putting his brother in his place. I see Miles shift from the corner of my eye, leaning against the door frame to what looks to lead into a massive kitchen. His back is against the wood, his ankles crossed, and his arms across his chest. I can't tell from here, but I swear I spot a small lift in his lips, so I'll count that as a win.

"Sin," Ezra warns.

Turning my head slightly so he can see my face over my shoulder, I lift my brow in wait. After a second, he sighs before turning me by my hips bringing me flush with him. His large hand encompasses my face, framing it perfectly to draw my eyes to his.

"Down the hall on the left, towels are on the shelves above the toilet. Don't make me come looking for you." Before he releases me, his lips take mine in a quick but bruising kiss trying to drive his point home.

Once he lets me go, I speed down the hall finding the bathroom he directed me to, voices pick up behind me. Ignoring the men's voices getting louder I close the bathroom door sinking against it.

Get it together, Athena. It's not that bad, is it? How the hell did I end up here? I can't bring myself to blame Oliver so the first person that comes to mind is Cindy.

I'm still paying for her abandonment even after all this time of her being gone. Drugs steal every ounce of hope, faith, and trust from you. From the people around you. Until you're an empty shell of who you used to be. The worst part is no one can help you, not if you don't want to fight for yourself. And Cindy? She couldn't fathom giving up the high she got from the white powder lined down the table. Swiping the stray tear that's made its way down my cheek, I stand straight looking around the bathroom.

It's an average size room with the toilet directly to the left near a small marble sink topped with a large mirror over it in a brass frame.

Unfortunately, there is no tub in here, only a deep walk-in shower with tiles the color of dark red brick lining it. The built-in bench calling my name. Turning to the cabinet above the toilet, I open it to reveal several stacks of fluffy towels big enough to wrap around me twice and I'm no thin girl. I have curves for days.

Setting a royal blue towel down on the toilet lid, I walk over to the shower turning on both nozzles and wait for it to warm.

Should I look through his shit? He deserves it. Screw it. I turn toward the cabinets to the far side of the wall opening them to find it bare except the basic toiletry items, toothpaste, toothbrushes, etc. Boring.

Moving past the mirror I come to a stop to take in my reflection, wide eyes stare back at me. The circles under my eyes more prominent now that the makeup has been smeared, my lips swollen and red but not from the lipstick I was wearing earlier.

My curls are long gone. The strands flat with knots littered through my hair. It's a wonder I don't have a rat's nest mangled in the back of my head. Steam starts to rise, so I turn away from the stranger staring back at me, stripping down to step in the scalding water.

It takes a minute for my skin to adjust to the water, turning it beet red in the process. Images of Ezra flash in my mind; the feel of his hands around my throat, his fingers deep inside me.

I can still feel the low throb of my clit under the pressure of his thumb that final move the catalyst that sent me over the edge. The fall so blissful it took my breath away. What scares me is how wet I was under the hold he had on me. Unable to take in a full gulp of air, the line between suffocation and breathing so thin that my pussy pulses to life at the thought.

This man is dangerous, and I've fallen right into his hands. He won't let me go until he's ready, but my fear isn't how long he'll keep me, it's of not wanting him to. I just got a taste of his control, but I want more.

Washing the soap from my hair, I step out of the shower to dry off but realize quickly that I have nothing but the dirty clothes on the floor. With the towel wrapped tightly around me I open the door, steam bellowing out into the hall, I call for Ezra.

"I need clothes—" I start to say until I see the stack in his hands.

Handing them over, he studies me dripping wet in only a towel standing before him. I can see the hunger flaring in his stormy gray eyes, so I grab the clothes and head back into the bathroom not fully prepared to face him yet.

"You can run, little sinner, but you can't hide." He chuckles. The sound of his steps getting further from the door.

Taking in a deep breath, fully clothed in a pair of his basketball shorts and a large, oversized t-shirt that swallows my entire torso down to my knees, I step out of the bathroom. Time to get this over with and I know just what I need to do. The TV must be off because the house is so quiet, I can hear my own heart pounding.

"Ezra?" I call out into the empty space.

Where the fuck is he? My bare feet slap against the marble tile, the sound reverberating through me, my nerves taking over. Only the light from the kitchen ahead of me is on, the rooms lining the hall all dark from the late hour. Anticipation spikes, my blood running cold, waiting for him to jump out of the shadows.

"Ezra!" I shout into the air.

Nothing. No sound other than the blood rushing through my veins. Walking further down the hall the kitchen opens into a massive space showcasing large steel appliances, a granite island in the center of the floor, and beautiful kitchen countertops lining the right wall. It's a chef's dream space and the need to bake in here calls to me.

With no sight of Ezra, I decide to let him come to me taking my chance to rummage through his cooking supplies. I've made it through the fridge, the stove, the cabinets, and all the baking sheets before the hair on the back of my neck stands on end. Standing on the tips of my toes, neck deep in his food cabinet, the warmth of his body encases my bare legs.

"Looking for something?" he asks against my neck.

"Where the hell have you been?"

"Looking for me already?"

My eyes drift closed under the pressure of his thighs against mine. Keep your shit together, Athena, this is business. Licking my lips, my mouth dry, I turn as much as possible with the limited space he provides me. Keeping my gaze trained on his chest, I state, "We need to talk about the contract."

The mention of said contract has him stepping back a few feet giving me the much-needed space to clear the fog his presence causes. Thank God for that.

"Thirty days for two hundred fifty thousand dollars. That's my offer."

He's so confident that I'll blindly accept that it shocks him when I fire back with conditions.

"No. I have my brother to think about I can't leave him with friends for that long."

"He can stay with us here. I have more rooms than I need."

I'm already shaking my head when he presses on.

"I'll provide all of your living expenses here: food, transportation, anything you need you'll get."

"Ezra, I can't just move in with a stranger for thirty days, dragging my brother into this with me. I have no idea who the hell you are or if you're a killer. Are you insane?"

"Insane? Maybe."

Shaking my head in disbelief I consider how to do this. I need to make it sound like a better deal.

"Five hundred thousand dollars for thirty days."

His laugh sends a thrill through my body and a pulsing between my legs.

"If you want this to go your way keep your pussy under control or I'll do it for you."

I groan, his command has wetness pooling between my legs.

He steps forward one step before I halt him.

Raising my hand to stop him. "Do we have a deal?" I ask.

"Half a million dollars for thirty days?"

"I'll be completely at your mercy. In the bedroom I'll bend for you in any way you want. Fuck me, fuck my mouth, teach me everything. I'll be yours for thirty days starting tomorrow."

"You have no idea what you're saying." he declares, visibly holding himself back from charging me right now.

"I can handle it. Do we have a deal?" I demand.

"Oh, baby, you had me at fucking you."

"Get the contract typed up by someone trustworthy and I'll sign it after I read every damn line," I state.

He moves toward me, taking slow steps, watching to see if I'll run. He loves to see me run and dammit if that doesn't make me soak his shorts.

"It's tomorrow," he says, looking at his watch on his left wrist.

Closing the distance between us he lifts me by the back of my legs setting me on the counter. My legs fall open welcoming him between them, my heels wrap around him pulling him in deeper.

"Fuck, baby, I can feel the heat of your cunt."

Smiling like a meek little thing, I look up batting my eyes. "No contract, no touching." My words are final.

Growling he kisses me hard before storming out of the kitchen. He may take what he wants when I'm willing to let him, but he knows that he's not getting into my pants or pussy until we have a signed deal, and my brother is safe with me. I just made a deal with the devil to save Oliver and I can't say I hate it.

CHAPTER TWENTY ONE
ATHENA

The sound of running water echoes from upstairs where Ezra stormed off to when he left me down here, giving me the chance to snoop. My bare feet slap against the flooring, not giving a shit if he hears me rummaging through his things, serves him right. Who leaves a stranger alone in their apartment?

A woman no less. We were born curious and nosy. I pass the living room not really interested in the large open space with couches, windows for walls, and the city lights down below. No, I'm on the hunt for something more interesting than a room built on money.

Peeking into the first bedroom I pass my eyes scan the room for anything of interest, but I only spot a giant king-size bed with all black bedding, blackout curtains, a small cream-colored rug at the foot of the bed, and a closet that's partially open.

From what I can see it only holds clothes but even with the thought of something lurking in the darkness I am pulled deeper down the hallway. Softly shutting the door to room number one that looks to be a very stylish guest room I move on to the second room on the left.

A warm glow shines from under the bottom of the door catching my attention but when the door swings open it reveals a large TV hanging on the wall. The background looping on different gaming system photos.

This room must be where the guys hang out most because the sofa chairs and small couch are worn down with ass prints, the TV is still on, and I can hear the hum from the gaming system.

So far nothing has caught my eye but a man like Ezra has to have secrets somewhere, right? The white walls lining the hall are bare. So he doesn't feel the need to cover empty space like most people.

At the end of the hall there's one room left I've already seen two rooms, the bathroom, the living room, the kitchen, and his elevator. This room has to hold something of importance. Like an office to go snooping through. *Or a sex room like in Fifty Shades of Grey*. I mentally shake myself from that ridiculous thought, scoffing at the idea.

The knob to this door chills my hand but I twist it and push anyway, too curious to walk away. Whatever's behind this door better be worth the panic I feel when utter darkness engulfs me as my feet carry me deeper into the room. I only get a step or two in the room before my knee slams into a sharp corner making me cry out.

"FUCK!"

Shit, shit, shit. I wonder if he heard me. Fumbling around for the light switch I try to listen for the water upstairs to see if it's still running. My breathing keeps me from being able to hear anything over the sound of the air being pushed out of my lungs. My fingers graze over something on the wall when finally, the light pops on revealing the most amazing view.

"Holy shit."

Spinning in a circle I take in the floor to ceiling shelves lining all four walls. The shelves a deep mahogany wood holding small succulents potted in the most beautiful clay pots. The corners of the room grab my attention when I spot the many marble hanging pots with their vines extending through the room.

Looking away from the greenery my gaze skims the books covering every inch of the wooden shelves, some look older than my grandmother would be, others appear to be classics, and fictional books that I recognize.

Taking my time to absorb the beauty in the room I fully submerge myself in the shelves. The tips of my fingers softly ghosting over the spines of several books, admiring the view in front of me. I don't know how I will ever bring myself to leave this room to do anything else other than read. The couch enough reason to stay, but a nagging thought at the back of my mind reminds me this is temporary.

I'm nose deep into the prologue of a beautifully-bound leather book about ancient gods when my body becomes aware of the presence lurking just behind me. I can already feel the heat of his body commanding the space between us.

"I see you found my library." His voice isn't as hard as it normally is and I secretly wonder if being in his personal space will allow him to let his guard down.

"Mmhmm," I murmur, closing the book gently before putting it back in its place on the shelf.

"I'll show you to your bed for the night but once you have your things tomorrow and the contract is signed, you'll be sleeping in my bed. Are you hungry?" His words are a soft statement.

Breathing in deeply to let the rising anger roll off my shoulders I turn to fully face him, letting him see every emotion on my face when I speak my next words.

I think about giving him attitude but remember that I did say that I would be his for thirty days. I don't answer though.

His breathing increases slightly, the longer I stay quiet.

I stare at the ground. The sight of his bare feet making me swallow harshly. Just now noticing that he's in nothing but sweatpants with his broad chest on display my breathing picks up.

"Eyes up here, Sin." His finger and thumb grip my chin, bringing my eyes to his. "I want your eyes on me when I'm speaking to you, do you understand?" he states.

I shrug my shoulders.

He steps closer, his thighs rubbing up against my own, my breasts grazing his bare chest. My nipples scraping over his heated skin causing chills to travel down my arms.

"Do you understand?" The words are spoken low in a whisper but the authority they hold makes my panty-less pussy soak my thighs.

I screw up my lips twisting them to keep from speaking which seems to light a fire in his ass.

His grip turns bruising, leaning down he nips at the dip in my neck where my shoulder meets my neck, biting down hard enough to leave a mark.

My yelp is smothered with a groan when he licks the sting away, his tongue swirling around in a painfully slow pattern.

"Do." Bite. "You." Lick. "Understand?" Bite. His hot breath fans across the wet spots on my neck.

"Yes, sir." My teeth are clamped tight but so are my thighs.

His hands slide down to my ass lifting me high enough to allow my legs to wrap around his waist with no effort. I don't fight it because his dick is hard and pressed right where I need it.

"Good, girl. My needy little demon. I bet you're so fucking soaked for me." His words are a mix between a grunt and a groan.

"Ezra," I whisper breathlessly.

Both hands squeeze my ass, his fingers wrapping around the bottom of my thighs. Oh, so close to my aching pussy.

"I bet you're dripping down your legs right now, aren't you."

His fingers inch closer, applying just enough pressure to cause my hips to roll forward using his hold on me to grind down on his dick.

"Sin," he grunts.

I roll my hips again chasing the feeling of his hands all over me. The need to feel his mouth on me overwhelming. Ezra has a hold on my body that chokes all common sense out.

He moves so fast my stomach drops with the speed of his steps thundering down the hall, doors slamming shut and open. The only thing that I register when each step rubs that sweet spot sending fire through my body. It's not until we reach the room with the bed in it shrouded in darkness do I register exactly what's going on.

"Ezra," I say, my voice a little frantic.

I'm not ready to have sex with this man. I have no idea what I'm doing or who the hell he is I need to stop this before it gets too far.

"Wait." My voice rises.

He pauses, looking down at me, shadows dancing across his face. I feel him relax his hold on me when he senses my hesitation.

"Sin, baby, I'm not fucking you tonight. I won't fuck that pretty pink cunt of yours yet."

My anxiety starts to fade until he speaks again.

"Now, lay your beautiful ass on the bed and let me taste you," he demands, dropping me on the bed roughly.

My teeth dig into my bottom lip, my pants drenched by now, I use my hands and the heels of my feet to move backward on the bed. Once in the middle, I lay back lifting my hips to scoot my pants down to my ankles.

Ezra growls under his breath, slowly palming his dick through his sweat pants.

He leans over the bed and stalks up the mattress between my legs, leaving the pants locked around my ankles. He grabs my hands and pushes them into the mattress above my head.

His other hand skims the outline of my left breast. His thumb grazing over my nipple, my back arches off the bed with the intensity of arousal that teasing causes. My thighs try to close around his torso but he's just too wide.

I'm damn near panting, lost in the haze of his hands all over my body, running down my bare legs, caressing my stomach, pinning my hands down, it's like he's everywhere all at once.

His eyes track each movement of my chest, his stare trailing down until he stops at my center looking at what I know is a very wet pussy weeping with want.

My ass lifts off the bed looking for something, hell anything, to relieve the ache he's causing. My chest heaves with each exhale my body thrumming with need.

He slowly dips one finger inside of me. I need more. More of his hands, more of his mouth on my heated skin, I just need more.

"Eyes on me," he orders, looking at me like a starved man. "I want those eyes on me watching me taste you."

I'm squirming against the mattress. When I don't respond fast enough he leans down to bite my inner thigh, making my legs clamp around his head. His tongue lashes out to sooth the pain, but the bite of pain is so good I don't want it to stop.

"Again," I moan.

"Say it."

Wanting him to do it again I clamp my mouth shut tight, watching his eyes on mine showing him just how much I want it. His pupils are blown with lust, his gaze never leaving mine when his teeth close over my soft flesh mere inches from my core, biting down hard enough to make me yelp but his warm tongue covers the spot in seconds.

My feet dig into the bed pushing my lower body right in his face.

"Say it, Sin, right fucking now," he demands against my skin.

His teeth close over my clit applying a little pressure, but he waits. He waits for me to obey him. Growling under his breath he clamps down on my clit making me see stars through the pain. I wait for his tongue to soothe it, but it never comes.

"Yes, sir," I blurt out, needing his mouth back on me.

As soon as the words leave my lips his mouth crashes down on me, his lips parting to let his tongue lap at my center.

His lips close over my clit, nipping and licking simultaneously making my legs close over his head.

Grabbing me by the hips he spins me so fast I'm not sure what the hell happened but the next thing I know he's flat on his back head between my legs and my knees are on either side of his face.

"Ride my face until you come," he says. "But if you stop, I'll take pleasure in punishing your perfectly pale ass. Got it?"

"Yes."

My legs wobbly before I lower down on top of him, his hands curling around my legs to hold me in place. He dives in like a man dying of thirst in a drought. His mouth is everywhere licking and sucking, my hips moving in rhythm with his tongue.

I ride his face chasing my release. My body thrusts repeatedly, grinding my pussy across his face, not caring that this is the first time a man has been between my legs.

Pressure starts building low in my stomach, my breaths coming quick. I can feel him tense under me, waiting to see if I stop and I'll be the first to admit I want to see what he wants to do to my ass, but I need to come more than I need to have my kinks discovered so I spread my legs wider opening to him even more.

He takes this chance to push his tongue inside me while moving his hand between us to press his thumb against my clit sending me closer to the edge but it's not enough. I need more.

"My girl is a fighter. You need a little pain with your pleasure don't you, baby? I knew you were a demon of my own hell."

His thumb moves from my clit, sliding down for him to push two finders inside of me, working in tune with his mouth. My legs start to shake, I don't know if I can hold myself up, so I don't. I fully sit on his face grinding my wet pussy across his face, trembling harder with each suck, lick, and twist of his finger.

"Please!" I shout, unable to hold it in. My orgasm is about to barrel its way out of me.

"Cum for me, Sin." His teeth clamp around my clit, biting down hard, my orgasm convulses through my body.

I ride his face until the tremors subside and my body slumps to the side. Ezra slides from under me flipping me on my back to watch me come down from my high.

I can see the satisfaction in his eyes gleaming back at me but I'm too high on my release to care about anything else. The bossy bastard may have gotten what he wanted but so did I.

"You came all over my face like such a good girl." His voice is dripping with unbridled want.

His hand traces my body, down my legs, over to my core, swirling my release onto his fingers. My sensitive flesh is flushed red and heated, but his touch still brings me back to life.

He slowly brings his fingers up to his lips to taste me one last time. He cleans me off his skin before he leans down taking my mouth in a deep kiss, the taste of me on his lips is a drug I crave.

"Get some rest, Sinner, we have plans tomorrow."

With that he gently pulls my pants up over my ass before walking out of the guest room leaving me with a sinking feeling in my gut and sticky thighs.

What have I gotten myself into?

CHAPTER TWENTY TWO
EZRA

The smell of bacon wakes me from a deep sleep, pulling my eyes open wondering where that smell is coming from.

Last night after sending Athena into an orgasm-induced sleep, I came up to my room to relieve myself. The image of her head thrashing around in ecstasy flashed through my mind the entire time my hand pumped my cock. I finished faster than a college kid getting his first real fuck.

Tossing the sheets off, I leave the bed in search of the delicious smell of food. Stepping out of my door the loud sound of off tune singing meets my ears and the low sizzle of something on the stove.

My feet continue to pull me closer down the stairs and into the hallway the sound of Athena singing a song about wanting a guy to drunk text her and her raspy voice mumbles around a few words before getting louder on what I would assume to be the chorus.

Reaching the doorway, I stop to lean against it watching each move she makes with rapt attention. She has a way of drawing you in like the perfect melody only to strike you down like a Venus fly trap.

She sways her whole body to the tune only she can hear. Her ass shaking with each movement of her hips causing a small smile to lift at the corner of my mouth. I stay silent watching and waiting to see how long it takes her to notice that I'm behind her.

There are ingredients scattered across my marble coun-tertop, littering the once spotless space with flour, grease, egg splatter, and seasoning but the way her smile shines through each word she sings pushes the clean freak in me to settle down. Athena turns on a spin stopping in her tracks when she sees me, her eyes wide with horror, mine however, I'm sure show my amusement.

"I see you felt the need to make yourself at home." I make a show of looking around as I push away from the doorframe.

Walking up to her, my thumb swipes at the flour on her cheek that must be from some sort of breading she's baking. I chuckle under my breath. Leaning down to steal a kiss, my lips planting at the corner of her mouth, sparing her from the fact that I haven't brushed my teeth yet.

"How long have you been there?" she asks, raising the spatula in her hand to point it at me.

Turning away from her I make my way over to the coffee machine to start up a brew when she says, "I need to go home today."

Home. Ignoring her I continue to get the coffee ready, she pushes my shoulder to get my attention.

"I'm going home today," she declares, her hand pointing that damn spatula, her lips pressed together.

"Sin, it's fucking eight in the morning, and I haven't had my coffee, relax for a minute." My words come out blunt but she's not deterred.

"Look, you big alpha hole bastard I have a life, a job, and a kid to care for. Until I sign on the dotted line, I can go when I want!" she blurts out, waiving that damn cooking utensil at me.

Sighing I turn to lean against the counter watching my little demon let that bratty little mouth of hers dig herself into a deep hole. Splatters of bacon grease go flying with each wave of her hand.

I lean in to breathe in the smell that is all her, running my nose up the column of her throat, leaving chills in my path. I press one kiss just under the corner of her right eye before I pull away.

Watching the fight leave her is like watching a birthday balloon slowly deflate, losing all her fight in mere seconds. The defiance in her bright eyes is still shining but she turns back to her browning food to make sure it's not burning.

I stand there watching her every move, tracking her with my eyes memorizing her process.

"I can't let you in." Her words are so low I almost miss them.

"What, baby?" I ask, standing from my relaxed position.

"I can't afford to let you in when I have so much already taking up space in my life. Things you could never understand and it's not on you to take away my problems. This deal, this contract, Ezra it's my one shot to get my brother out of here. We can't screw this up with getting personal because this... Us? It's just business, do you understand that?" Her words coming out fast, her voice sounding more emotional.

She's plating the food, a spread of toast, eggs, bacon, and little homemade biscuits when I walk up behind her, sliding my arms around her body.

"You don't have to tell me anything about you, Sin, let me tell you what I see." Pushing her hair over her shoulder revealing her smooth pale skin, I state, "I see a woman willing to do anything for her family. A woman who is fierce, beautiful, sings off key with pride." I laugh. "Athena, I see you."

"Ezra this isn't a game and I'm not a conquest you have to win. You already bought me. What more do you want?" she whispers, her body trembling under my touch.

"I want my thirty days with you. That's all I'm asking for. So why don't you eat and go take a hot shower before we leave to pack up some of your things. Where's your brother?" I ask, wondering who she trusts enough to keep her little brother.

"Listen, we may not know each other but I need to be able to trust you around Oliver. His safety is the most important thing to me and that's why you also need to know that he has Type One Diabetes that requires insulin," she informs me.

I don't know much about Diabetes other than what I've heard but he looked healthy at the park so she must have everything under control. I'll have to make sure to call the guys and have them pop over here while we're gone to get the guest room set up for a kid. The need to make him comfortable surprises me.

"How old is Oliver?"

"He's ten and a really good kid. He'll mind his manners while we stay here but I can't promise he's not going to bug you to death about playing Xbox with him."

I step away from her back when she turns to hand me a plate of food she made for me. We walk over to the island to take a seat and eat, giving us this time to talk, her words flowing without pause now that her attention is on food. So, it's not hot chocolate that gets her day started, it's either the cooking or the food that calmed her down.

"Tell me about him." Giving her a chance to talk about something other than herself I just listen.

She tells me about the things he loves, his favorite toys, the dreams he has, and everything else she can think of. It dawns on me at some point that having Athena here planning to bring a child into my penthouse doesn't make me break out into sweats waiting for the second she leaves.

My skin doesn't itch with the thought of sharing my space with her, even for a short amount of time. She has a sense of home about her that draws me in.

Once we finish eating, I take the plates and wash them in the sink while she heads to take a shower. Drying my hands, I jog up the stairs to my room to grab a pair of black sweatpants and a white muscle shirt to set on the counter for Athena to wear home.

Once I'm done, I pull out my cell and give Eros a call to fill him in on my ideas for the room and he's even more confused by the end of the call. Once he and Miles figure out just what I went through to get Athena in my clutches they may just have me committed.

Not that I give a shit what they think but it's going to be

hell to convince them I haven't lost my damn mind paying half a million dollars for sex, like she's a prostitute. My infatuation with her is beyond anything I have ever felt.

Once we are both clean and dressed, we head to the elevator, sliding my hand into hers craving her silky skin on mine. Her eyes move to the library on the way to the foyer, the dazed look in her eyes revealing just how much she must love books and reading. That's my girl.

We step into the elevator together, the mirrored walls giving me the perfect view of her face turning a sexy shade of pink.

Leaning down to speak in her ear, "You remembering the feel of my fingers sinking deep into your tight little pussy, baby?" I murmur.

She rubs her legs together trying to ease the growing tension but the need to fuck with her a little more has my lips skimming the crease of her neck.

"I haven't forgotten that I get to punish that pouty little mouth of yours as soon as we get back. You think I'd let you get away with that bratty attitude and not paint your ass red? Oh no, baby, my dick is hard just thinking about your lips wrapped around my cock."

Her chest starts to heave when I step away to give her air, the doors dinging when they open revealing the parking garage. With her heated stare on my back, I walk away leaving my little demon fuming and needy all at the same time.

CHAPTER TWENTY THREE
ATHENA

The drive to my apartment is made in silence, staring out the window watching people on the roads going on with their lives while mine makes twists and turns that could send us both crashing into the metal railing.

Ezra gives me this time to process everything from the last twenty-four hours but all I can think about is Oliver.

How is he going to handle being moved from the one place that reminds him of Cindy? Am I really doing what's best for him, for us, or am I doing what feels right for me?

These thoughts plague my mind until the view of our rundown home comes into view outside the tinted windows of his Bentley. He pulls into a spot close to the walkway leading to the stairs and turns the car off, looking at me before he opens his door to get out. Even standing here in his sweats and t-shirt, he looks out of place in this dump.

"Just grab the essentials for now. I'll send a check for a month's worth of rent to cover the time you'll be with me," he says, waiting for me to move from my spot.

I hesitate not sure I'm okay with showing him the fucked-up conditions we've been living in knowing that he has his plush shiny penthouse to return to at the end of the day. He must sense my hesitation because the next thing I know he's standing in front of me tilting my face to his, the heat of his stare makes me restless under his scrutiny.

"Sin, baby, look at me."

My eyes slowly make their way from his chest to peer into his deep gray eyes. We stand there for a moment before he speaks again.

"You are not where you come from. It may make you who you are, but it doesn't define who you become and that's all that matters. Trust me, even the richest people can come from the gutters but it's how you claw your way out that means something." His words are said with care and a finality that hints at a deeper, darker, meaning.

You?" I start to question but the moment my curiosity is seen I can see the lights shut down in his eyes.

"Everyone has a sad shitty story at some point in their life. Mine isn't on display but just know it's there under the surface."

With that, he backs away from me giving me just enough space to slip past him, showing him the way to my front door. Inhaling a calming breath, I unlock the door and slowly open it revealing our living room. Ezra walks by me making himself at home looking at everything on display for him to view and judge. Ignoring the shame and ball of nerves knotting in the pit of my stomach I walk toward Oliver's room to grab his things first.

While I sporadically pack things in bags tossing in clothes, gaming items, shoes, and bathroom supplies Ezra is off rummaging through who knows what. He doesn't talk or ask questions or make remarks on anything that might catch his eye and for that I thank the lord above. Nothing is worse than pity. Trust me on that.

After I make sure to pack all his important items I move on to my room, placing the three bags of Oliver's thing in the living room. Ezra looks over his shoulder at me from the kitchen, most likely seeing how minimal we live but I don't let that stop me from keeping my head held high when he peers at me.

"No judgement," I blurt, my nerves sparking my anxiety making me angry at this entire situation.

He holds his hands up in defense, but I can see it now, billionaire man-candy takes in poor woman and her medically sick brother, how amazing is he! Just seeing Ezra Finlay, the Sexiest CEO cover model standing in my rundown rusted kitchen makes my shoulders tense.

Until you've had your entire life on display for everyone to see your pain, struggles, hurt, and history you will never know how it feels to have their eyes on you watching and waiting for you to do something crazy, like the scum they think you are.

I turn away from his prying eyes before I let the staring get to me, storming my way into my bedroom to get what I need. Thirty minutes later Ezra leans against the doorframe propping his ankle up against his other foot with his arms crossed over his chest. I ignore him for the most part until he finally asks what he's been wondering.

"Where's your family, Sin?"

"Oliver is my family and he's with my friend." I avoid his questioning look by turning back to finish what I was doing.

"That's not what I meant, and you know it. Where is your family?"

"You really wanna know my poor-me sob story? My mom, the amazing egg donor that she is, loved little white lines more than me and Oliver, and jumped at the chance to run off with her supplier."

"I—"

"She left us long before that, left us to starve, to be abandoned in every way but physically until recently. I raised Oliver myself."

"Sin." His voice is gutted.

My head is shaking back and forth before he even makes it to me. My ass plants on my bare bed, the bedding already pulled off and placed in a bag. His face blurry when it comes into view. Breathe, T. In. Out. I can almost hear Sable in my head calming me down.

Ride the wave, T. In and out. It's going to be okay.

"Sin, look at me." Ezra urges me to open my eyes that must have closed at some point.

I look into his gray eyes but I'm not sure if I really see him. My vision is still blurry with tears that have started to pool in the corners.

"Athena," he barks out, grabbing my chin roughly.

Shaking my head, I look up at him again letting the cool gray color around his pupils pull me in. His thumb traces my bottom lip gently, pulling it down and letting it pop

168

back up repeatedly until my chest starts to rise and fall slower. We hold contact the entire time, waiting for my attack to fade into nothing more than silent tears.

"No one is judging you, baby. No one will ever judge you for being the strong woman your circumstances made you become."

He can see the disbelief in my eyes, so he continues speaking but my eyes stay entranced in the pit of gray that is slowly dragging me under.

"Only the strong make it out and you are as fierce as they come. My little demon will scratch and claw her way out of hell through scorching fires. I don't feel pity when I see you, I feel overwhelming pride and want. I feel need. The need to have you, to capture everything that you are, marking you as mine. The last damn thing I feel or see when I look into your eyes is pity."

He waits. Giving me a chance to see into him in search of the lie, knowing I won't find one, but I look anyway.

"Do you understand that? No one sees anything but you. I see you."

He kisses me deeply, taking my mouth with force. Nipping at my lower lip, making me gasp, giving him the perfect opening to slide his tongue into my mouth.

Both hands encase my head tilting until he finds the angle that gives him full access to every inch of me. I'm breathless when he gently pulls away, his teeth scraping against my lips in one final bite.

"Take a minute to finish up in here. I'll be outside packing Oliver's things into the car."

He walks out closing the door without a glance back and it takes everything in me to keep my ass planted on the bed instead of chasing him down begging for more. I sit on the bed a little longer playing over how we got here before

169

blowing out a deep breath standing up and putting on my boss-bitch face.

A short while later Ezra opens the door to see me standing at the foot of the ragged bed looking around the room.

"It's time to go, Sin, I have a few things to do later, and we need to head out."

Nodding, I bend down to grab two bags letting him grab the rest, turning to follow him out the door not looking back. It takes two trips down the stairs to get everything from the living room floor that I managed to pack into bags.

"That's all of it. Everything we'll need for now."

"Did you grab his medicine?" Ezra asks.

"Yes. Shit. Wait I forgot something." I jog back to my bedroom for my little brown box on my nightstand.

"Just leave it, I'll replace whatever it is we need to grab Oliver before we head back home."

The fact that he just called the penthouse home instead of "my home" makes my heartrate pick up.

"No, I need my box," I say, ignoring his previous comment.

"What's so important about the box?"

"It... my things are in there." I point to the small box as he tugs me toward the door.

"Can it be replaced?" he asks.

"I need my charger."

"You want to go back in for a charger? I could buy you hundreds of chargers, Sin. Let's go."

"It's not to my phone," I whisper. My cheeks feel hot, and I just know they are scarlet red right now because the way he pauses ahead of me, his hand tightening on my wrist lets me know he's aware of what item it goes to.

"Sin..." he utters.

Huffing out air, I stomp closer to him. "Fine but you owe me a new one since you're in such a rush to get back to your cushy home," I state.

One of these days my mouth is going to get me in a heap of shit but until then I'll enjoy the way it makes his eyes light up with hunger.

"You bet your sweet fucking ass I'll get you another. Hell, I'll get you a suitcase full of them and they won't just be for your pleasure." His words are feral with lust.

"Game on," I mutter under my breath.

I swear as the door shuts behind us, I can physically feel his dick getting hard and that's the one thing that takes my mind off everything else in this moment. To have Ezra Finlay hard as stone in the middle of the Bronx.

CHAPTER TWENTY FOUR
EZRA

Once Athena gave me the address for Sable's apartment, we left her place to head across town to pick Oliver up. It's been a twenty-minute drive of tension that's grating against my skin, but my girl is breathing fire today, so I back off for the first time in my life.

Normally I'd push until she gave me a reason to mark her ass with my handprint but now isn't the time. Not when she showed me more of herself today than she wanted to. The absolute rage I feel toward a woman I've never seen utterly blindsided me.

"Sin, we're here." My fingers brush her hair away from

her face, revealing a sleeping beauty.

"Mmmhm."

Her groan sets my blood on fire.

Biting the inside of my cheek to hold myself back from doing something stupid like forcing that sound from her throat while I'm balls deep down her throat.

Her eyelashes fan across her rosy cheeks fluttering open to look at me from the corner of her eye.

"Oh. I fell asleep."

Chuckling, I state, "It's okay, baby, you wouldn't be the first woman I put to sleep."

"So, is this you warning me that you're boring? Because damn, I was hoping for a good time not a bed time," she replies, always ready to give me shit and fuck if it doesn't make my cock rock hard.

"The mouth on you, my little demon. Such a pretty sinner, I can't wait to fill it with more than just sass."

"Asshole," she mumbles under her breath, assuming I didn't hear it.

Pulling into a parking spot near the corner of the slightly larger apartment complex, putting the car in park we both get out at the same time.

"After you." I waive my hand in a sweeping motion.

Rolling her eyes, the small smile lifts at the corners of her lips giving me just what I want. A distraction for her to feel like she's in a place of comfort while we completely move around her life just for her to come back home with me where I get to play with my little sinner.

I make a mental note to write two checks when we get back to get everything squared away. I have my attorney coming by to deliver the contract while the guys redo the spare room for Oliver.

That reminds me, I need to see where they are with that

project, not that they even remotely approve of this shit-show I got myself into. Eros is more concerned with the image of the business than anything else while we know the only thing that concerns Miles is his trust issues of newcomers.

We come to a stop in front of a door where shouting can be heard behind the thin walls, making Athena bang franti-cally on the door. "Sabby!" she shouts through the door.

My muscles pull tight waiting for the door to swing open revealing anything other than a happy, healthy little boy. After a few more bangs on the door, it opens to a red-faced woman I've seen at the club before. Her hair is in a state of disarray atop her head, makeup streaked down her face, and her cheeks are red with rage.

"Sable! What the hell is going on? Where's Oliver?"

Athena ambushes her with questions while simultane-ously shoving by her in search of her brother. Sable doesn't move from her spot at the door, her eyes connecting with mine and what I see has my blood turning to ice. Fuck.

"Sin," I bark out.

"Oliver? Ollie!" she calls out in search of her baby brother.

She's becoming frantic so I slide by a stunned Sable to help find her brother since her friend is of no use right now. Athena may not see it, but I do. This is no place for a child to be and I'll make damn sure Athena isn't left to her own devices around her either.

"Sable!" Athena spins on her heel, flames in her eyes.

Sable finally snaps out of her state of shock shaking her head before she rushes forward toward a room in the back, Athena close behind her. It takes me two seconds to finally notice a man standing on the other side of a small island in the center of a pale blue kitchen with off-white cabinets.

His appearance is rugged with a scar down the left side of his face, years old from the looks of it.

"What's up, man?" he asks, oblivious to the building tension in the room.

"Who are you?" I ask, ignoring his question.

He licks his lips, looking me up and down assessing me. Most likely looking for a weakness. His type always needs an advantage.

"I'm with Sable, man. She's my old lady."

His use of that term of endearment rubs me the wrong way, like he feels the need to place claim on his girl.

"Sin!" I shout

I don't take my eyes off him for one minute. The bastard still looking me over, watching and waiting to see if I can tell he's tweaking like a motherfucker. His lock-jaw a sure sign that he is.

This guy is my last concern but getting my girl and her little brother out of here is my priority because if he even moves an inch in her direction, I'll break his fucking neck but not before I cut his eyes from his head.

"Come on, Ollie. Let's head home." I hear Athena's raspy voice behind me.

"T, wait. It's not like that. We were just having a little spat, I promise. You know Ollie is always safe here with me," Sable says, her words rushed.

"I know. I trust you with my life, but I don't want him to be around the fighting. If you want to keep him again, I need you to do that for me."

My teeth grind together at the realization that Athena can't or won't see what's right in front of her. Sable is being hit on by a fucking tweaker piece of shit and she needs to get out of here and I know just who to call.

"Sin, let's go. We need to get home."

Three sets of eyes jump to me but mine stay trained on the man in the kitchen, watching him closely.

"Oh shit. This is—"

"Yes!"

Athena rushes out stopping her from saying *this is the man who bought you to fuck you for the first time* giving away way too much information in front of a child.

"Hi, I'm Sable." She puts her hand out for me to shake.

My eyes slide from the kitchen to hers trying not to be rude, her hand is cold in my large ones, her gaze roaming over me. She smiles looking between me and Athena with so many questions in her eyes and I bet my girl will be getting a call sometime tonight with all the shit girls talk about.

"Nice to meet you, Sable, but it's time for us to go."

"Ezra," Athena warns.

Having no choice but to give the bastard my back I turn to face Athena, giving her a look that brokers no fucking argument. She swallows down her words with a shake of her head not wanting to go at it in front of everyone here including the little guy standing next to her.

"Hey, little man," I say.

He looks up at me then back to his sister before he finally moves his eyes to mine not cowering from my stare. Color me impressed with his bravery.

"Oliver," he says, sticking his hand out to give mine a firm squeeze.

I hold back my grin not wanting to come off as an ass to the one guy I need to impress for his sister.

"You like to play Fortnite?"

His bright eyes light up at the mention of the video game, distracting him from the two women with their heads bent close whispering to each other. Making sure I glance over my shoulder watching whatever the hell his name is, I turn back to Oliver, his excitement palpable.

"Well, if you want to see a cool game room then let's go." I try for friendly over being creepy.

He looks over to Athena for approval and she just stares at me in wonder.

"Can we?" he asks.

Sighing, she nods her head looking back up at me with a small smirk that cracks something in my chest. I give her a moment to say bye to her friend with the promise of a call later with all the juicy details. My eyes roll this time, then we're finally headed out the door.

"Sin," I say in a low voice.

She shakes her head in one rough motion. "Not now. I can't right now."

So, she does see it. While she gets Oliver settled in the car around all the shit we loaded down in the car I stand outside the driver's door to call Eros.

"Hey, man."

"Hey, that thing I asked you to do, is it done?"

"We're just finishing up now. About to order some pizza for when you all get home. Figured kids love pizza and games." He laughs.

"Is that Ezra?" I hear Miles ask from the background.

"Yep."

"Hand me the phone."

I hear rustling mixed with a few snide remarks from both idiots before Miles's voice comes through on the other side.

"What the hell are you doing here, man?" he asks.

I take a calming breath reminding myself that this is my best friend. Someone I consider my brother and that he's just worried about where my head is.

"Miles I know what I'm doing. Athena will be staying with me for the time being and she will be treated with respect from anyone who comes into my home. That's the last fucking time I'll say it."

"Ez, she's a fucking stripper, with a kid and problems of her own. You really think she won't get attached? That she won't cause problems in the end. You have to see how insane this is!"

"That's enough! I know you're worried about me and the company, but this isn't a conversation I'm going to have. Athena knows what this is, and we have a contract being written as we speak to ensure neither of us fuck anything up."

"A kid is involved. Ezra, you can't be this stupid. What happens when he gets attached? Are you making him sign a contract as well? You can't pull a kid out of a shithole and into a castle just to toss him back in thirty days. This goes against everything you stand for and you know it. Stop thinking with your dick and do what's right. Let them go."

With that, he ends the call, not giving me a chance to respond but what would I say? He's right on every part except one. Athena isn't the one getting attached I'm the one unable to let her out of my sight. She's dead-set on going home in thirty days and I'm dead-set on making my place feel like her home.

I should stop while I'm ahead. Let them walk away before they get too deep in my bones. The thought of watching her walk away from me instead of running to me makes my flesh feel like it's being pulled from my skin.

Once she signs on that dotted line, I'll carve my name so deep into her silky skin she'll be scarred with my brand until we both perish in the flames. There is no turning back now, not when I've tasted the ambrosia and loved the feel of her pussy clamping down on my fingers. No. It's too late now. I'm in too deep.

If she, or anyone else, thinks I can let her go now they're out of their minds. My little sinner is dragging me straight to hell and I'll play with my demon the whole way down.

CHAPTER TWENTY FIVE
ATHENA

The drive back to the penthouse was spent in silence. Oliver passed out almost as soon as we left Sable's place, making my stomach churn with thoughts of how his night really went. I know he doesn't want me to worry but the look on his face when I found him huddled under the covers in Sable's bed made my blood run cold.

What the fuck was she thinking fighting like that in front of Oliver? She knows his past of watching Cindy fight with every Tom, Dick, and Harry she could sink her claws into.

Licking my lips, I turn my head away from the window

to glance at Ezra, the way his hand grips the steering wheel, his eyes trained on the road lost in thought. He's keeping something from me but why wouldn't he? We barely know each other but if I'm going to drag Oliver into this, I'm going to make damn sure I know just who he is.

"What are you thinking so hard about, Sin?" he says, not taking his eyes off the road.

"I don't know you."

"And I know you?" he retorts.

"No, you don't and that's the point. I'm bringing my brother into a home where I have no clue who you are."

He sighs. "Ask me whatever you want to know."

"Are you serious? You think twenty questions is going to solve all our problem? How do I know you're not going to lie? We're not teenagers."

His hand twists on the wheel, gripping it tighter.

"You wanted to know me and I'm giving you a free pass to ask what you want. I can see those wheels spinning in your head. Either ask or don't but this is the only chance you get."

I glance back out the window seeing that we still have a little way to go before we get back to his place. If I'm going to get information now's the time, I guess.

"Why?"

"Why what, Sin? Use your words like a big girl."

My eyes roll at his words.

"Keep rolling those eyes and I'll give you a reason to."

How in the hell did he see that?

"Why did you buy my contract?" I ask the question that's been bothering me.

He relaxes against the back of his seat accelerating the car at the same time.

"You want to know why I paid to fuck you when I could

get any woman in the city with the snap of my fingers? Why would I buy virgin pussy when I could fuck experienced women for free? Is that what you want to know?"

I nod my head once not trusting my voice. One of his hands moves from the steering wheel to inch up my leg, causing chills to break out down my arms. My teeth dig into my lower lip when his fingers ghost over my upper thigh getting closer to my center.

Before he moves any higher, he answers me. "Because of that, baby. You're so responsive and open for me, ready at the smallest touch. You, Sin, were made to pull me in and drag me down, my own brand of fucked up sin in a bottle. From the moment I saw you I knew I needed to touch you. My dick aches to be buried deep in your tight cunt and the moment I get the chance I'm fucking you until we both break, and it'll be pure bliss tearing us apart."

His words are rough. Each syllable cutting my skin with lust. My legs pressing together to relieve some of the aching pressure. My heart beats so loud I don't hear him so he must repeat himself because now he's looking at me like a man on fire and I'm the bucket of water.

"Ask me your next question."

My throat moves with my swallow, my mouth now dry. "Where's your family? I know you have Eros, but do you have any other family?"

I know from his reaction when we were at my apartment that his life hasn't always been perfect, so now's my chance to learn more about him and his life. I need to know something more than what I have in front of me.

"Eros is the only family I have."

"That's not what I asked," I state.

His hand moves from my lap back to the wheel putting distance between us once again.

"What happened to your mom and dad?" I ask, adding more to the question.

He rolls his lips hesitating before he surprises me by answering my question. "Eros and I went into the system at a pretty young age after our mother got hooked on drugs. It took me a few years to get my shit together enough for them to give me Eros to raise until he was an adult."

I don't immediately respond, feeling like an asshole for pushing him into telling me something so personal. My hand slowly reaches out to close over his on the wheel. With one in control of the car I pull the other down and place it in my lap. We don't speak, there's nothing left to say, I just give him what I can. Support.

A few minutes later we're parking the car in his reserved spot near the elevator and my stomach drops at the memory from last night in the glass box. After waking Oliver and grabbing a few bags we head upstairs to unpack.

When the door pings open it reveals Ezra's entryway with Eros and Miles standing there, waiting for us to come up.

I look over my shoulder my eyes connecting with Ezra's in question, not sure why we have a welcoming committee.

"What's all this?" I ask the guys, hoping one of them has answers.

Eros steps closer, his deep chocolate brown eyes shining in amusement,

"This, my lady..." He does a curtsy. "Is your introduction into the Finlay household."

Miles walks up and smacks him across the back of his head.

"Ow!" he yells, turning to shove Miles back.

They start wrestling around throwing punches and

smacks to the head until Ezra comes to stand next me, saying their names.

"This is Oliver, Athena's little brother. Why don't we show him his new room?" He eyes the guys giving them a silent message. Probably telling them to behave.

Oliver looks to me. "My new room?" he says. I can see the worry in his eyes. "Are you leaving me here?"

"What? No! Ollie we are both going to be staying here for a few weeks."

"Why?" His voice is low, but I can still hear the concern.

I look to the guys silently asking for help not sure what the hell we're supposed to tell a child about this fucked up situation. Ezra stands there staring into my eyes just as lost but it's not him or even Eros that says anything. It's Miles that finally steps up and gives me the break I needed.

"Your apartment has a plumbing issue, so it needs some work. Ezra and your sister are work friends, so he offered for you two to stay here. Is that cool with you, little dude?" he says, making it sound like a month-long sleepover.

"What about my games? All of my things are at home." He looks from Miles to me.

Eros and Miles step back motioning for us to follow them.

"We have everything you need in your room," Eros says, the excitement in his voice palpable.

We make our way down the hall following the three massive men into the spare bedroom that makes my cheeks warm at the reminder. Ezra peeks at me, my body heating under his scrutinizing stare but I just lift my chin in acknowledgement of last night. His answering smirk is the only response I get.

"Here you go, little man! Your own personal bedroom

filled with all the best," Eros says like a car salesman trying to sell his last car.

Oliver steps in before me his eyes opening wide in shock but it's not until I fully turn the corner into the room that I see what caused his reaction. Holy shit. The room is completely different from last night down to the bed and TV stand.

What was once a simple spare room is now a game room with a cool neon hanging light shaped like an Xbox controller, a lava lamp, a TV that's been upgraded at least four inches bigger than the last, a bean bag chair in the corner facing the TV, and three different kinds of gaming systems.

"No," I say.

No one looks at me. The guys go around showing off different items, cool attachments, new toys, but no one hears me.

"No," I repeat louder. Oliver is still to entranced in his own heaven to hear me, but Ezra is close enough that he turns my way.

"Sin?"

"I said no." My words come out louder this time, taking the room by surprise. "No. Oliver we need to leave. No, I can't do this we have to go."

Oliver's eyes drop to the floor but it's the look from Ezra that has both lust and fear spearing through me. Eros and Miles pull Oliver over to the gaming system to keep him busy while Ezra spins me around pulling me into the hallway shutting the door behind him all before the next words could leave my mouth.

"No what?" He cages me against the wall.

I swear you can hear my gulp in the dead silence

between us. The only movement made is our chest rising with our breathing.

"We can't stay here. I'm sorry, but this isn't going to work. The deals off I'm calling it off before we get any further."

He snickers. "Like you have a fucking choice, Sin. You really think after tasting you that you could walk out of here? You really think your body doesn't crave my touch? That you can walk away from me when we barely scratched the surface? Fuck no. So what's the real issue here?" His thumb pulls my bottom lip from between my teeth.

"He'll never be okay going back to his life after getting a taste of what you're giving him. He will never be okay with what little I offer when you hand him the stars."

"Baby." His voice is low. Guttural.

I turn my head unable to handle his attention.

He leans down closer speaking in my ear his warm breath fanning across my heated skin. "You give him everything."

It's not until the pad of his thumb wipes up a tear that I even realize I had one trailing down my face. I release a deep breath trying to calm the pieces of my heart that threaten to shatter under his touch. Finding comfort in Ezra is dangerous but the walls around my heart crave to test the limits with him.

He kisses the corner of my eye in the same spot as last night, making my heart flutter with the careful caress of his lips.

"Stop thinking about everything that can go wrong and go spend time with your brother. We will give you both space, but the pizza will be here soon, along with the contract. I'll come get you when they both arrive. Your name will be on the dotted line by tonight, Sin."

"And then what?" My voice is breathless with want.

"And then I'm coming for you and there's nowhere here that you can hide. You're welcome to try though, baby." He releases me, stepping back from the wall to open the bedroom door.

He calls the guys out of the room, leading them to the car to grab our bags, leaving me on the outside staring in at Oliver sitting on the bean bag chair playing his new game in his new room with a life we both know he can't keep.

CHAPTER TWENTY SIX
EZRA

Oliver shouts something incoherent from the other room, making Athena turn his way until his shouts turn into laughs.

"He's fine, Sin. They're just playing the game." I reassure her for the fourth time in the last hour.

My lawyer is sitting at the kitchen counter sipping on a glass of water watching us in rapt attention, probably wondering if he needs to be worried about my mental capacity to make decisions legally.

This is the first outrageous request I've made but the money I pay him is substantial, so he'll do what's asked of him morally gray or not he's getting paid to sell me Athena.

"So, here's where you sign, and this is where you initial." He points to a space on three different pages. Athena listens and pays attention to every word spoken, making sure she understands exactly what she's signing up for.

We negotiated on a few things with a little give and take I was able to force her hand on sharing a bed with me instead of one of the other rooms. Like hell was I about to sleep in this house with her under the same roof and not have her in my bed.

That was a hard no for me, so I had to give her a week to adjust but she agreed reluctantly.

My inner demon started counting down the days right down to the last hour the moment I signed the papers. Now it's Athena's turn and the way her hand is shaking is visible from where I'm standing near the coffee pot.

She's giving me her body in exchange for monetary gain but if she thought she would get her money up front before I received my part of the deal, she's fucking wrong. No, we made a deal for me to pay half now and half after the thirty days are up to ensure, she doesn't skip off with half a million dollars after I stain her white panties with the sin.

My hands twitch with the need to drag her from the brightly-lit room into my bed to mark her in all the ways my demon craves. She may not have been fucked by a man before, but my little Sinner craves pain just as much if not more than pleasure.

We both do. Athena is cut from the same cloth as me where pain and pleasure ride the same fine line crossing into each other, threading the two together with perfection.

Her green eyes are so bright under the lights of my kitchen. Her eyes go over each word on the paper, focused only on what's in her hands. I can sense her apprehension but the figure staring back at her is too large to turn down when she has a mouth to feed.

"What about school? I'm taking online classes."

"You can do that here. Anything you need, I have here."

"What about work?"

"If you mean the Café, then you can drive one of my cars or I can drive you. Take your pick and I'll make it happen."

"What about the club?" she says.

My spine snaps straight. "You want to keep working at the club after all of this?" I ask.

Her cheeks pinken under my stare. "I like dancing. I don't get to do ballet anymore. So, yes I want to keep my job at Deadly Sins."

My teeth grind together in frustration. "No."

"But—"

"I said no. No one touches you, looks at you, fucking thinks about you," I growl out.

"You can't—"

"I can and I fucking will. I'll kill each and every one of those fucking pigs if you even dream of stepping back through those doors as anything other than a guest." My hands curl around the edge of the counters

She straightens looking me dead in my eyes. "Ezra! You can't keep me from working where I want. If you want me to sign your contract, you'll bend on this condition."

She doesn't look away under the pressure of my stare she doesn't even flinch. Fuck, the little demon feeds off my anger absorbing it with glee. Her lips tip up in a smirk thinking I give in, but she doesn't know who she's dealing with.

I lean toward her, not moving my feet. "You want to work on stage? Fine, but I'll be there every night buying a private dance and fucking you against the glass wall until the entire club hears my name gasping from your mouth. The women will beg me to fuck them, and the men will beg to be me. And you? You'll be so sated with the feel of my cock fresh between your legs you won't be able to move."

Her mouth pops open in shock, either at my words or the fact that Ricardo, my attorney, didn't even bat an eye. Her tongue slips out to wet her dry lips drawing my focus to her soft pouty lips, pulling a groan from my throat.

"Stop," she whispers.

I lean back against the chair behind me giving her space to process my words because I meant every fucking one of them. If I have to shackle her to my bed fucking her senseless, she will learn to do as she's told.

"What if—" she starts to say.

"Athena." My tone is steel. Using her real name instead of my name for her is enough for her to stop her words mid-sentence.

Her red hair is piled high on her head with small strands falling loose around her face framing it perfectly. Her eyes trace my face watching me for several seconds before she gives in bending down to sign herself away to a desperate madman who's crazed for her.

My mouth waters watching her hand glide over the paper each swoop of the pen gets me closer to my end goal.

"There." She drops the pen on the counter, taking a step back.

Chewing on the inside of her lip, her stare clashes with mine when I shove off the chair I was leaning on to make my way over to her. Her breathing picks up, the rise and fall of her chest pulling my eyes downward on her heaving chest. The light purple shirt she changed into after her shower is pulled tight on her frame making the outline of her bra visible.

"Okay that should do it," Ricardo says, picking up the stack of papers on the counter and shuffling them into one neat stack.

"Send me a copy once you get into the office tomorrow along with my bill," I say, walking him to the elevator.

He knows his way around the building so there's no need for me to escort him any further, so I turn back to go deal with Sin but when I return to the kitchen she's gone.

I follow the sound of her footsteps leading me to Oliver's room where the guys are piled on the bed, floor, and bean bag chair each with a controller in their hand playing the game.

Athena stops at the doorway to look in watching them play, laugh, and have fun. Oliver's face is red from laughter his smile so wide it reveals a mouth full of teeth but it's the look in Athena's eyes at the sight before her that has my chest aching.

"He's never going to want to leave."

"Sin, you have a check for two hundred and fifty thousand dollars in your hands. You will find a way to give him everything he needs and wants," I point out.

She nods her head absentmindedly still watching the guys play and joke around, their laughter spilling out into the hallway. Miles and Eros are having the time of their lives entertaining Oliver and that gives me an idea. Athena may have bargained for a week to adjust but I've held back this long, what's another week?

With that thought, I start to put together a plan for seven days from now because once I get my hands on her naked skin, I'm aiming to sink my hooks in deep. Sin, you better pray to a god because the devil just made a deal and his little demon just sold herself to him.

CHAPTER TWENTY SEVEN
EZRA

I t's been seven days since Athena and Oliver got here. Seven days since she signed the contract giving herself to me for a month. Seven days since I touched her skin in anything more than a passing touch. The demon is rattling his cage in protest, but I wanted to give them time to settle in.

Times up. Unable to hold my attention on the files sitting in front of me I lean back in my chair. My office is quiet. The midday light barely peeking through the window.

My phone rings for the fourth time in an hour. Glancing down I see it's Selene again. She's been calling me several times a day. Ignoring the call, I finish with the paperwork on my final client for the day and start to clean up my desk before heading home.

Tonight's plans are already being put in motion. Right this moment, Eros and Miles are surprising Oliver with a movie and ice cream night out.

There's a knock on my office door then shouting before my office door slams open revealing a red-eyed Selene looking completely disheveled. She storms toward me barely giving me time to stand before she's slapping me across the face with an open hand.

"Oh gosh!" Bailey shrieks, rushing toward me.

Selene twists around lightning fast to shove Bailey, sending her down on her ass before my reflexes could reach out for her, but the surprise wears off fast my hand striking out to snatch her by the arm.

With one pull I jerk her away from my assistant, giving her the needed space to get off the office floor.

"What the fuck are you thinking?" I yell, shaking Selene with one hand and wrapping my fingers around her upper arm with the other hand.

She starts to shake, a mixture of rage and sorrow fighting for dominance behind her eyes. The latter finally winning. Tears pour down her face leaving black streaks in their wake, but I feel nothing for the woman in front of me.

"Selene, what the hell are you doing here? Hitting me and assaulting Bailey? Are you fucking nuts?" I pull her close growling my words into her face. I can taste the rage on the tip of my tongue.

Her lower lip trembles slightly under my harsh gaze. "How could you? I thought I meant something to you!" she screams.

"What in the fuck are you talking about?" Releasing my hold on her arm, I shove away from her.

The last thing I need is a domestic assault charge from her crazy ass accusing me of something that's not true. I know women like her, she's looking for something, anything, to get her back in my bed but that's not going to happen.

"I saw you moving her into your place! That's against the rules, Ezra!" She stomps a stilettoed foot.

"You saw what?" I demand.

"Uh... I saw... You were moving a woman into your place." She stumbles over her words.

Anger is laced in each word spoken. "You've been watching me, Selene?" I step closer. "How did you get into my building?" Another step. "How long?" Toe-to-toe, her eyes widen when she sees the venom in my eyes.

My body vibrates with the force of my rage boiling the blood in my veins.

"Ez, don't be like that. You know I love you. You love me too don't you, baby. You do." Her voice turns meek trying to pull me in.

"Selene, I'm going to say this once so make sure you're fucking listening to every damn word. Stay the hell away from her. Don't come within fifty feet of anyone connected with me. Do you understand?"

Selene doesn't move, her eyes don't blink, she's frozen in place.

"Selene! Do you fucking understand? If you even breathe near her or anyone close to her, I'll bury you and your father, and you know exactly what I'm capable of." My voice pure steel.

Her head jerks up. Her glassy, tear-filled eyes meet mine, mouth stunned silent by my threat. Sucking in a breath she nods her head slowly in a daze, likely from the adrenaline.

With a wet face and unsteady legs, she inches away from me until she's far enough way and spins away on her expensive heels, darting out of my office as fast as she came in.

"Bailey, are you all right?" I ask, my mousey assistant standing near the door her eyes never leaving mine.

"Yes, sir," she replies, her voice soft.

"Cancel anything left on my calendar for today and tomorrow."

"Yes, sir." She turns to leave when I stop her.

"Bailey," I call out. "Have Selene added to the list of people who are banned from the building. Have my team track her for the time being. And Bailey?"

"Hmm?" she hums out.

"She'll never touch you again."

She nods softly.

I storm by her, my hands itching for Sin.

Raspy giggles greet me in the foyer, the sound floating in from the hallway coming from the kitchen. The moment my eyes meet Athena's from across the room every muscle in my body relaxes, my shoulders dropping the heavy weight from the day.

"Ezra," she says, looking away quickly.

With her attention turned to her cooking, which I learned she loves to do, I let my smile escape.

"Where's the O-man?" I ask, loud enough for him to hear me from the other room.

Running is heard from the back of the apartment when

Oliver's strawberry hair is spotted dashing around the corner running straight into my side.

"Oomph," I grunt with the force.

His high-pitch laugh warms something inside me.

"Sorry, E!" he says, between fits of laughter.

He's started calling me E or Ez, picking up the names from the guys hanging around so much. Speaking of, where the hell are they? They were supposed to be here already picking up Oliver to head out for the night.

"Hey, O-man. Where's Eros and Miles?"

Right as the last word leaves my mouth a foam ball sails through the air, pegging me dead in the forehead. What the hell?

The entire room erupts in laughter. Eros and Miles come sauntering in. Oliver is on the floor, his face almost the color of his sister's hair, and Athena. Fuck me, Sin. Her head is thrown back with her long wavy hair flowing down to her ass. The milky skin of her throat begging me to sink my teeth into it, and her smile.

God had no hand in creating her because that smile. It's forged in sadistic desire made to bring gods to their knees.

Before I know what I'm doing, my feet carry me to her fisting her shirt in my hand I yank her into my chest taking her by surprise. A small gasp falls from her pink lips, her eyes turning a deep forest green with lust.

"Finlay." Her words are a plea.

She started calling me Finlay the day she signed the contract. She thinks it bothers me, like I bought her to own her but really, she owns every part of me without knowing it. Athena uses my last name out of spite to make me feel like her master but the way it fell from her tongue sounds like an archangel worshiping at the feet of the devil.

A throat clears from behind me, making Athena stiffen

in my hold. We both look in the direction the sound came from to find a smiling Eros standing there with a glaring Miles.

"We're going to head out. Oliver's coming with us to go see the new Mario movie," Eros says, addressing Athena.

She looks from him to and back again. "Wait. What? No."

"Sin, they're taking him to the movie and then to get dessert. He's with two of the only people I trust with my life."

Her stare bores into mine, staring, searching for the lie, but she won't find it. I can see the moment defeat sets in giving up on fighting what she already knows is going to happen.

"One scoop, Ollie. No more! When you get home, we'll check your blood sugar before we do your insulin."

He nods his head up and down in jerky movements bouncing in place, the excitement pouring off him in waves.

Athena walks over to give him and hug speaking in his ear too low for us to hear her. He slowly nods his head before kissing her on the cheek and rushing out the room likely to put his shoes on.

"One scoop of ice cream, Eros. Not because I'm a bitch, not because I don't trust you. Not for any other reason than he has to be careful with his Diabetes. Can I trust you to follow one rule?"

Eros knows she means well so he lets the conde-scending tone of voice and sass of her words roll off his shoulders with a smile batting his eyes for extra show.

"You can always trust me, T," Eros says, his voice low aiming for husky.

My fist clench picking up on his attempt to flirt with her

to get a rise out of me, not that its working until I see her beaming smile from the corner of my eye.

"Eros, I thinks it's time for you to leave," I declare.

The back of Athena's hand taps my chest. "Thanks, Eros. It's always a pleasure to be around a friendly face." She cranks up the smile full force, my teeth grinding together with each stretch of her lips showing more teeth.

"Brother," I mumble.

He just smiles at me before backing away with his hands up. Athena laughs beside me, finding humor in the entire situation.

"Don't test me, Sin," I say low enough for only her to hear.

"Oh yeah? Or what? You'll make me call you daddy?" Her words wake something inside me.

The image of her lying on her back hair fanned out around her head, eyes wide in pleasure, her skin flushed with her building orgasm, her raspy voice moaning for me, begging.

Daddy doesn't do shit for me it's not my style but when my girl calls me sir while her pussy clenches down on my fingers, fuck the way she'll feel gripping my cock torments me with want.

My jaw works back and forth trying to calm my hardening dick from traumatizing a ten-year-old in the middle of a kitchen with his sister cooking.

"Time to go." My words spill out.

No one moves for a second, so I say it louder sending them into motion heading toward the elevator.

With one last smirk over his shoulder Eros leads Oliver out the doorway leaving Miles to stare at Athena before his eyes meet mine, quickly dropping to the floor on his way out.

He'll need to get the issues with Athena figured out cause she's not going anywhere anytime soon.

As soon as they pile into the elevator and the doors close Athena bolts from her spot, her long legs shoving off the tile floor with force.

"I'll give you a head start, Sin!" I shout into the dark hallway, where her flaming hair slowly fades into black.

She doesn't make a sound. I yell into the shadows, "You have an hour to do whatever the hell you need to but tonight I'm ensnaring a sinful demon."

My shoes hitting the hardwood of the stairs that lead to my room is the only sound you hear in the entire apartment.

"It's my world now, Sin. Let's hope you can be a good girl," I whisper into the void, knowing she's listening to every sound.

CHAPTER TWENTY EIGHT
ATHENA

"**I** can hear your breathing, little sinner."

His voice bounces off the walls in the darkened hallway enticing me to come out to play. The whispers of sensually-charged air cascade across my flesh leaving chills in its wake. I've managed to escape him a few times since I left the safety of the hall bathroom.

It took me the full hour he gave me to shower, shave *everything,* give myself a pep talk, and then find the bad bitch I keep buried inside and drag her to the surface.

His words taunt me with each breath I take trying my hardest to silence each exhale by breathing out my nose slowly but at the rate my heart is beating it's almost impossible to remain hidden. Everything sounds so loud in the pitch-black space between us. When he teases me again while I slowly creep around the kitchen, I have to bite the inside of my cheek to keep from responding like a smartass.

The last thing I need to do is feed the beast by dangling my foul mouth over his head knowing he'll likely fill it to the brim with all he has to give.

"Come on, Sin, I can taste your pussy from here. The smell of your fear tainted with desire drips from you."

Damn. His voice is closer than before, so I attempt to pick up the pace my eyes not yet adjusted to the darkness. Why the fuck did he turn out all the lights? I'm the prey and he's the predator. My fingertips trace their way down the walls making my way through the doorway back into the hall, heading into the far room.

Was aiming for the library in the back of the apartment the smartest move? Probably not. Not that I can turn around now with nowhere else to go, my feet silently track their way through the open doorway thankful that the door wasn't shut.

There's no telling what noise it might have made when I tried to open it. It's not until the hair on the back of my neck stand that I realize I fell right into his trap.

"Oh, little sinner you fell right into my hands." The warmth of his breath fans across the back of my neck.

How the hell did he know I'd come here? My body tenses waiting for him to grab me but when he doesn't, I make my move not knowing that's exactly what he wanted. My feet slap against the floor pounding down the hall, the sound of my heart beating in my chest the only thing I can hear.

My bare thighs rub together with each stretch of my

legs. The liquid heat dripping down my leg proof of how much I love this.

My legs pump hard carrying me up the stairs two at a time not sure where I'm going since I haven't been up here before. Windows lining the hall cast just enough glow to keep me from falling into anything in my way. I spot a door to my right that's barely open.

Ezra's close. My pussy clenching with each grunt he makes storming up the stairs behind me.

"Run, baby, I'll follow," he growls out.

Why doesn't he sound winded? I'm fucking dying from exerting myself for the past thirty minutes but under the slight stain of fear a deeper emotion comes through.

Excitement, thrill, adrenaline, they all flood my system sending me spiraling. Barging through the door it hits the wall my feet skidding to a stop to take in the room I've entered.

Before I have the chance to look around Ezra slowly struts into room. The light from the window in front of us casting the perfect halo around him.

His shirt is gone leaving him in only sweats with his feet bare as well, the scene causes my thighs to clench his beauty too much to witness. How can the devil look so heavenly?

Spinning away from him I make dash for the four-poster king bed in front of me pushed against the floor to ceiling glass wall looking out over the city. Crawling on my hands and knees I scramble up the bed trying to get as far as possible with my ass peeking out from under the long, black button-down silk shirt I put on after my shower.

"Oh, baby," he groans.

A heated calloused hand snatches my ankle, halting my advance. With one strong yank he drags me toward him at the end of the bed, using his other hand he flips me like a pancake on a Sunday morning. Oh shit.

My pulse hammers under my skin. His gray eyes bore into mine letting a feral grin take over his face, showing his perfect teeth that glint in the low light.

"There's my little sinner." His voice is sinister.

The way his eyes track me from my feet up my legs, covered only by the length of his shirt, across my breasts that heave with each inhale, and landing on my mouth that's now parted, my teeth sinking into my bottom lip.

Swallowing down the lust that coats my skin I give him a devilish smile. "Looks like the prey has fallen victim to the predator." My voice is raspy, my words low.

Looking at him from under my lashes I watch as he steps closer, my legs falling open to allow him access, his knees hit the end of the bed.

Bending down until his mouth hovers over my leg just above my knee his hot breath beats down on my skin setting me on fire.

"Looks like the predator is starving for sin."

His hand leaves my ankle to ghost over my body sliding under the shirt until his warm hand finds my bare left breast. With his fingertips tracing my nipple in slow swirls, my hips jolt forward lifting my ass off the bed.

"Fin," I moan, not sure what I am asking for.

"Lie still and don't move. I'm going to devour every fucking inch of you." His teeth nip at my skin.

Trailing his lips up to the crease of my thigh his tongue flattens against me licking across until the tip of his tongue grazes my folds. Using his free hand, he spreads me open pulling back to take in my soaked core dripping wet for him.

Pushing up onto my elbows my eyes watch his every

move, taking in the way his mouth waters at the sight of me spread bare for him.

"Fuck, baby, your pussy is so wet for me." His words are a growl.

"Yes," I rasp.

"Yes what?"

My pulse kicks under my skin waiting for what I know will come so I bite my lip holding in my response, teasing the devil with my defiance.

A slap sounds jolting my legs from under me the pain shooting straight to my clit. Holy shit, did he just slap my pussy?

"Yes what?" he demands.

My breathing is erratic, unfamiliar with the sting of pain lacing its way up my spine making it impossible for my brain to focus on anything else.

Another slap has me shouting out into the shadows, cursing the man between my legs. Before the pain has time to overwhelm me two fingers are shoved deep inside me chasing the sting away, replacing it with white hot pleasure.

"Oh god," I groan.

Pumping his fingers in and out with ease my wetness dripping down his hand, he slaps my clit once again forcing a cry from my lips.

"Sin," he grits out.

"Yes... Yes, sir. Yes, sir," I chant.

"Good girl, that's a good fucking girl. Now fuck my hand and don't come until I give you permission."

"Please," I beg.

He groans closing his teeth around my clit, nipping while his fingers scissor inside me spreading me wider. My heels plant on each side of him pressing into the bed lifting my hips higher, shoving his meal in his face waiting for him to devour me.

Releasing my clit with a tug he dives into me drinking me down with each lap of his tongue. Twisting his fingers inside me he starts to pull out forcing a whine from my throat.

"Please!" I need more. More of his mouth, his teeth, his fingers. I just need more.

"Your pussy's squeezing my fingers so tight." His words are spoken against my heated skin slick with sweat.

Using every ounce of strength, I have I use my feet on the bed and my hands that are now entwined in Ezra's hair to ride his fingers while his tongue and teeth torture my clit. Shaking with the building force of my orgasm, I climb to the edge.

"No," he grits out, pulling away from my center, his eyes coming up to meet mine.

"Fin, please!" I blindly thrust against his hand trying to cause enough friction to send me spiraling over.

Grunting, he pulls his fingers out with a wet plop, shoves my legs wider, wraps his arms under my legs pulling me to the edge of the bed, while his knees hit the floor with a loud thud.

My ass is hanging over the edge with his head lined up with my waiting pussy weeping for him. Using his shoulders, he props me up on them, so I cross my ankles behind his head inching his mouth closer.

"Good girl, baby, now fuck my face until you're coming down my throat."

He barely gets the words out before his tongue is thrust inside me fucking me with it.

Using my new position, I clench my thighs around his head at the same time using my arms to hold me up so I can face fuck him. I'm so close. Just as my vision starts to double, his thumb comes up to press into my clit while his other hand joins his tongue in thrusting into me.

"Come for me right now, Sin."

With no other words needed, stars explode. My legs shaking with the force causing me to fall back on the bed. He continues to drink me down, the aftershock of my orgasm barreling through me.

"You did so good, baby. So good, Sin."

His fingers slowly slide out of me my breathing heavy and my legs hanging off the edge of the bed.

"Sin, you look like an archangel lying here tempting me to sink my dick so deep in you we'll be falling from heaven into hell." Feral. His voice his unbridled need.

Standing he reaches into his pocket to pull out a small packet, sending my heart into overdrive. Oh shit.

You can do this, Athena. It's time. It's just sex.

"Hey, eyes on me, Sin." Words thick with emotion, he calls for my attention.

Letting my eyes meet his gray ones wide with lust I watch him slide his pants down pulling out his long, thick dick and my pussy immediately pulses with hunger.

His large hand grips his dick, moving from the head down to the base in slow sure strokes giving me a show. Lifting the packet to his mouth, my eyes track each movement waiting to see what he'll do next.

His teeth bite into the plastic pulling down until it rips open. Pulling out the condom, he guides it down until it fully sheaths his beautiful, hard dick, his eyes never leaving mine.

"Move up the bed." His words are a short, quick order.

Scooting back until I'm at the top of the bed I watch as

he crawls toward me with a predatory gleam in his eyes, his smile turning into a snarl before my eyes.

He loves the chase the sick fucker but what does that make me? The hunted who loves to be caught. I can't deny the way my blood sings in my veins when I'm caught in his traps.

"Lie back and spread those legs wide."

I follow each direction he gives me needing his reward like I need the air I breathe.

"I want you to watch me fuck you. Do you understand?"

"Yes, sir."

"I want you to keep those green eyes open for me, Sin."

"Yes, sir," I moan.

Caging me against the mattress his hand grabs my knee wrapping my leg around his waist then bring that hand back down to my center, his fingers slide up and down rubbing my release around using it to make me slick.

"Eyes on us, Sin." He reminds me when I get lost on his face.

He leans down to pop my nipple in his mouth my back arching off the bed giving him more. Pumping his dick two more times he lines the head up with my entrance nudging my sensitive pussy, making me shiver.

"Watch my dick sink into your tight cunt, baby."

His words distract me from his forward movement, each inch stretching me further causing a burn to build low in my stomach.

"Fuck!" I yelp.

He pauses not even a good two inches in to pull back and look at my face, seeing the pinch of pain in the crease of my eyes.

"Open your legs wider and breathe through the sting."

Leaning down to take my mouth in a bruising kiss my

legs fall open wider the one wrapped around him hanging off his hip. Taking this chance to slide deeper into me he uses his mouth to absorb the pinch of pain until he's fully seated, and my teeth are clamped down on his bottom lip.

My teeth sink into his soft skin so deep the taste of copper spills into my mouth coating my tongue.

Releasing him with a plop I lick my lips swallowing down the taste of him high off the feeling of making him bleed for me. He stills, letting me adjust to the size of him, licking the inside of his lip to feel for the damage.

"Oh, you like to cause a little pain too, Sin?"

"Yes, fuck yes!"

I shout when he moves back to pull out while pinching my clit.

"What did I say? Eyes on my dick sliding inside your dripping cunt."

He pulls himself up on his knees, lying me flat on my back using his hands to drag my hips forward and back fucking me slowly at first.

"Yes, Fin, please."

"Please what, baby?"

"I need more," I moan, my words jumbled together with a loud groan deep in my throat.

My eyes watch as each pull of my hips has his dick spearing into me, his pace picking up.

He grits his teeth, his hand lashing out to grip my throat, shoving my head into the mattress while he pumps into me harder. Faster. Rougher. Squeezing tighter my eyes meet his, my lips part on a silent scream as he cuts off my breathing. My legs wrap him dragging his dick deeper, using my muscles from years of dancing to fuck him.

"Good, girl. Ride my dick, Sin. Fuck yes."

His hold loosens on my windpipe, the oxygen rushing

to my head. He slams into me hard sending me over the edge, a scream spilling from my lips. His thrust slows grunting into the darkness, his head thrown back with jerky movements. "I'm coming inside you, my sweet Sin. Feels fucking amazing."

Sweat covers his skin shining in the light from the buildings outside, giving him the appearance of a dark god bathed in holy water. Damn. I'll never be the same after him.

He inches out of me slowly the sting making me grimace, the void from him pulling out echoes around me.

CHAPTER TWENTY NINE
EZRA

The warmth from Athena heats my skin with every touch as she sleeps next to me, her hair fanned out in every direction. The strength it takes not to trail my fingers up her thigh into her tight little cunt is almost unbearable but even the demon that wants nothing more than to claim her as his knows she's sore right now.

She's been in an orgasmic coma for the last few hours after I carried her to the tub for a hot bath.

The way her body melted into me fully submerged in the water settled something deep in my bones in a way nothing has before. My little Sinner gives as good as she gets but I knew what she needed once I had my fill.

I take in her high cheekbones, long lashes splayed across her pale skin, observing the way her chest rises and falls pulling on my shirt that's covering her.

My phone vibrates from the table to my right, turning over to grab it before it wakes Athena, I see it's Eros calling. Fuck, Oliver.

"Hello?" I answer the call.

"Hey, man, were headed up. The coast clear?" Amusement lines his words.

"Come on up, fucker. Athena's asleep so keep it down."

He ends the call without saying anything else. I swing my legs over the side of the bed standing to pull on some work out shorts lying on the chair in the corner of my room.

Not bothering with a shirt, I pad down the stairs turning on a few lights along the way not knowing if Oliver is afraid of the dark. It's weird having a kid around when it's usually just me and sometimes the guys.

Making my way through the apartment I come around the corner as the doors open revealing a smirking Eros, and Miles holding a knocked-out Oliver in his arms.

There's dried ice cream circled around Oliver's mouth with what looks like a new football in his arms.

"Here, I'll take him to his room," I say, making my way closer to them. I reach out to take Oliver when Miles pulls back, stopping me.

"I've got him." He looks down with a slight smile. "I'm going to go get him settled in his bed."

Walking away without another glance in our direction Miles continues to the guest room to put him to bed, leaving me and Eros to stare after him in shock. Miles and kids aren't used in the same sentence.

"He's been like that all night," Eros says, my expression giving away my thoughts.

Nodding my head, I motion for him to follow me into the kitchen so I can pour us a drink. I sure as fuck need one after the night I had with Sin, holding back isn't easy for someone with my particular taste, but being inside her knowing I'm the only one to ever touch her skin has me doing things I don't normally do.

"Want one?" I ask.

"Do you have to ask?" he replies, always the smart ass. "So…"

"I'm not talking about Sin with you." I cut him off before he can even start.

He lets the issue go, tipping his glass to swallow his drink. We stand there for another few minutes before Miles comes back out minus one sleeping little boy in his arms.

"He's out. You ready to go?" he asks Eros.

"You want a drink before ya leave?" I ask, offering him the extra glass I poured.

Sliding it on the counter toward him he grabs it up and tosses back the entire thing in one go. Eros and I watch him waiting for him to tell us what's on his mind, but he just sets the glass down and walks toward the elevator without another word. The broody fucking dick.

After saying bye to the two I head back upstairs, climbing in behind Athena who's now sound asleep on her side giving me the perfect chance to wrap my arm around her waist to spoon.

The heat from her mixed with the fire in my chest from the whiskey has my eyes drifting closed moments after closing them.

～

My alarm wakes me up at seven in the morning, going off on the end table beside my bed but it's the cold sheets next to me that has me sitting up in a rush.

"Sin?" I call out.

Getting out of bed, I dress for work knowing I need to get some shit done at the office today. There's no smell of food so she isn't in the kitchen and the shower water isn't running so where the hell is she? I walk over to my closet opening the door to grab some black slacks and a white button-down shirt making sure to dress up for the client meetings I have today.

With Athena fulfilling her side of the contract last night it crosses my mind that she could have run but why would she with the promise of another two hundred and fifty thousand on the line.

Once I'm dressed and done getting ready for work, I make my way to Oliver's room only to find it empty as well. Now I'm starting to get annoyed.

After taking my time looking through the entire apartment, I come up empty-handed. They're not here. Why the hell didn't I get her to give me her number last week? Slamming my hand down on the counter I storm out of the apartment heading down to the parking garage.

It only takes me fifteen minutes to get to the office with the way I drove through the city pissed the hell off. I'm going to paint her ass red if she decided to go back to the piece of shit apartment with my cum still fresh in her pussy.

She thinks I'm done with her? I'll make it to where no man will ever be able to make her orgasm like I do.

I'm halfway through my second meeting when my

patience runs out, making me shove my chair back sending it toppling over behind me.

Bailey and Eros look up from their files both of them startled by the sudden movement but I'm past giving a shit.

"Bailey pass anything pertinent to Eros for the day. I have business to take care of," I snap, charging out of the conference room.

I've told her once and I'll say it again. You can run but you can't hide, Sin.

CHAPTER THIRTY
ATHENA

The sun beats down on my back, the seat of the bench pinching my thighs sitting here watching Oliver play with a few other kids on the swing set. The huge smile on his face has one spreading across mine knowing he's happy and healthy right this moment. We made a deal a while ago that on days I have no school or work we'd do stuff just the two of us or us and Sable.

As I wait for Sable to meet us here, I can't help but to think about last night, the twinge in between my thighs a steady reminder of what I gave up. After we finally pulled away from each other fully sated Ezra carried me to his massive bathroom with an oval jacuzzi tub that was filled to the brim with hot water and bubbles that smelled of lavender.

The thought of a dominate, bossy, alpha like Ezra taking care of me after sex still sends flutters shooting through my stomach. I can't let him get to me, not when I'm so close to finishing this entire deal. I glance down at my phone for the third time in the past five minutes wondering where the hell Sable is.

I'm not sure what's going on with her and Mike, but it's not good. That I do know. Making a mental note to keep an eye on her, I put my phone back down.

Tomorrow I have to go back into work at the café while doing a night class so I need to find a sitter for Oliver. I also have to make sure he doesn't get too comfortable where we are because it's not a permanent situation.

Looking back over to Oliver, I watch as his head is thrown back in a full belly laugh making my chest hurt with the sight in front of me. I'd do anything for him.

"T!" I hear Sable's voice shout over the kids yelling around us.

My head swivels trying to spot her in the busy crowd of the afternoon rush. The hair on my arms stands on end, my body lighting up like a live-wire like it does anytime Ezra's around, so I take in my surroundings wondering if he tracked me down.

The need for space when I woke up drove me to grab Oliver and rush out of the apartment early this morning to give myself time to think without the overpowering presence of him.

"Sable?" I call out, still not seeing her or Ezra.

A hand lands on my shoulder a few seconds later making me jump from my seated position.

"Whoa, it's just me," Sable says.

"You scared the shit out of me!" Shoving her, we both laugh.

She walks around the bench plopping down hard on the seat, leaning back to close her eyes. Taking this time, I look her over searching for something, anything, to give me a clue as to what's going on with her but the only thing I spot are dark circles under her eyes from sleepless nights, most likely from working at the club.

"How are the girls? Raven and Sasha?"

It's only been a little over a week, but I miss seeing them and I know Oliver misses Raven even though he has the guys to hang out with now. He hasn't stopped talking about Miles and Eros since he woke up, telling me all about his night out with the boys. I mentally roll my eyes at his phrasing for the entire situation.

We talk for what feels like hours just joking around and catching up, not used to being away from each other. Being with Sable right now makes me feel like the old Athena for just a short time. Shortly after Oliver spots Sable on the bench he runs over mentioning food. Typical boy.

"How are you and Mike?" I ask in a low voice.

Oliver hasn't said much about the other day, but I still don't want him to hear what we're talking about. Sable keeps walking toward the small pizza place down the street. Her eyes looking everywhere but me, making apprehension settle in the pit of my stomach.

"Sabby, you can tell me anything," I say, reaching out to grab her hand giving it a squeeze.

Her head bows down, staring at the ground before she rolls her shoulders lifts her head high and sighs. Seeing Sable like this isn't normal. She's my badass. Always ready to stand her ground, willing to do whatever it takes to protect herself or those she loves.

But this? Shying away from her issues, not sleeping, fighting with a guy? She would never stand for this.

Assessing her as we keep walking, I also notice the way she looks leaner or skinnier than normal.

"Sable." My voice is stern this time.

I'll push if I have to because we don't back down when it comes to the two of us. She looks at me then back at Oliver making sure he stays close to us before she finally acknowledges that I asked her a question.

"I don't think this thing with Mike is going to work out.

We're fighting all the time and I swear I found drugs in his dresser the other day. That's why we were fighting because you know me and my history, I can't be around anyone with a drug problem." Her words spill out.

"What kind?" I ask, my voice hard.

If there's anything we don't mess with, it's drug addicts. We have both been abused and abandoned by them before so we know first-hand how their lifestyle could affect someone else.

"I don't know. I'm pretty sure it was cocaine, but it's not like I tested it to make sure. So, of course, he denied that's what it was." She rolls her eyes.

Biting the inside of my cheek we pause the conversation when we enter the diner, walking up to the counter.

"How many?" a short woman behind the small podium asks.

"Three," I reply.

Oliver stands to my right with Sable on my left, waiting for the hostess to show us to our seats when the hair on the back of my neck stands on end. Someone's eyes are on me, burning my skin.

I subtly look around the building trying to spot anyone who looks familiar, but coming up short. Shaking off the feeling of being watched, I follow the woman when she grabs a couple menus and walks off without saying another word.

Once we're seated, Oliver and Sable sit across from me, with my back toward the door we pick up our conversation. Oliver plays with my phone, hoping to keep him interested in something other than what we're talking about.

"You can't stay there. Drugs always leads to violence, abuse, theft, or trouble."

"I have nowhere else to go." Her eyes stare at the menu.

I take both her hands in mine, pulling her gaze to my face. "Move back home with us. Stay until you can get your own place or hell stay until we can get a house together. We're sisters. We stick together."

"I can't do that. You have so much going on in your life and now you have your bossy bastard in your life."

I waive off her excuse, "Sabby you come before anything else. Do you understand me? Ezra won't be a factor after our time is up." A twinge of pain squeezes my heart at the thought of never seeing him again, but it's just the way things are.

"Are you sure?"

"Always."

"Come hell or high water?" she whispers.

"'Til Kingdom come," I vow.

The air turns thick with emotion, but she nods her head anyway agreeing to move back home to stay with us setting my anxiety at ease.

"But not until you're back home."

"What do you mean?"

"I'm not going to stay there alone so I'll come home

when you fulfill your contract with bossy bastard." She smirks, her mood lighter now.

I rub my lips together in thought. That's another three weeks. Should she really wait that long?

"I only have three weeks left before I can move back if I want the other half of my money."

The itching sensation on the back of my neck returns. The heat from someone's stare scorches my skin. I'm being watched. Before my mind could conjure up any insane ideas, I feel the warmth of someone's breath fan across the back of my neck shooting fear down my spine.

Sable's eyes shoot wide before she relaxes in her seat, looking over my shoulder. Meaning I know just who it is. Ezra-fucking-Finlay managed to track us down.

"E!" Oliver shouts, looking up from the phone to see who just sat down next to me.

"What's up, O-man?" he asks in a light tone, but I can hear the hidden fire beneath it.

Our legs are pressed together. The heat from his body flowing into mine, overheating my skin. The hands resting on the table, looking across the table, watching Sable with an assessing gaze.

I can sense the buried distrust for Sable and anger toward me just below the surface. Knowing he's only hiding his emotions because Oliver is here. So, what do I do? I push his buttons because who are you to get mad at me for taking my brother to the park.

"Fin, how was your morning?" I turn toward him, watching the side of his face for a reaction.

The only one I get is the slight clench of his jaw, most likely biting back the response he had. His right hand leaves the table landing on my knee, using his fingers to draw small circles on the inside of my leg distracting me.

My mind clouds with each swirl of his skilled finger, my thighs twitching with each inch he moves up. My eyes flit over toward Oliver to see that he and Sable are playing videos on the phone. Thank God for her keeping them from listening in on our conversation.

"I woke up to a cold bed and empty apartment, Sin." His voice is relaxed but he's anything but calm.

"Your keeping tabs on me now?"

He turns his head, gray eyes locking with mine. "Until your time in my bed is up, you do as I say," he declares, trying to keep his voice low.

My eyes look down to his lips, the tip of his tongue peeking out. He smirks when he notices what grabbed my attention. My thoughts drift back to last night when his head was between my legs and that sinful tongue was deep inside me.

"Unless you're fucking me, I don't obey shit you say." I whisper, my voice raspy.

He leans in, giving me a feral smile. "Oh, I'll be fucking you, but it won't be that tight little cunt, it'll be your smartass mouth. Have fun with your friend because when you get home, I'm giving you ten minutes before I'm facefucking you while you fuck yourself with those pretty little fingers you love to point at me."

His words are pure filth, lighting defiance and anger deep inside me. So why is my thong soaked all the way through? I can feel my face getting pink, but is it because of his words or being pissed that he has the nerve to demand my obedience.

I look up at him batting my eyes at him with a soft smile, letting him think he has me wrapped around his dick like a bitch in heat.

Licking my lips, his eyes catch on the movement. "I'm

going to love watching you try to control me," I say in a soft purr.

His left-hand closes over my throat just under my jaw pushing my head to the side, my eyes roam the room making sure no one's watching us. His lips ghost over the skin just behind my ear. His hot breath giving me chills with each word spoken.

"I'm going to love watching you get on your knees for me, little demon, watching you fuck yourself, begging, pleading for me to replace your fingers with my dick. Your pussy is going to weep for me, dripping down your thighs getting ready for me to fill you, but the ache of being empty is the only thing you'll get."

My pulse pounds in my veins, my breathing ragged with each twirl of his finger that's almost at my center now.

"Just when you're about to cum all over your hand with my dick shoved deep in your throat, I'll pull away taking every ounce of your release from you making you watch me cum knowing you can't chase the feeling of having me buried in your aching cunt."

With those words he kisses me just under my eye, his favorite spot, before pulling back with a smile on his face leaving me to recover from whatever the hell that was. My clit throbs with the need to go in the bathroom to ride my hand with the image of his dick in my mouth, his head thrown back in pleasure, my lips wrapped around him. Damn.

"Why don't you bring Sable back to the penthouse so you can take Oliver swimming? We have a heated pool on the roof with a grill for cooking," he offers.

My mouth drops open but no words escape. My mind still on his previous words but Sable jumps in, eager to accept the offer. Her love of water and swimming coming to the surface. Oliver lights up at the mention of having a full day of nothing but fun.

"Can we invite Eros and Miles?" Oliver asks, looking over at Ezra then back at me.

I open my mouth to respond when Ezra cuts me off with his own answer. "Already done."

Great, I'm attending a pool party horny and thirsty for the controlling bastard's dick. How original, the stripper and the rich guy. What is this Pretty Woman? I know one thing for sure, the end of our agreement won't end the same way. No one falls in love and lives happily ever after with the gutter girl from the Bronx.

CHAPTER THIRTY ONE
ATHENA

"Cannonball!" Oliver yells, running full speed toward the shallow end of the pool.

The sun is high above us, shining bright enough for me and Sable to lie out on pool chairs to sunbathe. I'm still mesmerized by the fact that we are outside without actually being outside in the winter air.

Ezra's rooftop pool area has a large dome type shape over the top, blocking in the heat while letting the sun through the top. I won't lie and say it makes sense, but with the summer feel in the middle of winter I really don't care.

"This is so amazing!" Sable squeals with excitement.

Laughing at her wide-eyed expression, I take in the

room right along with her, noticing every detail. Like how Ezra is standing next to a grill that looks like it could cook enough hamburgers for a football team all at one time.

The grill stands beside a long granite counter with all the same equipment as an actual kitchen, but more. Just more.

"This place is insane," I whisper to Sable.

"I'd never leave from up here if I was you."

"I can't believe he's just now showing me this."

The dome covers the entire room with the pool in the center of the room, the shape of a huge tear drop more so than an oval, with crystal blue water and black lining or concrete I'm not quite sure.

Oliver is wading in the shallow end, most likely counting down the seconds until the guys show up to hang out with him.

"Should I be worried that he thinks two grown ass men are his best friends?" I ask Sable.

Sable stands to adjust herself on the long pool chair we are using to get a tan, if that's even actually possible through the covering. Once she's done fixing her spot, she lies on her stomach before she turns her head to look at me. Her gaze roams from me to Oliver and back again, her mouth opening to speak when excited voices boom from the far end of the room.

"O-man!" Eros shouts, walking out in swim shorts and a white muscle shirt, revealing a few tattoos I haven't seen.

"Ollie!" Miles yells, walking straight for my little brother.

Miles gives him a wide smile, showing two curved dimples placed perfectly in the center of his cheeks. Holy shit, his smile could knock a girl off her feet if she wasn't prepared for it. I wonder why he doesn't show it more.

"Eros! Miles!" Oliver says, trying his best to run in water barely moving a foot with his efforts, making us all laugh.

Turning away from the guys I look back at Sable to continue where we left off, but her sight is on something... or someone else entirely. Miles lifts Oliver up, throwing him over his shoulder before jumping into the pool, taking them both under.

When they pop back up, I notice that Miles is shirtless, wearing red swim shorts showing off strong powerful legs with a toned body.

"Look away, Sable. Down girl." I shove her, laughing at the way her eyes cloud over.

"Who the hell is he and where can I buy one?" She snorts on a giggle.

"Bitch! He's Eros and Ezra's childhood best friend but other than that I don't really know anything about him. I know he doesn't seem too fond of me, but he really likes Oliver from what I've seen so far," I tell her.

The truth is it does bother me that Ezra's best friend doesn't like me, on the other hand I don't really care. I won't be around for long and unlike what he thinks I'm not here to take advantage of Ezra, in fact it just might be the other way around.

Damn. Now my mind is on a completely different half-naked man, one who is watching me like a hawk hunting his prey. My tongue swipes out wetting my dry lips, gray eyes following every move I make.

"Damn, girl, it's getting hot in here," Sable murmurs.

Smiling, I turn my head to face her, keeping my eyes forward on my guy. "Should I take off all my clothes?" I wink at her, knowing I have my suit on under my tank top and shorts.

My guy? What the hell am I thinking?

Our laughter bounces off the walls, echoing through the entire space, our heads thrown back without a care. I've missed her so much over the last few days. We needed to spend some time together.

"Sin," Ezra calls out, grabbing my attention and effectively stopping our foolishness.

Looking up, he nods at me to come over. I swing my legs over the side of the chair pulling myself to a stand. My bare feet pad across the cool floor.

"Ezra," I state, when I stop in front of him.

His eyes are shining with an air of playfulness, but the hidden shadow screaming danger still floats around him.

My eyebrow raises in question. "Yes?" I ask.

"Yes?" he questions.

I know what he's looking for, but he isn't getting it out here with everyone around us. I just nod my head once not looking away from his intense stare.

"Why don't you introduce the guys to Sable since she's going to be around more now that you live with me."

"Temporarily staying with you," I retort.

"What?" he asks, confused.

"You said live with you but I'm not. I'm staying with you for the time being. Living together isn't the phrase I'd use."

Stepping forward to erase any space between us, he uses his forefinger and thumb to pinch my chin tilting it up, giving him full access to my entire face. He leans down bringing his mouth mere inches from mine so close I can taste the mint on his breath.

"Sin, for all intents and purposes you live with me. That's the fucking definition so get over your issues with it and watch that pretty little mouth of yours. Now call your friend over here and introduce her so I can drag your ass away from her. My hands are itching to show you what happens when you disobey me." Before he pulls away his lips touch mine so briefly, I think I imagine the kiss all together.

It takes a full minute for my ears to hear anything other than my heart beating in my chest.

Beneath the fear of what he has planned excitement festers into curiosity, and we all know what they say about curiosity killing the cat or in this case the pussy.

"Sable!" I yell, not taking my eyes of the devil in front of me.

Pulling her away from what she's doing, motioning for her to come to me while Ezra leads me over to the guys taking my hand in his. Miles is the first to spot us coming, his stare stopping on Sable who's walking up on my right with her short hair bouncing with her steps. The deep maroon of her bathing suit complementing the slight tan she holds all year, both colors making her eyes pop.

"Sable, this is Miles and Eros. Eros, Miles, this is Sable my best friend and sister." I point from the guys to her.

Bending down to extend a hand she shakes Miles's hand first, his hand engulfing her small dainty one. He holds onto her for a few seconds longer than a normal greeting, his eyes traveling her entire body pausing at her chest before coming back up to her face.

I look between the two, Sable smiles wide giving him her flirty grin that can make a man do whatever she wants.

"Eros," she says, reaching out to take his hand when Miles finally lets her hand go.

"So, you're the best friend?"

"Looks like it." She quips not able to hold back her smartass comments.

"Is that so?" Eros asks, his eyes glinting with mirth. "Good to know."

With one hard yank he pulls Sable into the pool, splashing Ezra, Miles, and me all at the same time. Oliver laughs from the other side of the shallow end when Sable comes up for air, her hair hanging in her face covering her eyes.

"You son of a bitch!" she screams, launching at him with a huge grin on her face. Her laugh maniacal.

Ezra moves to stand behind me, placing both hands on my hips. The feel of his body flush against mine makes me lose my train of thought. Dipping his fingers into the waist-band of my shorts he trails them in circles on my hip bone playing with the bikini string tied there.

Just in case the two idiots playing in the water decide to drag me in next, I step forward and to the side staying away from the edge of the pool.

From the side I see Miles move to walk down the stairs, getting back in the water. Ezra turns to face me with a heated look in his eyes, ready to consume me.

"Where are you going, Sin?"

"Who said I'm going anywhere, Fin?" I tease, keeping my voice soft and low.

Using both hands I unbutton my jean shorts slowly pulling the zipper apart, watching his eyes darken as I let the shorts drop to the group. His eyes are glued between my legs. Turning, I give him a perfect view of my ass and legs without flashing my little brother.

"Sin," he growls in warning, his voice vibrating deep in my bones.

. . .

Turning my head towards him licking my lips as I step out of the shorts to reveal deep forest green bottoms hugging my ass while matching the color of my eyes.

He takes a step toward me, then stops, watches intently when he sees my hands grip the edge of my shirt ready to pull it over my head.

"That's it, little demon strip for me," he says, entranced in my every move.

Having Ezra's full focus solely on me has my pussy clenching with need. His stare feeding my lust, leaving me wet and wanting. It's exhilarating knowing how it feels to have his hands on me, his mouth grazing across my skin, his devilish tongue inside me, and oh fuck his dick crafted by Satan himself.

I'm going to use this time to learn everything I can about being worshiped by him, learning how to make him moan, using his groans to fuel me, pushing us both over the edge.

"Yes," I tease, not fully giving him what he craves.

My hands tug the edge of my shirt up until my vision is blocked by the shirt completely and I realize my mistake. I gave him exactly what he wanted when I blinded myself by slowly stripping for him.

The second my eyes are covered he strikes, gripping my hips, tossing me over his shoulder putting my bare ass on view with my suit barely covering it.

"Fin, put me down!" I shout, but even I can hear the smile in my voice.

"Oh no, baby, you belong to me," he replies.

Using a free hand that's not trapped under his arm I pull the shirt off my head letting it drop to the ground, not giving a shit if it gets wet. Using that same hand, I reach down smacking his ass, loving the way it feels under the palm of my hand.

He tenses under me for a split second before we go airborne. His powerful legs launching us off the ground and a few seconds later we hit the water jostling me off his shoulder.

I sink to the bottom not bothering to go back up for air yet, letting my thoughts take a backseat while I enjoy the feel of the cool water surrounding me. I've always been a swimmer. It's just hard to do living in the north, but this is pure heaven.

I open my eyes letting them adjust to the pressure of the water, blinking a few times Ezra comes into view swimming down grabbing my wrist to pull me to the surface.

We both reach the top gasping for air Ezra's hand still pulling me toward the shallow end where the others are crowded around talking and playing even Oliver is a part of the chatter. Stopping just past the deep end where he can reach, he spins around shoving me toward the edge of the pool caging me against the hard concrete.

"You're lucky we're surrounded, because I'm fucking starving."

Water drips down his face, the blue from the water pulling out the blue in his gray eyes mesmerizing me. My hand lifts from the water, little droplets sliding down my arm while my fingers trace his face, down his cheek, over the sharp edge of his jaw line, until my finger finds its way under his bottom lip.

Our breaths mix in the air between us, my core soaking through my bathing suit bottom.

"Wrap your legs around me," he orders, his calloused hands lifting just under the crease of my ass.

With one smooth jump my legs close around his hips,

my body making contact with his hard dick, enticing a groan from my throat.

"Good, girl," he praises, pushing me closer to the wall until there is no space between us.

From the corner of my eye, I can see Sable glance over here a few times while trying to keep the guys occupied. Thankfully my bestie knows how to hold a man's attention. Without warning Ezra slams his mouth down on mine, absorbing all my thoughts and replacing them with him until all I see, hear, smell is the devil between my legs.

His fingers pinch my ass making me gasp, giving him what the access he wanted. The only thing holding me up are my legs and his hips pressing into me. Biting my bottom lip Ezra sucks it into his mouth sending heat down my spine.

"Fuck." I rasp.

I'm overwhelmed with sensation of him everywhere, his mouth still on my flushed skin, my core pressed against him, it's all too much but not enough all at once. My chest heaves with each pass of his lips over my neck.

"Shit!" I utter, when water drenches us from the side, a smiling Eros standing a few feet away.

"Thought I'd help cool you two off since we have little eyes around," he says with a wink.

Damn it. Ezra turns my brain to mush every time he touches me. I almost forgot everyone else was on the other side of the pool. His presence encompasses me, erasing the world around me.

Sable snorts from the other end of the pool, looking at me with knowing eyes while she holds Oliver on her shoulders gearing up to toss him under.

"Who's down for a game of chicken?" Eros claps his hands wickedly.

Before I know it, my thighs are gripped tight around Ezra's head, Miles has Oliver on his shoulders, and Eros has Sable on his with Miles tracking each roaming finger on Eros' hand. Shit's about to get really interesting.

CHAPTER THIRTY TWO
ATHENA

My eyes burn from staring at the bright light of my laptop perched on my knees which are bent toward my chest. I've been studying for hours preparing myself for an online test in a few days, the silence throughout the penthouse grabs my attention, Ezra is keeping Oliver busy in his room for me.

It's been three days since everyone came over to swim and since then the guys have barely managed to stay away for longer than twenty-four hours.

I wonder what the boys are up to now that I think about it, so I decide to go find out, setting my computer and fuzzy blanket to the side.

Getting up from the couch I make my way through the apartment until I come to Oliver's temporary space with the door cracked just a tad. Making sure to keep my steps quiet I try to sneak up on them by slowly opening the door not making a sound.

What's revealed behind the wood door makes my heart drop into my stomach, melting me completely. Across the room in the beanbag chair Ezra is leaned all the way back with a black controller in his hand with Oliver sitting between his legs on the floor with a matching white controller beside him.

I pull my fingers to my mouth gently pressing my lips closed so I don't make a sound as light tears roll down my cheeks. Oliver's head is resting on Ezra's lap, both of them sound asleep with the TV playing in the background.

My chest caves in at the thought of them losing each other because I've seen Ezra open up with him lately. The way that they bonded, how Ezra looks after him during his medical tests and insulin intake, he's always checking in on him and offering to watch him.

"Fin," I whisper, trying to grab his attention.

Wetting my lips, I bring the edge of my shirt up to swipe at the stray tears that managed to drip down my chin. Moving into the room a little further my hand rubs down the side of Ezra's back trying to wake him without waking up Oliver.

"Fin." I nudge him again.

"Hmmm," he groans, his voice deep and full of sleep.

Oliver shifts until he's fully on the floor giving me the needed room to shake Ezra so he can go get in his bed and off this small chair.

"Come on, Fin, let's get you in bed."

His arms encase me pulling me down on his lap shoving

his face in my hair in the process, sighing before he drifts back off. Struggling to get out of his hold I pinch his arm to get him to release me.

"Go get in bed." I try for stern.

"You trying to get me in bed, baby?" he whispers back, his voice close to my ear shooting arousal straight to my core.

"Don't be a perv. I'm trying to get you off the floor," I retort, rolling my eyes.

In one quick motion he's standing with my legs wrapped around his waist, a wicked grin on his beautiful face taking my breath away. The way God took his time crafting this ungodly man makes it hard to look at him, the power of his presence overwhelming.

"Oh, Sin I'll never stop wanting you and I believe I still owe you a punishment," he murmurs in my ear, slowly making his way out of the room not waking Oliver in the process.

His words sink in filling me with anticipation for what's to come, thrilled with the thought of learning more of his body, what he needs, and more importantly what lines I'm willing to cross for the devil.

He calls me his little demon and that's just what I plan on being for him. A temptress bathed in his blood drinking him down and absorbing his soul. If I'm his then he's mine and I plan on devouring everything he has to offer me.

Squeezing my legs tighter he can feel the way my thoughts drift to the plans he has for me, my mouth watering at the prospect of having him in my mouth. Pulling back, I watch his face. His steps sure and strong with his gray eyes darkening with each second.

Powerful legs climb the stairs not struggling to carry my weight as if I weigh no more than a child.

CAMIE PARRISH

Leaning forward I run my tongue up his neck and back down again, pulling a growl from his chest. The vibration of his need traveling through him into me going straight to my needy center that's now drenched.

"Sin," he warns, barely holding back his hold on my ass biting.

"Yes?" I ask sweetly.

"Patience."

I nibble on the edge of his jaw before moving to his full lips, pulling him into a kiss right as he slams me into the wall outside his room not quite inside the doorway.

My eyes drift closed taking anything he offers. Our tongues battle for dominance but I willingly give that to him for now, I pull back taking in air. Hovering just over his open mouth our breath mingles in the space between us. My eyes open to watch the way he takes me in.

Damn, the way he sees straight into my soul. My teeth pull his bottom lip into my mouth sinking into it until the tinge of copper spills into my mouth coating my tongue in his blood. Licking at the small cut I groan, loving the feel of his pain dripping down my throat. My clit throbs, craving the same feeling.

"Fucking, little demon." He grits through clenched teeth.

Dropping me to my feet he pulls back, his gaze dark with wicked thoughts watching a small drop of his blood drip at the corner of my mouth. He leans in licking me from one corner of my mouth to the other, cleaning all evidence of him from me.

"On your knees, Sin," he orders, his tone ferocious.

Licking my lips on the way down I don't take my eyes off him, letting him see how willing I am to drop down and worship him for the devil he is. I'm giving myself to him fully in this moment, letting him take control of my body to use how he pleases and begging for the pain mixed with pleasure he has to offer.

Looking over his shoulder he checks to make sure Oliver hasn't come out of his room before his hand closes over my throat dragging me into the room, slamming the door behind us.

"You're mine, Sin. Do you understand?"

"Yes, sir."

"You do what I say, when I say."

"Yes," I groan, my chest heaving with each breath.

"Keep your eyes on me and your mouth open. Follow my directions and I'll let you come, disobey me and I'll paint your ass red. Got it?" He squeezes my throat tighter to push his point.

"Yes... yes, sir," I whisper out, unable to get any louder.

"That's a good fucking girl. Now take my dick out." He motions to his gray sweats.

My hands reach out, my nerves coming in full force but when his thumb tips my chin up forcing my gaze to lock with his, all thoughts fly from my head leaving nothing but Ezra Finlay to consume me. Lust, greed, wrath, they all reside between us.

Pushing his pants down just past his ass freeing his long, thick, dick hard that's now eye level with me my pulse kicks up under my skin, the heat from my skin burning.

Looking up, I watch his face as my hand closes around him not able to fully grip him due to his size, but the sight I swear makes my pussy convulse on the spot.

"Open that pretty mouth for me, Sin. I want you to swallow down my dick just like your pussy is going to when I'm done fucking your sinful little mouth."

Oh god. His words are so dirty yet just what I need to

drive me forward, wrappings my lips around the head of his dick swirling my tongue around to wet it. His pupils are blown with lust, his teeth sinking into his bottom lip.

"That's it, baby. So fucking good." His praise spurring me on with the need to please him.

Pushing him in further I work my jaw and throat making room for him in my mouth, trying to take all of him down my throat.

Using my tongue, I trail it on the underside of his cock bringing my free hand up to cup his balls making his head fall back against the wall, sending pride shooting through me. My thighs shift trying to rub together with a mind of their own.

"Mmm," I groan around his dick.

My pussy throbs just seeing what I do to him, bringing Ezra pleasure is enough to make me cum on the spot, I fucking love it. I only go down one more time before his hands spear through my hair on each side of my head tipping in a way that widens my jaw giving him more access.

"Keep that mouth open and watch me while I fuck your face," he demands.

I nod once before he groans, pumping in and out of my mouth. Spit spilling out the corners of my lips as he goes deeper with each thrust. Swallowing around him to keep from choking tears leak from my eyes but he keeps going. My thighs drenched, leaving me wanting so I slowly move one hand between my thighs ready to relieve the pressure.

"Fuck yes, Sin, you're such a good little fucking sinner. That's it, swallow around my dick."

Opening my mouth further I use my tongue with each thrust in and out, I trace the underside of him feeling him pulsing in my mouth so close. My eyes move back to his, loving the way he watches me with pure need. My fingers sliding into my shorts under my underwear until I feel my heated flesh damp with my arousal for the man before me.

"I want you to fuck yourself while you take my dick down your throat," he says, giving me just what I want.

Gliding my fingers between my folds I swirl the wetness around my entrance before two fingers slip inside me, almost sending me over the edge that fast. He pumps harder the force of his thrust shoving my head back further, but that doesn't stop me from lifting up on my knees fully to drop down on my hand.

"Ride your fingers just like that. Fuck your hand like you're about to ride my dick."

Following his directions, I ride my hand with pure abandon of anything but me, Ezra, and our pleasure surrounding me in this room. The force of our presence mixing together makes me shudder under the suffocating feelings that drown me. My legs twitch with the force of my climbing orgasm. I'm so close to finishing, but I need more, and I think he knows it.

One hand moves to the back of my head twisting my hair around his wrist yanking my head back and then forward again shoving my mouth down until my lips reach the base of his dick, swallowing him completely.

Dropping down on my fingers one more time, I shatter while he simultaneously grunts his release down my throat, filling my mouth and spilling out the side all at once.

"Fuckkkk," he rasps.

We're both breathing hard, our eyes never leaving each other he releases my head pulling out of my mouth to bring his thumb across my bottom lip, wiping away the droplets that escaped only to shove his thumb in my mouth for me to suck clean.

"Fuck, Sin, your mouth is my fucking heaven but your pussy? That's Nirvana, so damn good."

Bending down, he lifts me to my feet walking me backwards until my knees hit the bed.

"Strip off your clothes and lie on your back."

Walking away he heads into his massive walk-in closet for fuck-knows-what not that I care I'm too busy trying to gain composure from having my face fucked for the first time. Who knew having a dick shoved in your mouth could be so fucking rewarding?

Unable to restrain my smile I do as he says, peeling my clothes off before climbing to the center of the bed and lying down, I decide to pull my feet up bending my knees with my feet planted flat on the bed. Exposing every inch of me.

My head turns when I spot him walking out the door with two things, the first makes my heart speed up in excitement, but the other sends a shiver of fear through me with the thought of having it used on me. Fear must fuel the darkness buried deep inside me because once the chills dissipate only raw eagerness remains.

"That's right, baby, relax for me. I know just what my little demon aches for." His words feel like a prayer answered that I didn't know I made.

He makes it to the foot of the bed his stare dropping down to my waiting dripping center, licking his lips as he watches me draw circles on my clit with one finger. He looks back up at me with a feral sneer.

"Hands off, Sin, your pussy belongs to me. Only me, understand?"

I nod, unable to form words with his declaration.

He leans forward to drop the two items on the bed letting me have a good look at them both. The blindfold I can handle and even want to try but the leather whip makes my heart stutter in my chest.

"Don't worry. The pleasure is just as strong as the pain."

His hands close around my ankles yanking me to the edge of the bed, my lungs pulling in a large gulp of air. This is going to hurt so good.

CHAPTER THIRTY THREE
EZRA

Athena's spread open on my bed looking at me like I'm her salvation if she only knew it's the other way around. Her tits bounce with the force of my pull, the grip on her ankles bruising, but I don't loosen my hold.

Her lips part in surprise with the sudden movement, her eyes watching the whip and blindfold I just sat on the bed.

"Don't worry. The pleasure is just as strong as the pain."

Her eyes widen, flitting from me to the offending objects making my lips turn up in a smile with the way her chest rises and falls in excitement. Bending down I blow lightly on her pussy watching her squirm under me, my girl so fucking needy for me.

"Don't move," I order, my words harsh.

Pulling her legs until her ass is almost off the bed, it's my turn to drop to my knees at the feet of my Sinner, ready to worship every inch of her. Her hip lifts just enough to grab my attention so I reach out for the whip, not taking my eyes off hers.

"Sin, when I tell you to do something you obey me. In here I am the only God you bow to."

She nods in quick concession.

"Say it."

Lifting the whip, I bring it down over her inner thigh with a crack the sound harsher than the sting preparing her for what's to come. She yelps but her body stills when I lift a brow reminding her of the rules.

"Sin."

"Yes, sir."

"Good girl."

Rewarding her, I close my mouth over her clit flattening my tongue over the pulsing bud applying pressure with each flick against it.

Her hands fist the sheets holding herself to the bed to keep from moving, but fuck if I don't wish she would. Using my free hand my fingers slide inside her slick heat, sucking them in hungry for more.

"Fuck, baby, you're soaking wet for me. You love sucking my dick, Sin? Does it make you wet watching me cum down your throat knowing you fucking consume me?"

No words, just noises spilling from the back of her throat, her head thrashing back and forth on the bed.

Pushing my fingers deeper to curve them against that sweet spot in her tight little cunt, my teeth close over her clit adding enough pain to have Athena lifting her hips shoving my face deeper between her legs.

The hand holding the whip comes down on her thigh next to my head, not taking my mouth off her pussy adding more force with this hit her scream is orgasmic, my dick pressing into the mattress.

"Fuck, yes!" she yelps, my little demon bathing in the pain.

Not wanting her to cum from my mouth on her I pull back, wiping my mouth with my hand licking my fingers in the process letting her watch me with hunger. I give her the chance to taste the pure bliss that is her. Pumping my fingers back inside her, I twist them against her G-spot, her legs twitching with the feel of me inside her.

"Open up, Sin."

She opens her mouth, sucking in my fingers swirling her tongue around the two digits cleaning every drop of her from my skin.

"Fuck, you're such a good girl. So responsive and ready for me."

Grabbing her by the hips I move her up the bed, ordering her to grab the headboard while I tie the blindfold on her, cutting off her sight.

"If you let go or move, I'm going to whip your pretty pale skin. If you cum without my permission, I'll flip you over and fuck you from behind while I mark your fucking ass watching as your flesh turns red."

She moans with the threat, and I damn near explode with the image of fucking her from behind with her head thrown back, but I shake my head to clear the vision floating around.

Her fingernails are embedded into the wood holding her in place, blind folded and ready for me. Crawling up the bed to rest between her legs I spread her open taking in the view, my dick weeping with need.

"You're a wet dream laid before me, my own personal temptress ready to drag me to hell. I love the burn from your fire, baby."

Sliding my hands up her sides watching her body come alive under my touch, her breathing picking up pushing her tits in the air.

Her nipples are hard peaks just begging to be played with, so I bend down taking one in my mouth, pinching and pulling the other one between two fingers.

"Fin!" she squeals, scratching the wood.

"Don't move," I remind her.

"Yes, sir. Please!"

"I love to hear you beg for my dick, baby."

Releasing her nipple with a wet plop, I lean back on my heels lifting her ass, sliding her down on my dick, pausing to keep from coming on the spot. Fuck, her pussy is so tight, like it was made for me. The sound that escapes her throat with the slow glide out and back in makes my dick twitch inside her.

"Please, Fin!"

"Tell me what you need, Sin."

"More. Please. Harder."

I grunt out an incoherent response slamming into her, trailing one hand up to her throat, using my hold on her to hit a new angle making her move with me.

Raising the whip with my free hand I lean back watching my dick pull out and slowly pump back in, her chest heaving right as I bring the whip down on her inner thigh a few inches from her pussy. The bite of pain clipping my thigh driving me deeper inside her.

"Yes! More!" she exclaims, her cunt quivering around my cock.

Bringing the whip down across her nipples slightly softer, screaming out my name, using her feet to lift her up and slam her down on my dick, eyes rolling in the back of my head.

"God damn it, Sin, your pussy grips my dick perfectly."

"Again," she begs.

I thrust into her harder, bringing the whip down across her pussy. The edge of it hitting just above her clit. The force of the blow has her cunt soaking my dick, squeezing me so tight my grip on her throat tightens, my thrusts becoming erratic.

"Fuck!" I growl out, yanking her forward pulling her off the bed, her hands releasing the headboard.

Holding her to me, I fuck her relentlessly, her pussy still gripping me with the aftershocks but I'm far from finished with my little demon.

Her new position allows her to rest her body weight on me but it's not enough, so I spin her pulling out flipping her on her stomach shoving her chest into the bed leaving her ass in the air.

The view is enough to make my mouth water. Not sparing a second glance before my dick is buried balls deep in her pussy.

"Hold on tight, baby."

"Fin!" she groans, her voice needy.

"What do you need, little sinner?"

"Whip."

One word turns my world black. The elation of her asking for what I need makes my blood boil, my dick twitching I'm so close. Picking up the whip with one hand I grab her hair with the other leaning down to whisper in her ear.

"You belong to me, Sin. I'm your God, your salvation, your fucking master. This pussy is mine and I'm going to fuck you until you learn your place."

Sitting up I pull her head back fucking her hard and fast, my balls drawing tight with each thrust. My hand lifts bringing the whip down on her ass harder than the others. My gaze falls to her milky skin watching it turn pink with the mark. The demon in his cage roaring with the sight.

"Fuck me, Fin!"

With each thrust the whip smacks across her skin with a loud pop, leaving marks in its wake, her legs shaking with the force of her orgasm.

I'm on the edge, my vision blurring, the corners of my eyes covered in black spots.

Needing to send her over the edge I release her hair, shoving her head into the mattress allowing her to turn her head sideways for air.

"Harder! Please, please, please," she chants.

"Cum for me right fucking now, Sin," I demand.

The whip cracks across her skin. Once. Twice. A third time when she explodes, milking me dry, our bodies soaked in sweat.

We ride out the aftershock of our orgasms together. Pulling out of her gently, making sure not to rub against her smarting ass that's painted the perfect shade of red matching her hair. The fucking irony isn't lost on me.

"Holy shit." She giggles in a post-orgasmic haze.

Pulling her front against my chest I push her damp hair from her face searching for signs of fear, pain, or anything else that would make her run from me. I couldn't handle her leaving me right now, not when I've just begun to show her all we can be together.

"Sleep, Sin," I murmur against her lips.

Her eyes droop, completely and fully sated she starts to doze off with a goofy grin on her face. If this is what hell feels like I never want to go to heaven. Athena is crawling her way inside me so deep I'm scared she'll pull out my heart on her way out.

"Sin."

"Hmm."

"Let's take Ollie to the zoo tomorrow."

"Mmhm, okay, Fin. Okay."

Her eyes never open, she just trails off her words slurred and raspy. Watching her sleep pulls me into a deep rest, slowly falling into the blackness with my arms holding Athena, pulling her closer not willing to let her go. I'm not sure I'll ever be ready for her to walk away I guess I'll have to find a way to make her stay.

CHAPTER THIRTY FOUR
ATHENA

Agiggle escapes me when I read the next line in one of my favorite books. My legs draped over the arm of the couch head upside down, I smile with each word. Getting lost in the pages of sassy females and morally gray men has always been the one escape that helped me let go of everything weighing me down.

Turning the page, my phone goes off vibrating against the glass table in the center of the living room.

Rolling off the couch I see that it's my alarm reminding me that Ezra convinced me to go with him and Oliver to the zoo today. A slow smile creeps up at the memory of him slipping the question in after he put me in an orgasm-induced coma. Fucker.

Folding the soft white fuzzy blanket that I brought from my apartment I pad through the living room to start a pot of coffee for Ezra to have and making myself a large cup of hot chocolate. Once the coffee maker is going, I head into Oliver's room to wake him up for the day. Slowly pushing the door open I reveal a still sleeping Oliver spread sideways on his bed.

"Ollie," I whisper, walking further into the room.

He doesn't budge when I sit on his bed. My hand reaching out to brush his hair out of his eyes, my eyes roaming over his smattering of freckles across his face.

"Bubs." I nudge his shoulder.

He mumbles a few words before turning on his side to face the wall.

"Wanna go to the zoo?" My voice is light with excitement.

The way he shoots straight up almost knocking his head with mine make me break out in a fit of laughter.

"I'll take that as a yes?" I say.

"Can we really go?"

"Of course. Ezra's going to take us. Go get dressed and we can have breakfast."

Ruffling his hair before I leave, the door's barely shut when he bolts off the bed with a huge grin on his face rushing to get ready for the day. Going back into the spacious kitchen to pull out all the ingredients I need, I start to make French toast, eggs, and bacon.

The bacon is sizzling in the pan spreading the greasy aroma throughout the penthouse when Ezra walks up behind me crowding me closer to the hot stove.

"Morning, Sin," he murmurs against my neck, his voice rough with sleep.

The effect his voice has on my body is enthralling, each syllable pulling me into him deeper. I could drown myself in him and still thirst for more, begging for each drop that hits my tongue. I'm getting too deep I need to claw my way out before he sinks too far unable to release me.

"Hi," I squeak.

Warm hands land on my hips, making me jump with the sudden movement. Pulling the bacon off the stove, I use cooking to distract myself from the way his fingers trace the line of my shorts moving tantalizingly slow across my bare skin. My ears buzz with awareness when he leans in to nip at my earlobe.

"Ez!" Oliver yells, rushing into the kitchen.

"What's up O-man?" Ezra walks over to ruffle his hair.

Letting them dive into their own personal conversation I start dishing out plates on the island in the center of the room. Moving over to the fridge I pull out some orange juice for Oliver pouring him a small glass.

"I need to check your blood sugar after breakfast. We need to keep an eye on it if you want ice cream after the zoo," I say.

We all take a seat to eat our breakfast, Ezra groans around a mouthful of French toast, he turns to me his gray eyes soft and assessing. Syrup drips down his chin licking my finger I lean forward to wipe it off, popping it in my mouth with a sly smirk.

He goes to pull me in, but I dodge his grasp shoving a bite of bacon in my mouth with a laugh.

"I'm going to head upstairs to shower before we head out. Oliver brush your teeth when you finish, and we can do the test after."

He grumbles a response around a forkful of eggs, shaking my head at the sight I turn to Ezra, bending down I trail a kiss over his cheek.

"I'll be back down shortly. Thank you for this."

With that, I rush up the stairs needing to escape the wave of emotion that overtakes me every time I'm around him.

~

Leaving the zoo in Ezra's SUV I turn to look back at Oliver, who is now passed out in the back of the car covered in sweat, face paint, and dirt. The soft expression on his face melts my heart, bringing me a sense of relief that I'm able to see him this relaxed and happy.

"He's knocked out." I laugh, turning back in my seat.

Ezra looks over at me while backing the SUV out of the parking spot, the sun hitting his window in just the right spot, his gray eyes shining.

"We had so much fun today. I know I said it before but thank you so much, Fin. Oliver really needed this." My words are low.

Reaching out, he grabs my hand, intertwining our fingers, resting it between us. Using his thumb to rub small circles against my skin, sends shivers down my back.

"Anything for you. You know that. I'd do anything to see that boy smile." His eyes are now trained on the road unable to bring them back to me.

His voice is filled with emotion, but I don't allow myself to assume anything, not when we are so close to being done with our contract, I can't risk my heart right now.

It's me and Ollie against the world and the stone walls I've built around us have small dents and dings in them from my time with Ezra. He's breaking down everything I worked so hard to build. The need to protect the little boy sleeping in the back is my first priority.

Reaching in my pocket to pull out my cell I check it for the one hundredth time today, waiting for Sable to get back to me but when nothing's there my heart sinks.

"I need to go check on Sable. Can you drop me and Ollie off at her apartment?" I ask him, keeping my gaze trained out the window.

"Why don't I keep him and have the guys come over to hang out while you go check on your friend?" he offers, peeking over at me from the corner of his eye.

Hesitating, I think about his offer to keep Oliver knowing how close Ollie's gotten to all the guys and not wanting to keep that from him. My thoughts also go to the need to check his sugar and make sure he's doing okay.

"His sugar needs to be checked after all the sweets he's had today. I have to keep an eye on him."

"You think I would let anything happen to him?" he says, pulling my attention with a tug on my hand.

My mouth opens, but no words come out, not knowing how to respond to his question.

"Look at me," he demands, coming up to a red light giving me his full attention. "Oliver has become important to me over the last couple of weeks. I would never put him in harm's way and I will always make sure to care for him in the way he needs. You're mine Sin and that makes him mine as well."

The way his words spill from his lips, each one spears its way into my heart has heat crawling its way up my legs to settle between my thighs. My tongue slips out wetting my dry lips. The all-consuming need to show him how much I appreciate his declaration has my fingers twitching to wrap around his dick.

"Fin..." I whisper. His name a prayer on my tongue.

He pulls me toward him, meeting me in the middle of the SUV to press his mouth on mine, kissing me desperately, pulling in every last drop of my sanity and swallowing it down with each kiss.

Our tongues clash like a tidal wave sweeping us apart and back together again until the wave pulls me down, drowning me in his overbearing shadow.

"Sin," he groans against my mouth, sucking on my bottom lip. "Come back to me in one piece, do you understand me?"

I nod, still lost in the taste of him, not quite ready to pull away. I dive back in, gripping his shirt in my hands.

"That's an order, little demon," he states, pulling away when a truck behind us honks.

My cheeks flush. "Yes, sir," I reply.

Our joined hands cling together between us. The rest of the ride to Sable's apartment is spent in silence, both of us lost in our own thoughts. I'm stuck between wondering what he's thinking about and how I feel about him.

Every day that I spend around him brings me closer to wanting to stay. Even Miles has started to slowly grow on me because of his adoration of Oliver.

Pulling up to the complex I swear the weather dampens. The clouds coming out to shadow the building, taking away the blazing sun that's been following us all day.

My mood shifts when I spot the rundown area. I am not missing being on this side of town but it's like ice water pouring down my spine bringing me back to reality. Because this picture? It's painted on me. Its colors are bleeding into my skin, this is where I come from and it's where I belong.

I'm not meant for large penthouses with massive, heated pools, walk-in closets as big as my bedroom, and SUV's that cost more than a house.

Seeing Ezra's car parked in the apartment parking lot brings a new wakeup call all together, like an *aha* moment that takes my breath away.

I'm the rundown apartment begging for a makeover and updates while Ezra is the pricey beautiful SUV worth thousands and loved by millions of people. We just don't belong. I let that thought settle in my bones, sinking all the way into the marrow.

Us? Ezra and me? We don't belong in the same world, so I need to stop letting my walls down. Opening the door, I drag my hand out of Ezra's, letting me go so I can get out. Walking to the back door I open it to wake Oliver up and let him know the plan.

"Sin," Ezra says, sensing my mood change.

The way he can read my signals that I've let him get too close to me, allowing him to learn more than I was willing to share so I ignore him.

"Bubs."

Nudging Oliver awake, his sleepy eyes look at me in confusion that cracks my composure letting a small grin through.

"Ezra and the guys are going to hang out with you for a little bit while I stop by to see Sabby, is that okay with you?" I ask, giving him the chance to stay with me.

Yeah!" He jumps up, sitting straight to look around the seat at Ezra.

"Is that okay, Ez?" he asks, smiling shyly.

"Hell yeah, O-man! We're going to order wings and have a guy's night." Ezra winks at him playfully.

Holy shit the way he handles Oliver not only makes me want to fuck the shit out of him but also makes my heart melt. Stepping away from Oliver with a slight nudge to his shoulder to shut the door I step up to the window, waiting for him to roll it down.

The tinted window slowly opens giving me the perfect view of tousled brown hair and mesmerizing gray eyes. His beauty makes my heart stop.

"I'll be back to pick you up tonight, Sin."

Instead of arguing with him on the fact that I plan to take an uber I just smile before walking away. Not looking back.

It's not until I reach Sable's door that I hear the sound of tires driving over gravel, my hand lifts to knock but before my hand makes contact the door is swung open, revealing a disheveled-looking Mike.

"Where's Sable?" I demand. My words harsh and my stare of pure fury.

CHAPTER THIRTY FIVE
EZRA

The sound of yelling has my eyes rolling, mimicking Athena's dirty little habit. Miles shouts followed by a grunt from Eros making me smirk knowing that Miles most likely just killed him on the game. Oliver is chanting for Miles to win so he can go against the winner. They're all piled into his room by the gaming system.

Oliver's lying on the beanbag chair with Miles next to him on the floor with his back against the bed while Eros is lying across the bed, his head landing right between the two.

"Pizza's been ordered," I announce to the room from the doorway.

"About time!" Eros grumbles, always ruled by his stomach.

I swear any woman that feeds him a good meal will end up stuck with the fucker.

"Eros."

His eyes meet mine, motioning with my head I signal him to step out of the room. With a small nod he lets Miles kill him in the game.

"Well, shit!" he whines to play it off, handing Oliver the controller.

"Your turn, little dude."

With Miles and Oliver playing the game, I walk out of the room headed into the hallway with Eros on my heels. Opening the door to the library, I walk in walking around the room, observing all the books I've collected over the years.

A smile creeps up thinking about Athena running in here that night, trying to hide from me as if I couldn't sense her with my eyes closed. I could find her anywhere.

"What's up, man?" Eros says, pulling me from my thoughts of Athena.

"We need to discuss the client from Moe's bar. I'm not sure it's a good idea to take them on right now."

Before I have the chance to finish, Eros is already shaking his head. I knew he would push me on this because of the nature of the job, but I plan on making him see reason.

"No, man. We have a responsibility to them, and you know it! We have the power, money, and means to do something about it and you just want to walk away?"

"No. I'm not saying we do nothing; I'm just suggesting

we outsource the work to another company. We don't have the time to take on this big of a job."

He scoffs, shaking his head again. "You mean YOU don't have the time. You're so pussy-whipped that you've barely been in the office! Now you want to let down an entire group home? The same one that took us in and took care of us? You may be able to turn your back on them, I sure as hell won't."

His finger points at me and if I was closer, I'm sure it'd be jammed in my chest by now.

"Don't drag Athena into this, Eros. You know I love those kids just as much as you, but taking down an operation like that? What the hell are we supposed to do with a hundred kids? Pile them all in here?" My voice rises with my frustration.

I'll be damned if he tries to throw this on Athena, as if she's a problem to be solved. She's not moving an inch out the door unless she wants to leave. Even if it was her idea, she'd have a hell of a time making her escape. The devil himself would have to drag her out of my hands.

"We can't just ignore the fact that there are dirty people working there, abusing the ones they swore to protect from the streets they're pulled off of. How could you think this is the right decision?"

He looks at me as if he has no idea who I am, but he won't see reason no matter what I say or who I tell him is behind it. I created this life for us so we would never have to live the life we did before.

I poured my blood into the world for him. Risking everything to make sure he survived the fucked-up hand we were dealt, and I never held that over him, but I won't risk everything to do what he's asking.

"Eros, there are things about this job you don't know

about. People behind the scenes pulling the strings that we can't predict. You think it doesn't make my skin crawl and my blood boil with the need to take them out? It does, but it's a risk right now!"

"There's no risk greater than letting those kids suffer! Hand me the files and point me in the right direction, but I'm going to do everything I can to do what's right."

He steps closer, bringing himself only two feet from me, the brown of his eyes looking obsidian in the stark lighting in the room. His rage flows off him, beating against me with a blinding heat. Taking a step toward him, placing my hand on his shoulder, I look him in the eyes, dropping the wall around us so he can see the struggle on my face.

"You really want to step into this mess?" I pause, letting him see the raw panic in my eyes, knowing who's going to meet him at the gates of hell.

"I need you to hear me loud and fucking clear, Eros. I do not support this, but I support you. I'll back you all the way, but you're running point. Have Bailey give you everything on Brookhaven Group Home, even the files in my office."

"You know I can handle this, so I don't understand why the hell you're acting like I'm still your kid brother who used to get into stupid shit."

A small chuckle escapes. "That's because you're still my kid brother and this is you doing stupid shit. Honorable? Brave? Maybe, but stupid either way."

Pulling my hand back, I walk around the room again needing to pull those walls back up making sure to be the Ezra Finlay that built an empire to spite the words of a dead man.

"If this affects our family you pull out, do you hear me?" I warn.

Running my finger across the black shelving holding my

horror book collection to see how much dust is resting there. Inspecting my finger, I can still feel his eyes staring into my back knowing he won't let this go for long, but I keep my attention on needing Christie, my house cleaner, to come dust in here.

"Ezra."

"Yeah?" I ask, keeping my back to him.

"You're really worried about this job?"

My shoulders stiffen for a split second before I relax them, not willing to show weakness. "It's a job I don't take lightly, so you need to remember to do the same."

He starts to walk toward the door, his footsteps getting further, before I call out to him.

"And Eros?"

"Yeah, Ez."

I stop him before he heads out the door, turning to take in my little brother. "I'm proud of you."

"Yeah."

His voice is hard, but the gleam in his eyes show his true feelings, so I turn back to my books to give him space. We may not be good with showing our emotions to anyone who isn't us or Miles, but I'd never let him forget how proud I am of him.

Hearing him move down the hall, I wait until the door closes to Oliver's room before I pull out my phone to check the time.

Being away from Athena is like being in arms reach of air but not able to pull the oxygen hose closer. The panic of being so close to what's going to save you is unfathomable.

She's been gone for a few hours now and with each minute my patience for allowing her to make her own decision wears thin. The sound of the elevator dinging has me making my way to the front of the apartment expecting to find our pizza, but what I see has my blood turning to ice.

"Sin?"

Rushing over, I pull her into me checking her to make sure she's okay, but once my arms close around her she breaks down, shaking with a force that rattles me.

"Eros! Miles!" I shout.

Miles comes sliding around the corner eyes wide with alarm. "What the fuck?" He pauses when he takes in Athena sobbing against my chest.

"Keep Oliver in the room and don't let him come out. Do you understand?"

"Yeah, man, I've got him. Eros!" he calls out while he rushes back into the room before Oliver decides to see what's going on.

Eros storms into the entryway, his gaze tracking Athena, a questioning look passing between us. Walking Athena to the couch making her sit, she pulls back and the look on her face has my heart skipping a beat in my chest. Mike better pray to the fucking saints that he didn't touch my little demon.

"Sin, baby. Look at me. What's going on?"

My finger hooks under her chin, forcing her to look at me. Her eyes are bloodshot from crying, the evidence of tears tracking down her face.

"Baby, talk to me. Breathe. I've got you."

Her lip quivers, tears streaming down her cheeks again. My girl's chest heaving with an oncoming panic attack. Moving my hand from her face to wrap around her neck, I know just how to pull my little demon back from the darkness trying to consume her.

In order to break the attack, she has to become the darkness she fights.

Squeezing her throat until her eyes widen with the force, I watch the pale flesh spanning up her neck, turning red to match her eyes.

Leaning in, I trail a kiss up her jaw landing at the corner of her eye, right in my fucking spot. My spot. She's mine to protect.

"Tell me what happened, Sin."

Waiting for her tremors to subside, I release my hold a little, allowing her to inhale the air I stole from her, filling her with the oxygen I give to her only with my permission does my Sinner get to breathe.

Licking her lips, I can see the light coming back into her eyes, reviving the emerald green that was being drowned out by her fear.

"Ezra let her go," Eros says with a soft voice.

"Back off and let me handle my girl," I grit from clenched teeth.

"It's okay," Athena murmurs, reassuring Eros or herself I'm not sure.

"You being like this isn't fucking okay, so I need to know what happened now, Sin."

Her small soft hands grip my wrist, pulling my hand from her throat, knowing I'm only releasing her because she's calmer.

"Don't fucking demand shit from me."

"There's my Sin." I brush her damp hair off her face.

I knew bringing her back to me would shake off any fear or shock she was stuck between, having her anger be the remaining emotion to use as a defense. Sitting back against the couch, I track every movement slowly looking for any marks, handprints, or bruises to indicate she's hurt. When

I'm satisfied there's nothing to see, my stare darts back to her face.

"It's Sable."

With that one name I know what the next words out of her mouth are going to be, souring my stomach with the realization. If I could have protected her from finding out that her friend has become a victim of abuse I would, but there's no easy way to handle these situations.

"What about Sable?"

The question pulls three sets of eyes to the kitchen doorway where Miles is standing with his arms crossed over his chest. His stare is steel waiting for her to continue.

"Where is Oliver?"

"He's watching a movie. I told him we have adult business to handle and to hang out for a little bit. Now, what the hell is going on with Sable?"

"What do you care?" Athena snaps, finding a target for her rage and lashing out full force.

Hopping off the couch, she storms toward him before I can pull myself off the couch.

"What is wrong with Sable?" he asks again, each word forced out.

Once she reaches him, she brings pushes up on her toes trying to reach his six-foot one height. Miles doesn't move from leaning against the doorframe not threatened by Athena, but I know how lethal she can be for the people she loves. I stand just behind her waiting to see how he handles it. Miles may be my brother, but I'd put a blade in his throat if he even breathes too hard on her.

"You have no business asking me anything when you refuse to even speak to me when you're here! You have no respect for me and for what? Because you see me as some stripping, money-hungry-whore?" She's rattling with the force of her words, but she doesn't back down. "You have no idea who I am, yet you judge me."

"I don't trust you," he retorts, looking over her at me then back to her. "Ezra is like a brother to me. No, he is a brother and I'll be damned if you swoop in and get him wrapped up in your pussy just to ruin everything he's built."

I step up to Athena not taking my eyes off Miles, but needing to see how she handles him before I lay his ass out.

"You have no idea what the hell you're talking about. Ezra is a grown ass man. He doesn't need you to handle his business. Get out of my face."

She has her finger in his face, her red hair fanning out around her giving the appearance that she's covered in flames, making my dick twitch in my pants. Miles would never touch a woman, but I won't tolerate him disrespecting her either.

Pulling her away from him, I shove Miles against the wall, getting in his face to show him just how far he's crossed the line this time.

"You're my brother, but I'll put you on your fucking ass if you pull some shit like this again. That goes for you too." I point to Eros, "Athena isn't going anywhere anytime soon, so get on board or get the fuck out!"

Athena manages to yank me off Miles, forcing me to stumble back a few steps, wedging herself between us to grab him by his black crew top shirt. She uses all her strength to pull him down to her level, and he lets her.

"I'll let this shit slide because you're protecting Fin, but next time you insult me, I'll let him beat you within an inch of your life." Pushing him back to release his shirt, she turns to walk away.

I stay there watching his gaze track her before his eyes

meet mine. The entire thing must play back in his mind because his eyes widen for a split second before he starts to open his mouth.

"Now's not the time for your shit."

Walking over to Athena, who's now standing at the glass wall looking out over the city, Eros is on her left side talking to her in a low voice.

"Sin, what's going on with Sable? Does she need our help?"

With a heavy exhale she turns to face me, her stare so hollow and sad it cracks something within me. In this moment with the city behind her and the glow of lights casting a halo behind her, she looks like a fallen angel that's broken from the fall.

"She's in trouble, but she won't let me help her. How could she not tell me? I don't understand!"

"What happened?"

"It's Mike. He's got his claws in her so deep! When I got there, she was lying on the bed badly beaten, but when I mentioned her leaving to come stay with me, she lost it. She went insane scratching herself and screaming for me to leave and that I wasn't welcome there anymore."

Her voice waivers on the last word, but it's the ding from the elevator that pulls all our attention to the foyer. Without a word, Miles steps in before the doors close, not saying another word. Athena has started to pace, following the wall next to her and back again.

"Where the hell does he think he's going?" she asks, continuing her pacing.

"He has a history that's not my place to tell."

"Athena, do you want us to go get her?" Eros asks, his tone soft.

Shaking her head, she doesn't speak, just continues to

walk back and forth against the glass, her stare cast down to the street below.

"Athena." Eros says her name again, almost pleading.

"Please." She looks to me as if she thinks I'd tell her no.

"She's your family, Sin," I remind her, trying to break through the anger simmering off her. "That means she's my family."

Her steps pause with my statement, taking her off guard with my declaration.

"I'm not your problem to solve."

"No, you're not a problem to solve. You're the fucking air in my lungs."

CHAPTER THIRTY SIX
EZRA

"**A**re you sure?" Athena asks, looking at Eros.

We've both gone over what she wants to do and settled on dragging Sable back here to stay with us until we can figure something out.

Eros is in the middle of convincing Athena that he can handle keeping an eye on Oliver, who's asleep in his bed, while we go to Mike's apartment. He steps up to her placing a hand on her arm making my fingers twitch with his proximity to her.

"We'll be okay, T, I promise." He uses Sable's name for her to show her how much he means it.

With a shaky nod she smiles before giving him a hug

that makes the demon inside me rattle the bars of his cage demanding me to yank her away from his hold.

"Let's go, Sin." Forcing her attention back to me where it fucking belongs.

She laughs. "Always so possessive. Okay, let's go."

Eros winks at her before walking away, making sure to toss a smirk at me over her head. Grabbing her hand, I pull her into me, watching the way she stumbles over her feet in the process.

Waiting for the elevator doors to open, my fingers trail her arm loving the way her body is so responsive under my touch, the chills that slowly spread across her pale skin making my mouth water.

"Fin." Her words are a warning.

Fuck, I know it's not the best time but my dick aches to be buried deep inside her with my fingers wrapped around her throat.

When the doors open, we step in, Athena moving to the corner of the mirrored box trying to keep her distance. As if that'd stop me if I really wanted her on her knees begging me to fuck her.

It's the appearance of her bloodshot eyes that have me pausing, mentally shaking myself for not being able to control myself. I have no control when it comes to my little demon.

"Come here, baby." I aim for gentle.

She rubs her lips together in thought, I can see her sinking into herself, beating herself up with guilt. Reaching forward I press the small red button bringing the moving elevator to an abrupt stop. Athena's head jerks in my direction, her eyes assessing me.

"What are you doing? We need to get to Sable."

"Come here now," I order, my words sharp.

Expecting her to refuse, I'm taken aback when she moves forward without hesitation. I'd be lying if I said that didn't make me hard as a rock, knowing she's willing to bend to my demands. Spinning her to press her up against the wall. My hands run up and down her arms, watching as her lids start to droop.

"I need you calm before we walk into a situation I can't predict, so I'm going to help you with that."

"Fin, we can't."

Taking both her wrists in one hand to pin them above her head, my gaze rolls over every inch of my Sinner, reveling in the way her tits strain against the tight gray tank she has on. Each breath she takes pulls at the thin material, pulling my eyes back down to her chest with each inhale.

"We have time."

One step closer is all it takes to force a moan from her pink lips, the sound raspy. Leaving no space between us, my free hand tilts her head to the side giving me the perfect angle to run my tongue down her neck, stealing the taste of her sweet skin like it's a drug.

Fuck, it's my drug. She's my own brand of whiskey.

"Fuck," she utters.

"I bet your panties are drenched for me."

Only sounds come from her throat with every pass of my lips on her skin, my fingers drawing circles on her hip bone making their way lower.

Slipping into the band of her leggings past her thong to trace her pelvic bone, making her wait for more and loving the way she wiggles her ass against the glass.

"You love getting on your knees for me, don't you?" My words are growled into her skin, biting down on her throat.

"Yes." Another moan.

"Such a fucking slut for me."

My fingers slip lower feeling the heat pooling from her wet pussy, parting her lips her head falls back, I dip my fingers into her dripping cunt, my dick straining with the feel of her gripping the single digit.

"I don't want you on your knees for me this time. I want you to see a real fucking king fall to his knees to worship at the feet of his queen. Fuck my face while you watch, surrounded by the view of me between your legs, showing you how God-damned obsessed I am with your tight cunt."

With each word her hips swivel on my finger silently asking for more, so I add another finger twisting twice before I curve them to rub against her favorite spot.

She clenches around me, already so close. I ease out of her pulling my hand free of her pants, but I wait until her green eyes come back to me before I suck them in my mouth letting the pure bliss of her cunt soak my tongue.

"Oh shit." Her words are lost on a long groan.

Rubbing her thighs together she pleads with her eyes, asking for what she wants with one look. I'm not one to deny my girl anything. Stepping back, my hand releases her hands allowing them to fall to her sides.

"Strip your pants off."

She does as she's told, pulling her pants down to her ankles before kicking off her flats then her pants the rest of the way.

"Keep your eyes on the ceiling. I want you watching how much I love the way you fuck my face covering me with your cum. Do you understand?"

"Yes, sir."

My dick jumps in my pants with her obedience, precum leaking from the tip at her words. Our eyes connect while I lower to my knees my mouth level with her pussy, watering with how close I am to burying my tongue in her.

"I want you to ride my face hard and fast. Don't stop until your sweet pussy empties every drop down my throat. I'm at your mercy just once, Sin, don't waste it."

"Fuck, Fin." Her hand itches to touch herself, but I hold her back, not able to handle watching her fuck her own hand.

Lifting her right leg to place over my shoulder, I dive in not giving her a second to process my movement. My mouth closes over her clit using my tongue to flick it over and over until she relaxes fully.

"Eyes on the ceiling," I order.

"Fin!"

Her head hits the wall behind her, the reflection above damn near enough to have me finishing in my pants like a horny teen.

Her skin is flushed pink, her green eyes hooded with lust, but it's the way her body responds to mine that has my soul caving. Each fiber of my being reaches for her with each taste, each grip of her thighs, each grind of her hips, it's Nirvana.

Both hands spear through my hair, twisting the strands to pull me in deeper, her other leg shifting open to give me full open access to her.

Plunging my tongue inside her I bring my thumb between us to put pressure on her clit, sending convulsions through her body.

"Fuck! Oh god." Her screams make my skin burn, the pinch of her pulling my hair not enough.

"I'm no god, Sin."

Moving her other leg over my shoulder I stand, leaning her back against the glass wall, both legs hanging down my back, my mouth still locked in place taking everything she's willing to give. I'd steal everything from her with no remorse. Athena's in my bones.

"Please. Please. Oh shit." Her chants fuel me.

Using her thighs, leaning hard against the glass for leverage, she fucks my face with frantic thrusts, finding her high with my tongue deep in her cunt.

Taking away my thumb to add two fingers inside her she starts to shake with the force of her release. Shifting my forearms under her ass, we move in tandem, but it's the not until my teeth sink into her clit that she shatters like the glass surrounding us.

"Finnnnn!" she screams, her moans rattling the walls around us.

Shit, I thought I'd taste her and be done, but the way her pussy floods my throat with her ambrosia heat, my dick craves her taste. Not giving her time to come down from her high, I drop her on her feet, spin her around forcing her to catch herself with her hands against the glass, dropping my pants below my ass in one move.

"Fuck, Sin, I need my dick inside you now. Take my cock like a good fucking girl."

Slamming into her I pause to adjust to her cunt pulsing with her orgasm, trying not to move too fast. Once we both adjust, I start to thrust into her uncaring of how rough I'm being, my fingers digging into her waist.

"Yes, baby, soak my dick. You're such a good fucking girl, just like that. God damn, Sin, your pussy was made for my dick."

"Fuck." Thrust. "Squeeze." Thrust. "My." Thrust." Dick." Thrust.

Sensations take over, the view of her mouth open, head thrown back, her large tits pressing against the glass, her red hair spilling down her back. I need more. My hand itches to wrap around her throat, so I do just that.

Pulling her head back, my hand grips her throat cutting off all air, the power of having her oxygen in the palm of my hand has my dick pulsing inside her.

Athena can only grunt with each punishing thrust inside her, the pink of her skin turning a soft shade of red with the pressure of my hand on her throat.

"You're mine. No one touches your pussy but me. Ever."

My movements become jerky so close to release. Her face bright red. The shallow inhales dying down, with every thrust my grip gets tighter.

Speaking against her ear, "Your air is mine. This pussy?" Thrust. "It's mine. Your orgasm is mine."

She's shaking, tremors roll off her in droves until she's close to passing out.

"Soak my dick. Come for me, little demon."

Her head thrashes trying to pull in air, but I refuse.

"Come for me. Now!"

That's all it takes for her pussy to convulse all over my dick, pulling my release from me so hard and quick that my vision turns black. Releasing her, she gulps in air filling her lungs while my cock fills her with every drop. Pushing her hair to the side, my lips land in their spot kissing her below her eye.

"Your cunt fucks me so good, baby. Always so fucking good for me."

Stepping back, I turn her to me the color on her cheeks fading with each breath she takes until her eyes come to mine, showing me just what I do to her. My demon feed hers and fuck me if she doesn't swallow down all my fucking sins.

"Holy shit."

Adjusting my pants with a smirk on my face, I bend to help her pull her pants back on waiting for her to step into each leg hole. When I'm satisfied that she's good my feet move back, my stare bouncing back to her, before I press the red button.

Kick starting the elevator it starts to slowly move down to the parking garage when she bursts out laughing.

"What's so funny, Sin?" My eyebrow arches in question.

"I'm about to go save my best friend from an abusive piece of shit with cum dripping down my legs."

Well, fuck, now my dick is hard again with the thought of my cum dripping from her cunt.

CHAPTER THIRTY SEVEN
ATHENA

The ache between my legs fades with each mile the closer we get to Sable, where that abusive son of a bitch is. My heart pangs with hurt at the way she looked when I walked in her room after forcing my way in the door. Mike didn't want to let me in. The idiot thought he could actually keep me away from her.

It wasn't until I got closer to the bed that I saw each bruise spread over her body, like her skin was a canvas that he painted with his fist. The stark realization hitting me that she was ignoring me the past couple of days so I wouldn't see her like this hurts.

It cuts deep. Instead of festering in my feelings on how she could keep this from me, I plan out how to get her out of this. Short of killing the bastard, I have to convince Ezra to end our contract early so I can go back home with her.

Shit. The ache vibrating through my bones a reminder that I've let this bossy, broody, stalker in too deep. Ezra's wormed his way into each fiber of my being, identifying with every part of me until it's almost impossible to undo the stitching.

Worrying my lip with thoughts of leaving him in a week, seven short days, that's all we have left of the deal. I didn't count on feeling like this when I signed my name on that dotted line.

"Sin, where's your head at?" Ezra's voice pulls me from my musings.

"How could she not tell me what was going on? We're family. I could have helped her sooner!" My words tremble on the verge of tears.

The skin around my eyes is already raw so I force myself to hold back the tears that threaten to fall. Ezra looks over at me, for a brief second the streetlights casting a soft green hue across his face showing so many emotions pass before he settles on anger.

"Women in these situations often feel like they're to blame even when the people they care about remind them they don't deserve this. It's hard to escape when all you want is for the person abusing you to change. To show you that they really do love you behind the smoke and mirror show going on."

Fidgeting with my seatbelt, my gaze goes back out the window trying to pull a thick blanket of strength over my skin like armor. I wouldn't be surprised if he turned this fucking car around once I get the courage to tell him that I'm going to leave.

Pulling Sable from Mike's grasp isn't going to be enough. She will need someone to help her get through it. Making sure she doesn't run right back in to one of his traps.

"Ezra there's something we need to discuss."

His eyebrows raise in a silent question waiting for me to continue. We edge closer to her apartment only ten minutes out, so I decide to just rip the band-aid off risking losing the other half of the money. It's not like I've already cashed the first check. Not yet. It's sitting in a drawer back at home.

Dammit. I called his place home. I'm falling in too deep.

"I think it's best if Ollie and I go stay with Sable at my apartment. She's going to need us to be there for her."

"No. Seven fucking days, Sin." He stops me. "We have seven days left. I have time left..." His words trail off, both hands gripping the steering wheel, knuckles turning white with the force.

"Sable is more important to me than money. I still have the check of the first half. You got what you wanted. My cherry has officially been popped. Now my family needs me." Turning sideways in the leather seat the pinch in my heart at the sight of his frantic look takes my breath away. "Ezra, it's what's best for Sable. You have to understand that."

"What about what's best for us?" he states angrily, bringing his fist down on the dash making me jump.

"This was never a permanent situation, and you know that! We are nothing more than an arrangement, a deal made in the dark. It was always meant to end even if it burns along the way. Accept it for what it is. You don't belong with someone like me, and I'd never live up to the woman you deserve, so please just stop."

"No, I won't accept this, but if you thought I would let you go, you haven't learned a damn thing. Sin, you truly believe you'd walk away from me? Good fucking luck." Breathing hard, his words are spit from between gritted teeth.

"You can't keep me like I'm a pet. Oliver deserves a real family!"

Flicking on his signal, he swerves over to the fire lane throwing the SUV in park. His head swinging my way, stormy gray eyes glaring into mine. Hands shake against the wheel. The beast he's becoming spiking fear down my spine.

Lighting something within me, the fear coats my inner darkness, begging me to demand he fold at my feet.

"Athena, let me get one thing through to you loud and fucking clear. You better listen closely because I won't repeat myself. You and Oliver are MINE. Oliver has a family with me. You want a place to call home? Done. You need a beacon to lead you through a storm? Fucking done. You need a family for Oliver to grow up with? I can name two men who adore him, not including the fucker sitting right in front of you begging you to stay. You need me to worship you, begging on my hands and knees? Done! Say the word and I'll beg. I'd beg for you as I crawl on my stomach taking anything you throw my way."

His gray eyes widen with each word. The guttural sound in his voice searing me to my core.

Reaching out to cup my face with a large, calloused hand his thumb pulls at my bottom lip. The way he uses my real name instead of Sin has me holding my breath.

"My soul is yours, little demon. You were always my Sin

to live and die by. You've carved your way into my bones, embedding each initial in the marrow with a dagger. There is no end, only more. We are more, Sin. You stole the air from my lungs and fuck I don't want it back."

"Stop. Just stop. You don't know what the hell you're saying. Please, Ezra, please. We can't do this right now. Sable needs us."

Moving his hand until it's at my throat, feeling every divot in the curves of my neck, he pulls me to the center of the car, "This conversation isn't over I promise you that. I'll chain you to the bed and fuck some sense into you and trust me baby your pussy will love every goddamn second, so remember that when you try to run. I'll always bring you back to me."

Quivering under his touch, my core heats with the vision of being spread on his bed bound under his mercy with every inch stretching me over and over again. My thighs rub together with the need to ease the ache.

"Yeah, my girl likes the sound of that. I wonder if you'd soak my dick while I carve my name into your milky skin, branding you as mine."

He leans in licking the skin under my bottom lip before pulling it into his mouth, giving it a harsh bite before letting it go with a wet plop. My fingers come up to rub the area in shock at his declaration unable to process what just happened, but I know one thing. No matter how bad my body calls out to him, I can't stay.

~

Pulling up to the apartment Ezra curses, whipping the car into a spot, he tosses it in park right before jumping out. The door slams rattling the glass window, rushing after him my fingers just out of reach to pull him to a stop.

"Ezra what the fuck is going on?" My words are whispered, trying to avoid causing a scene.

Ignoring me, he runs up to the door to Mike's apartment stopping in his tracks. Those appraising eyes stuck ahead of him. Before my mouth opens to ask what is going on I see it and a scream rips from my throat. Rushing forward through the open apartment my legs carrying me over to Sable, who's lying on the living room floor unconscious.

"Sabby!" Pain shoots up my spine with the force of my knees slamming to the floor.

From the corner of my eyes, I can see Mike on the floor with a body over him the sound of meat on bone makes my ears ring. Flesh on flesh. Fist breaking skin. Bones crack. My ears ring. And ring. My hold on Sable slips, her weight dropping back down to the floor.

"Sable, please wake up!"

"Miles, stop! He's done."

Ringing.

Bone and flesh and blood.

"Miles, man, that's enough!"

So much blood.

Sable's eyes are swollen but shut. Still Shut.

"Sable, please. Please wake up. Oh god."

Grappling sounds from behind me two sets of voices screaming at each other. The ringing getting louder. Sable's chest rises. *Thank fuck.*

"What the fuck are you doing here?" Ezra.

Ezra's voice pulls me back into reality and the full situation that's unfolding in front of me. "I need help!"

"Fuck, the cops are on the way."

"Shit. Did I kill him?" Miles? When did Miles get here?

Sable's chest continues to rise, none of the blood is hers, only Mike's.

Something pulls on my arm, but I shove them off unable to move with the weight of Sable on my lap. How did we get here? Sable's the strong one.

"Sin, baby, please let me get to her so I can see how bad it is."

The heat from his touch dulls the ringing in my ears, my eyes focusing back in on my surroundings making my stomach drop with awareness.

"Oh my god!" I shriek when the room finally comes into view.

Miles is sitting on his feet staring at his hands as if he could wash away the blood and skin with just a look. The lines of his face fierce with rage but it's the hollow look in his eyes that has my blood turning cold.

"Miles?" My words are raspy and low, but he hears me.

"Hmm?" he replies.

Crawling over to him, my small hands close over his large ones not shying away from the raw, gruesome sight in front of me. Holding both his hands, attempting not to hurt his knuckles that are likely broken, I bring them to my chest.

"Look at me."

Licking my lips, my gaze flits back at Sable, who is now in Ezra's arms standing beside me, her head hanging from the side.

"Hmm?" Still no words spoken, but his blue eyes are on mine.

"We've got you. You saved Sable, that's all that matters. I owe you everything for saving her."

"Is he dead?" The emptiness in his tone has the hair on my arms standing on end.

Crawling over to a beaten Mike, my stomach rolls at the sight of his face. Extending my hand, I reach for his neck, feeling a faint pulse. The low thump feels like a curse. Nodding I look over my shoulder, sharing a look with Ezra full of questions.

"He's alive, for now, so let's get the fuck out of here."

Miles stands, his stare not moving from his hands inspecting them like their foreign objects unable to be controlled. Stepping closer to him I wait until he looks up from the blood, meeting my gaze.

"He could have killed her yet she's alive because of you. I don't know why or how you're here, all I know is Sable is alive and going home with me. Thank you for that."

My arms wrap around his large frame, hugging him, my body clings to him, allowing Miles to break through the haze of what he did to hug me back. It's not until I feel the burn of Ezra's body heat at my back that I pull away, releasing a jittery Miles.

"We have to get out of here. Sin, I need you to drive Miles's car back to the penthouse. He's not in any state to drive right now."

Nodding my head in agreement he has Miles toss me his keys. Ezra carrying Sable, we rush out of the apartment leaving Mike in a pool of his own blood with a note warning him to stay the fuck away from Sable. Ezra also left a wad of cash, against my wishes, to make sure Miles didn't go to jail.

My hands shake on the steering wheel, the images from tonight continue to flash through my mind branding me for life. Things turned bad so fast, but there's still two questions that keep nagging me to find out the answer.

The first one: Why the fuck was Miles there?

The Second: How the hell did he know where Sable lived?

I don't know the answer, but I will by the end of the night, or I'll kill him myself.

CHAPTER THIRTY EIGHT
EZRA

"You need to back the fuck off and give her more time." Athena's voice is cold and detached.

Her steps are quick, pacing back and forth, stopping only to glare at Miles, who is leaning over the couch nails dug in deep. Most likely the only anchor he has holding him in place when all he wants is to rush back to Sable. Who is sleeping in my bed, where no other woman but Athena has been, but I push that thought out of my head for my little demon.

Athena's on a warpath, prepared to cut anyone off at the knees who dare to fuck with Sable. Eros walks in from checking on Oliver making sure he's still sound asleep.

Questions in his eyes, walking over to sit on the couch Miles is leaning over.

"Why don't we all calm down and have a drink to take off the edge."

Nodding my way, I take his lead going into the kitchen to grab a few glasses and a bottle of Macallan from the top shelf of my bar area.

Pouring three glasses, handing them off to Eros and Miles, they take theirs. Eros sipping his, while Miles tosses the entire thing back. Athena storms over, snatching the glass I have at my lips before a drop touches my tongue and knocks it back before shoving it into my chest.

"Pour me another one."

Her words are a demand not giving a shit who she's talking to and under different circumstances I'd punish her, but right now she'd have my balls in a choke hold if I denied her anything. We have to get to the bottom of this shit tonight because I have plans with my girl in a few days that require her to trust Miles and Eros with Oliver.

"Miles, you have questions to answer. Starting with what the hell was your plan tonight?" I ask.

Athena pauses her steps to grab a second drink from me. This time taking sips. Her lips parting against the cold glass, the amber liquid flowing down her throat with each swallow. Licking her lips, she catches me staring at the movement of her throat.

"No. The question that matters most is how the hell you know Sable or where she lives. You don't do what you did for a stranger so break it down for me. I want to know everything."

Athena walks closer to Miles, who's now standing straight not backing down from her hard stare.

"We met at my bar several months back, way before we

ever met you. She came in late one night with a tall, lean girl with jet black hair. They were both there for a good time."

"Raven," Athena says, more to herself than anyone. Nodding her head, she motions for him to continue.

Rolling his shoulders, he says, "They stayed at the bar until closing, tossing drinks back and having a good time. When it was time to shut the doors, I didn't feel right letting them drive so I took her friend home, but before I could get Sable home, she passed out in the car, so I took her to my place above the bar."

Holding his hands up at the look on Athena's face, he assures her no lines were crossed. Knowing who Miles is, it's easy to believe he didn't do anything to her outside of letting her crash in his bed or on the couch. I trust him with my life.

"When she woke up, I assured her of the same thing. Nothing happened that night, but we talked for a while even had breakfast together.

Nothing outside of a casual friendship was started, but once she walked out the door she was gone and I didn't see her again until you came along."

Eros leans back on the couch propping his feet up on the table, catching my eye when he does, only to slide his feet back off a second later.

Miles walks around the back of the couch to sit next to him, placing his elbows on his knees. Crossing my arms over my chest, I watch as Athena continues to wear a path in the floor with her continuous pacing.

"Sin, sit down."

Flipping me off, she addresses Miles once again.

"Have you slept with her? When's the last time you saw her before tonight? And for the life of me, I can't see how you knew where she lived! She lives with Mike, Miles. So, how did you know where their apartment was?"

His head falls forward, the silence deafening. My girl is only going to wait so long. The little demon is at her wits end. My need to stop this bullshit and rush over to comfort her makes my hands clench.

"I've seen her a twice since the pool. Yesterday when I followed her home from the club because she was refusing to dance, and that's when I saw that things were not okay. She was hiding something, but wouldn't let me in. Until you stormed in here earlier, I couldn't piece it together. I thought it was someone at the club, because to be honest I didn't know about Mike."

"She never told you about him?" I ask, my gaze watching for a lie.

Shaking his head, his eyes find mine. "I fucking swear. We never slept together, but Sable means something to me. I've let her in, and I won't apologize for protecting her. You'd do the same if you were in my place."

Fuck, I'd do worse. The bastard would be six feet under by now if he had put a finger on my Sin.

"He'd be dead." My words are final.

Athena stops to look at me with wide eyes, so I move from against the doorframe to meet her halfway. She's walked her way back to the window overlooking the streets below. Her flaming red hair is tied back in a braid down her back, perfect for me to wrap around my wrist. Her small soft hand pulls me from the vision I'm having with her on her knees right here.

"She's going be okay, baby," I reassure her.

Pulling her into my arms, she settles against my chest her breathing ragged.

Eros finally speaks, "Do you think he'll go to the cops?"

Scoffing, I reply, "Not a chance. I left a stack of cash and Miles left him beaten half to death. He'll know not to say shit to anyone. It's Sable we need to worry about. She needs to see a doctor tomorrow and we need to bring a bed in so she has somewhere to sleep."

Athena opens her mouth, but I cut her off.

"She's not sharing our bed and if you think I'm letting you leave after tonight, think again. I won't have this talk with you tonight, but that decision's been made. You and Oliver are my family."

She turns away, her eyes shining with tears, to look out at the night sky.

Eros, Miles, and I plan for the doctor to come in tomorrow to take a look at Sable and to make sure nothing is seriously broken. I plan to set her up a space in the library until further notice, but a small voice stops all other discussion.

"I'm not staying here," Sables rough voice says, pulling everyone's attention to the doorway.

Miles jumps up rushing to her, Athena not far behind. Sable's hair is a wild mess, her eyes are dark with no life in them, but a glimmer of fight shines back giving me hope that she's still in there somewhere. She's covered up her bruises with a long sleeve shirt and leggings, trying to hide the truth, as if none of us saw it for ourselves.

"Sabby!" Athena cries, pulling her best friend and sister into a hug, being as gentle as possible.

Miles stands back giving them a moment before yanking her into his chest where she breaks down into full sobs.

"Shhh it's okay, killer," Miles whispers against her hair.

We all watch as she falls apart clinging to Miles while Athena stands a foot away with confusion written all over her face.

"You're staying here with me," Athena declares adamantly.

Making my way to stand at her back, my hands rub up and down her arms, allowing her to relax into my chest for support.

"Let's give her some space, Sin. She's been through a lot."

"I'm not leaving," Miles states, his tone and his stare determined.

Sable pulls away, placing a hand on his chest. She looks at Athena with soft eyes begging her to see reason. "T, please. I love you, but I can't stay here with you and Oliver. This is where you belong."

Hearing those words has me damn near falling to my knees ready to thank her for seeing what Athena refuses to. What's right in front of her.

"You can't go back to that apartment. I won't let you!" Athena twists her hands, pulling at the skin with anxiety.

My need to protect her beats at my chest. "That's enough. You can stay here, Sable. Go get some rest so we can talk more about it in the morning. We've all had enough for tonight."

"Can I go with you? Just for tonight?" Sable is looking at Miles.

Eros stands from the couch, taking each glass back to the kitchen where I hear the water turn on at the sink.

"That's not even a question. You're coming home with me where I can keep an eye on you." Addressing Athena, he waits until he has her full attention. "I'll bring her back tomorrow for the doctor to look her over and I promise to call you if anything happens. You've trusted me with Oliver, you can trust me with Sable."

She looks from Sable to Miles, looking for any sign not to let her go but she doesn't find one. With a hard nod, she storms out of the room. The sound of her feet pounding up the stairs settles something in my chest.

Knowing she's going to find comfort in our room has my inner demon roaring with satisfaction.

"Eros, come over tomorrow with Miles. We can have a family breakfast and I have something I need to plan with you both for Sin."

With that, Miles walks with Eros back to the elevator. His arm around Sable's shoulders, holding her to him like she's, his lifeline. I know the fucking feeling. I head into the kitchen to start making dinner when Athena comes in, making my heart stop with the sight in front of me.

Wearing nothing but my shirt, she pads over to me with a dark look in her eyes.

"I need you, Fin. I need something to take away everything from tonight."

Her raspy voice is like silk rolling over my skin. So fucking smooth and soft, ready to move in any way I demand.

Reaching out for her I pull her against my chest. "You need an escape? I can give you that. Always."

She pats my chest and says, "Whatever you say, Finn." Her ass peeks out from under my crisp work shirt.

CHAPTER THIRTY NINE
ATHENA

P atting his chest. "Whatever you say, Finn." I start to move away from him.

"You need someone? Come to me first, always." His words cut deep, pulling at my chest.

"Needing someone isn't what I signed up for. This is a means to an end. After everything is said and done, I'm walking out that door and going back to the Bronx where I belong, and you will stay here in your pristine penthouse looking down your nose at strippers like me."

Backing me into the kitchen island, he grips my chin in a bruising hold. "You'd walk away from me? From us? After everything?"

"That's the deal, Ezra. It's what we agreed to. This is the bed we made. You have to let us go."

"What if I'm asking you to stay?"

Breaking eye contact, my gaze glances over his shoulder to the doorway where Ollie is in the next room sleeping. Finn isn't having it though. He moves his large hands to wrap around my thighs and lifts me onto the counter. Shoving everything to the side he steps into the apex of my thighs and dips down to nip at my neck.

His lips run up and down and back again, pushing a soft mewling sigh out of me.

"Stay, Sin." His warm breath ghosts over my skin, sending a shiver down my back, causing him to smile against my collar bone.

"Why? What is it you want from me?" My eyes search his, looking for something hidden in his stare.

His hand closes over my throat, leaning my head back to meet his eyes. Deep, cloudy gray eyes draw me in until his mouth lowers, barely touching my bottom lip. Finn's teeth nibble at my lip, our breaths mixing in a heady combination of his need and my fear. The darkness under my skin swirls with each squeeze of his hand, loving the way my air is sucked from my lungs.

"Let go, Sin baby. Let me worship you. Stay here with me and Ollie as a family."

He slams his mouth down on mine in a clash of teeth and tongue so wild he steals the only oxygen left in my lungs. I can't pull away, drowning in my need for this powerful man standing before me. I take all he has to give until our control snaps.

Pushing me down flat on the counter with his rough palm, my head falls back on a moan. Those calloused hands

I love so much grab my ankles and caress their way up to my thighs, sending tingles up to my core.

Wetness coats my inner thighs soaking the red lace thong until it's dripping. My hands come up to intertwine in his soft hair pushing him down to where I need him.

His chuckle against my skin sends a zing straight to my center. "Let me take my time on you. This is where you belong, right here under me. My fucking Sinner stealing the soul from my body."

Teeth nip at their way from the crease of my knee to just inside the crease of my hip and groin.

Fuck.

One of his hands slips up to squeeze my throat while the other plays my nipples like a master pianist plays their favorite tune.

The slip and slide of his silk work shirt over my bare nipples overrides my nerve endings until my head is thrashing against the hard granite. Applying more pressure to my throat, my breathing begins to shallow in that way that makes my blood sing in my veins.

"That's it, baby. Relax this beautiful body for me."

God, he drives me wild, my wetness drips down my legs when he moves the hand that was teasing my nipples to pull the thong down my legs. Before I can catch my breath, his hot mouth is on me lapping up everything I have to give. Every inch of his mouth is on me, biting, kissing, sucking, until my legs are shaking, and my skin is hot with pleasure.

"Ezra!" My voice is raspy and needy.

"That's my girl. Let me have every drop, Sin. Let it go."

He slides one of his thick fingers inside me at the same time his teeth close over my clit, and I see stars. The hand on my throat moves to cover my mouth to keep me from waking Ollie.

He laps at me until he has cleaned every last drop of my release and my legs are shaking from my orgasm, but before my body has time to cool, he snatches me up, flips me over on my knees with my ass in the air and his mouth closes over me again.

"I never said I was full." His words vibrate against my sensitive flesh, forcing a deep throaty moan from my lips. Using the edge of the island in front of me, I grip the counter and push my ass back into his face riding him and taking everything he has to offer.

"Finn, yes, please."

His tongue thrusts inside me in sync with his fingers until my whole body is shaking for the release that is more powerful than the last.

I'm on the edge just before I can let go, he pulls away and I hear him pushing his pants down before his arm bands around my waist to pull me down, sliding me to the floor.

"Rest your hands on the counter and don't move. If you move, you don't come, is that understood?"

I try to form words, but my chest is heaving with my breaths and my center aches with needy want. His hand comes down on my ass in a bruising smack that has my clit pulsing.

"Do you hear me?"

"Yes...yes, sir." Another moan.

"Good girl." His words are a praise settling deep in my bones.

He presses me into the counter flat on my stomach with my feet on the ground, his thighs touching the back of mine as he slides into me slowly. So fucking slow it has me arching back into him.

"No." He pauses his movements and damn if I don't want to cry.

I force myself to stay still and he continues to push into me until he is seated as deep as he can go, stretching me fully, sending chills across my skin. One hand wraps my hair around his fist and the other reaches under my stomach to hold me in place as he pounds into me in strong strokes making my toes curl.

Biting my lip until blood spills in my mouth, his hand slides from my stomach to between my legs rubbing at my swollen clit.

"Please. Please. Please." I'm chanting and begging and I don't even care if I sound like a bitch in heat. It's so. Fucking. Good.

Leaning down until his body lays over mine his breath blows across my skin. "Come for me. Come all over my dick. I want your cunt to squeeze my dick."

My release explodes out of me with his wicked words and darkness clouds my vision as spots dance in my eyes.

I can feel him pulsing inside of me with his own release, groaning and grunting with it. His breathing heavy but he doesn't let himself crush me. Standing to pull out of me he spins me around, kissing me hard and fast picking me up under my ass he sets me back on the counter.

"Have I convinced you to stay?" Those knowing eyes observe me in the way only he can, watching and waiting for me to answer.

"Finn." It's not an answer yet he finds his anyway.

Letting out a breath he spreads my legs again and kneels until his face is eye level with my core.

"You are dripping with our come, baby. Let me clean you while you decide what closet you want. I'll give you the world on a platter, Sin."

His wet mouth closes over my flesh and it's almost too much to handle after everything. He flattens his tongue to swipe up everything we left behind sending aftershocks through me down to my bones.

"Finn, please. I can't, it's too much." Gasping over the pure pleasure overload, my legs close around his head holding him there.

Growling out his approval he eats at me like a starved man with both hands gripping my legs pulling me impossibly closer to his waiting mouth.

Sucking my throbbing clit into his mouth and nipping at it sends me over the edge and I swear I blackout for a minute or two because when I come to Fin is carrying me to his bathroom to fill the bathtub with warm water.

My head rolls to the side with my eyes slightly closed in an orgasmic coma. I grin up at Ezra watching him take care of me in everything he does. His beauty has my heart knocking against my ribs and I swear he can hear it beating in my chest.

Everything in me screams to run away from this feeling but I can't. Not when he touches me brushing my hair out of my face, not when he kisses that spot just under my eye, and not when he pauses to take me in, the gray pool of his eyes reflecting the same feeling in my chest.

"Take a bath with me." My voice comes out soft and subdued, causing him to let out that low laugh I love so much.

"Anything for you, Sinner."

I'm falling in love with Ezra Finlay and there's nothing I can do to stop it.

I don't want to stop it.

CHAPTER FORTY
ATHENA

Moving around the kitchen pulling boxes, bags, and cartons out of different cabinets and the fridge to cook. My mind is all over the place, each thought pulling me in a different direction.

Sable's been with Miles for three days now, my nerves are spread thin on that entire situation and Oliver is with Eros today at the park to give me some space. Ezra is upstairs in the shower preparing to go into the office. Everyone else seems to be on the same page leaving me to be the bad guy.

I called Marie at the café to take the week off, needing time to get everything under control. My classes are done for the semester, being able to do them online has saved me from completely failing.

It's turning from winter to spring over the next few weeks so the weathers starting to hit the fifties. Oliver senses that something's off but we've been able to keep him busy with school work, activities, and guy's time.

It shouldn't bother me that he's gotten so close to the guys but some place deep under my skin chafes with irritation that it was so easy for them to connect with him so quickly.

When the curtain is pulled back and the other shoes drop, because it will, he's going to be devastated. We only have a week left. Cracking an egg over a glass bowl my heart mimics the sprawling lines over the shell stealing the breath from my lungs. Even the mere thought of losing Ezra has my knees ready to crash to the floor.

"Sin," Ezra says from the doorway.

Looking over at him I take my time admiring his bare feet up to his black slacks hugging his strong thighs. My eyes travel up to his bare torso, the large expanse of his chest making my mouth water. He hasn't buttoned it leaving it open for me to see every inch of his spotless skin. The sleeves of the white buttoned-down shirt that hugs his forearms are rolled up just under his elbows.

"Fin."

Damn, even I can hear the raspy moan in my tone. By the smirk sliding over Ezra's face, he heard it too. With damp hair and smokey eyes he saunters over to me with that fuck-me grin he loves to use against me.

"Need some help?" He raises an eyebrow in question.

Biting my lip, I hold back my smartass remark knowing it'll only start something we don't have time to finish.

"Yes, please." Batting my eyes at him I turn back to my task, pointing him in the direction of the pancake mix.

"Can you go ahead and mix up the pancakes? I'll get the eggs and bacon started. What time do you need to leave for the office?"

"When we finish eating."

By not giving me a time, he's showing me that I'm his priority. My heart speeds up with the realization that no one will ever make me feel like this. The way he touches my skin sending my pulse soaring with even a feathered touch in passing.

We work in tandem moving around the kitchen cooking each item to place them on the island in the center of the room. Pulling the orange juice and milk from the fridge to place it next to a plate of fruit, he steps up behind me slowly turning me to meet his stare.

"Sin." It's a plea falling from his lips.

The need to lighten the mood has me doing something stupid and wild. Reaching beside me my finger dips into the batter on the counter pulling it back to swipe it across his cheek. Ezra's eyes widen my smile falling an inch waiting for his retaliation.

"Oh, you little minx." He laughs.

Hauling me against him holding my arms at my sides he pinches some flour from the bag behind him at wipes it across my nose before leaning in and licking the side of my face. Heat pools in my core with his mouth on me.

"Fin, we can't."

"No, we can't. Not right now but I do have plans for you later. I want to try something, show you a piece of me, without you running." His words are spoken softly.

Both of his warm hands encase the sides of my face, his gray eyes swimming with intent. Slowly, so slowly, he leans down kissing me with such care. Every kiss before this one has been ravaged, reckless, and wild. But this one? It's slow, soft, intent on bringing me to my knees.

Opening for him we don't fight for dominance. I release it willingly letting him take control of my mouth, my body, and ultimately my heart. With each lap of his tongue his teeth slowly pull at my lower lip not quite biting. Our heartbeats pound in my ears, the staccato of his overpowering mine until they both sync into one loud bass between us.

"Athena."

The use of my name has me pulling back to take in every line of his face. My throat works to swallow down my surprise at the moisture in his eyes. His thumbs rub each side of my jaw, his gaze traveling down over every square inch until he finds what he's been looking for. Gently brushing a kiss under my eye in his spot, my legs start to shake.

"Me too, baby. Me too."

Without words we both step back, my tongue between my teeth, I pull my fingers to my lips spinning around to give myself a moment. Clearing my throat, we get back to work cooking, cleaning, and plating our food. Once we have everything finished and together, we sit at the island eating, laughing, and spilling secrets to each other.

Learning about Ezra is like cave diving into a deep dark hole unsure of what you might find but then somehow you come across these massive gems buried in the cave walls just waiting to be polished, cleaned, and shared with the world. His dreams of saving people from a troubled past, to bring money to the poor communities, and to help other troubled youth makes me melt for him.

I share my love for ballet along with my dreams of

opening my own studio one day that kids and adults from lower income neighborhoods can afford to go to. The art of ballet and dancing has always been a passion of mine.

It may sound crazy but a small piece of me misses the club solely because it was the only way I could dance for people.

After we finish eating he heads to work, reminding me that Eros won't be back with Oliver until later tonight giving me the day to relax. He kisses me senseless outside the elevator leaving me standing there long after he's gone.

My smile hasn't faded yet, the weightlessness I feel being here is like an addiction. Spending my day cleaning, reading, and taking a nap, I finally give up, calling Sable. She's had enough time.

"Hey," she answers.

She sounds better.

"Sabby."

"T, what's going on?"

I hate small talk. We don't do small talk. The awkward air between us grates at me.

"Sabby why don't we get together tonight? I don't have Oliver and Ezra's at the office until later. I need this."

Silence.

"Sable?"

"I'm ashamed, T. You don't know what it's like to have people, men, see you lying on the floor beaten and bruised. How could I let this happen? What did I do?"

"Don't you dare! This was not your fault. Not at all. Please just come spend the evening with me. I've already been here for hours by myself; it's driving me nuts!"

Rustling is heard on the other line, then she sniffles. "Just the two of us?"

"I promise. We'll hang out here and eat junk food."

"Okay. I'll be there soon."

After ending the call I get a few things ready for tonight to make sure we have everything we need for a much-needed girls night in. An hour later the elevator dings signaling Sable's arrival.

"Change of plans!" She sings in a loud voice.

Oh boy, reckless Sable has shown up to the party.

"And what might that plan be?" I wonder out loud.

"Oh, trust me you'll love it. We are going out tonight!"

This is not what I had in mind for us when she said a night out but what the hell. I could use a few drinks to take off the edge not to mention spending time with Sable was my goal.

Sable strolls up the sidewalk, her happy mood has me concerned with everything she's been through, so I make a mental note to keep an eye on her tonight.

A large blue flashing neon sign that reads *Grayve Yard Bar* aptly named after the owner Miles Grayson. Was coming here a risk? Yep. Does Sable give a shit? Nope. We decided to put our phones on silent, only checking them once an hour to make sure Oliver is okay.

Sable twirls on the sidewalk her short skintight black leather skirt not moving an inch. She looks stunning under the city lights. The shine of her brown hair flowing just past her shoulders now that it's grown out.

"You ready for this?" Her smile is stretched across her face.

The skimpy red top barely covering anything rides up a little further when she tosses both hands over her head. She's manic and I'm worried if this is just blowing off steam trying to forget or if this is something else. The look in her eyes tugs at something in the back of my mind but I shove it away not daring to call attention to it. I can't.

"Hell yeah." My smile feels weak.

"You look smokin hot, T!"

Nudging my shoulder, she nods toward my outfit. "That dress looks amazing on you. It makes your boobs looks great." Winking at me, her eyes trail down the royal blue thigh-length dress with the back out.

"All right, all right let's go inside." My cheeks feel hot with embarrassment.

The bouncer standing at the door lets his eyes wander over both of us.

"IDs?" he asks.

We both fish our license out of our purses, mine hung over my shoulder, passing them both to him along with the cover charge to get in. Handing our cards back we step inside the dark hallway with music pouring from speakers on the wall.

"Let's stop by the bar to get a drink," Sable suggests.

Nodding in agreement we make our way through the large crowd to the bar where a guy no older than us is handling the sea of people shouting orders at him. We stand at the corner waiting our turn until he finally makes his way to us with a flirty smile he most likely gives every girl here. Anything for a tip, I'm sure.

"What can I get you two beautiful ladies?"

He eyes our wristbands before he makes a move to grab our orders.

"I'll have a Malibu Rum with pineapple juice." I order my favorite drink.

"And for you, gorgeous?" her asks with a big smile.

Sable leans in to make sure he hears her. "Jack and coke, babe."

She goes straight for the hard shit. Bar guy, who never gave his name, walks off to make our drinks and continues to manage the building crowd. This place is full of people of all ages dancing in the center of the room, filling the booths lining the edges of the room, and an upstairs space for higher clientele.

The railing leading to the top floor is swarming with women waiting for the chance to be pulled upstairs with the men who pay for a fun night.

Bar guy returns with our drinks, setting them down on the bar top. Before he can leave Sable stops him.

"Keep a tab open for us."

He doesn't get the chance to respond before she's pulling my arm toward the dance floor, drinks in hand, our bodies moving with the flow of the music. It only takes her two swallows to down her glass, slamming it on a table near us, her head is thrown back with a laugh. My glass is next, setting it on the same table, the rum has heat flooding through my chest.

We dance until sweat spills down my back and my legs aching. I'm seconds from pulling her off the floor when a chill crawls down my spine, the hair on my arms and neck twitching with awareness. He's here.

Fuck, how long has it been? After three drinks and ten songs I've lost count of the time.

"Fun police just walked in," Sable shouts into my ear over the song blaring around us.

We laugh, my head numb to anything other than our bodies gliding together, rolling with each lyric from the song playing. What is the song playing? Bar guy, who we've learned is Logan, brings us another round this time it's courtesy of a group of men in a corner booth at the back of the room.

"I made it myself. It's the same drinks you've been ordering they just paid for them."

He reassures us when we both hesitate to take the glasses from him but the cool liquid calls to me. My throat dries from exerting myself. Tossing back the full glass I hand it back to him with a wink. Sable is slower to drink hers, so he walks off leaving the glass with her.

"Are they just going to watch or come over to yell at us?" She tries to whisper.

We laugh, stumbling a few feet before righting ourselves our arms holding on to each other.

"I've missed you, T," Sable says, sadness entering her tone.

"No, no. We can't do this here. It's a fun night, so let's have some fun!"

My last words were a yell grabbing a few people's attention but the feel of his eyes on me never leave. The way they trace every inch of my body while we move around to the beat has me drenched.

My body craves his touch, the need for him to walk over here and punish me has my thighs rubbing together, I want him.

Is that the alcohol talking? Shit.

My eyes drift closed, hands twisting and twirling over my head, letting my movements flow freely. It's not until I feel the heat of someone at my back that my eyes pop back open startled from the hands on my waist. These hands don't belong on my skin. I can feel how wrong they are touching my bare flesh.

"Keep moving, baby."

The voice is wrong. It's all wrong. Sable's gaze flies behind me and back to me shaking her head.

"Get off me." I shove his hands off in jerky movements.

My head pounds, the fuzzy feeling flooding out all common sense. Turning in slow motion my stare clashes with a stranger standing over me with wicked eyes and a smile that makes my skin crawl.

"Come on, baby, we're just having a little fun."

His breath fans across my lips. The smell of nicotine and whiskey makes my stomach roll and I know he saw the disgust flash over my face when he snarls at me. Both of his meaty hands grip my arms yanking him to me, pulling me in until my breasts are flush against his chest.

"Let her fucking go, you pig!" Sable yells, shoving on his arm.

It takes one look to have the color draining from her face sending her back to that night with Mike. This stupid bastard has her spiraling while holding me in a bruising hold.

With one look over his shoulder my eyes connect with smokey grays that hold fire in them. The alarm on my face is nothing compared to Miles and Ezra storming through the crowd without a care.

"You're going to regret ever touching me," I say with a smirk.

His mouth opens but no words come out. His hands are pulled from my skin in one hard tug, bringing a fuming Ezra into view. With nothing standing in his way he slams the guy into the floor landing blow after blow into his face.

Miles rushes up to Sable taking her face in his hands. People backing away from the commotion, Ezra still on top of the bastard.

"Miles stop him!"

"Fuck no. He had his hands on you, Athena. There's nothing that's going to stop him now."

People start to pull out phones when they realize it's Ezra Finlay business CEO fighting over a woman. No, I can't let this happen to him. Jumping into action, I throw myself onto his back, pulling at his arms, begging him to stop. Nothing works.

"Miles!" I scream.

Sable is still in a state of shock standing behind Miles, who has his arm behind him holding her hand.

"Fin, please! Stop!" My shouts fall on deaf ears.

People are watching in sick fascination. Sliding off him I drop to my knees pining myself between him and the guy as his fist is coming down.

"Fin!"

My scream snaps him out of his haze. His fist sails past my head into the flooring, splitting the skin. My body trembles with adrenaline mixed with fear. Wide eyes take in the room around him, his fist still bawled and his breathing ragged.

"Sin, are you out of your fucking mind?" he yells, yanking me into him.

He stands with me in his arms, my feet barely reaching the floor. He moves backward until we're at the edge of the room, leaving the guy on the floor for Miles to deal with he drops me to my feet. One hand wrapped around my throat forcing my head back.

"What the hell were you thinking? I could have killed you." His words are barely audible behind his rage.

His whole-body shakes with anger. "I'm going to take pleasure in your punishment, Sin." Pulling me in, he slams his mouth down on my mouth in a biting kiss that feels like the beginning of what's to come.

"Let's clear out. I have the team handling that prick for us. I'm going to take Sable home and get her sober. Eros is going to keep Oliver for the night, I called him and told him what happened. Get her out of here," Miles says before dragging Sable away with a vacant look on her face.

"The Devil and the Sinner." That's all he says before he leads me to his car, opening the door, and walking around to the other side.

If he's the Devil I must be Persephone, damned to love the darkness.

CHAPTER FORTY ONE
EZRA

Athena leans back on the leather seat, her long legs showing the wide expanse of her creamy skin. My knuckles throb on the wheel, my grip pulling at the busted skin, blood drying around the opening. Taking a few turns in the wrong direction, it's not until the city lights fade that Athena perks up, her eyes staring out the window.

Glaring at the side of her head, my heart pounds in my chest.

"What the fuck was that? Do you know what I could have done to you if my fist connected with your skull? In what world do you think it's okay to step in front of a man taking a swing at another man?"

I can feel the venom dripping from my tongue with each syllable. Athena could have been hurt. I could have hurt her and not in the way my hands shake to punish her right now. No, my fist could have done serious damage.

"You weren't going to hit me, Fin. I knew you would do anything to keep from hurting me."

"What if I couldn't stop in time? If my body shifted just an inch? Your ass is due for a spanking. Why didn't you tell me you and Sable decided to go out?"

Her head swings in my direction, her eyes cutting me down on the spot with the daggers she's shooting my way.

"Last time I checked I am an adult who *can* and *will* make her own decisions. You didn't hit me, and no one was hurt so take a step back."

Whipping my hand out I grab her jaw, pulling her face within inches of mine our lips a whisper away.

"I could have killed him. I would have killed him for you. He'll heal but if you were hurt I wouldn't. So next time refrain from doing stupid shit, and I don't have to learn to live without you."

Her eyes blink in quick flutters. "I'm fine, Ezra." Her words hoarse.

I plant a kiss under her eye. The move settling the raging demon beating at his cage demanding I go back to kill the fucker who put his hands on what's mine. Letting her go to focus on the road ahead, my foot accelerates past the stop sign we were sitting at.

"Where are we going?" she asks, her words filled with anticipation.

"Take off your panties," I order.

Her head swivels toward me, the streetlights ahead casting a glow on her face showing the hesitation.

"What?"

"I said take off your thong and hand it to me. Now."

Licking her lips her eyes never leave mine. Reaching under the tight dress hugging her frame, she lifts her ass for leverage. Both hands disappear under the hem of the blue material slowly bringing her black thong down her legs. I can hear the wet suction of the material pulling from her dripping pussy releasing what's mine.

"All the way off."

Her breathing turns ragged, the little demon lifting her legs to show off the toned muscles. Once the offending piece of clothing is removed, she lets her legs fall open. The dress has ridden up her to her hips giving me a glimpse of heaven. Holding out my hand she drops them in my palm and fuck, I was right, her pretty, pink cunt is soaked for me.

Pressing down on the pedal to bring us closer to eighty miles an hour, I turn on the cruise control now that we've reached a long stretch of highway. The vibration of the car has her emerald-green eyes darkening into a deep forest green. Lust clouding her gaze. My eyes dart to the road keeping up on course, but the pull from my Sinner has my fingers itching to sink into her.

"Touch yourself."

Her inhale echoes through the silent car speeding down the road, each rev of the engine forcing a shiver from my girl. She loves the feel of my car under her while I control her moves.

"I want you to fuck your hand until I tell you to stop."

Biting the inside of her cheek she nods her head eager to give me what I want. Inching her hand down her stomach, her stare locked on the side of my face, she pulls her dress up over her waist giving me a mouth-watering sight. My hands squeeze around the steering wheel, my mouth watering to be where her fingers are.

"Keep going, Sin," I order.

Her smile turns into a wicked smirk, those sinful fingers spread open her wet folds revealing her pink swollen clit, ghosting over it to reach her opening. Plunging two fingers into the knuckle her mouth falls open in the shape of an O letting out a small gasp.

"Feel how wet you are for me, Sin?"

"Yes." A moan escapes.

"Fuck your hand for me. Ride your fingers while I watch your cunt drip for me."

"Oh god." Another moan.

Speeding up the car jerks her back, pressing her into the seat. Her eyes drifting closed with the hum of the car, fingers still deep inside her. Teeth digging into her bottom lip, she starts to move.

"Open your legs wider, baby. Let me see your tight little cunt pull your fingers in begging for my dick to replace them."

She starts to ride her hand, hips lifting meeting her palm thrust for thrust only pausing to graze her clit with her thumb. Fire red hair falls from her clip in curtains, tempting me to tug on the silky tresses. Looking back out on the road, my speed evens back out kicking the cruise control on again I relax my foot.

"Fuck, Sin," I grit.

Her chest heaves, the tight material stretching over her round breasts. My mouthwatering with the image of her nipples pinched between my fingers.

"Fin," she pleads, needing more.

"Use your other hand. I want you to ride your fingers while you play with your swollen clit."

Obeying my every word Athena's head rolls to the side, her hazy eyes locking with mine, the shine in them pulling me in. Curling her fingers using her feet planted on each side of the floorboard she pushes down with each thrust.

"That's it, baby. Good fucking girl."

My dick is steel under my dress pants. The bite from the zipper barely felt behind my overwhelming need to sink balls deep inside my little demon. Her tight cunt grips my dick so perfectly. Just imagining that perfect vision makes my cock leak.

"Oh god. Oh god." Raspy pleas fall from her sinful red lips.

"I want you calling my name when you come, Sin," I demand.

Hands shaking, her legs twitch from holding herself off the seat, her other hand pinches her clit. Two more plunges onto her dainty fingers and she shatters, yelling my name over the rev of the car.

"Fin!"

"Oh, fuck baby. Look at you my little sinner drenching my seat."

Reaching out, grabbing her hand before she tries to wipe off her fingers, I take them into my mouth swirling my tongue around them sucking every last damn drop of her release from her skin. Her come belongs to me. Leaning back against the seat, her knees fall closed hiding her from view. The dazed look in her eyes proof of her orgasm.

"Watching you let go is like watching stars fall from the sky. Breathtakingly beautiful leaving me wishing for something more."

Taking her thong from my lap I wrap it around my gear

shifter letting it hang between us the entire ride home. Athena's bare ass on my seat and the taste of her cunt on my lips. The taste ambrosia doesn't fade from my tongue until long after we reach the city again. It takes an hour to reach the penthouse parking garage, pulling into my reserved spot, I park the car and jump out walking to the passenger side.

Opening Athena's door before she gets the chance to step out, my hand reaches down to pull her to her feet, watching the way her ass peeks out from under the dress still at her waist.

Her cheeks turn pink still holding on to the appearance of being shy, but I know my girl loves my eyes on her. I wait for her to adjust her dress, pulling her forward when she turns to retrieve her panties, forcing her to leave them where they are.

"Those belong to me now. I think I'll keep them there to remind me of how it looks when you push yourself over the edge."

Slapping my chest, she moves around me heading for the elevator, but she can't hide the satisfied smile that spreads across her face. I'm not the only one with an addiction. We reach the elevator pressing the button to call it down when she spins around to me bringing herself face-to-face with me. Smiling, she rises up on her toes to loop her arms around my neck using her momentum to pull me down.

"Fin." She breathes against my lips.

"I know, Sin."

She kisses me long and deep until the doors open. She kisses me even after we shuffle into the glass box. Her lips caress mine the entire way up to the penthouse, lighting my blood on fire.

Soft lips travel from mine, down my neck leaving bites along the way, over to my ear where her teeth graze my lobe. Pouty red lips close over my throat, biting and nipping along the column making my dick hard again.

Pulling back, her green eyes trace over my face in search of something. Athena looks at me like she's seeing deep into my soul, finding the man I hide away in fear of rejection.

She can see through my walls, breaking them down until nothing's left but dust and rubble. Dropping her head to my chest, she sighs into my shirt, the heat from her touch burns.

"Come on, Sin, I have a surprise for you."

The door opens to the foyer, but she stops me pulling me to the hall bathroom before I can show her our bags packed sitting in the living room waiting to take us far away for the weekend. A surprise that's had my pulse thrumming through my body in anticipation.

"I need to clean up your hands first," she declares, her hold on me unwavering.

My heart beats for the woman in front of me. The way her body sways, it's hypnotizing. My eyes drift closed for a second, wishing this time with her would last forever. Because the organ in my chest? It belongs to my Sinner. The realization that I love her has my eyes shooting open, staring into her piercing, emerald green eyes.

CHAPTER FORTY TWO
ATHENA

A private jet. Soft, plush, cream-colored leather seats in a private jet are what my cheap legging covered ass is planted on. My thoughts shift to our conversation hours earlier when he ambushed me with our bags packed and Eros on the phone damn near shoving me out the door. It took him and Miles forty minutes to convince me that leaving Oliver with him and Eros was a good idea and that they could manage his Diabetes regime.

I smile thinking about Eros going over what food Oliver can and can't have and how often he has to check his blood sugar. We all laughed when he gagged at the thought of Oliver having a needle stuck in his stomach but after everything was said and done, I felt comfortable with leaving him there for two days.

Licking my lips my eyes jump over to Ezra, who's off to the side on a business call with an intense look on his face.

He has yet to give me any clues as to where we are headed. I only know that the flight is six hours, giving me no clues on our destination. The blinds are pulled down on the windows giving the jet a nighttime feel.

My curiosity is peaked, being my first time on a plane let alone a private one, I decide to go look around. Looking back at Ezra to see he's still on the phone I make my way over to a small bar area with one woman handling any orders we might have.

Giving her a small smile, I order a Malibu Rum for the ride to take off the edge. My heart is torn with this entire trip. Could it really be this simple? Dropping my walls to let in a man who has shown me time and time again that he would always choose me. From the moment he met Oliver, he's taken him in with open arms accepting us for who we are and not where we come from.

My heart skips a beat at the memory of me realizing that Ezra had the entire fridge stocked with insulin for Oliver all paid for by him. This was the first week we moved in.

It was never asked for, it's just something he did for us to make our life easier. My only question is why? Why me? Why does he push so hard to break down my walls?

"There you are, baby."

Ezra's lips skate over the skin on my shoulder, sending good shivers down my spine. I've made my way into the back of the plane where a bedroom is tucked away, the door closed so I can't see in. Stark white walls spread through the jet with gold trim from ceiling to baseboard travel the full length of the aircraft. Not a speck of dust in sight.

"What's back here?" I ask, more to myself than to him.

He chuckles against my collar bone. "Always so curious, Sin."

Using his hand, he turns me with a firm grip on the back of my neck bringing me eye level with his chest.

Leaning my head back far enough to see those startling gray eyes assessing me, my ponytail holding a bundle of curls, sweep across the door. Backing me into the wood at my back he smirks down at me, loving the sight of having his prey at his mercy.

"Why don't I show you? Our plane doesn't land for another few hours and I do believe I owe you a punishment."

Adrenaline pumps through my veins. My heart picking up speed with the promise of what's to come.

"Are you finally going to tell me where we're headed?"

His smile stays in place, his free hand reaching behind me just above the small of my back to grab the doorknob and slowly opening the door with his stare still pointed at me.

Walking me in the room backward, only guided by his control my knees hit the edge of a mattress only a few feet in the door. Taking a moment to survey the room around me.

A large circular bed is at the back of the room, taking up most of the space, covered in black bedding with gold swirls scattered over it. There is a small table and chair area near a window to the left and what seems to be a stand-up shower to the right, with just enough room for a bench inside the shower.

"Wow." My tone is filled with astonishment.

Releasing his hold on me, Ezra steps back, crossing his arms over his chest. The look in his eyes flickering from amusement to dominance in an instant. It's like he hit a switch changing the air in the room from relaxed to charged with possession, control, and lust. My thong is immediately soaked all the way through from the heat of his stare.

"Strip and kneel for me," he orders, not taking his eyes off me.

The pull of his black Henley shirt outlines every muscle in his biceps, dragging my attention from his face to his perfectly sculpted form. The short sleeves stop just above his muscles, displaying his corded forearms.

Stormy eyes watch me intently, tracking the way my hands grasp the bottom of my shirt, slowly pulling it up to reveal my body.

Being aware of his attention on me, the heat of his penetrating stare is exhilarating.

Keeping my movements steady, my gaze doesn't leave his until the gray of my bookish T-shirt blocks him from view. Dropping the soft cotton shirt to the floor, my fingers ghost over the waist of my leggings, gently dipping into the crease to pull down the fold.

"That's it, baby. I want you bare for me."

His words are an order but the way his eyes flare, it's almost like he's pleading for me to obey.

Giving my hips a shake, my leggings slide down to my feet and I step out of them. The sound of his inhale when he spots me bare under the thin pants has chills spreading down my arms. Kicking my discarded clothing to the side, my gaze searches his out waiting for those steamy, grey eyes to hold mine before I gradually drop to the floor on my knees.

"Good fucking girl," he praises. "Spread those thighs for me, Sin. I want to see how wet you are for me. Show me what a good little slut you are for me. Slide your fingers into your cunt and feel how soaked you are for my dick."

Oh god. His words are filthy and everything I need all at once. The pulsing need in my center intensifies when my fingers graze over my hip bone slowly sliding down to brush over my clit.

"Ohhhhh," I groan softly.

Ezra adjusts his stance, widening his feet with his arms still crossed over his chest, but it's the burning stare focused on my body that sets me on fire. Everything's hot, my pussy clenching with the need to be filled, and my mouth waters for a taste of his skin.

The tips of my fingers finally reach my opening setting me on edge. With my fingers inching inside me at a torturing pace my head rolls to the side.

"I can see how wet you are, baby. You want my dick, don't you?"

Lips parting on a groan I plunge my fingers inside my pussy, clenching around them needing more so I twist and scissor them adding pressure. Easing them in and out at a slow pace, my legs spread wider, my knees grinding into the hard floor. Lifting my hips to drop back down on my hand, giving me the perfect angle to grind my clit against my palm.

"Oh god!"

"Stop," he orders.

A whine leaves my lips as I pull my fingers out of my pussy.

"I want you to taste yourself."

Without hesitation I follow his order, loving the way my body obeys his every word without question. The way he commands me has my legs shaking. My tongue wraps around the two digits, tasting myself while his sights are fixated on my mouth.

Unfolding his arms, he reaches in his pocket to pull out something small in the palm of his hand. Using one finger he motions for me to come to him. I stand, stretching out my legs to adjust from the hard floor. He waits for me come within inches of him before his hand snakes around my back, something cold pressed into my spine.

Leaning down he nips at my ear before whispering, "I want you on the bed spread open for me waiting for me to fuck you. I'm going to show you what happens when you step out of line. And putting yourself in danger? That's unacceptable."

"Yes, sir." Is my automatic response.

The bite of metal scraping my skin has fear and wonder fighting for dominance in my mind. I can't see what he has but I can feel it and the thought of what's coming has liquid heat seeping out of my body.

"So eager for your punishment. My little Sinner wants to play."

His free hand clamps around my throat lifting me onto my toes stealing the air from my lungs.

"Crawl on the bed and spread your legs. Show me that pretty pink cunt dripping for me."

Releasing me to drop back down to my feet I back away two steps before I turn and slowly climb onto the bed crawling up to the head with my bare ass in the air.

I'm almost to the top when I'm stopped by two calloused hands gripping me by my legs, his fingertips meeting in the middle of my inner thighs. Yanking me back down to the foot of the bed, still on my knees, one hand shoves my chest into the mattress.

"I just want a taste."

He says his words barely out before he bends down closing his mouth over my pussy. My ass is in the air, his mouth on me from behind, with my face in the mattress. A low buzz of bliss travels from my head to my toes with each suck on my clit. His palms slam down on my ass, shooting pain and want through my body.

"Oh yes. Please, Fin!" I'm begging like a whore, but I want more.

Growling against my skin he bites down my clit, shoving two fingers into me rubbing up against the spot that has my knees shaking. Pumping his fingers inside me twice he pulls them out and flips me over so fast the emptiness almost has tears springing to my eyes.

"I want to show you how your body craves to be touched. Don't move."

He waits until I give him a jerky nod to strip his clothes off and crawl between my legs on his knees hovering over me.

My bottom lip is between my teeth, grey eyes trace over my face looking for fear, he only finds my obedience. The click of something metal opening grabs my attention, looking over at his left hand resting on his thigh.

"Close your eyes and keep still. I want you to feel everything. Let go of everything and just feel how your body begs for me."

My eyes drift closed, listening for his movements so I can try to anticipate them but when a cold object grazes my bare nipple I'm startled. The feel of a blade scrapes down my breast making my center pulsate, looking for any way to take away the pressure. A sharp bite of the blade digs into my stomach on the way down to my pelvic bone.

"Open your legs."

My knees automatically fall open waiting to be filled with his dick. It never comes. His hand grabs my hip pushing me into the mattress while the other hand holding the blade drags it down right over my clit. Digging the tip of the blade into my skin, my hips lift with the pain chasing that feeling.

"God, Sin. You're such a good girl taking my marks and begging for more."

Twisting the blade into my skin I yelp but it rolls into a moan when he shoves two fingers into my pussy.

"Oh fuck!" *Holy shit.* My bones vibrate with each thrust inside me mixed with the heady feel of being cut. I want to watch the blood roll down my skin. Opening my eyes, I look down to see each small cut not quite deep enough to draw blood.

"More," I groan, my head pressing into the bed.

"Such a filthy little whore. You want me to cut you? I'll carve my name into your bones if you let me. Pushing my knife into your skin with my dick buried deep in your tight cunt. Is that what you want?"

"Yes. Yes, sir. Oh god yes." Each word is a plea falling from my lips.

Removing his fingers, he pulls my bod down, moving me to line his dick up with my center and with one hard thrust he's seated deep stretching me over his thick cock.

Before I can fully adjust to his size, he has the blade twisting and curling over my nipple, one hand on my neck squeezing the air from my throat, and his hips thrusting into me.

Each sensation is so overwhelming black spots form at the edge of my vision, pulling me deeper into the darkness yet it's still not enough. Using my heels to lift of the bed I meet him thrust for thrust dropping down on his dick with harsh movements.

"That's it, baby, ride my dick. Fuck me like a good little girl. Yes, fuck, Sin!"

Pulling the knife down my stomach he applies more pressure, pulling my eyes from him down to the knife while we both watch a small bead of blood roll from my stomach down to my pelvic bone. My eyes start to roll with each press of the blade into my skin. The cold bite of metal spurring me on.

"Fin! Yes, oh yes," I chant, my words a whisper-scream.

Growling, he leans forward completely cutting off my airway supply leaving handprints on my throat. With no way to inhale and the overpowering feeling of my orgasm building low in my stomach my movements turn jerky riding him with reckless motions.

"Your pussy grips my dick so good, baby. You. Are. Mine. My dick is the only one you'll ever fuck."

"Yes. More. Please." My words are whispered unable to speak with the pressure on my throat.

I'm not even sure what I'm asking for, but he knows. Of course, he knows what I need. He can read my body, my needs, my wants better than me. Adjusting his grip one hand stays on my neck and the other moves the knife down to my pussy flipping it in his hand replacing the blade with the metal handle.

"That's it. Slam that ass down on my dick. Ride me rough, baby girl."

With each order my pussy drenches his dick, the handle of the blade is now at my entrance pressed against his skin and mine. My heart lurches in my chest at the feel of him sliding the handle into me alongside his hard length.

"Keep moving, Sin. I want you to fuck me while I fuck you with my knife. I hold your life in my hands. Only me."

Tremors wrack my body, my orgasm so close. I'm cresting over the edge. Slowly sinking the handle in deeper, my eyes track the blade in his hand watching as his grip has him bleeding from the creases of his fingers.

His blood mixes with my wetness damn near sending me over the edge. The heat from him combined with the chill of the handle has my legs shaking with each thrust.

He lets go of my neck allowing me to take in a large gulp of air my chest heaving, my hips still rising and dropping with ragged motions. Using his free hand, he grabs my hip forcing me down onto him and the handle, his head falling back on a groan.

"Come for, Sin. Soak my dick. I want your pussy to squeeze my cock."

"Oh my god, Fin!" I scream, my voice hoarse.

"Now. Come on my dick now." He demands shoving the handle deeper in my pussy.

My eyes roll in the back of my head, my pussy convulsing with the force of my orgasm, my screams echoing through the room. Coming back into focus Ezra is pounding into me the blade tossed to the side, his bloody hand pressing into my chest holding me down, his stormy grey eyes boring into mine.

His eyes don't leave mine with each thrust into me. He drives us higher up the bed, his groans wild and guttural.

"Fuck yes. This is my pussy. You feel so goddamn good. Mine."

With one last roar he slams into me dropping down on my chest still holding most of his weight. Blood and cum mixing between us. A bloody handprint on my chest has my pussy twitching with him still inside me.

I'm spent, in an orgasmic haze unable to move, his body covering mine pressing me into the bed. Placing both hands on each side of my head, he leans up to look over me, taking stock of any injuries he might have caused from the knife.

Our eyes meet sharing something deeper. A connection between two dark souls that yearn for each other. My soul has reached out to his stitching themselves together.

"I love you, Sin. With every fiber of my being, I love you. You were made for me. Sculpted from my dreams brought to life when I needed you most."

My eyes widen with his words, unable to comprehend how we got to this point.

"I can see you wanting to run, to build those walls back up, but I'll break every one of them down each time. I love you." He repeats those three little words.

My heart shatters into small shards before slowly piecing back together in the shape of Ezra. "I love you too, Fin. Me too."

CHAPTER FORTY THREE
ATHENA

The woman's bright, wild eyes peer at me intently. The green of her eyes familiar yet the light shining in them is a breath of fresh air. She smiles at me, a real tooth-baring smile, the crinkles around her eyes proof of her happiness.

Both of my hands scrape through my hair, twisting and pulling until the frizzy mane is pulled back into a messy bun on top of my head. She tracks my every move, pink cheeks flushed with color, and small cuts across her abdomen that has my core clenching with each one.

Reminders of how it feels to relinquish control of everything, mind, body, and soul into the hands of a devil who thirsts for me. Licking my lips, my gaze follows her tongue wetting those puffy swollen pink lips. The woman in the mirror observes me, looking for the Athena from a month ago, but unable to find her.

"You ready, Sin?"

Ezra stands behind me, his grey eyes free from the dark shadows that haunt them most days. Seeing how free he can be with me and Oliver warms my heart. Being able to open up to him, letting him break down those walls, and giving up all control has lifted a weight off my shoulders.

"Can I know where we are yet? It's hard to plan an outfit around an unknown destination."

Stepping into my back, his hands gently stroke the back of my arms, making me break out in goosebumps. Trailing soft kisses up my neck to the shell of my ear, his words are whispered into my flesh.

"Anything you put on will be beautiful, but if it helps I set out an outfit that I picked up for you."

Meeting his stare in the mirror ahead, the confusion on my face is met with a smirk. The playful gleam in his eyes giving me a light feeling.

He slowly turns me into him, kissing me breathless for a few moments before pulling back to graze his lips just under my eye. Reaching out a hand, I place mine in the palm of his, allowing his fingers to intertwine with mine.

"We need to finish getting ready. The plane will be landing soon," he reminds me.

On the bed is a clothing box. A gold bow tied around it is standing out against the black of the cardboard. Dropping my hand, he steps toward the bedroom door, slightly opening it, his eyes never leaving mine.

Rubbing his lips together with a sly grin, he says, "I'll be waiting for you in our seats. Hurry back to me."

With that he walks out, only pausing to firmly shut the door behind him, leaving me alone with all my feelings spilling from my chest. I never wore my heart on my sleeve before Ezra, yet here I am dropping everything to hop on a plane, going places with him in the middle of the night.

I remind myself that Oliver is happy and doing better with his medicine. Sable has Miles looking after her. It's finally my turn to find happiness.

Ezra is my happiness. The comfort I find in him is unlike anything I've ever known to be possible. When he touches me, it feels like my soul is trying to climb from my chest in search of his. When he's inside me, carving his name into my bones, forcing me to face the darkness building under the surface I feel powerful. Unstoppable.

And when he's with Oliver? I can't breathe. If this is what love is like, I can't imagine ever wanting to lose it or being able to survive without it.

Tugging on the bow until it unravels, the gold straps fall flat on the bed. My fingers quiver around the top of the box not sure what's going to be under the lid.

Lifting it up, the first thing I see is a breathtaking, silver dress folded in the center of the box, but what is on top makes my heart drop. The small velvet box sitting next to a long gold case causes my hands to sweat at the idea of what could be inside.

Our time is almost up with only one day left of the contract. He's asked me to stay and I've been unable to give him an answer.

Gradually my hand closes over the soft box holding it to my chest for a moment, giving myself time to breathe.

My teeth sink into my bottom lip, worrying the skin

with bated breath. My fingers flip open the box, bringing tears to my eyes.

"Holy fucking hell," I murmur, as I stare down at the most beautiful, uniquely-designed ring I have ever seen. Gently lifting it out of its case, I take in every single detail. The deep grey anatomically-correct heart that cages a stunning emerald green gem, holding it in place with such care. My face is wet with tears. My heart hammering in my chest, but the air in my lungs is stolen when I see the tiny inscription inside the band. *My heart belongs to you, little demon.*

Smiling behind the flow of tears I slide it on my middle finger, a perfect fit, of course he knew where I'd place it. *Fuck, Fin.* Swiping at the mess on my face I drop the box on the bed, and lift out the short, flowing, silver dress that shimmers when it moves.

Pulling the silky material over my head, it glides down my body, perfectly falling into place.

The dress is an A-line with a princess-cut lace bodice cocktail style. The open back drops all the way down to right above my tailbone. I twirl around in it, not caring how childish it may be. Laughing freely, I'm stopped when a throat clears behind me.

"Ma'am, Mr. Finlay is wondering how long you might be," the same woman who served our drinks asks from the doorway.

My cheeks redden. "I'll be out in just a moment."

Shaking myself mentally, I return to the box grabbing a pair of cute white and silver sandals. Flats, which means we might be doing some walking, thankfully he thought of everything.

The only thing remaining in the box is the long, gold box, but after the ring I'm not sure how much more I can take. Knowing the plane will be landing soon means I need to be back in my seat shortly. I quickly yank up the box and flip back the lid to reveal a dainty silver chain that is settled in the center, sparkling under the light.

"Oh my god," I whisper under my breath.

My fingers pinch the chain, gently pulling it out of the case to hold it in front of my face for a better view. It appears to be just a plain chain from first glance until you look closer there's three small jewels imbedded in the middle of the chain held by sterling silver clasps.

Each jewel is a different color. The center one a beautiful stormy grey, the one to the right a bright emerald green with darker green flakes inside, and the final one to the right is a light blue.

Each color represents the three of us and it's all too much. Spinning toward the door ready to find Ezra, my body jerks to a stop when I come face-to-face with the man in question.

"What is all this?" I ask, overwhelmed with emotion.

He moves toward me, reaching out to take the necklace from my hand, motioning with his finger for me to turn around.

"Move your hair back for me," he states.

With shaky hands, I pull my long unruly hair over one shoulder, giving him access to the back of my neck. Dropping the chain in front of me, he works his way around my handful of hair until he has the necklace firmly locked in place.

Dropping a soft kiss to my bare skin, he gently turns me, forcing me to drop my hair. He admires the outfit he's selected, pausing on the necklace, before searching out the ring he'll find on my middle finger. On my left hand.

"One day you'll have two rings on that hand, but for now I'll settle for you holding my heart."

His fingers twist in my hair tilting my head back, providing him with better access to my mouth. Heat pools in my stomach, my thighs clenching with the way his nails scrape against my scalp. Before my body can enjoy it, he pulls away too soon leaving me wanting more.

"Let's go, baby. It's time to land."

With our fingers entwined, his thumb rubbing my ring, he leads us to the front of the private jet where a glass of wine is placed next to my seat. A smile finds a place on my face, the warmth in my chest spreading down to the tips of my toes.

Dublin. Dublin, Ireland, to be exact. That's where we landed early in the morning on a private landing strip that's surrounded by beautiful old-style stone buildings bustling with life. We unload from the plane to get in a town car that was waiting for us on the strip. I'm in complete shock and awe with how he made this possible because I don't have a passport.

"How?" Is all I'm able to say.

He laughs. "I have my ways."

He gives me nothing else as our car begins moving through the streets at a slow pace, his hand squeezes my knee distracting me from my questions.

"Where are we going? I can't believe I'm in Ireland!" Squealing, I can't keep my legs from bouncing.

"One thing at a time, Sin." He shakes his head, but that smile still stuck in place.

Watching the buildings go by outside, each one looking older than the next. People are out today enjoying the warmer weather with the sun shining, heating up the chilled morning air.

Ezra points out a few places. He's been telling me all

335

about his experiences and promising to bring Oliver and me back again soon.

Not long after we leave the airport area, we start to see the city fade away, the shops and diners getting further apart from each other. We eventually pull up to a castle-shaped building that stands out against the old brick.

"Wow," I blurt out.

Admiring the red wood wrapping around the front bottom half of the café with the top portion stone arching up into sharp points like a tower on a castle. Each window has a long, deep obsidian basket housing colorful greenery growing wildly up the side of the building.

My gaze reaches the top where a sign hanging above a small black awning state: *Rustic Stone Café*.

Ezra has the car pulled over to the side, stepping out of his side to walk around, he opens my door offering me a hand.

"Let's get you some food."

My lashes brush across my cheeks, blinking away my awe. I grab his hand as I slide out of the car. The smell floating through the streets has me inhaling a deep breath, holding it for as long as I can. Is this real?

I'm tempted to pinch myself to make sure I'm awake and not back on the plane sleeping in the bedroom.

"Fin." My words are soft.

Looking over his shoulder, he pulls me forward. The look in his eyes start to change into an emotion I can't quite place. Hesitating for just a second, he turns fully raising an eyebrow at me in question.

"Sin."

"Yes, sir," I reply.

The surprise on his face has me stifling a laugh, even when my grin slips through. He opens the door to the café releasing my hand to let me in ahead of him like the gentleman he tries to be.

I know the filthy man behind the suits, so I'm not fooled. Walking through the doorway, my words die in my throat unable to speak. It's breathtaking.

CHAPTER FORTY FOUR
EZRA

The fire in my chest burns hotter with each doe-eyed look from Athena. She hasn't stopped gawking at everything since we landed, but her fascination with the inside of Rustic Stone takes it to a new level.

I knew she would be mesmerized by Ireland, so when I decided to bring her inside one of my favorite places to eat when I visit, I was hoping she'd love it just as much as me.

"This has always been my favorite place to dine."

My words pull her from the daze she was in, her green eyes bouncing from one corner of the café to another, finally landing on me with an astonished look.

"You eat here all the time?"

A chuckle slips past my lips. "I wouldn't say once or twice a year is all the time, but when I do travel here this is one of my first stops."

Our waitress walks over to take our orders. My hand tightening on Athena's knee, stops her before she can give her order.

"She will have the French toast platter with scrambled eggs, bacon, breakfast potatoes, and hot chocolate please."

"And for you, sir?" she asks, her eye flitting between the two of us.

I'm sure she's wondering why I'm ordering for Athena and most likely thinks I'm a jerk. Athena needs to see that people care about her, pay attention to her, and genuinely want to be with her.

By ordering her favorite things, I'm proving that even when all I want to do is be buried deep inside her, I'm still aware of what she wants.

After giving her my order, she walks away to go make our drinks.

All this time Athena hasn't taken her eyes off me, her emotions guarded behind her eyes. Our table is pressed against the glass wall providing us with a stunning view.

Athena's tongue peeks out from between her teeth. "You ordered for me without asking me what I wanted."

Reaching forward to sweep her hair out of her face, I reply, "I know you."

Mashing her lips to the side in thought she hides the sly grin, forcing its way onto her face. Her beauty often has me frozen in place unable to move. Her left hand sits on the table showcasing the ring that makes my heart beat erratically in my chest.

The need to replace it with something more permanent makes my skin itch.

We talk while we wait on our food to be delivered to the table, our drinks are almost gone and in need of a refill. Athena picks up her cup, bringing the now warm hot chocolate to her pink pouty lips and swallowing down the last drop.

Once our food arrives, we dive into eating, my knee bouncing with anticipation at our next destination. Knowing my little demon this is going to be her favorite place here. Dublin is known for a lot of things, but this particular building is famous for its size.

Fork poised at her lips, she smirks. "So, where to next?" Popping the bite into her mouth she chews, waiting for an answer.

"It's a surprise."

With that being my only answer, she pouts funneling food into her mouth in an attempt to hurry.

Our waitress stops by to refill our cups, her eyes widening when she catches sight of Athena trying to fit almost a full piece of French toast in her mouth. Smiling at her around the forkful, Athena mumbles thank you after the waitress walks away.

Shaking my head. "Slow down before you hurt yourself."

Gulping down the last of her eggs she flashes a toothy smile at me.

"You don't mind when it's your dick being shoved down my throat."

My knee slams into the table, jostling forward in shock at her words. Her smart-ass mouth knocks me off balance yet makes my dick hard at the same time.

Gaping at the little demon sitting in front of me

attempting to look innocent, my fingers ache to grab her by the throat and fuck her mouth just to prove a point. Although it might just be proving hers.

"I'll be sure to show you how well you choke on my cock later. For now, we have somewhere to be."

After cleaning off my hands with the wet wipe given to us along with the check, we stand to head out the door. Athena takes one last look around, the light in her eyes shines brightly.

Once the bill is paid and a hefty tip is left for the wonderful food and service, we meet the driver around the side of the building.

Opening the door for her, she pauses, turning to meet me head on, reaches up on the tips of her toes, she kisses me quickly. Once she's seated inside, I close the door making my way to the other side telling the driver where our next stop is.

The drive is thirty minutes too long. The need to have my hands on Athena's skin driving me insane. Pulling her closer by her inner leg she glides over the leather seat with ease thanks to the new silky dress she's wearing.

Her milky skin is on display drawing me in. My teeth ready to sink into her soft flesh. My dick twitches with the image of my teeth marking her perfect skin.

Speaking in her ear, I mumble, "Don't make a sound."

My fingers trail up her thigh, drawing circles along the way, loving the way she shudders beneath my touch. My girl is so responsive and always so ready for me. I bet she's wet right now.

Inching her dress up higher she watches my hand travel up to her center. The heat has me groaning into her neck, nipping at the skin.

"Fuck, I bet you're soaking wet for me."

"Yes."

Pushing her panties to the side, I part her folds, growling at the feel of how wet she really is for me. Swirling her wetness around her clit, she lifts her hips chasing after what she wants.

Slowly my fingers push into her, my teeth clamping down on her neck, her pussy gripping the digits.

"You're always so wet for me, Sin. Goddamn the feel of your cunt gripping my hand is heaven. You're sweet Nirvana."

Pumping my fingers inside her in slow strokes her body twitches, her head pressing into the back of the seat, eyes squeezed shut. Parting her lips on a sigh she lifts her hips up only to drop back down, trying to fuck my hand for her release.

"You want to come?"

Trailing kisses and nips up and down her neck I wait for her to answer. My tongue presses down on her skin licking from her shoulder up to her ear in swirling patterns.

"Yes, please."

"I want you to beg for it, Sin. Beg me to let you come. Say it."

Her legs tremble every time my fingers slide across her sweet spot.

"Please, Fin. Please."

Her hips lift, dropping down harder this time, her clit grazing my palm. She attempts to grind against my hand needing the pressure to send her over the edge.

"That's it, baby. Beg for it. I want you to know that only I can make your pussy feel this good. Only. Me." Pumping into her faster this time, my fingers curl finding the spot that has her shaking.

"Please, Fin. Oh God. Yes, only you."

Her words are grunted out, each thrust is met with the roll of her hips until her legs are trembling too much to hold her up. My other hand spreads her wider, my eye dropping down to watch my fingers sink into her pink cunt.

Her clit is throbbing and my teeth ache to bite into it. I unbuckle my seat belt, moving to kneel on my knees in the cramped space. The sight of her dripping for me, skin flushed red, with her eyes wide pointed at my fingers pumping inside her makes my dick leak in my pants.

"Put your legs over my shoulders. I'm fucking starving for you, Sin."

"Oh shit," she moans, sliding back against the leather turning her hips to give herself room to prop her legs over my back.

My face is eye level with her cunt and my mouth waters at the sight in front of me.

Slowly pulling my fingers out, my thumb adding pressure to her clit, I shove my fingers back inside hard. A deep raspy groan escapes her throat traveling down my spine straight to my dick.

"Be a good girl and fuck my face. I want you coming down my throat before this car stops. Do you understand?"

"Yes. Yes, sir. Please."

She barely gets the words out before my mouth closes over her clit and my tongue lashes out at her swollen nub. Her hands grab the sides of my head, her fingers twisting and pulling at my hair.

While I am plunging my tongue inside her, she uses her grip on me to grind her pussy on my face. Growling into her wet skin, I eat at her like a starved man unable to control his hunger.

"Yes. Yes. Yes!" Her chants are frantic.

Adding my fingers inside her with my mouth still

devouring every drop she gives me, her heels dig into my back, the pain almost causing me to come on the spot. Shit, I might not be able to hold back. My need to be balls deep inside her too strong.

Pulling away from her, I lick my lips, my eyes dark with intent. Reaching forward to grasp her throat, I pull her forward.

"Open that pretty little mouth," I order.

Shoving my fingers in her mouth, I state, "Suck. Now."

She does as she's told and fuck me if it doesn't make me smile knowing that she bends at my will.

"Good girl. Now come sit on my dick."

Undoing my belt to pull out my dick, my attention is pulled to the front making sure the blackout glass is still in place. Sitting on the seat with my fist gripping my hard dick squeezing it while I watch my little demon hike up her dress to pull off her drenched thong.

"That's it, baby. Now come plant that ass on my cock and fuck me like a good little whore."

Her eyes flash at the challenge. Heat spreading through my body at the defiance, but she does as she's told if only for one thing. My dick to be buried deep in her tight pussy because Athena loves to fuck me.

Placing her knees on each side of me her eyes meet mine watching with rapt attention as she sinks down on my dick, inch by inch her cunt pulls me in deeper.

"Fucckkk," I groan.

She tilts her head to the side with a wicked grin, inching up and down in tortuously slow movements. My hands grab her waist, pulling her up until she's barely on the tip before I slam into her, dropping her down at the same time. My eyes roll to the back of my head in ecstasy.

"Ride me."

I smack her bare ass roughly, just the way she likes, to spur her on. She plants her hands beside my head on the back of the seat, leaning forward she starts to bounce in place, fucking me into the seat. Lift. Drop. Lift. Drop. Twist. Lift. Drop.

My balls pull tight, her cunt gripping my dick so tight I see stars. She lifts all the way up and drops back down. Her head falls back, exposing her long creamy neck.

"You feel so fucking good."

She glows at the praise, so I keep going pushing her closer to the edge with my dirty words while she rides me. Shoving her down on my dick, I stop her from moving up. Instead, I use her hips to grind her pussy against me, my thumb pressing into her clit. Her whole body vibrates with the building release of her orgasm.

"That's it. Soak my dick like a good girl. Squeeze my dick baby. I want to feel you come all over me."

Pressing down harder, she speeds up in jerky movements riding me harder.

"Yes!" She screams.

Using my thumb to spread her wetness over her clit, I move my hand just under her ass. Gripping her throat with one hand, my other spreads her ass cheeks, planting my thumb at her hole.

"Don't stop riding me, Sin," I state.

Using her own juices as a lubricant, I slowly press my thumb into her hole and back out again.

"Dear god!"

Squeezing her throat tighter, my teeth clench together unable to hold back much longer.

"Goddamn your pussy was made for my dick."

Pressing my thumb into her, all the way this time, she

shatters. When she finally finishes coming all over me, milking my dick of every drop, she falls forward on me.

We sit there for a minute, the car coming to a slow stop, to gain control over our breathing. It's not until she climbs off me that she starts to laugh uncontrollably.

"What do you find so funny?"

She blinds me with her smile. "You just had your finger in my ass!"

Giving her a wicked grin, I lean down while she straightens her dress. "I plan to have more than my thumb in your ass. Soon. You're going to let me fuck it."

Her laugh dies off instantly, sending me over the edge. My head drops back with a loud laugh. I can't remember the last time I felt so free in my entire life yet with Athena, nothing can touch me.

With her, my thoughts and nightmares are shoved into the corner, blocked by her presence. Once we're cleaned up, I get out of the car. Walking around to open her door, I move back to give her room to slide out.

"Whoa," she gasps.

With everything going on in the car she didn't see where we were, but now that it's right in front of her, I can see the wonder in her eyes. Bringing her here was the right choice. She looks from me to the sign on the stone building.

It expands past what we can see but the opening is so grand with the large archway top coming to a point. She steps forward onto the walkway, turning from me and back again, unable to find words.

"Is this...?"

"It is," I reply with a smile.

Leaping into my arms, she hugs me tight and whispers in my ear, "I can't believe you brought me here. Thank you, Fin, it means the world to me."

Clearing my throat to keep the moisture in my eyes from falling, I set her back down on both feet, pulling her to the doors.

As we pass the sign, she trails her fingers over the gold name plate that reads: *Trinity College Library*. One of the largest libraries in the world and the largest in Ireland. It dates back to the year 1592.

"Let's go take a look."

She heads down the path, tugging me along the way. The sheer joy flowing off her is enough to have my heart pounding in my chest. I love this woman.

CHAPTER FORTY FIVE
ATHENA

My legs ache from walking the isles, but I push the soreness to the back of my mind to take in every last row of shelving. The massive expanse of books spread for what feels like miles has my fingers aching with the need to reach out to touch the spines.

Long rows are laid out ahead lined with velvet ropes blocking people from touching any of the old first editions on display.

"Down here you'll see a small spiral staircase that leads to what we call The Long Room," our tour guide says.

He's an older gentleman dressed in his Sunday best showing us around on a private tour of the more popular areas of the library. Deciding to opt out of the climb up the narrow staircase he moves us through a few doorways leading into a dark room with a bright light shining down on a glass case.

"It's a beautiful display," I murmur to Ezra.

"It's the new Book of Kells Treasury and display that were recently unveiled. Why don't you both take a look around and I'll be right through this doorway."

Walking away without looking back, Ezra turns toward me with a soft gaze, that smirk I love so much sliding into place. He brings both of his hands up to cup my face, tilting my head back forcing me to see only him.

"I have something for you."

My face must show my confusion because he lets out a low chuckle that shoots through my body lighting it on fire. This man will be the death of me one day.

"You've given me enough, Fin. This is all too much. I'm not here with you right now for your money."

Raising an eyebrow, he retorts, "Isn't that how we got here in the first place? Because of money?"

Before I can get a word out, he's smirking at me. I feel my lips tip up with a smile, never quite able to be mad when he's so open and light like this.

His eyes gleam with a mischievous look. Gently rubbing his thumbs in circles on my cheeks he slightly nods his head to the left toward the box where the book is under the single spotlight in the room.

"Go look on the case, baby."

Releasing me, he takes a step back gesturing with his hand toward the black case with the glass top.

I slowly walk toward the center of the room. Stopping

to look over my shoulder, the feel of his grey eyes staring at me has me pausing.

"Over here?" I ask.

"Just take a look, Sin," he says, urging me forward.

Only a small space away from the box I see a beautifully crafted envelope with a seal holding it closed. The vibrant gold of the seal shines under the light. Lifting the envelope to inspect it further, my mouth opens in awe realizing that the wax seal is in the shape of a stiletto heel. Hinting at a joke of where this all started. Next to it there's one lone lily lying on the glass in full bloom.

Looking at him from my spot across the room I can see his anticipation in the way he flexes his hands at his sides, wishing that he could tear open the paper for me.

I decide to mess with him by moving my hands in a slow manner. My finger barely grazing between the opening and the wax seal, gently peeling it open hoping to save it from breaking.

Once I've opened it, I pull out the single gold slip of paper with one small sentence on it followed by a beautifully carved butterfly.

With one sentence my heartrate picks up, excited for what's to come. I'm learning to always be on my toes when it comes to Ezra Finlay.

Have dinner with me to celebrate. Grafton Street, Dublin. WILDE Restaurant.

Licking my lips, I look from Ezra to the slip of paper and back. "What are we celebrating?" I ask.

Not sure I'm prepared for the answer, this is all moving so quickly. One minute we're in the penthouse following through with our contract the next I'm in Ireland. I'm away from my brother for the first time, receiving gifts that I haven't earned. No one prepared me for how it would feel to lose myself in him so deeply.

He finally moves from his place taking slow steps toward me. My chest rises and falls in sync with his movements. Watching and waiting unsure of what his next move will be. His warm hand closes over mine intertwining our fingers.

"We'll celebrate at dinner tonight."

"But what are we celebrating?"

My question hangs in the air still unanswered. At this point I'm not sure if I could handle his answer.

"We're only here for a night, let's enjoy it while we can because we fly home tomorrow."

The way that he mentions home so casually has my pulse picking up. The blood rushing through my veins heats my skin with the thought of having to leave the penthouse where Oliver and I have made a home.

A place that we cherish. The image breaks my heart. He's carved his way in too deep and now he's made it impossible to escape him. The hooks are too deep to remove so I'll bask in the scars they may cause.

"Yes, home," I whisper under my breath but the tightening of his fingers on mine holding me tighter make me wonder if he heard the longing in my voice.

Lifting the card and the lily from its place on the stand I decide then that this is where I belong. We make our way through the archway running into our tour guide who's leaning against the wall waiting for us. We follow him back through the enormous library. My thoughts return to all the beautiful works of art lining the walls.

Our private tour lasts for another hour where we are shown every private room available. My favorite is the private room where the new Book of Kells Treasury is on display.

Once our tour is finished, we head outside where the sun is starting to set. When we head off the library grounds my attention is pulled to the beautiful sky. Lit up in stunning orange and pink hues is a magnificent sunset we both pause to take in the sight.

Ezra pulls me to the left where I spot the town car parked waiting for us and I wonder if our driver's been sitting outside the entire time.

"Are we headed back to the plane?"

"Our bags have been picked up and moved to the trunk we'll have an hour to clean up before dinner."

Once we reach the car the driver starts to get out of his door when Ezra waives him off, stepping forward, he pulls open my door. Brushing the back of my arm as my body drops down into the seat, he bends down to my eye level, the grey in his eyes growing darker.

"I can't wait to be inside you again but until then I want to taste you."

His filthy words stun me for a second until his mouth takes mine. Kissing me deeply his lips turn up into a knowing smile when he pulls away to leave me rubbing my thighs together the entire ride to our next destination. The cheeky bastard.

CHAPTER FORTY SIX
EZRA

T he way that silver material flows with each step she takes captivates me. Her tempting curves sway with each step, my eyes trailing down her back over the large opening in the back of her dress. Fuck, I didn't think about how low it went when I picked it up. Tonight is about keeping her. Ensuring that after tomorrow, our last day of the deal, she'll still call our penthouse home. Fuck asking, I'm not giving her a choice.

I take in the people around us feeling the familiar rattle in my chest, demanding every man to keep their eyes of what's mine. The hostess stops at a small table in a secluded corner of the room giving us some privacy.

"Your waitress will be with you shortly." She smiles, her stare traveling over me.

The heat from Athena's glare feeds my inner demon knowing my girl is ready to stake her claim on me. She swears that she'll walk away after tomorrow, but her actions say otherwise. Reaching out to pull her chair back, she lets out a sigh as she sits. Taking my seat, the breath leaves my lungs following her lead.

"It's been an eventful day." She grins.

She chews on the inside of her lip. Releasing her cheek from the bite of her teeth, she asks, "What are we celebrating? I'm all for a good meal and drinks but it's usually known to both parties that there's something to celebrate."

Resting my elbows on the table, my hands fold under my chin. Leaning forward a few inches my smile turns into a sinister grin.

"That mouth of yours is going to get you in trouble, Sin."

Her eyes light up at the threat and fuck if I don't love when she gets turned on by the thought of pain. My perfect little demon. Our waitress arrives to take our drink order and to drop off bread rolls in the center of the table. Athena orders a glass of sweet tea while I use the night away to relax ordering

Sitting back against the chair, her lip's part on a small sigh. "Tomorrow, our deal ends."

That's the only words that leave her mouth as she watches me intently. The emerald, green fading into a dark forest green. Reaching into my pants pocket I dig out a small, square, cream-colored box that's been burning a hole in my pocket all day. It makes a small thud sound when I drop it on the table in front of her.

"Open it," I order.

My little demon squishes her lips to the side, looking me up and down before her hand closes over the small box. My fingers itch to reach out and caress her skin, just to have my hands on some part of her.

Holding it in front of her she tilts it back and forth trying to figure out what's in there, but she'll never figure it out that way.

"Sin, open the box."

Pursing her lips, she uses her thumb to lift the top, letting it fall to the table without a second glance.

Her stare is zoned in on the small metal item nestled on the foam inside the box to hold it in place. Her eyes widen when she finally catches on to what it means. What I'm asking of her.

"Fin." My name rolls off her tongue softly.

Pulling the old-style skeleton key from the box she flips it over and over, trying to piece together what it goes to. Peering over at me, her eyes are filled with confusion when the waitress walks up setting our drinks down between us and proceeds to take our order.

Athena hasn't set the key down yet, her eyes darting from me and back to the waitress, placing her order. Once she walks away Athena uses the silence to jump into asking questions.

"I don't understand. What's the key for?"

She looks so stunning tonight. Her flushed cheeks a soft pink against her green eyes and long red hair that's braided to the side. Athena is the definition of natural beauty. Tapping the key on the table to grab my attention, it pulls me from my thoughts.

"I've already asked you to stay so this is me making that permanent. I want you and Oliver to live with me in the penthouse so I'm giving you a key."

She rolls her eyes. "The penthouse is controlled by a keypad, so I don't understand the use of an ancient rustic key."

"Always such a smart ass. It's the meaning behind the key."

Closing the key in a tight fist her eyes drift closed so I give her a moment to process what this means for the both of us. For all three of us. I'll lock her in my room and throw away the key, literally, if she tries to back out but I know what my little demon wants and it's not to leave.

"Say you'll stay, Athena. You'll never be alone again. I'll fight for you, fight with you, and protect you no matter what. Oliver would be safe and loved. You'll want for fucking nothing. Say yes and I'll drag your ass back to the plane right now and fuck you senseless."

Her long black eyelashes flutter revealing tear-filled eyes. "Okay."

That's all she says before picking up her drink, those puffy pink lips closing over her straw to pull in a sip of sweet tea. Extending both arms across the table to grab onto her wrists our eyes lock sharing a silent conversation.

"Yes?" My smile spreads wide.

Nodding her head, she starts to chew on the straw giving herself something to do to keep from being overwhelmed by emotions. The way her tongue twirls the offending item around in her mouth, her teeth sinking into the plastic, has my dick growing stiff in my pants.

"You had me at fuck you," she declares.

A growl builds low in my chest at her words. The same words I spoke to her thirty days ago when we started this contract. Now, I have my Sinner right where I want her. In the palm of my hand ready to bend when I say. She'll take everything I have to give her all while begging for more because she was made for me by the devil himself. Signed, sealed, and delivered in perfect packaging.

Athena's phone rings right when the waitress comes over to bring our plates, so she silences it placing it back on the table. My phone buzzes in my pocket so I pull it out to glance at it, seeing that it's an unknown number, I hit ignore. We start eating, sharing heated looks with each forkful. She raises a bite of medium-rare steak to her lips when her phone rings again. This time I see the name on the caller ID, it's Sable.

"She's called twice now so I may need to take this," she says.

The ringing stops so we pause waiting to see if she calls back again, knowing that if she calls three times in a row it could be important. Half a second later my phone rings, Miles's name popping up on the screen, at the same time Sable calls Athena. Our eyes meet, pausing before we both snatch up our phones to answer.

"Hello?"

Heavy breathing comes through the line. "We need y'all to come back home. Now."

Miles sounds out of breath and scared making my stomach drop at the possibilities of what could have happened. The only reason Miles would call me, and Sable would be calling Athena is if it involved Oliver. Our food instantly forgotten.

"What the hell is going on?" I demand.

"Shit. Sable!" I hear on the other line. Eros is heard in the background along with another voice I'm not familiar with confusing me on where they could be.

My fist clenches around the phone. "Miles talk to me. What is going on?"

. . .

A heavy exhale. "Oliver is in the hospital. He got really weak and passed out. We think we missed his dose this morning, so we busted ass to get to the hospital. They need Athena here to do anything major, so right now they are just running tests to be sure everything is fine. She needs to get here fast in case he needs something done."

By the time he's done I can hear Athena railing Sable with question after question, both of us on edge through it all.

Not waiting for Miles to say anything I end the call not wanting to waste time talking on the phone. Tossing a few bills on the table I grip Athena's wrist to pull her out of the building. She's frantic unable to focus on anything, her phone still in her hand, Sable's voice heard on the other side.

"Come on, baby, we need to get to the jet right now."

The vacant look in Athena's eyes the entire way home pulls at something in the back of my mind. Barely talking on the flight home just small words of comfort whispered in her ear as she lay in my lap as tears soak the sweat pants I changed in to.

Unable to pull her from the darkness she's still in her silver dress. The nine-hour flight back home felt like years unable to get updates on Oliver's condition.

"I won't survive if anything happened to my baby brother. I won't make it," she murmurs against my chest.

CHAPTER FORTY SEVEN
ATHENA

Pounding. My heart beats against my ribs, fighting against the cage in a steady beat that echoes in my ears. My eyes watch the numbers climb one, two, three. The light shines on number four, the ding of the elevator doors opening startles me, revealing all white walls with a desk just ahead.

I rush forward in search of Sable, praying she's here with Oliver. Ezra isn't far behind, the calm he excludes is setting me on edge. How could anyone be calm while my baby brother is in the hospital.

Reaching the desk an older nurse looks up flashing me a smile. "How can I help you ma'am?"

My fingers tremble at my sides, unable to keep still with the thought of Oliver lying in a bed on this floor looking for me. He's here sick while I was off fucking around in Ireland having the time of my life without him.

What was I thinking losing myself in a man and leaving my brother behind to be kept by men who are practically strangers? I would have never done this before I met Ezra, so how could I have let this happen?

"Miss?" the nurse says.

"I'm looking for my brother, Oliver Drakos."

"T!" a scream comes from my right just down the hall.

Sable is there flagging me down. I bolt away from the nurse, running the rest of the way, my shoes slapping against the tile floor. Ezra is close behind me, still sticking with his silent but supportive shit.

Sable's breathing heavy, her eyes wide, the black of her pupils overtaking any color from showing. My lips twitch, the whites of her eyes slightly red, but it's the grind of her teeth that has my skin crawling.

My hands open and close trying to gain composure. "Where the hell are Miles and Eros? I want to talk to a doctor right now." Shoving past her, I storm into the room.

There in a hospital bed settled in the middle of the room is Oliver sleeping soundly, hooked up to an IV. The skin under his eyes a light purplish hue. My legs eat up the distance coming up the side of the bed I drop down in the chair at his head. Brushing his strawberry-blond hair out of his face, a sad smile lifts the edges of my lips.

"I'm here, bubs. I won't leave you again," I whisper, leaning down to drop a kiss on his cheek.

Turning back to Sable, I notice that she's in leggings and a baggy shirt with tears smeared across her face. My mouth opens to ask what happened when Miles and Eros walk in with what looks like snacks and food from the cafeteria, sending me over the edge.

"What the fuck happened? Is this all a big joke to you? My brother is lying in a hospital bed right now and all you can think about is food?" I declare.

From the corner of my eye, I spot Ezra making his way to me, so I thrust out a hand stopping him from getting any closer. I can feel the walls closing in on me pulling my skin tight, the black spots in my vision spreading. My whole body starts to shake with each passing second.

"Don't come near me," I whisper-yell at Ezra, unable to stop the words from spilling out of my mouth. Each one like poison.

I glare at Eros and Miles. "How could you let this happen? I trusted you all!" My words are laced with ice.

Pointing a finger at Sable, I state, "You are supposed to be family. How could you let this happen? And you." I thrust my finger at Ezra. "You drag me away from Oliver to take me out of the country. For what? A quick fuck? I want all of you out. Now." Slashing my hand through the air I then point to the door.

Miles and Eros take everything I throw at them, which pisses me off even more. How could they have nothing to say while Oliver sleeps behind me hooked up to different machines? Sable has her hand over her mouth, tears pouring down her cheeks.

"Sin," Ezra says softly, sending my rage higher.

"Do not placate me, Ezra," I blurt out.

The use of his first name has his back shooting straight his eyes darkening, pulling me in, but I'm too far gone to the fear to stop now.

Standing from the chair I walk up to him, we come nose to nose, snatching the ring off my middle finger roughly and shoving it into his chest.

"Leave and don't come back, all of you. I've blinded myself into thinking I could have this life with you, but the truth is I left my brother in the hands of people who can't care for him like I can. I should have known better." My gaze flicks over to Sable. "I shouldn't have trust any of you with the care of the most important person in my life."

Stepping back, my heart tears with the loss of contact from Ezra, but there's no going back. Not now when all I can see is red. I'm angry, but what I'm not admitting is I'm more upset with myself than I am with them.

Allowing myself to be so invested in Ezra that I forgot who was more important. Making me a failure just like Cindy. Are we cursed to always put men first? Am I becoming her?

"T, it wasn't anyone's fault," Sable says, ready to stand up to me.

Shaking my head. "You're right, it's not any of y'all's fault. It's mine for thinking that this was a good idea. It is over. All of it. Leave. I need to focus on my brother right now and I can't do that with everybody here." My voice breaks.

Before anyone else is able to speak, a male doctor knocks his knuckles on the open door, a concerned look on his face.

"Who is the guardian of Oliver Drakos?" he asks.

Stepping forward, my eyes meet his. "I am. My name is Athena Drakos."

Sticking out my hand, he takes it in a firm hold. Eros stands from his stance against the wall, his eyes burning into the side of my face waiting for my attention to turn to him, but I refuse to give in.

After a few seconds he and Miles step out of the room, but not before speaking to Ezra in a low voice. Sable is still focused on me. Her eyes moving from me to the floor, unable to keep her attention on one thing.

The hair on the back of my neck stands when Ezra brushes past me to sit with Oliver while the doctor goes over his medical information, verifying his routine. From what he's told me, it appears that Oliver missed a dose or two of his insulin and that mixed with not telling anyone he was feeling sick caused him to go into what's called diabetic ketoacidosis.

"So, what do we need to do?"

Looking from me to Oliver's sleeping form, the doctor says, "We need to focus on replacing his fluids and electrolytes right now and go from there."

Nodding my head automatically my body feels numb. "How long will he be in the hospital?"

"He shouldn't be here longer than a day or two, depending on how well he does." He smiles in an attempt to calm any fears I have.

Shortly after he leaves a nurse comes in to check over all of his vitals and IV. I've moved to the other chair at the back of the room, allowing my head to fall into my hands, closing my eyes. Sable's pacing the wall by the door, unable to sit still, sparking red flags that flash in my head.

"Go home, Sabby."

Her steps pause, keeping my eyes on the floor at my feet, she walks to the door, gently opening it.

"I don't know how three adults could let this happen, but right now I can't be around you," I say.

With my words she sucks in a deep breath and walks out, shutting the door behind her.

Ezra sets Oliver's hand down on the bed, dropping his into his lap. Keeping those gray eyes on me he stands to move closer. Jumping to my feet, my hands come up to stop him. Backing into the far wall, I motion for him to stop a few feet away, not able to handle him any closer without falling apart. The adrenaline that was flowing through my veins earlier is wearing off.

Licking my lips, our eyes connect. "You need to leave, Ezra. It's over. The game we played was fun, but it's time to get back to the real world where I'm just a stripper and you're a CEO. This was never going to work and right now all I can see is how I neglected my responsibilities to bury myself inside you."

He reaches out, tipping my head toward him. "I'll give you the space you need, but you're crazy if you think you can walk away after everything we've been through. I'm leaving for now, but I'll be back for you, baby. Nothing can keep me away."

His words are firm, leaving no room for argument. Letting go of my chin, he takes two large steps back before making his way to the door.

"Don't keep me waiting long, Sin," he says, pulling the door shut the door behind him.

With everyone gone from the room, my legs give out, my ass slamming onto the cold tile in the hospital room. I could have lost Oliver today and that thought has me sick to my stomach.

I'd give up the world to keep him safe, so why does it

feel like I just lost everything that meant something to me. My heart sinks, shattering into shards of glass, the chill in my bones spreads goosebumps over my skin.

My heart is broken just as I knew it would be, yet the one I should have been protecting it from was myself.

CHAPTER FORTY EIGHT
ATHENA

S mall hands wake me from a restless sleep, my head lying across Oliver's lap. Lifting my head, my neck stiff, our eyes connect. It's been twenty-four hours since I got back to New York, all of which have been spent by Oliver's side. When he first woke up, he had so many questions about where the guys were, where Sable went, and more, but after a while I think he finally realized that I sent them away.

"You stink." Oliver giggles, the sound is music to my ears.

Sitting up, I ruffle his hair. "You saying I need a shower, shorty?"

Color has started to return to his face, his freckles standing out against the pink of his cheeks. Pushing up on his hands, he scoots back sitting up fully.

"I think you need a shower." He wrinkles his nose.

Flicking his nose, a wide smile takes over my face hiding the pain in my chest. The doctor told me he could go home today, so now I have to tell him that we won't be staying at the penthouse anymore. The thought reminds me that I need to have all of our stuff moved back into the apartment if they'll let us go back.

"I can help with that." A deep voice says from behind me.

Oliver's eyes light up, the toothy smile he flashes at the doorway makes my heart skip a beat, his excitement is palpable. Logic of the situation starts to sink in, but my pride stands in the way of me being able to face him.

The sound of footsteps gets louder the closer he comes to me, stopping at the foot of the bed. His eyes caress my skin in a scorching path, leaving heat in its wake.

"Sin." His name for me falls from his lips.

Oliver's stare bounces between us trying to read the room. Blue eyes shine up at me from his place on the bed. The feel of both sets of eyes tracking my movements makes my skin crawl, hating the feeling of being watched at every moment.

Deciding not to ignore him, I come to a stand turning to face Ezra, his beauty still managing to take me by surprise. He's still in the same clothes as yesterday, but the white of his eyes are a slight red from no sleep.

So, he's having just as much of a hard time as I am. He calls my name again, only this time the tone was a little sharp.

"Outside," I say.

Walking past him, I don't wait to see if he follows me, instead just heading for the door. Once we are both in the hallway with the room door shut, I allow myself time to admire the devil in front of me.

Stepping into me until my heels run into the wall behind me, my head tilting back not moving my gaze from his. Placing both hands on each side of my head, Ezra bends his head in closer, ghosting his lips over mine.

"I gave you time, now I'm here to take care of what's mine. Letting you push me away yesterday was the hardest thing I've ever done, but I understood the need to feel in control when everything was falling apart." His thumb pulls at my bottom lip.

"The love I have for you can't just be tossed out when you feel like running. Me and you, baby, we were inevitable," he says, kissing the corner of my eye.

That one simple move has my walls crashing down, my knees giving out, sending me falling into his chest. He catches me with ease, hauling me closer, enclosing me in his massive frame. I inhale the scent that's all him. He holds me for a while, letting me get all my frustrations out. Whispering reassuring words against the top of my head, he makes no move to pull away.

"The guys feel horrible about what happened, but I told them to give you more time. We all understand how important family is, so they don't hold it against you, but Eros and Miles are crushed at the thought of you taking Oliver away."

The tears keep flowing so he continues, "Miles called me this morning. Sable came back to his place, but he's worried about her."

Shaking my head, I pull away knowing my face is probably a mess right now. Swiping away the wetness on my cheeks, his hands cup both sides of my face, the gray in his eyes swirling into a storm, waiting to come crashing down.

He gives me a sad smile. "She's your family too, even when she messes up. Family will disappoint you and let you down sometimes, but Sable loves you. I know you love her too. I'll always be in front of you shielding you from those who want to cause you harm. I'd rip out the throats of anyone who stands in your way, but Sable isn't one of them."

Not giving me time to process his words, even when they ring true, his mouth slants over mine taking me by surprise. Prying my lips open with his tongue, he sweeps the inside of my mouth, proving his ownership in the way he dominates me. One hand slides down the column of my neck, his fingers pressing into the skin at the base of my throat.

"Next time you push me away, I'll make sure you can't sit for a week," he says against my mouth.

Kissing him back with just as much force, our breathing turns ragged, my chest pressing into his. Pulling away to catch my breath, he watches me like the stalker he is.

Licking my lips, I state, "I need to go see her."

He's right. Sable is my sister in every sense of the word, nothing should be able to ruin our relationship. She loves Oliver as much as I do and deep down, I know she'd never do anything to hurt him so it's only fair that I go make things right.

Nodding his head, he grabs my hand leading us back in the room giving my fingers one quick squeeze.

It's not long after the hospital serves dinner that Oliver is discharged to go home. I sent Ezra down to pull his car around while the doctors push a sleeping Oliver in a wheelchair to load up. Policy states that patients must be escorted out of the property in a wheelchair for safety.

Ezra pulls up in the SUV, jumping out to put Oliver in the back seat.

"Can you take me to Miles's place?" I ask.

The drive to Miles's bar, that also doubles as his apartment, takes around fifteen minutes. That time is spent in a comfortable silence, his hand in my lap drawing circles on my thigh. The bar is dark at the back of the building with no street lamps providing light.

Parking, I slide out, meeting Ezra at the driver side door. He gets out gently, not wanting to wake Oliver. Taking in my surroundings, I don't see him coming until it's too late. With both hands gripping my forearms he spins me pushing me up against the driver's door. Stepping into me and not leaving an inch between us, nose to nose, his breath whispers over my skin.

"Come back to me, Sin. Promise me no more running."

Exhaling a shaky breath, my eyes fall closed. "I promise."

Cupping my face with his hands, he tilts my head back, resting his forehead on mine.

Sighing, he rumbles out, "You're mine."

It's not an ownership like before when he calls me his, no, this is a declaration of what we both knew all this time. Our souls are bound in darkness, only the shining light to guide the other home.

"Me too, Fin."

"Yeah, baby, me too."

Kissing me slowly, yanking at the strings in my chest, the organ thumping behind my rib cage burns with love for him. He pulls back, only leaving a few inches between our lips, my favorite smirk sliding into place, he steps back.

Moving around him to head to the door, I don't look over my shoulder until my hand closes over the handle.

Turning to look back at Ezra, I state, "I'm trusting you with him."

It's the only comment I make before pulling open the tall metal door that leads to the rear of the bar. A bright light shines above, blinding me. Black spots in my vision clear to reveal a disheveled-looking Miles.

He stares at me with a sneer. "What are you doing here?"

Jerking back in shock at his tone, I take in his tired eyes.

"I'm here to see Sable."

He scoffs, rolling his eyes, running his fingers through his blond hair, before bringing those stark blue eyes back to mine.

"Well, you're a little too late. After the shit you said to her, she ran off to God-knows-fucking-where. She hasn't returned any of my calls, but I can bet on where she went."

Holding my hand up, I yell, "Wait. If you know where she is, what the hell is stopping you from going to find her?"

Turning to rush out the door, not giving a shit about his feelings regarding me, I'm prepared to take his car to go find Sable. His hand snatches my wrist when I reach for the door handle, stopping me.

"She's with Mike. If we go out there, I'll kill him this time," he grits out, venom dripping from each word.

Turning to fully face him, my eyes clash with his, waiting for him to see every emotion crossing my face. Shoving my shoulders back, my smile is feral, filled with dark truths.

"You won't have to because I'll do it myself. Now, let's go find Sable."

CHAPTER FORTY NINE
EZRA

I've been pacing the living room floor for the past hour, waiting for Athena to come home. She's been gone for hours now with no word on what the hell is going on. I can feel the demon pounding his fist on the metal bars of his cage, demanding to go in search for what's his. Oliver's asleep in his bed, so I'm stuck here in the unknown drowning in worry and impatience.

Pausing to look out the wall of glass, I sit watching the night life down below, as if I could see Athena in the tiny people way down on the street. Irritation eats at me until my phone is at my ear calling Athena once again. It just rings and rings with no answer.

Trying Miles, his goes straight to voicemail, sending me into a blinding rage. Spinning, I storm to the kitchen snatching a glass from the cabinet to pour a shot of Jack, tossing it back. Welcoming the burn gulping it down before pouring another.

Looking down at my watch, I see that it's almost midnight now. Where the fuck is she? Images of her bent over my lap, ass red from her punishment flashes in my head. Her promise to come back to me repeats over and over. Fuck it. I call her one more time before deciding if I should go out looking for them or not when someone picks up the line. Only it's not my little demon.

"Hello?" A woman's voice says on the other end.

"Who the hell is this and where is Athena?" I snap at the voice on the other line.

Loud noise comes through the other end before her concerned voice says something that stops my heart completely. "Sir, this phone was found at a crime scene. That's all we can tell you over the phone."

My lungs stall in my chest, my next words stuck in my throat, but the ding of the elevator door pulls me out of my stupor. Eros's wide eyes set my body on full alert. The hand holding the phone starts to shake.

"Where is the woman who had the phone? Can you just tell me that?" I beg.

"I'm sorry, sir. All we know is two women were trans-ported to Montefiore General. That's all I can give you. But, sir?" She pauses.

"Yes?" I rasp on the verge losing every ounce of control I possess.

She hesitates before saying, "I would hurry if I were you."

With that she ends the call, most likely to put the phone

in evidence. Eros is standing in front of me, but my vision tunnels until all I see are Emerald eyes floating in front of me. Everything goes numb, coating my skin in terror at the thought of losing my soul.

My entire body shakes.

"Ezra!"

The trembling worsens.

"Fucking hell, Ezra, we need to go!"

Cold darkness seeps into my bones.

"Shit."

Red hot pain spreads across the left side of my face, snapping my head back.

"Look at me."

Brown eyes clash with mine, fear and worry spilling out a reminder. Eros has both hands on my shoulders shaking me while yelling for me to snap out of it. How can I? I'm falling into darkness.

"Ez?" A soft low voice fills my head, snapping me back to the room in front of me.

Searching out the one who called me my gaze meets a startled and tired looking Oliver. Shit. Oliver.

"Hey, man, what are you doing up so late?" Eros asks, walking over to him.

I'm unable to move. My feet feel like they're stuck in cement. Eros walks Oliver back to bed so I spring into action, forcing myself to move forward in my need to rush to Athena. Eros is walking back toward me by the time I've thrown my shoes and a shirt on.

"I have him watching a movie. Go," he urges me. "I'll be here with Oliver."

Pressing the button to call the elevator I turn to ask, "How did you know something was wrong?"

He looks away for a second before his brown eyes come back to mine. "Miles called me then his phone died."

I'm immediately on edge. "Called you to say what?" I demand.

"Sable was at Mike's apartment where Athena and Miles were headed."

Ice runs through my veins. I'll kill them both if a hair on Athena's head is out of place.

CHAPTER FIFTY
ATHENA

Blood. Blood has a way of spreading when it's spilled over cloth, overtaking the material completely. Crimson stains my hands seeping through my fingers. All I see is red. Every part of my body aches, screaming for relief from the soul crushing pain.

There is nothing left. No light or dark, only empty space leaving me suspended in agony.

Screams are all I hear. Where are they coming from? My mouth opens but no sound escapes. My throat is dry. The screams are coming from me. My voice now hoarse and stolen from me by the pain. Blacking out is the only semblance of peace I get. The darkness taking over until nothing's left.

I silently pray there's still something left of my soul when Ezra comes to pull me from hell himself.

CHAPTER FIFTY ONE
EZRA

Adrenaline fuels me forward. The hospital doors opening into their lobby that's cold as fuck. Fear the prominent emotion spilling from me. Sick people are lining the walls in the emergency room waiting to be seen but I don't stop to think about all the ill people here. People at the desk shout for me to slow but my legs pump faster in search of any sign of Athena or Miles.

Rounding the corner, I spot Miles with his head in his hands covered in blood that stains his cream-colored shirt. Or what used to be. I can see him visibly trembling, not slowing down, I reach him at the same time his eyes lift to meet mine. The empty look in his eyes has me stumbling back a step in sheer devastation.

"Miles. Where is she?" My voice breaks cracking on the last word.

He raises his head to look me fully in the face, his finger pointing to a room down the hall. My knees wobbly with each step forward but my heart drops in the next second. It happens in slow motion like being pulled into quicksand. I can hear the code blue call, nurses and doctors flooding into the room at a fast pace, but that's all I see from the hall.

"Move! Move!" I'm shoving everyone out of my way to get to Athena.

A handful of nurses step to the side and what I see has my heart sinking in my chest. Athena is hovering over Sable, who is being given CPR. Her cries are haunting, each wail shattering something deep in my gut. The doctors try over and over to shock Sable back but nothing's working. Falling to her knees Athena pulls at her hair screaming so loud the glass shakes in the window behind her.

"Time of death," the doctor starts to call ,but Athena jumps up so quickly she startles him.

"Don't you fucking stop. Save her!"

No one in the room moves, no one can with all the air being sucked out, Athena's pain suffocating. Ravaged with debilitating grief she jumps on the bed doing compressions herself, begging Sable not to leave her. Tears are falling all around the room with each plea.

"You swore it was me and you. Please, Sabby, don't leave me! Please!"

The crack of a rib.

"How could you abandon me?" Her hands shake with the force of her compressions.

Another rib cracks.

"Athena," I call, unable to watch her continue.

"No. She isn't gone. She can't be. Please someone help her!"

Thrusting her head side to side as if she could shake the image in front of her away, she starts to rattle Sable's still body.

Her red hair falls in curtains around her face blocking the tears I know are falling. Her arms are growing weak with each press down. Stepping past the nurses who don't know how to stop this, I step up behind her placing my hands on her arms, but she just tries to knock them off.

"Come on. Don't leave me all alone. I can't do this without you!"

Moisture builds behind my eyes, but I refuse to let them fall. Not while Athena is being sucked into the worst pain of her life.

A doctor steps up ready to yank her off the bed but I wave him off, prepared to grab her myself. Sable's short hair has less shine, her eyes are sunken in, her clothes are baggy and ragged.

"Baby, she's gone. Please let the doctors through." I try to coax her out of the room.

"I can't leave her," she declares hoarsely.

Pale green eyes peer up at me, leaving me feeling cold. Falling forward, she lies completely over Sable's body hugging her into her chest. Everything in me fights to comfort her, sobs wracking her lean frame. She lifts her head and presses her forehead to Sable's, eyes drifting close. Athena's body is still trembling, the adrenaline probably wearing off, leaving her exhausted and in shock.

"Please. Please. Please." Her cries are gut-wrenching.

Wrapping my hands around both her arms I start to lift her off the bed in an attempt to clear the way for any medical staff. The look on her face with both her arms stretched out screaming for her sister sends me into a spiral. My mind breaking at the reminder that this could have been Athena, I thought it was, instead she's lost her best friend, a sister.

Hugging her to my chest she clings to me like a child with her legs gripping my waist. Burying her head in the crook of my neck she sobs uncontrollably. Using one hand I rub circles into her back watching as the nurses start to file out of the room giving us space to take this all in. From the corner of my eye, I spot Miles standing in the doorway the dried blood startling to see on him.

What the fuck happened tonight?

Sitting down in one of the chairs against the wall Athena nestles into me soaking my shirt. I do everything possible to comfort her even though there's nothing in the world that could remove this pain. She'll feel empty inside. The darkness clouding her vision will try to pull her under, but I'll be here every step of the way to drag her back to us.

It's not until she's still, not moving an inch, that my mind lets it click that Oliver would have no idea what's happened tonight. Miles is covered in blood that isn't his, yet Sable doesn't have a drop of blood on her. So where is Mike and is he dead? Will Miles end up in jail this time? The air in the room is sucked out with Miles tears rolling down his face. I don't think I've ever seen him cry.

"Athena?" I say, concern evident in my voice.

"How could she leave me all alone?" she asks, broken.

Kissing the top of her head, I state, "You will never be alone again. You will never be abandoned."

CHAPTER FIFTY TWO
EZRA

The frame of the door digs into my back, watching Athena cuddle with Oliver, their silent cries have my fist clenching. My instinct to shield them from this hurt is overpowering. After Athena cried herself to sleep next to Sable's body, I was able to haul her back home. I got her cleaned up in a hot shower before she crawled in bed with her baby brother. Oliver knew something was wrong the moment he saw her face, but I'll never forget his horror at what happened.

It's been a few hours since they lay down together, but I can't bring myself to move from watching over them. Not until Miles comes into view from the hall walkway motioning for me to follow him. Meeting him and Eros in the living room we try to speak quietly so they don't hear us.

Seeing Miles look so haunted doesn't stop me from rushing him, snatching him up by his shirt to haul him into my face.

"What the fuck were you thinking?" I ask, my hands straining to hold up his weight. "What the hell happened?"

Eros jumps into action hauling me backwards forcing my hold on Miles to release. Standing between us my eyes find Miles's over his head. Dull blue eyes stare back at me, the vacant look startling.

"I... I don't know, man. Athena went in blazing hot rushing Mike. He took a swing at her, Ezra what was I supposed to do? And Sable." His voice cracks.

"What did he do to her?" I demand.

Shaking his head pressing his palms into his eyes as if he could rub the memory away.

"She was gone the moment we walked in the door. Athena found her first, in the bedroom on the floor, the needle still in her fucking arm."

Drugs. I was fucking right, and that confirmation makes me sick to my stomach because if I would have told Athena what I suspected we could have tried harder to save her. Every person in this room will feel the regret of what happened because this is what we do for a living yet it's so close to home.

Athena is going to struggle with the loss more than any of us but what hurts the most is Oliver. He's lost so much already with his mom leaving them and now Sable was stolen away from them.

"And Mike?" Eros presses.

We both look at Miles waiting for him to say what we

all know. That much blood doesn't spill without consequences. Anger flares in his eyes the blue like the depths of the sea dark and void.

"He'll never taint the world with his fucking vitriol again."

That's all he gives us before walking out heading to the elevator door.

"Miles," Eros calls out.

Worry for his best friend clear in his voice. We've always been tied together shouldering each other's pain, but this is something Eros can't hold for Miles. Knowing the fear that ate at my soul when I thought it was Athena in that hospital room, so I don't pressure him for anything more right now. Letting him go, we watch the doors close with a soft ding.

"Fin," my name is murmured from the doorway.

Athena stands there calling to me with a blanket wrapped around her shoulders.

"Sin, come here, baby," I say, opening my arms to welcome her in.

She rests her forehead on my chest, her small hands clutching my shirt. "He's asleep. Please take me to bed." Her voice is raspy from crying.

"Of course, Sin."

Kissing the top of her head I sweep her feet from under her heading to the stairs. Yelling over my shoulder at Eros to ask him to stay for now. Making our way up the stairs, careful not to bump her head, my foot pushes open our bedroom door. Gently setting her down on the bed I start to tug off her pants getting her ready for bed. Lifting her hips, forest green eyes stare back at me, the green growing darker.

"Take the memories away. Please, Fin. Make me forget." Her words a plea.

My eyes roll over her bare body. "Baby, not tonight. You need to rest."

Biting her lip her nose flares. "I want to bury myself in you to erase the pain. I need you."

Tugging both her ankles, I drag her to me until her legs wrap around my hips, her doe eyes waiting and watching. Smiling, my fingers close around her wrist pulling her chest flush with mine loving the way she fits against me perfectly.

"Come take a bath with me." Kissing my spot just below her eye, my heart pounds in my chest.

She stiffens against me ready to fight with me on this, but I lift her up my hands planted under her bare ass.

Her skin feels like silk against me, and I fight like hell not to give her what she's asking for. Walking into the bathroom to sit her on the counter, I turn on the water pouring in soap to make a bubble mixture. Turning back to my girl who watches me make my way back between her legs, I cup her cheek with one hand.

Pulling her bottom lip down. "Don't fight the pain, baby, just give it all to me. I'll shoulder everything you have to give. Always." I drop a kiss on her lips.

She nods her head, moisture pooling in her eyes, dropping her head forward to release the dam on her emotions.

"That's it, Sin, fall into me. I'm not going anywhere," I reassure her.

Her and Oliver will never have a reason to doubt me. They'll never wonder if one day I'll walk away to leave them all alone. Never again will my girl feel the need to carry the weight of the world solely on her shoulders. Cutting the water off after testing that it's not too hot I help Athena off the counter.

Once we're both completely submerged in water, I nudge her forward to wash her back. Smooth strokes up and down her arms, over her chest, and down her back. Repeating that pattern until I can feel her muscles finally relax.

"Lean your head back," I whisper.

Following my directions, she lets her long hair fall into the water. Reaching around us to grab the shampoo I lather some into my hands. Using my fingers to massage her scalp I start at the top and work my fingers through to the tips of her hair. I repeat this same action with the conditioner.

"What am I going to do?" she wonders out loud.

Not sure what she's asking. "Breathe. That's all I need from you, baby; I'll do the rest."

Shaking her head, "No, I mean about her funeral. She has no family and we never..." She inhales. "We never thought this would happen."

I can't see her face, but I know there are tears rolling down her cheeks staining them with wetness. Twisting her head with my finger on her chin, her eyes meeting mine. The lost look in them breaking my heart.

Leaning in to brush my lips over hers. "I'll handle that, Sin. You just worry about helping Oliver heal. You and he are my only concern right now."

Taking her mouth in a bruising kiss, my teeth sink into her flesh needing the anchor to hold me here, our tongues twisting in a brutal war. We pull away breathless matching lust-filled eyes, so I look away not wanting to use her need to feel something other than pain to get what I crave from her. Pulling the plug from the drain we sit there until the water runs out not moving even when the bubbles go with it.

After a moment we use the shower sprayer to rinse all the soap from our bodies before climbing from the tub. Wrapping her up in a large white towel I reach over to grab my own, never taking my eyes off Athena. She rubs her lips together not sure where to go from here, so I take the pressure off her by stepping out of the bathroom to give her space. Using that time to get dressed in gym shorts.

"Get in bed, I'll be right back," I say to her through the door.

Taking the steps two at a time I open Oliver's door to peek inside, checking on him. His hair is fluffed up on his head with a small amount of drool falling from the corner of his mouth making me smile. Walking into the room further I can see under his eyes are red and puffy from crying, my hands ball into a fist. He is such a strong kid. It's then that I come up with a plan on what needs to be done. I know the perfect way to make sure I never lose Oliver or Athena.

CHAPTER FIFTY THREE
ATHENA
ONE WEEK LATER

Sable's bright smile shines against her tanned skin, the happiness still reflecting in the gleam of her eyes. The hole in my chest aches with the empty space where she used to be, where she should still be. Tracing my fingers over her face I try to place a smile on my face like everyone keeps telling me to do. Be the good little female with a pretty smile. Fuck them. My entire world just crashed to the ground with the loss of Sable.

My hand clenches bending the memorial card in my hand, the one that lists only me and Oliver as surviving family, my hurt turning into anger. Ezra put together a beautiful service with the help of his assistant Bailey, who I met earlier in the week. Going over what Sable would have wanted crushed every fiber of my soul until there was nothing left but tatters. I know Ezra wishes he could shoulder the burden and steal away the pain, but I won't let him.

I'm here living my life with the one who feeds my soul yet my best friend, my sister, is being lowered into her grave. There are no more tears left to cry. Oliver's small hand clutches mine with a tight grip. He hasn't said much since I told him about her death, he's only asked questions. Questions that none of us could fully answer with his age. The only thing keeping me functioning is making sure he doesn't end up back in the hospital, so his medical care has become my obsession.

"Sin."

Ezra taps on my thigh gaining my attention. Snapping me out of my thoughts he stands, offering me a hand. I've tuned out the noise, the guest, the tears, everything. Now it's my turn to paste on a fake smile to place my rose over her casket. My legs weak from not being able to stomach food, I squeeze his hand, Oliver's hand still firm in my other one.

"It's our turn," I tell him.

Walking to the front of the row we pass Eros and Miles, the latter looking like a zombie, sitting in the front row as if they knew her like I did. All of the people here cry over Sable as if they had any clue who she really was. Raven and Sasha showed up earlier with warm hugs and teary eyes, but all I could feel was anger.

Stopping at the open hole where they lowered her large black casket, I let go of Ezra's hand to pick up a small white rose off to the side on a small stand with a photo of her. In the picture she is laughing, the short bob haircut framing her beautiful face, joy written across it. She was so full of life and sass. Swallowing down my scream, I drop it into the hole, watching the rose fall.

"Come hell or high water," I whisper.

Stepping to the side I let go of Oliver so he can do the same, my hand reaching out in search of Ezra's. Needing his support my body leans into his, welcoming the scent that has always smelled like him. Home.

"'Til kingdom come."

Oliver's soft voice whispering Sable's half of our saying sends me over the edge until I'm collapsing in on myself. Ezra wraps his arm around my waist to haul me against him, keeping me from falling to my knees on the damp grass. Oliver steps up to us silently crying, gripping my hand in his, holding on for dear life.

"Let's get you two home," Ezra says.

Everything passes by in flashes. The walk to our cars. Ezra sitting in the back with me and Oliver. Eros taking Oliver to play games in his room. Guests eating and chatting in the penthouse. People offering their love and condolences. Everyone clearing out of the apartment. Cleaning. Scrubbing everything. Images of Sable's body on her bedroom floor. Screaming for her to stay. Cursing her for abandoning me like everyone else. Passing out on Ezra in our bed.

His body heat wakes me with sweat covering my skin, so I gently get out of bed to make my way downstairs. Stepping into the kitchen I jump when I see Miles sitting at the island, drinking a glass of whiskey. Pausing to see if he looks up at me, my fingers twitch at my sides with the need to keep my hands busy.

"Drink?" he offers.

I step forward, taking the stool across the counter from him.

"Where's Eros?"

Swirling the amber liquid in his glass. "He fell asleep in Oliver's room at the foot of the bed."

That brings the first smile to my face all week knowing that through all this Oliver has people who truly love and care for him now.

Miles downs his drink before pouring me a small glass sliding it over to me. Lifting it to my nose I smell the over-powering stench of alcohol my nose scrunching from the burn. Tossing back the drink my tongue pokes out to catch a stray drop.

"I loved her," Miles says, his eyes cast down.

The glass in my hand dropping from my fingertips clinks against the marble. Giving myself a moment to process the declaration, pressing my lips together before my eyes lift to meet his ice blue ones.

"You blame me for her death. No one will ever blame me more than I do myself," I say, knowing it's the truth.

His jaw grinds holding back his next words through clenched teeth.

"I blame the piece of shit who pushed her into the drugs. Nothing you said or did could have changed what happened. Sable was fighting for her life everyday under the smiles, jokes, and smart-ass mouth. I tried to pull her back, to be enough for her to want to stay, but in the end, nothing could have helped Sable but Sable herself."

His words sting because how did I not see it before now? Was I really so wrapped up in Ezra that I couldn't see what she was dealing with?

Shaking his head his finger points at me. "Don't do that.

Don't sit here and wonder what you could have done or why you didn't see that she was in pain. Stop. This isn't about you Athena this is about Sable, so grieve her but celebrate her life, because she lived it for you and that little boy in the other room." His words sound hollow.

Raising an eyebrow, I stare at him. "And what about you? Do you just keep moving forward after everything and not feel regret?"

His eyes leave mine spotting the man standing over my shoulder, forever my stalker, watching him stand in the dark doorway.

Ezra's eyes burn a hole in my back, but I don't turn to address him, instead I stare at Miles waiting for him to meet my eyes.

"I'll feel Sable in everything I do. She'll be in the music I listen to; the shitty drama shows that I watch, but no matter what happens she'll always have my soul bound to hers. We shared something no one will ever understand. A sort of trauma-bond that pulled us together."

Clearing his throat, he picks up the whiskey to pour another glass gulping that down in one shot. Using his fingers to wipe his lips he puts the top back on, stands, and clears the island. Stopping at the bar cabinet, he looks over his shoulder at me.

His blue eyes peer into mine. "My brother loves you and that makes you family, Athena. Families have their issues, but this family is forever."

With those last words he walks into the living room, leaving me sitting there staring after him. My body feels him long before he reaches me. Ezra steps into my back, brushing my hair off my shoulders.

"It seems that my stalker hasn't quite retired yet," I joke.

Bending down to kiss up my neck, his breath tickles my skin right below my ear. Stretching my head to the side giving him more access my breathing turns ragged.

His lips tip up against my skin. "I'll always follow after you, Sin."

∽

Hot water from the shower beats down on my back loosening the muscles that have been pulled taunt for so long. Tipping my face toward the water, my eyes close exhaling on a long sigh.

My body buzzes with awareness when his tall frame slides in behind me brushing up against my slick skin. I don't tense, my body doesn't move, I give him no reaction to his presence. There's only the slight change of my breathing that gives away my excitement with having his sinful body near mine.

Large, calloused hands glide over my wet skin his fingertips ghosting over my thighs up my legs to rest on my waist. Blowing air on the back of my neck he causes chills to cover my entire body. Moving one hand to push my hair over my shoulder his mouth trails nips and bites across my neck to my ear.

"So fucking beautiful," he murmurs.

Biting my bottom lip to keep from speaking my feet slide backwards pressing my bare ass into him feeling how hard he is from just my touch. Coyly bending to grab the shampoo bottle my ass lines up in just the right spot causing him to growl out a curse.

"Looks like my little sinner wants to play."

His words are vicious ready to punish me any way he can, knowing that I crave the pain he's so willing to give.

Looking over my shoulder still bent at the waist my cheeky smile flashes at him.

"Make me feel something, Fin," I challenge him.

His head falls back on a groan, attempting to still give me space that I don't want, his eyes fall back down to my ass. Dropping his head back down I see the feral smirk fall into place ready to play my wicked little game. He gives me no warning when he grabs my hips and slams into me stretching me so fiercely a scream is ripped from my throat. Giving me no time to adjust to his large size, the burn sparks the darkness I try to keep buried.

"Shiiitt your cunt was made to take my dick." He thrusts harder. "That's it, baby, grip me like a good girl. Your pussy weeps only for me."

Oh god. Each filthy word that falls from his lips pushes me closer and closer to the crest my core is begging to be shoved over. One hand moves to twist my hair around his wrist pulling my head back with each long powerful thrust.

"Yes. Yes, please."

My moans bounce off the shower walls creating our own song while he plays my body like an instrument.

"That's right, baby. So fucking needy for my dick. Ohhh fuckk!" he groans out, yanking my hair harder.

His free hand comes down hard on my slick skin the loud smack echoing. My core tightens with the force of my building release. His strokes pick up speed, each one met with his hand lashing out across my skin, the sting making my pussy clench around him. Reaching around his fingers slide between my thighs flicking my clit.

Lifting my head up forcing my back flush with his front, he bites down on my neck, grunting against my skin.

"Come for me, my little demon. Soak my cock like only you can."

CHAPTER FIFTY THREE

"Fuck me, Fin," I mumble, my words garbled.

Pinching my clit at the same time his teeth skin into my throat my orgasm slams into me, my eyes clouding over. My ragged breathing mingling with his is the only sound left in the shower to be heard over the running water.

He pulses inside me, giving us both time to come down from the high. Pulling out of me in one stroke that leaves me feeling empty he spins me to face him. Water cascades down our faces, flooding my eyes in the process.

"Out of the shower, Sin," he orders.

Each word sends shivers down my spine with anticipation. Stepping out of the shower water rolls down my bare skin covering me in goosebumps. He's not far behind me shutting off the water then handing me my favorite white fluffy towel that swallows my entire body. Using the other towel, he twists it around his waist.

Crowding me into the counter, he smiles as he says, "Go somewhere with me." Gray eyes stare back at me.

I raise an eyebrow in response, waiting for him to give me more information. He bends kissing me in his spot making my heart ache with the move. Cupping my face in both hands his smokey stare takes me in.

"Come somewhere with me. You and Oliver, we can take some time off, but I want to take you away for a while."

He can see the fight in my eyes, so he stops me before I get a word out.

Ghosting his lips over mine, he states, "You can take a few weeks off. It'll be good for Oliver to get away from the city. Trust me, Sin."

My lips curve up in a smirk, his eyes darken with one look.

"I'll always follow after you," I repeat his words.

Ezra Finlay owns every piece of my soul. I'll never regret signing it over to the devil himself.

The End.

CHAPTER FIFTY FOUR
ATHENA
ONE MONTH LATER

The click of Oliver's door echoes down the hall. His eyes closed the second his head hit the pillow, worn out from our flight home. It's been three weeks since we've been home at the penthouse. Six weeks since we lost Sable. My palms start to sweat with the feeling of being in the city, knowing I'll never see her here again.

"Sin."

The deep baritone soothes my soul with just one word, chills skate across my skin just like every other time he's near. The devil who caged my heart in chains that match his smokey grey eyes. A warm smile pulls at my lips, looking over my shoulder I see him, our eyes clash in the dim hallway light. He holds a hand out calling me to him.

I will always follow him.

"Come to bed baby."

His thumbs rubs the ring that still sits on my middle finger, twisting and turning it the entire way up the stairs. My heart hammers in my chest at the reminder of our time spent on his private jet. Images of his blood spilling into me with each thrust of the cold steel handle of his knife heat my skin boiling my blood below the surface.

Pulling me to a stop he spins me until he has me pressed up against the wall by our bedroom door. Leaning in to run his nose up my neck, inhaling me, he leaves a trail of fire across my flesh scorching every inch of me.

"What's on your mind, little demon? I can practically hear your heart racing."

Memories slam into me from the past few weeks. Water parks, amusement parks, valleys, mountains, beaches. You name it and we went there. Ezra spent the past month making sure me and Oliver know that we would never be alone. Our hearts are still healing from losing Sable, but the hole where she used to be is being glued together with pieces of him. Never replacing her only sealing the gaps she left.

"I need you." My words are raspy filled with want.

His hand slips beside me to open the door wide enough for us to shuffle through the doorway. Kissing and nipping down my neck he nudges me to the edge of the bed before he steps back to take me in. His eyes are light with an ease I wasn't sure he would have after everything. Giving Eros their shared company, Finlay Execs, has brought out a side of him I haven't seen before.

Ezra still has say in the company and technically still works with his little brother but he is taking a step back to spend time with us. Eros took the news well, I think he was hoping for this so he could start this new project, even when Ezra doesn't support it. Their long talks over the phone on the subject often got heated.

Ezra walks over the the closet stepping inside without turning the lights on. The sound of metal on metal screeches in my ears shooting anticipation through my bones. Biting the inside of my cheek my mind conjures different images in my head on what he might have planned for tonight. My leg bounces with impatience.

Slowly stripping off my clothes from the day, my black leggings are pooled at my feet when we returns, with an arm full of different items that has my chest rising and falling faster. He drops my favorite whip on the bed followed by a tie, blindfold, long gold handled knife, and a green fishnet outfit.

My eyebrows raise at the last item.

Tugging my shirt over my head for me he throws it in the corner of the room, his body heat causing chills to spread down my spine and arms. Picking up the outfit he motions for me to step into it his fingers brushing over my new ink sending me into overdrive. The tattoo is nestled just to the side of my left breast on my ribcage. The air gets stuck in my throat at the reminder.

The week after we buried Sable, Ezra and Eros took me to their tattoo shop so I could get something to remember her by. I can see the photo of my tattoo so clearly in my head without needing to look down. The intricate way he drew a castle with a large wave rising behind it still takes my breath away. Her initials are planted in the door of the castle. Our own personal kingdom.

Come hell or high water, til kingdom come.

Stepping into heels Ezra has sitting next to the bed my gaze connects with his and I know he can see it all over my face. His large hand clasp the back of my neck tugging me into him until my breast are pressed against his chest . The rough feel of his shirt rub against my nipples through the fishnet pushing my senses into overdrive.

"On your knees." He orders, his voice hard.

Inhaling a gulp of air that sticks in my throat I drop to my knees instantly with no hesitation. I can already taste his addicting flavor on my tongue, the urge to take him in my mouth without being told is overwhelming, but I wait for his next orders.

Tipping my chin up to look down at me, he admires what he sees kneeling here on the floor before him. Waiting and ready to do whatever he asks me to. My mouth waters when he starts to strip his shirt off revealing his lean cut torso.

"Don't move. Do you understand?"

Licking my lips I nod my head, the words getting lost in my throat.

Gripping my ponytail he pulls my head back exposing the long collum of my neck, "Say it."

"Yes sir." I groan.

He turns and walks out the room leaving me on the floor to wait for him to come back. Numb tingles spread through my knees up to my thighs from the hard floor, but my body stays in its place not moving an inch. On my next exhale the door opens to Ezra carrying in a chair from the table downstairs.

Setting it down in the center of the room he takes a seat spreading his legs to rest his forearms on his thighs. My thong is instantly drenched at the sight of this powerful man before me. Leaning into the back of the chair his fingers twist in a circle on his legs.

"Crawl to me."

My hands slap against the floor with each move, my gaze stay on his the whole way there, until I have to sit on my heels in front of him. Palms on my knees, my stare never waivers from his. The cloudy grey in his eyes swirl has my pulse singing in my veins. He unbuttons his pants before his hand brushes a stray hair from my eyes.

"Pull my dick out."

Doing as he says my cool hands close over his heated skin causing a groan to slip past his lips. Using his thumb and forefinger he pinches my chin in a bruising hold.

"Be a good girl and suck it."

Needing no other push, I jump forward taking him in my mouth, using my tongue to swirl around the tip. Wetting his shaft, my lips fully close over him, slowly getting closer to the base. Moaning around his cock my eyes roll with the taste of Nirvana flooding my mouth as his precome drips onto my tongue.

Twisting my hair around his wrist he grits, "Fuck, your mouth is mine."

Lifting his hips to thrust in and out of my mouth I open my jaw wider welcoming the sting of tears rolling down my face. Each moan vibrates down his length making his leg twitch. Another hand comes up to grip my face holding me in place my head unable to move at all.

"Eyes on me, Sin. Watch me as I fuck your pretty little mouth. God, you're always so good for me." Each word spurs me on taking him deeper. "Yes, just like that baby."

Flattening my tongue against the bottom side of his

shaft he grunts out my name until he's shooting down my throat. Each thrust shoving his cum deeper down my throat. Swallowing around him my eyes never leave his. His head falls back when he pulls out of my mouth with a wet plop. Licking my lips my thumb comes up to catch a drop at the corner of my mouth pushing it back in to drink the last of him down.

Sitting up he tracks my movements, "Stand."

Once I'm on my feet I step between his legs needing his hands on my body but he stops me by pushing me backwards. Shoving out of the chair he turns me forcing my ass into the seat he just left, the leather still warm. Walking to the bed, grabbing the whip, blindfold, and tie he steps back into me.

"Hands behind your back."

My heart pounds in my chest the steady thumping like music in my ears. Moving to stand behind me, the silk of his dark navy tie slides against my damp heated skin with each knot he ties. Once I'm secured to the chair he comes back to stand between my open legs. The opening of my fishnet providing the perfect view of my wet thong.

He sneers at the offending fabric as if it did something to him. Bending down his fingers trace my inner thigh inching his way to my core. Using his finger to pull the soaked cloth away from my skin he yanks in once, ripping it from my body with little effort. Did I say I was drenched? Fucking flooded is more accurate. Wetness coats my thighs now with no barrier to hold back my arousal.

Standing back up he grabs the blindfold and slips it over my head making sure it's in place before leaving me shaking for him. Every single noise he makes has my head spinning in that direction. Each pass of his fingers over my skin sends me into overdrive. Ghosting his fingertips over my collarbone forces a moan from clenched teeth.

"Tell me what you need."

My chest heaves with each inhale unable to clear my nose of his intoxicating smell. "Mmmhmm." Is the only sound I make.

With no sight I don't see it coming until the swish of leather brushes air over my face, landing on my inner thigh with a sting.

"Tell me what you need."

"Yo..You." My words are uttered behind bated breath.

A loud thud makes me jump, my hands pulling at the back of the chair sends pain shooting through my arms. "Fuck!"

Swish. The whip lands on my other thigh matching the pain of the right leg.

"Don't move." He demands.

A calloused hand glides up my legs pushing them apart to welcome him between them. Gripping my hip he tugs me to the edge of the chair leaving me at an awkward angle with my ass hanging off while my back is extended. The sound of tearing pulls my attention to movement between my legs the cool air hitting my damp sweat slick skin.

A chill breaks out over my body, something cold is rolled over my leg, rubbing back and forth. The knife. Biting my lip I wait for the pain, in anticipation, needing him to consume every inch of space inside my body. The darkness swirling in my chest beats against its cage, rattling the bars.

"Is this what you want, Sin? To bleed for me? Or do you prefer to watch me bleed for you?"

"Oh god." I rasp.

Teeth sink into my flesh, matching the sting from his

blade digging into my other leg, but before the pain takes over its gone completely. Replaced by his mouth closing over my dripping center. He eats me like a man dying of thirst in the desert, as if I were the first glass of water he's had in days.

"Oh yes.. Oh fuck yes, dear god."

My hips lift chasing his mouth in an attempt to ride his face.

"Please." I start to beg.

"My needy little slut needs more. Always so greedy."

Twisting the tip of the blade into my thigh he pulls it down cutting the skin at the edge of my pelvis sending my eyes rolling to the back of my head. His tongue plunges into me replacing the pain with blinding pleasure while his other hand brings the whip down over my nipples causing me to lift off the chair.

"Fin!" I scream.

Thrusting my hips, my pussy grazes over his lips, but the pressure isn't enough. Forcing a growl from my throat out of frustration. His chuckle vibrates through my wet core, a finger finally joining his tongue in fucking me. Twisting his finger, he opens me wider, the sudden shock of cold metal being brushed against my hot skin makes me jerk to a stop.

His other hand brings the whip down over my thigh sending me reeling from the sensations of him everywhere. The handle of the knife pushing inside, joining his fingers and tongue, pushing me closer to the edge. My legs start to shake, but the need to see him devouring me takes over my whole body, squirming with the thought.

"Oh shit. Please Fin, I need to see." My words are a plea, falling from sinful lips.

The thud of his whip falling to the floor has me pausing

when his fingers close over the blindfold on my eyes. With a yank he pulls it free, my gaze falling to him between my legs, the sight alone has my orgasm rolling closer to the edge. I'm panting like a bitch in heat with Ezra on his knees for me, hand bleeding from the knife digging into his skin, while his mouth covers my pussy. It's a heady feeling having him in this position for only me.

"Untie me."

It's not an order but I keep my eyes on him showing just what I want with one look. Pulling out of me he leans back on his heels a smirk falling into place with the knife in one hand and the other reaching behind me. It only takes one pull and the silk tie slowly falls to the floor under the chair.

"On the bed."

His smirk turns into a sneer flashing me his teeth, but he does as I say anyway. Our gaze lock holding each other in a snare. He pulls his pants completely off in the process of walking backwards to the bed. His dick springs to life drawing my eyes downward for a split second before I remember what I was doing. Nodding my head I motion for him to climb on the bed.

"Lay on your back."

My skin buzzes with confidence, each step I take towards him fueling me forward, knowing that this man belongs to me. Light bounces off the blade, glinting in the dark room, still in his hand. I bend down to grab the whip before I join him. Crawling up his body my legs dip the bed on each side of him, opening my fingers dropping the whip near his head.

Staring into dark grey eyes, "I'm going to fuck your face."

Before he can respond I drop down over his mouth my thighs closing over his head. Two hands wrap around my thighs with a brutal grip, holding me to him, but leaving enough freedom for movement. My head falls back my hips start to move on their own searching out what my body needs. One hand tangles in his hair holding him in place while I grind my pussy on his face.

"Oh yes. Shiiit."

I'm unable to form words when his teeth nip at my clit sending my eyes to the back of my head. Legs shaking, I fully sit on his face, uncaring on if he can breath. My body only looking for what it craves.

"God, I need.. I.."

What do I need? Swiveling my hips then dropping back down pulls me closer to the edge but I can't reach it. Growling out my frustration I pull on his hair shoving his face deeper between my legs but nothing's enough. I need him inside me like my lungs need air. Lifting from his face I move down until my center is lined up with his massive dick.

His hands land on my hips halting my movement, our stare connects, he lowers me on him, stormy eyes focused on watching the way I pull him in deeper.

"That's it baby, your cunt was made for me. You always take my dick like a good fucking girl. Fuck, your pussy grips me so tight."

Reaching beside him he grabs the knife and with the other hand he picks up the whip. His eyes darken every time I drop back down taking him deeper. Reaching out with his long arm his hand closes over my throat, the leather of the whip pressing into me. Pumping in and out in hard thrust he squeezes until my throat closes, not taking any air in, with the other hand he drags the blade down from my collarbone to my belly button. Cutting my skin enough to have drops of blood seeping through the slices.

"I love the color red on you." His words are feral, "I want to paint your milky skin bright red."

Moans slip past my lips, riding him harder, the pain mixing with the pleasure of him stretching me. I can feel the burn of my lungs needing my next breath, but the buzz covering my skin urges me on. Panting in small gulps of air, I lift off him and drop back down in rough jerky movements. It must not be enough because he lifts me off him the ache of being empty forcing a cry from my throat.

Releasing me he flips us until I'm on all fours and he's on his knees behind me lifting the whip only to bring it down across my ass. Dropping my chest into the bed I bare my pussy to him.

"Fin please." I wiggle my hips.

Whip.

Pushing back into him I search out his length.

Whip.

My hand slips between my legs to rub my clit.

Across the back of my thighs.

I shove my fingers inside my dripping pussy.

Across my hip.

I finger myself harder my palm rubbing my aching clit.

Across my ass.

Jolting forward my thumb pinches my clit hard.

Another hit across my ass.

The cool handle of the blade touches my hand. Ezra's pushing it between my fingers.

A sting on my thighs.

"Fuck yourself with the handle. I want to watch you cum all over over my knife."

My head falls forward with his sinful words.

The whip bites into my ass cheeks.

Doing what he said I spread my slick wetness over the

top of the handle before slowly pushing it inside me. The chill from the brass has my core clenching around it, my entire body shaking with the reaction.

"So fucking beautiful."

Pumping the handle in and out, my lungs stall when his dick pokes at my entrance, gliding against my hand. Pulling the handle out to the tip allowing him to push into me from behind. Ezra fucks me in tandem with the knife. He brings the whip down across my ass on one hard thrust shooting stars behind my eyelids. Dropping the whip, both hands grab onto my hips, slamming into me over and over dragging me to the edge of a cliff.

"Keep fucking the knife. I want you to soak my dick and the knife at the same time."

Forcing the handle deeper the blade cuts into my palm, my teeth dig into my bottom lip drawing blood the taste of copper fills my mouth. The sensation of being so utterly full is surreal.

"Good girl. Come all over me. Squeeze my dick."

"Oh god!" Screaming, my orgasm barreling through me.

Thrusting into me harder and faster he grunts out, "Fuck yes, Sin"

He stills, emptying into me until our mixed cum starts to spill out all over my hand.

Gently pulling the knife handle out I give him room to come down from his high.

It takes us both several minutes before we move to clean up, our breathing mixing in the air between us, charging the space surrounding us.

After we clean up and we are both naked from head to toe, he pulls me into his chest planting his lips under my eye, in the spot that still makes my heart skip a beat.

"I love you." I whisper into the darkness.

CHAPTER FIFTY FOUR

"Me too." He mumbles against my hair.

I fall into a deep sleep with the feel of his fingers tracing my tattoo, bringing the rising wave to life beneath his caress.

C ome hell or high water, Til kingdom come.

Watch for Eros and Miles' stories coming soon! Sign up to be notified when releases are announced here:
https://authorcamieparrish.wixsite.com/thecoven

Keep up with The Coven and all they have to offer in Camie's Reader Group:
https://www.facebook.com/groups/3490545267848805

More by Camie Parrish

Series:
    The Coven Series
    Misfits- Out now
The Wicked- Fall of 2023

Standalone Books:
    Starving for Sin.

Want more from the guys? Stay tuned for more stories involving the Finlay and Grayson men. You won't want to miss this!

Acknowledgements

Erin! I am forever in your debt. You managed to keep me afloat and my train on the tracks LOL. No one could have helped me through this mess other than you! Thank you so much for being my rock, the best PA ever, and a truly amazing friend.

Apollo and Bells! Without you there would be no Camie Parrish and what a sad world that would be. The magic we have created together is unmatched. I love you guys to the moon and back. Til Kingdom Come.

To all of my readers, Alpha's, and loyal supporters, thank you! Starving for Sin would not be what it is today if not for all of you. This story means the world to me so for all the help and honesty I am truly grateful.

Milton Keynes UK
Ingram Content Group UK Ltd.
UKHW010120011223
433552UK00004B/186